PSYCHO ALLEY

Recent Titles by Nick Oldham from Severn House

BACKLASH
SUBSTANTIAL THREAT
DEAD HEAT
BIG CITY JACKS

PSYCHO ALLEY

Nick Oldham

This first world edition published in Great Britain 2006 by
SEVERN HOUSE PUBLISHERS LTD of
9–15 High Street, Sutton, Surrey SM1 1DF.
This first world edition published in the USA 2006 by
SEVERN HOUSE PUBLISHERS INC of
595 Madison Avenue, New York, N.Y. 10022.

British Library Cataloguing in Publication Data

Oldham, Nick, 1956-
    Psycho alley
    1. Christie, Henry (Fictitious character) - Fiction
    2. Police - England - Blackpool - Fiction
    3. Detective and mystery stories
    I. Title
    823.9'14 [F]

ISBN-13: 978-0-7278-6383-6
ISBN-10: 0-7278-6383-5

All Severn House titles are printed on acid-free paper.

Typeset by Palimpsest Book Production Ltd.,
Polmont, Stirlingshire, Scotland.
Printed and bound in Great Britain by
MPG Books Ltd., Bodmin, Cornwall.

For Belinda

FRIDAY

One

The last thing Henry Christie needed to be doing on a bitter, wind-chilled Friday evening was traipsing from pub to pub around Fleetwood town centre. Not that he had a problem with Fleetwood, though it did seem to be over-populated by surging masses of extremely inebriated young women, many of whom appeared to be pregnant, with a desire to fight, and could well have been descendants of fishwives; nor did he have a problem with a pub crawl. In fact, that was one of his favourite pastimes.

What was bothering him was the fact that a three-month major crime investigation he'd been heading had come to this: trawling through dens and dives in an effort to root out a suspect, and only a suspect at that, who had constantly been eluding him. 'Clutching at straws' was the negative phrase which kept whirring through his grey matter. And on top of all that, because he was on duty he could not drink any alcohol *and* he was in the company of someone he would rather have avoided.

'Don't see him in here,' Henry said. His eyes scanned the faces in the Trawlerman public house situated at the top of Lord Street, Fleetwood's main shopping thoroughfare. He had spoken both for the benefit of the person he was with – she was much smaller than he and his height gave him an advantageous viewpoint – and the tiny microphone affixed to his bomber jacket, connected to the personal radio (PR) covertly fitted under the jacket. This was transmitting on a frequency exclusively allocated for the use of his team of cops dotted around other Fleetwood pubs in this farcical search. The bar Henry was surveying was throbbing with hundreds of sweaty Fleetwoodians and the ear-bursting din from the house DJ whose equipment was set up at the far end of the room, playing thumping music which sounded like mobile phone ringtones to Henry's uneducated ears.

He sipped his iced mineral water, then blew out his red cheeks as a wave of exhaustion swept over him. He had been heading this investigation for over eleven weeks without a proper break, often toiling twelve hours a day, and he needed some respite. He decided that if tonight's search was negative, he would take a minimum of three days off. Put some charge back into his lifeless batteries.

'You all right?'

Henry turned to look at Detective Inspector Jane Roscoe standing next to him. 'Yeah, why?'

She shrugged. 'Looking a mite peaky.'

'I'm OK.'

'Sure he isn't here?' Jane was a good head shorter than Henry and was forced to stand on tippy-toe to get any sort of view. She was therefore having problems seeing through the crush of bodies.

'As eggs,' Henry said.

'Ever seen him in the flesh?' she asked, having to compete with a classic record sung by a crazy frog.

'Nope.'

'So how can you be sure?' Jane quizzed him, as was her way with Henry these days. He was always on the ropes, a legacy of their past intimate relationship.

He paused, blinked, sighed impatiently. 'I'm sure.'

Jane's tut of disbelief was carried away by the shrieking laughter of a gaggle of noisy women. One of them staggered drunkenly into Jane, only to be heaved away and subjected to one of her fleeting, but killer, put-down glances.

If there was one thing Henry Christie was certain of, it was his ability to pick out someone he might only have ever seen in a photograph, recent or otherwise. His aptitude to recognize faces was one of the few 'gifts' he considered he had as an investigator. Though he had never come face to face with his elusive suspect, George Uren, predatory paedophile of this parish, he was convinced he could pick him out of a crowd.

'If you're so sure, shall we move on?' Jane shouted into his ear. 'This place is doin' my head in and the people are horrid.' She looked disgustedly at the group of women.

'Let's.' Henry emptied his glass, ice-cubes clattering against his teeth. He yanked up the zip of his jacket and turned to leave. Jane slotted into his slipstream as he threaded his way

4

out between revellers. On reaching the double exit doors, he became aware that Jane was actually not at his heels. He looked back. Squinting through the cigarette and cannabis smoke he saw she was head to head with a scantily-clad female who wore a miniscule skirt, had fat thighs and acres of tubby belly-flesh on display. The woman was making broad, aggressive gestures towards Jane, her face twisted into a menacing snarl, the like of which Henry had often seen associated with alcohol.

'Shit,' he uttered and pushed his way back.

He recognized the woman as the one Jane had propelled away and been the subject of one of Roscoe's 'looks' moments earlier. Obviously she had taken umbrage and was now challenging Jane in the best traditions of Fleetwood, something confirmed by the first words Henry heard when he emerged from the crowd.

'Come on, you stuck-up, snooty old bitch!' she was yelling insanely into Jane's impassive face. 'Who the fucking hell do you think you are, pushing me – me! – and giving me a look like I was shit on your shoe?'

Jane stayed cool, passionless. 'Sorry,' she said sensibly, aware it was probably the best tactic to back down, though without losing face – and get out in one piece. To stand up to her would have meant being torn to shreds by a pack of hyenas, as the woman's group of friends hovered dangerously, expectantly, hoping for a fracas. Jane knew of too many people who had ended up with a broken glass gouged in their face in A & E because of a 'look'; she also realized that her warrant card would offer no protection in these circumstances.

If only she could extricate herself.

Unfortunately, her apology wasn't good enough. The woman was on the scent of blood.

'Sorry, you ancient bitch?' she wailed, which was rich coming from someone aged somewhere between forty and forty-five, dressed twenty years younger than was sensible, with a fast-expanding midriff, tattoos, and an array of cheapo golden jewellery adorning her. She also had a bottle of WKD in her right hand and Henry's eyes were fixed apprehensively on it as he approached from downwind. 'You will be, you stuck-up cow!'

To her credit, Jane remained chilled.

Henry edged into a position where he could easily grab the drunk from behind if necessary.

Then it happened very quickly. The woman's right arm arced through the air, bottle in hand, aimed at Jane's head, accompanied by a scream. Jane ducked. Henry lunged for the woman, his left hand grabbing the neck of her skimpy tee shirt, his right trying to stop, deflect or otherwise interfere with the trajectory of the bottle heading towards Jane. He yanked her off balance as Jane did a neat side-step and the bottle whizzed harmlessly through mid-air and Henry discovered he now had a tigress in his hands . . . and another one on his back as one of her friends launched to her defence, scratching, kicking, kneeing, trying to rip off his ear with her teeth.

Henry roared, spun round, threw the original assailant to one side, tearing her tee shirt as she went, exposing a large, floppy bosom – whilst doing his utmost to dislodge woman number two from his back, who was riding him for her life. She seemed capable of clinging on there, like a lioness on the back of a zebra, despite his attempts to shake her off.

The whole pub erupted with a roar of delight.

Henry and Jane found themselves in a vortex of punches, kicks, screams and beer glasses being thrown everywhere. Henry was the recipient of numerous, but ultimately useless, boots, thumps and slaps, and he caught a quick glance of Jane stumbling under the weight of two women who had piled into her.

It seemed that the whole of Fleetwood was up for a fight that night, and it was a long time since Henry had witnessed such fun.

However, though he rode his assault without too much pain, he was worried that one of the hands at him might be holding a knife and he knew he had to get himself and Jane out of there quickly. He surfaced mightily from beneath an avalanche of blows, bellowing as he found the inner strength of self-preservation. He grabbed hold of Jane's arm – the one she wasn't using to punch another woman's lights out – and howled, 'Let's do a runner!'

Out of the corner of his eye he'd caught sight of a trio of black-suited bouncers elbowing their way fairly nonchalantly, but effectively, through the crowd. Best to get a move on, he thought, tugging hard at Roscoe.

At that precise moment, Henry took a punch delivered by he knew not who. It landed smack-bang on his left cheekbone, jarring something at the back of his head and behind his eyes, sending a pulsating shockwave through his brain, spinning him backwards between several women. As he fell he saw once more the floppy breasts of the drunken female who'd started it all, followed by the flashing disco lights whizzing past his eyes, then he landed hard on his coccyx and caught the back of his head on the edge of a table.

After that, things became slightly less clear.

'Didn't see that one coming,' Henry admitted with a short and bitter laugh, then groaned as a sharp needle of intense pain seared through his cranium. 'Dear me,' he added stiffly. He was sitting on a low wall surrounding flowerbeds in Fleetwood town centre, holding the side of his head, cradling it in his left hand. The front of his face below his left eye was tender, already slightly swollen, his eye starting to close. His cheek-bone felt like it could have been fractured, but then he was always one to exaggerate the extent of an injury. 'I can't take you anywhere,' he moaned.

An unruffled Jane Roscoe sat on the wall beside him, philo-sophically inspecting the knuckles on her right hand, which were grazed and sore. 'Sorry,' she said. 'It was an instinctive thing. I just swung in the direction of whoever grabbed me. Unfortunately it just happened to be you.'

'You pack a good punch.'

'Sorry, again . . . but then maybe I actually knew it was you who got hold of me and maybe punching you good and hard is something I've been wanting to do subconsciously for a long time. Y'know – a sort of Freudian thing?' She grinned maliciously. 'But I guess neither of us will ever know, until maybe I go for some deep counselling.'

'Let's hope it's out of your system, then.'

She shrugged doubtfully. 'Who knows?'

Henry touched his face gingerly and winced. 'Gonna be a shiner,' he said. 'God, I hate fighting women. So much nastier than blokes.' He checked his watch: ten thirty-five p.m. 'What d'you think about calling it off for the rest of the night?' he asked Jane. 'Maybe we could get a drink somewhere decent on the way home?'

'You asking me out?'

'For a drink . . . in the workplace sense, not the romantic sense . . . I thought we'd moved on from that,' he said, hoping it didn't sound too cruel.

She nodded. 'OK, I'll have that.'

Henry spoke into his new Generation 2 TETRA personal radio. He ensured the rest of his team, who were scattered about in various hostelries about town, were receiving and stood them down with instructions to resume duty at nine a.m. on Monday. They all acknowledged Henry and he breathed a sigh of relief. 'Phew – a weekend off. I think I'll have Monday, too.'

'Going to surprise Kate?' Roscoe probed, her mouth twisted rather like the metaphorical knife she was holding.

Henry shrugged, not wanting to answer. The affair he and Roscoe had was a thing of the past, for him at least, but there were still some raw nerve endings exposed. He could tell from the tone of her voice that she still had 'issues' to deal with and put to bed, so to speak. It didn't help matters that they worked in such close proximity. Sometimes it was hard to get away from each other, as tonight had proved.

They walked in silence back to Fleetwood police station where their cars were parked in the back yard. Henry's eye throbbed painfully, the swelling growing, maybe a visit to A & E on the cards, but not tonight. Friday meant busy with drunks, accident victims and a long wait. Maybe he'd get Kate to run him in in the morning if it was still a problem.

'We did well to get out of that place,' Henry said, breaking the silence. He had a hazy memory of himself and Jane staggering out of the pub – which had been still fighting in lumps – as the uniformed police contingent arrived en masse. 'We'd have looked pretty stupid in a cell, wouldn't we?'

Jane did not respond, her face cold, her attitude now icy.

Once in the yard, he and Jane stood awkwardly by their cars. Jane scraped the toe of her shoe on the ground and looked up at Henry. 'I know I've given you a hard time since we . . . y'know . . . since you dumped me, but that's because it hurt . . . it hurt me so much, you hurt me. I thought we were on the verge of something,' she said quietly. 'But it didn't happen. I fell in love with you and it hurt, OK? Still does.'

Henry nodded dumbly. He was trying not to do 'feelings'

any more, because he was basically very bad at 'going there'. All he wanted to do now was get on with his life, not get involved with anyone again, concentrate on making his life good with Kate, buy an expensive hi-fi system, maybe indulge in a plasma screen TV, collect films on DVD and go away for as many foreign holidays as possible; he was due to retire in three years – when he reached the grand old age of forty-nine – and he wanted to approach that time with a light heart and an easy existence. He'd had enough trauma with feelings, enough of making a fool of himself over women, he hoped, yet he did have a weakness of character that meant he had a tendency to press the self-destruct button without thought of consequence. Something he had to fight.

He sighed. 'Maybe going for a drink isn't a good idea.'

'Maybe not,' she agreed. 'Get a bit of alcohol down me and next thing you know, we'd be shagging. See you Monday.'

'Oh, about Monday . . . can you cover for me?'

'Cheeky bastard,' she uttered through gritted teeth. She regarded him chillingly and exhaled a long, aggrieved breath, very close to telling him where he should stick it. 'OK,' she relented.

'Thanks, appreciate it.'

'I wonder what Chief Superintendent Anger'll say about you not being there on Monday?' she teased.

Anger was Henry's boss. Jane and Anger had formed a close alliance, both seeming to want to get Henry ditched, each for their own reasons. 'Depends on what you tell him, I suppose. You could just say I've worked like hell for the past three months and I deserve a break. How about that?'

'Or I could tell him you're a lazy git who hasn't got a cat in hell's chance of getting a result and should be replaced as SIO. Mm,' she said, tip of her forefinger on the cleft of her chin. 'I wonder which one?'

'Follow your conscience,' he said abruptly. 'Whatever, I won't be in on Monday.' He strutted angrily to his car, his brittle mood not made any the better when he saw how busy the seagulls had been on his windscreen.

He watched Jane reverse, or lurch, her car out of the parking bay, slam it into first with an angry crunch and screech dramatically out of the police yard with a squeal of rubber. He had

9

a friend, a frequently divorced friend, who had once told him without a trace of irony that women were not worth the hassle. 'Henry, me old mate,' he'd said drunkenly once, 'losin' it all for the sake of a wizard's sleeve is bloody crass stupidity.' He'd gone on to explain what he meant by 'wizard's sleeve', but with a bit of imagination Henry had already worked out what he meant. Henry believed that if he and Jane had tipped over the 'verge', as she had called it, he would now be living to regret it. He would have lost his family, which included two great daughters, and would have been nowhere near buying a plasma screen TV . . . all for the sake of a wizard's sleeve. He allowed himself a chuckle at his friend's crude metaphor, started his car, cleared the screen of bird shit and allowed it to warm up before setting off into the night.

· He drove to the Esplanade, Fleetwood's seafront promenade, then did a right past the North Euston Hotel on to Queen's Terrace, the Isle of Man ferry terminal to his left. Way across the mouth of the River Wyre were the lights of the sleepy village of Knott End on Sea, and in the far distance to the north the hulking structures of the nuclear power station at Heysham, illuminated by an eerie orange phosphorescent-like glow.

His intention was to trundle down on to the romantically-named Dock Street, cut right across town then head south towards Blackpool and home, hoping he could make it safely with just the one good eye.

Henry's bleat to Jane about having worked long, hard hours for the past three months had only been partially true. With the exception of a two-week family holiday jaunt to Ibiza, he had actually been hard at it for nine months. For the first six he had been running a complex and particularly dangerous investigation into large-scale corruption and murder within the ranks of some Greater Manchester Police officers. This had entailed much overtime – all unpaid, of course – and several trips to Spain. During the course of the investigation, headed nominally by Lancashire's chief constable, but run directly by Henry, his life had been threatened twice and his firm's car had been regularly damaged whilst parked unattended in Manchester. These worrying occurrences had not deterred him from completing a job which had sent shockwaves through GMP. There were some loose ends, as there always are in such

10

a far-reaching enquiry, but Henry was as satisfied as he could be at the outcome . . . and then he returned to the force, immediately being handed the reins of his present investigation and a new posting to boot.

He was currently a temporary detective chief inspector, a member of the Senior Investigating Officer (SIO) team which was based at force headquarters near to Preston. Or at least he had been. Whilst busy in Manchester, there had been some changes to the SIO team and its remit. It had been renamed the Force Major Investigation Team (FMIT) and in order to ensure there was an even better response to serious crime, the staff had been divvied up and given responsibility to provide cover to specific police divisions in the county. In the shuffle, during which Henry had no say, nor was consulted, he had ended up with responsibility for 'A' and 'B' Divisions, covering the west and north of Lancashire. He had been turfed out of his comfy headquarters office and relocated to Blackpool nick, where he had ended up in a shoe-box of an office with no heating and initially no phone or computer.

Having spent much of his career in Blackpool, and living there, the move wasn't entirely unwelcome. At least he did not have to do the forty-odd mile round trip each day through increasingly horrendous traffic. But in his paranoia, he did suspect the move could be the first step in ousting him from FMIT by putting him at arms' length and giving him an investigation to run which he had overheard described as having gone 'tits up'.

'Tits up.' A phrase to conjure with. It had been up to him to reverse the grim way in which the investigation had gone so far, and so far it had not gone well.

He gripped the steering wheel tightly as his thoughts spiralled around to his boss, Dave Anger, a man who made the phrase 'intrusive supervision' look like something a nanny did. Anger was forever on Henry's shoulder, overseeing everything he was doing, questioning him, making him feel unsettled, making it known that if Henry did not pull the investigation out of the bag, he would be going on a sideways jaunt. He had made it clear that he did not want Henry on FMIT, for reasons that still remained unclear to Henry; what Henry did know was that although he detested Anger with a vengeance, it would take a crowbar to prise him out of the job he loved and was passionate about.

11

As Henry cruised along Dock Street, he tried to relax and put these things out of his mind. On reaching the roundabout at which he intended to swing right through town, he stopped at the give-way lines whilst waiting to see what the car coming on to the roundabout from the opposite direction was going to do. At first Henry thought the driver would loop right round, but at the last second, the car carried straight on in the direction Henry had just driven.

'Thanks for the signal, mate,' Henry muttered, aiming his best glare of contempt at the man behind the wheel who turned face-on to Henry for the fleeting moment that the two cars were side by side, door by door. The yellow street lighting illuminated the man's face, very brightly for a flash – just long enough for Henry's one good eye to go for a ninety-five per cent certainty.

The man driving the car was none other than the slippery Mr George Uren.

As the cars passed in the night, separated by maybe four feet, and the man's head turned away, Henry caught a flick of the ponytail at the back of his head; Uren was known to sport such a haircut. Henry also caught sight of the dark profile of another person in the car, a man sitting low alongside Uren in the front passenger seat. He could not make out any of that man's features.

'Shit,' Henry blurted, a flush of cop-adrenalin gushing into his system. 'Even with one good eye,' he congratulated himself.

He stabbed the accelerator and raced around the roundabout, losing sight of the car for a few seconds. As he drove back up Dock Street, Henry thought he might have lost him. He decided not to race, just cruise easily around – and there he was, stationary at the side of the road, brake lights on, smoke puffing out of the exhaust. Henry sailed past, sneaking a quick sideways look at Uren, who was in deep conversation with the passenger, who remained in shadow. Henry pressed the transmit button on his PR, still on the same exclusive channel as previously.

'DCI Christie – anyone receiving?' He would not have been surprised if no one answered. The team would all probably have switched off as soon as he'd stood them down. No one answered. 'Rory? Jane? Deppo?' Still no response. Henry cursed silently, annoyed that his radio was inaccessible at the moment inside his jacket and he could have done with changing channels. He swore and drew into the side of the road a hundred metres ahead of Uren's car. He switched his lights off, kept his foot off the brake pedal and adjusted the rear view mirror so he could observe Uren and partner. They were still chatting. About what, Henry wondered. 'Anyone receiving?' he asked hopefully into his PR.

'Henry? That you?' It was Jane Roscoe's dulcet tones. Henry's face screwed up in frustration. Why did it have to be her? Still, any port in a storm . . . a saying which had often caused him to get into trouble in the past.

'Yeah, it's me. Just sighted Uren. Where've you got to?'

'Almost at Poulton-le-Fylde.'

Henry raised his eyebrows. To get so far in such a short time she must really have been motoring. He had obviously rattled her cage. 'Can you start heading back? He's currently sat in a car on Queen's Terrace, more or less opposite the ferry terminal. In a dark-coloured Astra, blue, I think. Don't have the registered number yet. One other person on board, male, no other details. Uren is in the driver's seat. I'm parked further up the road, facing towards the North Euston Hotel.'

'Sure it's him?'

'As eggs,' Henry said.

'Be with you as quick as I can.'

Henry sat back, hoping she'd be as speedy returning as she'd zoomed away.

The two occupants in the car continued their discussion, head to head. Henry watched all the while, speculating what subject matter required such deep discussion. Whatever it was, he hoped it would go on and on, giving him and Jane time to get into a position from which they could nab the perv; however, Henry was acutely aware that situations like these were more often than not dictated by the actions of the suspect, not the cops.

The passenger door of the Astra opened. Henry tensed up. The second guy climbed out on to the footpath, then leaned back into the car again, said a few words, then turned away, pulled the hood of his jacket well over his head and set off into Pharos Street, which ran towards the town centre. There was something strangely discomfiting about the hood thing, which Henry could not immediately interpret.

13

He got himself ready to move, thinking that Uren would now be ready to roll. He was wrong. Uren stayed where he was.

'Where've you got to?' Henry asked Jane over the radio.

'Just passing Morrisons.'

'Roger.' Only a couple of minutes away, Henry thought. We might just get lucky here.

Just then the dark hooded figure of Uren's passenger re-appeared from Pharos Street bearing the unmistakeable carrier bag which screamed 'takeaway!'

Henry snorted and allowed himself a wry smile, causing his facial swelling to twinge. Clearly he would not be belly-laughing for a while.

The passenger got back into the Astra. Again, Henry got ready, but Uren and friend were going nowhere fast; they began to feast on their fast food, making Henry's stomach grumble jealously at the thought. He hadn't eaten a proper meal for days. Not that a doner kebab could ever have been classified as real food, but just at that point in time, it would have hit the mark for the ravenous detective.

'They're eating a takeaway,' he informed Jane. 'We could be in luck here.'

'What do you mean? Confiscate the meals?'

'Yeah, that and arrest Uren. A double-whammy. Position?'

'Just passing Freeport,' she said, referring to the massive riverside retail outlet on the outskirts of town.

'When you hit the roundabout, carry straight on, then as Dock Street bends into Queen's Terrace, pull in. They're parked just before Pharos Street. You know it?'

'Yeah, gotcha.'

It seemed to take forever before the set of headlights belonging to Jane's car appeared in Henry's mirror, then stopped at the side of the road about seventy-five metres behind Uren, and were then doused. She had arrived.

'OK – what's the plan now?'

Always a good question, Henry thought. 'Simple: pincer movement, sort of,' he said. 'You come up from behind, I'll saunter down from here. Uren doesn't know me, so we ought to be OK. By the time we meet up we should be at his car. You do the passenger door and I'll slide across for the driver's door and ignition keys.'

'Sounds a wonderful, well thought out approach.'

'Stop being a cynic and let's get on with it.'

He climbed out of the Mondeo and began strolling towards the Astra, Jane doing the same from her car. They actually closed quite rapidly on their target, Henry already fingering his warrant card, ready to slap it into Uren's face so there would be no doubt that he was the good guy.

Twenty metres away it went wrong.

Henry heard the engine of the Astra rev, the crunch of gears, saw the headlights come on full beam . . . somehow Uren had been spooked and was going to do a runner . . . the car moved and Henry came to a halt, wondering whether he should leg it back to his car, then realized the Astra was accelerating towards him. It had mounted the pavement with the nearside wheels and yes, it was definitely aiming at him. Not that an Astra could gather too much speed and momentum from such a short distance, but that wasn't the point. Being struck by half a ton of moving metal was not something to be taken casually. For a moment, Henry did not react, his brain did not compute the facts, but then his disbelief diminished and he knew that Uren was intent on mowing him down. There could be no other explanation.

The car grew as it approached, engine screaming in first gear.

For a split second, through the double glare of the headlights, he saw Uren's face clearly behind the wheel, but not the face of the passenger; and then the car was only feet away and Henry was stumped as to what to do. His feet had become clods of clay, heavy and cumbersome, and he could not command them to do anything to get out of the way. In a second he was going to discover just what the chassis of a Vauxhall Astra looked like from a mechanic's point of view.

It was at this prospect that his legs suddenly found their raison d'être. He could not move to his right or he would be flattened against a building, so he twisted himself towards the road. But not quickly enough or far enough. Uren yanked the steering wheel down and followed Henry, catching him a glancing blow on his thigh with the front offside wing of the Astra. Not for the first time that night Henry went into a spin. He found himself on all fours in the road, stunned by what had happened, then further horrified to find that Uren had not finished with him.

The white reversing lights came on and the car sped backwards, slithering dementedly as it raced to flatten him.

'Henry! Look . . . !' he heard Jane scream.

His head spun up to see the back end of the Astra bearing down on him, virtually on top of him. He felt his eyes widen in fear and amazement, almost popping out of his skull. He started to scramble as though he was on starting blocks for the hundred metres. The toes of his trainers slipped on the tarmac road, but he found enough grip to propel himself out of the way, scrambling into an untidy forward roll as his shoulder thumped the ground. The Astra missed him – so close he could smell the car – braked, then surged forwards, tearing away down the road towards the seafront, its lights extinguished as it went.

Henry was left sitting on his backside on the cold, but dry, road, slightly confused by what had just happened. And why it had happened.

If he read it right, George Uren had just tried to murder him.

But there was no time to reflect on that.

'Henry!' Jane screamed, running up to him. She swooped down on to her haunches. No other words came out, so shocked was she.

'I'm OK,' he gasped, grateful for the hand she held out to assist his battered body to its feet. He stood unsteadily, swaying slightly. 'Let's get the bastards.'

'He tried to kill you,' she uttered.

'I gathered that – with a bloody Vauxhall Astra. Now get your PR on to Fleetwood's channel and let's get some bodies looking for it.'

He pulled his own TETRA out from inside his jacket and tuned into the local frequency, Jane doing likewise with hers.

'Did you get the number?' she asked.

'Oh aye,' he breathed unsteadily. The registration mark was as clear as day in his mind's eye as the little projector in his brain re-ran the scenario of the car coming backwards to crush him to death. 'It's imprinted on my head – almost – shall we say?'

Initially the adrenalin rush eased the pain, but as that wonderful self-administered drug evaporated from his system, Henry's leg began to throb dreadfully, making him suspect that some damage might have been done.

It was twenty minutes since the car had driven off. An immediate search by all the local available cops had failed to find it. Henry and Jane had criss-crossed the streets, also without success. As they sometimes do, the car had just disappeared. Now he and Jane were back in the yard behind Fleetwood police station, sitting in Henry's motor, discussing what had happened. Henry found himself starting to shake as the pain grew in intensity.

Jane noticed. 'You all right, Henry?'

'No,' he gasped. 'Jeez – I think I might've hurt myself.' He touched his leg and jumped. 'Not having a great night, so far.'

'Come on inside the nick and let's have a look-see,' Jane suggested. 'You might have to drop your pants in front of me.'

'Nothing new there, then.'

She assisted him to get out of the car, then provided a shoulder to help him hobble in through the back door of the station, where he propped himself up against a wall in the corridor. His face was screwed up agonizingly.

'Let's have a peek.' Jane reached for his belt buckle, but Henry checked her hand.

'I can manage.'

He unfastened his black leather belt and began to flick open the buttons on his Levis, his eyes holding hers as his fingers moved down the fly. As he reached the bottom rung, Jane's eyes looked down and her eyebrows arched.

'Let's see what's behind the façade, shall we?'

Painfully he eased the jeans down to his knees, exposing his Marks & Spencer Y-fronts, new ones, unstained, he was glad to report, and his thighs.

Jane's playfulness left her suddenly as she laid eyes on the side of his right thigh where the car had glanced him. He looked down and saw a thick lump of flesh turning purple and black and swelling up. 'That needs looking at and quick,' she said.

Henry felt quite faint.

Over the years Henry had spent so much time on business in the casualty department at Blackpool Victoria Hospital that he had got to know the long-in-the-tooth staff there pretty well.

This was fortunate, because the unit was heaving and under real pressure when he landed there just before midnight.

It was the usual fare. Drunks who'd been assaulted, drunks, drunks who'd drunk too much, more drunks, sober people who'd been assaulted by drunks, drunks, drunken drivers who'd crashed their vehicles and mangled themselves, victims of drunken drivers and an array of uniformed paramedics and cops coming in on the back of the assaults and road crashes. It was not a location for the faint-hearted, this unit that resembled the chaotic scenes from MASH but without the army helicopters and the constant sound of artillery. This was the place where the offenders and the victims of the town that was the country's biggest holiday resort were dumped, and could be one of the most violent places anywhere on a Friday night if the combination of people and drink was just right.

Henry was tossed into the middle of this, limping through a melee of smelly people to find his way, eventually, to a stern-faced triage nurse, who he did not know. She quickly assessed him – 'You walked in, can't be that bad, can it?' – handed him two paracetamols and dispatched him to X-ray. Jane snaffled a stray wheelchair for him, which seemed to have a mind of its own, and pushed him through the corridors. It took half an hour to get that sorted, then he was pushed back to the main waiting room where Jane reversed him into a tight corner. He glowered in a depressed way when he saw the scrolling LCD message announcing that the minimum wait for treatment was two hours.

'Drunken fucking pissheads,' he moaned.

'Now, now,' Jane admonished him. 'This is your community. The people you serve.'

He grunted and shook his head. 'I need to call home.' He eyed Jane hesitantly. She nodded and walked away.

'Tell her I'll run you home,' she said over her shoulder. Henry opened his mouth to protest. 'No . . . it's all right,' she said. 'If you give me your car keys I'll get one of the section lads to pick your car up from Fleetwood and get it dropped off at your house.'

'Thanks . . . you don't have to, y'know?'

'I know I don't.' Jane left him.

Henry fumbled for his mobile phone, called home and spoke to a sleepy Kate Christie. She was still his ex-wife, actually, the mother of his two daughters. He lived with her and was trying to keep to the straight and narrow, trying to get his wayward life into some semblance of order once and for all.

As he talked to her, he heard his name being called by a nurse. At first he thought he had misheard. When it was called again, he shouted 'Here!' as though he'd just won a full house. The stressed-out, pretty nurse, who was holding his notes, walked towards him with a look of resignation on her face.

'I thought I'd be here two hours at least.'

She regarded him and sighed. 'The doctor knows you, apparently,' she said in a way which made Henry believe she was somewhat pissed off at him.

SATURDAY

Two

'Henry, it's me, Jane. Sorry to wake you at this time.' Henry Christie closed his good eye tightly and rubbed it, feeling woozy and confused. Kate had actually handed him the bedside phone, having answered it by reaching across him, then shaking him awake from a deep, drug-assisted sleep. He had not heard it at all, hadn't even moved, even though the thing was only inches from his ear. He tried to look at the clock, focusing his uninjured eye, unable to do much with the one Jane had punched, which was swollen and caked up. It was five fifteen. At first Henry thought he'd been in bed over twelve hours, then his heart sank when he realized it was more like four. It was five fifteen in the morning.

His voice sounded disconnected to him when he replied, 'It's OK, what is it?'

'I deleted your name from the scratch pad, put mine down instead,' Jane explained, meaning she had amended the call-out rota at HQ comms so that her name was on first instead of Henry's. Had she phoned to tell him that? Very nice and thoughtful, but . . . ? 'So they've called me out,' she said.

'Right,' he said dubiously, brain groggy, not with it at all. He sat up slowly, the pain in his leg numbed by the strong analgesics doled out to him at A & E.

'They've found the car.' Henry did not respond to this statement. 'The one Uren was driving, the Astra, the one that clipped you. Been found burned out.'

'Oh great.' To be one hundred per cent honest, he wasn't completely interested. He wanted to be asleep. Desperately. 'And? Have they caught him?'

'No, but I presumed you'd want to turn out with me . . . I know we've had bog all sleep.'

'Why do we have to turn out for an abandoned car?'

'Because your instinct about Uren was on the button,' she said.

'Explain.'

Briefly, she did.

'In that case, I'll come. Are you en route to the scene?'

'Er, sort of . . . if you look out of your window, you'll see me.'

Henry stood up and staggered to the window with the cordless phone, pulled back the curtain and saw Jane outside in her car in the grey dawn looking up at him. Her mobile phone was clamped to her ear. She smiled and tinkled her fingers at him. He waved, dropped the curtain.

'Be with you soon,' he said and thumbed the end-call button.

Kate was propped up on one elbow, her pretty mouth twisted sardonically. She was wearing a long tee shirt bearing a slogan about how dangerous women can be when their hormones are in the ascent. Her hair was ruffled. She looked sleepy and gorgeous.

'Mm?' she said.

'I know, I know,' he said glancing down at his naked and rather sagging body. Too much time spent on long investigations wreaks havoc with diet and fitness regimes. There was a massive, ugly bruise which had spread in an oval shape around the outside of his thigh, almost up to his waist and down to his knee. It looked worse than it was, the A & E doctor had assured him, but it felt pretty bad just at that moment. He crossed the bedroom and began to dress, pulling on the exact same clothes he had divested earlier. When dressed he bent over and gave Kate a kiss, inhaling her intoxicating night body aroma which often drove him crazy. 'See you later, honey.'

'Ho-hum,' she mumbled. 'Don't wake the girls.' She flopped back into bed, asleep before Henry had even closed the bedroom door.

'How did you explain the shiner?' Jane asked with a smirk.

Henry shrugged. 'Winged it.'

'You do a lot of that, don't you?'

'What?'

'Winging it. "Wing" could be your middle name. Henry "Wing" Christie.' There was a brittle edge to her voice.

Henry stayed silent, his head resting, eyes closed. Jane gripped the steering wheel, her mouth twisted down with disapproval.

'You don't have to do this to yourself, you know,' Henry said.

'Do what?'

'You know – work with me. You've got Dave Anger's lug-hole . . . there's no need for you to be working the same cluster as me, is there? You could influence him easily enough.'

'I didn't have any choice . . . we all got posted around the county when the SIO team became FMIT. As much as possible people were posted where it didn't cause too much inconvenience.' She shrugged. 'I live in Fulwood. Not too much of a hardship to get into Blackpool down the 'fifty-five.'

'Or Preston, or Blackburn, come to that,' Henry pointed out. 'Or is it that you're still spying on me . . . Anger's little mole?' He squinted through his good eye.

'Don't be ridiculous,' she said, her neck reddening.

'Whatever,' he said tiredly, past caring.

Jane had driven from Henry's house, down through Blackpool on to the promenade, then turned north, the sea on her left. The tide was a long, long way out and the clearing dawn was windless and tranquil, the weather having eased since last night. The huge expanse of beach looked for all the world like something from a glossy travel brochure. There were times when Blackpool actually looked beautiful, but Henry did not cast a glance to his right so as not to spoil the illusion. The tacky Golden Mile would bring anyone crashing back to earth. Instead he tried to imagine he was somewhere tropical.

'Shit.'

Jane slammed on the brakes. Had it not been for his seat-belt, Henry would have been catapulted through the wind-screen. He was literally jolted back to reality, brought back from his dreams of distant shores.

A scruffy black mongrel dog trotted across the road, a dirty look directed at Jane's car. She had managed to avoid flat-tening it more by luck than judgement.

'County dog,' Henry remarked, referring to the semi-mythical creature which had been used ruthlessly as the explanation for many otherwise inexplicable police vehicle accidents: 'It was a dog, Sarge, a big black one, came from nowhere.'

'I didn't see it coming . . . I was almost asleep,' Jane admitted, sounding cross with herself. She set off again with a long exhalation of breath.

Henry sat up straight, aware that tiredness could get you killed. 'Whatever happens today,' he announced, 'we'll both take a couple of days off . . .' But even as he spoke he had one of those pit-of-the-stomach premonitions that indicated to him there would be fat chance of that happening. 'Anyway,' he continued, hoping to keep Jane awake by way of discussion, 'what else do you know about Uren's car?'

'Other than the body in the boot, you mean?'

She drove north through Bispham, then Cleveleys and up into Fleetwood. All charming, romantic-sounding names, Henry thought sardonically, rather like the names of the towns along Route 66. Jane threaded through the streets of Fleetwood and emerged at the roundabout where Henry had originally spotted Uren and his unknown companion in the Astra not many hours before. Just off the roundabout was newly-built superstore, next to which was Fleetwood's well known retail outlet, Freeport, which sold brand names at much reduced prices. Henry had been there a few times as a customer, but in the many clothing stores on the site he had never yet found anything that actually quite fitted him. He always ended up back in Asda or Debenham's.

Jane spun round the roundabout, now heading out of Fleetwood, Freeport on her left. Just beyond Freeport and a few large, untidy warehouses, she turned left into a service road which ran towards Fleetwood docks. This led through a series of tatty, run-down buildings which were once fish-packing sheds and other warehouses, all bearing the hallmarks of a once thriving fishing industry.

A couple of serviceable trawlers were berthed in the dock itself, but the quayside was littered with several rotting hulks of fishing boats which had once provided a living for the people of the town, together with huge chunks of unidentifiable scrap metal. The place looked and felt desolate, overseen by the ghost of a bygone age of profitability. Jane drove past a scrapyard, at the gate of which stood the classic, stereotypical scrapyard hound; a mean-looking mongrel, a cross between the Hound of the Baskervilles and Scooby-Doo, all bones and bollocks. Then there was a caravan storage facility behind high, chain link fencing.

After the dock, Freeport could be seen away to their left, and between was a newly refurbished marina in which was berthed an array of yachts and motorboats. Henry was struck by the juxtaposition, old and new, poor and wealthy, clean and shite. A microcosm of Lancashire, he thought.

Jane drove on. Out to their right was the mouth of the River Wyre. The road narrowed to a cracked, concrete track, then bore right towards the river itself. Ahead of them was a police van with two uniformed constables lounging tiredly against it. Jane drove up to them and stopped. She got out, flashing her warrant card. Henry stayed where he was, looking out across the estuary. With the tide out, huge, dirty-looking mud bars were exposed. The area was wild, rugged, quite barren, the silence broken only by the call of gulls.

Following a brief conversation, during which the officers pointed directions, Jane returned to the car, shivering.

'Surprisingly cold out there.'

She continued the journey, taking the car along an ever-narrowing track, past the remnants of old buildings, their foundations now merely outlines in the earth, some areas of flat concrete, some bricks that had once been part of walls, reminding Henry of the remains of a Roman fort. Maybe one day this area would be of historical and architectural interest.

'How far?'

'Another hundred yards and this track stops, then we're on foot. You up to it?'

'Aye,' he nodded.

Jane pointed. 'Across that hillock, between those trees, then almost down to the edge of the river, apparently.'

Looking to where the track petered out, Henry saw two more vehicles, one a liveried cop car, the other plain, probably belonging to the on-call local detective. They were parked nose to tail.

'Let's stop here, walk the rest of the way.'

Jane stopped the car. She knew Henry liked to stroll up to major crime scenes from a distance: 'With the sun at my back,' he would say. He always thought that such an approach gave him and edge, although he could never quite qualify or quantify that with any tangible evidence. But as Jane knew, when dealing with a crime and any subsequent enquiry, gut feeling was not always to be sniffed at.

Henry climbed out stiffly, his leg hurting, his eye throbbing. It was cold out here at dawn, near the banks of the river, a cutting if intermittent breeze coming in from Morecambe Bay.

They walked to the point where the track disintegrated and became part of the scrub; then they continued up the small hill Jane had pointed out between some trees. At the top of this rise they paused and took stock. The land ran away from them, harsh grass and scrub, then became muddy sand at the edge of the river, intercut by a number of narrow and, at that moment, waterless creeks. The tide being out, the main channel of the river was the only water to be seen as they looked up towards the big ICI works a mile or so north.

'Beautiful,' Jane commented.

'Spooky.' Henry was momentarily mesmerized by three more hulks of trawlers abandoned in the mudflats, lying there like the rib cages of some giant, mythical monsters. It all seemed very Dickensian, and if there had been mist or fog rolling in, Henry could have believed he was in the opening chapter of *Great Expectations*. He almost expected to see the fleeing figures of escaping convicts and hear the rattle of manacles.

Away to their left was where police activity was taking place. They made their way toward it. Three police officers were huddled together in a conflab near Uren's burnt-out Astra, which had been abandoned there; two uniformed, the third a detective who, when she saw Henry and Jane approaching, broke away and came to meet and greet.

'Hi, boss,' she said to Henry. Her name was Debbie Black. She was one of Henry's protégés, having worked with him when he was on CID at Blackpool. She'd done a spell on Child Protection and Special Branch; promotion to sergeant had brought her to Fleetwood, where she was a DS. She noted his eye and limp, but, diplomatically, said nothing. After acknowledging Jane with a curt nod, she said, 'Not good, this.'

'What've we got?'

'Well, you circulated this car last night.' She pointed to the Astra. 'So our patrols have been keeping an eye out for it.'

'Splendid,' Henry said.

'About an hour ago we got a call from a man walking a dog on the opposite side of the river.' Debbie pointed across to Knott End. 'Said he could see a car on fire here . . . Fire Service turned out and doused it down before we got here, then they popped the boot, hatchback,' she corrected herself, 'and found the body.'

'Fire brigade been and gone?' Jane asked.

Debbie nodded. 'They got called to a house fire in Cleveleys, but they'll be back.'

'What are your initial thoughts?' Henry asked. As much as he was eager to go rooting about, he liked to gather facts and opinions as he went along.

The DS shrugged. 'If there hadn't been the body, it's a pretty normal run of the mill thing. Abandoned car gets torched. We get quite a few dumped here. It's a popular spot for it. Another unusual thing is that the fire brigade said the car had been set alight with incendiaries of some sort, plus accelerant, probably petrol.'

'Incendiaries?' said Henry thoughtfully. 'Unusual.'

'Which route did the car take to get here?' Jane put in.

'Same way as all of us, we think, except that where the track disappears, he kept on driving. It's bumpy, but driveable, until you reach the sand and mud, that is.'

'Have you organized a search of the area yet?' Jane asked.

'Not yet. The lads've had a scout round, but nothing structured.'

'Was anyone seen at the car?'

'No.'

'In the area?'

'Nope.'

'What've you done about securing the scene?' Jane asked.

Debbie looked squarely at her. 'I've only just arrived.' If she'd said it any slower it would have been spelled out. The two women regarded each other coldly and a confused Henry decided it was best to step in.

'Let's have a look.'

Debbie spun haughtily and set off towards the Astra, Henry and Jane in tow.

'You got some sort of downer on her?' Henry hissed. 'Why are you bustin' her balls?'

Jane's head turned and she gave him a cynical look. 'Why are you defending her? Is she another of your conquests? I thought I was asking reasonable questions about crime scenes.'

'Jane,' he said bristling, 'I have not shagged every police-woman in Lancashire, no matter what you might believe.'

'Just two-thirds of them.'

'And anyway, what business is it of yours?'

'None, I suppose,' she snarled.

'Exactly.'

The vehicle, although still recognizable as a Vauxhall Astra, had been burned to a crisp. The fire had gutted it. Everything that could have been burned had burned. The tyres had melted. The seats were just springs and metal frames. The dashboard was a gooey mess, the windows molten glass. Henry had seen numerous torched cars and was not surprised to see how little remained, just a charred metal shell. Cars burned extremely well.

The hatchback was open. Henry assumed the Fire Service had done that, which was something to check on – and the body was inside there. Debbie Black led him up to the car and, keeping his hands in his pockets – an old, but trusted approach to a crime scene – he peered in.

Sometimes the brain does not immediately compute what it is seeing. For a fleeting moment, Henry's mind needed to make some adjustments; rather like staring at one of those multi-patterned optical illusions that need to be stared at for a length of time before hidden, recognizable shapes emerge in 3D.

At first Henry could not configure what he was seeing. It looked like a black and brown, singed, burnt mess . . . and then a shape emerged; a head, body, arms, legs; a seared, scorched, distressing sight. And then the smell hit him: burned human flesh, instantly recognizable, once inhaled, never forgotten, forever remembered by the olfactory sense.

'Jesus!' Jane uttered, putting a hand to her mouth.

Henry turned to see her stagger away, hands covering her face, retching. 'Make sure you puke a good long distance away,' he called after her, rather cruelly.

He caught Debbie's eye, who, under her breath, said, 'Wouldn't want to contaminate the crime scene, would we?'

Henry smiled, looked again at the body. It was a truly awful sight, but the real horror to Henry was that its size told him something that made him shiver inside, made his throat constrict. Obviously it would have to be confirmed by the pathologist and the post mortem tests, but there and then Henry would have bet a month's salary that he was looking at the body of a young person. Maybe eight, ten years old, somewhere round there. What sex he could not tell. Not that it mattered. Henry's tired eyes – or good eye – which had seen a multitude of deaths, became sad as he inspected the murdered body of a child . . . and he now realized why Jane had maybe reacted so badly. She too had seen enough death for anyone and was usually unaffected by it. But even the most hardened detective is moved by the death of a child.

'You think this death is connected to the enquiry you're running?' Debbie Black posed this question as she drove Henry south towards Blackpool. After apologizing to Jane about his lack of sensitivity, a gesture received with a sneer of contempt, Henry had delegated the task of crime scene manager to her for the time being, much to her obvious annoyance. He had then commandeered Debbie Black and her car to run him back to the Major Incident Room (MIR) from where he had been running his inherited investigation. To be straight, he should have given the CSM job to Debbie, but Jane was making him feel uncomfortable, so his decision was purely personal. If called to account, he thought he could justify it professionally if necessary.

Now, with the Irish Sea to his right this time, Henry considered Debbie's query. He blew out his cheeks, gave it some application of grey matter.

On his return from the Manchester murder/corruption enquiry, he had been given an investigation that had been going down the pan. Not, he was at pains to admit, that he'd been doing much better with it since taking over. Problem was that it had taken the police too long to see that there even was a problem, despite the much-heralded problem-solving approach Lancashire Constabulary claimed it took, so by the time Henry became the SIO, he'd inherited a mess.

The whole thing had begun some six months earlier, whilst Henry had been knee deep in corpses and bent coppers across the border.

The beginning of spring. Days growing longer. Kids staying out later, parents inside, or sat on patios, beers in hand.

There had been four attacks in one day around Blackpool, each more horrific and violent than the last.

Saturday lunchtime: the first attack, an attempted abduction. A man in a car, a young girl skipping along a street. The man stopped, asked the girl for directions. She was wary, though, despite being a tender eight-year-old. When he opened his car door and she saw his trousers were unfastened, his penis out, she screamed as he lunged for her. She evaded his outstretched hands and ran for home. The man and car disappeared and the descriptions obtained were poor.

The second attack, two hours later: same MO and same result. The child escaped unharmed, although the attacker did manage to drag her to him, but he disappeared empty-handed.

Two more attacks took place that day. The fourth was the most horrifying, but this time the man – if it was the same man – was on foot in a local park, not far from the seafront at North Shore. He made no mistake and grabbed a girl who was walking alone through the park. Within seconds he had bundled her terrified into the boot of his car and driven away. She was released three hours later after suffering a brutal sexual assault. Again, the police had little evidence – that the man had a silver car was about the best they got – and after an intense, but short-term enquiry, they got nowhere. The man went to ground. No arrest was made, but then again there were no more attacks. After a short period of hi-viz patrolling, police resources were channelled into more productive activities. Within a month, the attacks were all but forgotten, except by the victims and their families.

Six weeks later there were two more attacks on the same day – attempts, unsuccessfully, to entice young girls into a silver car by a man with his pants off and penis in hand. These were half-hearted attacks, less serious than on that first day, and it was assumed that they might not have even been committed by the same man. The only evidence linking the two days was the silver or grey car. The problem was that these were not unusual occurrences. A man driving around, flies undone, pants removed, approaching young girls, was the sort of thing that happened quite regularly, unfortunately.

Then nothing. Not one incident for three months.

Then he was back with a vengeance.

A Saturday morning in midsummer. One of the hot days. Scorching sun, people letting their guard down. Nothing bad was supposed to happen on such days, not in England, surely.

He struck hard and brutally.

The girl he abducted was found three hours later, left for dead in a grass verge next to a lay-by, having been strangled and raped. That she lived was a miracle.

It was only then that the police started to click the pieces of the puzzle together, realizing there was every chance they had a serial offender on their hands, someone who could possibly kill on his next outing. In a very short space of time an investigation team was cobbled together and a proper enquiry was underway. Better late than never. By judicious use of skilful bullshit and lies, they managed to avoid too much criticism from the local press, who were ever willing to kick the cops at every opportunity; internally there was some searching questions asked and a lot of arse kicking. A ferocious chief constable insisted on a result, or else.

The results did not come. The local DCI in charge of the investigation found himself miserably sidelined on to a neighbourhood policing project – shamed, basically – and replaced by the newly-returned-to-the-force Henry Christie.

For Henry, this was an unexpected and unwelcome development. He had known about the restructuring of FMIT and his transfer to Blackpool, but had not expected to be handed a poisoned chalice so quickly.

His first two days back in the force had been spent doing his defensive tactics refresher training, which included a great input on how to slap someone, which was both highly amusing and effective; there had also been a demonstration by the Firearms department of the taser stun gun, which was also impressive. On day three he was unwillingly helping out with promotion interviews at headquarters, forming one third of the panel assessing potential sergeants. This was not up Henry's street, but he had only himself to blame; foolishly he had once volunteered to be trained to carry out recruitment and selection interviews in a moment of weakness several years earlier. Now it was payback time as he found himself press-ganged on to a panel asking inane questions to bright-eyed bushy-tailed constables who believed they had the qualities to be sergeants if they gave the answers the panel wanted.

He became so bored so quickly by the whole, dry, mind-numbing process that he started to apply his own assessment criteria. He started scoring highly if the candidate was female, blonde, slim and attractive, whatever they said in answer to his less-than-probing questions. Just so long as they had a modicum of intellect. His approach was soon spotted by the rather snooty other members of the panel, straight-laced, rod-up-the-arse HR types. He was quickly taken to one side and lectured to by a scary lady who threatened him, but could not actually really prove what he was doing. She looked as though she could have plunged a knife into him, which gave him a warm feeling inside.

'You can always find someone else,' he suggested, knowing she was well and truly stuck with him as all the other eligible high-ranking officers had scattered like cockroaches from a light when they saw this task coming up. Just like he would have done if he'd been pre-warned. However, he took heed of the dressing down and when he returned to the interviews he amended his criteria to be more inclusive: redheads, brunettes *and* blondes.

By three p.m. on the second day of interviews – Thursday of that week – having seen an average of three people an hour over six hours, he was mentally screwed and physically crumbling. The panel were taking a well-earned coffee break, Henry avoiding all small talk about human resource issues, when his mobile phone vibrated silently in his pocket as a text message landed . . . and by three fifteen p.m., having given his fellow panel members a cheery wave bye-bye, he was sitting in the chief constable's office wearing a wary expression and wondering if he would be better off choosing blondes or brunettes. Also in the office was Detective Chief Superintendent Dave Anger, head honcho of FMIT. Even before conversation commenced Henry's eyes roved the room in search of the metaphorical chalice, or was it the Sword of Damocles?

'Henry,' the chief constable began. He was sitting on one of the four low leather sofas arranged into a square, for those less formal gatherings. He leaned forward with his fingers intertwined, facing Henry who was on the sofa directly opposite. Dave Anger was on the one to Henry's right. 'I just want to say again that you and your team did a cracking job in GMP.'

'Thanks, boss.' The Chief did not hand out praise readily; mostly he insulted Henry, so Henry realized immediately he was being softened up, therefore remained on guard. In terms of the Manchester job, the Chief had actually headed it, though Henry had done the donkey work.

'No point slacking now you're back, though,' he went on.

'Hadn't intended to. I've just redone my defensive tactics training and I'm involved in PC to PS interviews as we speak.'

34

'Very commendable,' he said insincerely. The Chief's name was Robert Fanshaw-Bayley. Henry had known him for many years. FB, as he was known in the force (and it was not necessarily an affectionate term, because most people called him 'Fucking Bastard' behind his back), had spent virtually all his service as a police officer in Lancashire. He had been a career detective up to the rank of chief superintendent, then became an ambitious high-ranking chief officer, ending up in his present position quite swiftly after one or two deft career moves. Henry had worked for FB several times over the years and they had developed an unhealthy, one-sided relationship, one in which Henry's skills were used and abused by a ruthless FB, often to the detriment of Henry's well-being, mentally and physically. Henry had actually believed FB had gone a little soft on him, but that gentleness seemed to have gone up in smoke. Now he was back to normal, the pleasantness just an unexplained blip on an otherwise uncompromising bastard's character; FB had resumed his role of devious, manipulative, scheming, result-driven git, and Henry guessed that FB did not possess a conscience.

Henry smiled stupidly from one high-ranker to the other, raised his eyebrows and waited for the punchline.

'Dave and I have been talking . . . about you,' FB announced. 'And as you're now pretty hot in terms of your investigatory skills, what with this GMP thing under your belt, we want those honed skills to be put to good use for this force now.'

'Oh, save me the rhetoric. Cut the crap and cut to the chase.' The words hovered on Henry's lips, but were left unsaid. His eyes narrowed with suspicion, realizing he was definitely being set up for a stinker. 'Oh dear,' he did say, looking sideways at Anger. Anger had been fairly recently transferred into Lancashire from Merseyside to run FMIT. Despite his best efforts, he could not dislodge Henry as much as he would have loved to. With close-cropped grey hair and tiny round glasses, making him look like a fully-paid-up member of a Gestapo hit squad, Anger smiled venomously. Despite Henry's success in GMP, Anger still did not give him the benefit of the doubt. It was something Henry could not understand; just what did he have against him? Whatever it was, it was about to be unleashed. Anger's next step in his master plan to oust Henry off FMIT.

'We want you to take on the enquiry into the child rape and attempted murder in Blackpool and the associated abductions,' Anger said without blinking.

'I thought Tom Banner was heading that.'

'Was. As of now, you are.'

'Does Tom know this?'

'He's gone on the neighbourhood policing project.' Anger gave a twitch of his nose. 'Good for his CV.'

'Why me?'

'Fresh perspective and all that,' FB intercut. He knew Henry and Anger did not see eye to eye, that there was a palpable tension there. Once FB had been bothered by the clash; now he wasn't. He had more important things to do than get involved with the petty squabbles of his subordinates. Rather like Pilate, he seemed to have washed his hands of the affair. He was chief constable, for God's sake. 'The investigation seems to have stalled, so we want you to take it on, and,' – for some reason FB inspected his watch – 'get a result within a month.' It was said in an offhand, almost unimportant way.

A chill of fear rippled through Henry's lower intestine. 'A month? It's been going on six months already.'

'All the more reason to wind it up quickly. A lot of people are getting extremely twitchy about it and we want to be seen to be doing something,' Anger said.

'Hence me,' Henry said glumly.

'There is a carrot,' FB announced.

'Shock me,' Henry said.

'Substantive chief inspector. I'll fix it.'

Henry was a temporary chief inspector which always had the possibility of being taken away from him. 'And if I don't get a result in a month?'

FB pouted. Anger half-shrugged. Neither seemed to have an answer.

'Do I have a choice?'

'Nope,' they said in unison.

And so Henry inherited a major investigation getting nowhere which he secretly named 'Operation Wank', because he was sometimes just plain childish.

Henry sniffed, nostrils flaring, and turned to look at Debbie Black's profile. She was a pretty woman in her mid-thirties, with oval eyes and a thick, meaty mouth. Henry half-recalled that she had separated from her husband, but couldn't remember the exact details. Since she had posed the question, Henry had been mulling it over for so long that they had reached the multi-storey car park next to Blackpool Central police station, one level of which was leased for police use only, secured appropriately.

'Good question,' he said finally. 'Does it have any connection?'

'Taken you long enough to reply,' she smirked.

'Deep thinker, me.'

'So?' she queried, negotiating the car around the tight corners and high kerbstones of the car park. 'What do you think? Connection or not?'

His shoulders jerked, a non-committal gesture. 'Who knows? I don't think I'll be able to say until later in the day, but my gut feeling is that it's not connected with the investigation into the abductions . . . or then again, it could be. Uren could be our man for both . . . maybe . . . vague answer, but it'll have to do. I really want to get the scientific side boxed off properly, get the body identified and find the unpleasant Mr Uren PDQ.'

The MIR from which Henry had been running his investigation was situated on the fourth floor of the station. Henry and Debbie made their way to it by way of the lift and found the room, unsurprisingly quiet, devoid of personnel. Or, at least that's what Henry thought until he saw a dark, bulky figure lurking behind one of the computer terminals. A man rose slowly as he and Debbie entered the room. Henry's boss. Dave Anger.

He should not have been astounded. Although he had not personally informed Anger of the latest developments because he had not yet had time (or inclination, if truth be known), it was something very near to the top of his mental 'To Do' list. Henry guessed that Jane Roscoe may well have done the deed already in her capacity as Anger's snitch, though Henry did not know for sure. And even though he did not know if this was truly the case, his feelings towards her hardened anyway. It confirmed to his slightly paranoid mind that she and Anger were still in league, Roscoe because he had dumped her and

37

it still smarted; Anger because of some unknown, unfathomable reason that completely eluded him.

The two men faced each other across the computer terminals. Henry could see Anger looking at his injured face. Debbie hovered back behind Henry.

Anger addressed Debbie, speaking across Henry's shoulder.

'Leave us. Close the door behind you.'

'Sir.' Meekly, head bowed, she withdrew, confused by the tableau, leaving Henry with a man he had grown to hate. But why? Henry knew Anger wanted his chosen few on FMIT and Henry did not come into that clique, but that surely did not really explain the utter dislike.

'What've you got, Henry?'

'Abandoned car, body of a young person in the boot. Car was being driven earlier by George Uren, someone we wanted to question.'

'How do you know?'

'He tried to run me down.'

'You get hurt?'

'A bit.'

Anger looked disappointed that Henry wasn't lying on a mortuary slab. 'Are you the SIO?'

Strange question, Henry thought. 'Yeah,' he said unsurely.

Anger's head rocked. His lips drew back, revealing his teeth. 'Your job is to tell me about it all, I believe.' He sounded supercilious and Henry half-expected him to lick the tip of his finger and mark a 'one up to me' in the air. 'I've had trouble with you before about this, haven't I? Not keeping me informed.'

'I was actually going to give you a ring now . . . and anyway, it seems you already know about it, otherwise why would you be here?'

'Pure chance, pure coincidence, Henry. I only know because I came in early to have a mooch, as is my wont.'

The temptation to say, 'Yeah, right, pull the other one – that cow Roscoe told you, didn't she?' was strong, but Henry refrained as he was also a little gobsmacked by the phrase 'as is my wont'. Did people still say that? Henry, who enjoyed words and sayings from yesteryear, thought it sounded quaint, but coming from Anger it was more like a threat.

The pause lengthened uncomfortably, until Anger said, 'So? What else have you got? Time's ticking, Henry.'

Henry could easily have reeled off the course of action he was going to take by quoting the chapter headings of the Murder Investigation Manual. Instead, he said, 'I know what I'm doing.'

'OK,' Anger conceded with a long sigh, but remained tight-lipped and lizard-eyed behind his round glasses. 'But you keep me in the loop, Henry. That's an order.'

'I know my job.'

Anger nodded curtly, weaved past the desks and brushed past Henry on his way out of the MIR. Henry turned as Anger's hand dropped on to the handle of the door. 'What is it? What the fuck have I ever done to you?'

Anger stood still, his hand squeezing the handle tightly, knuckles white, blood vessels in the back of his hand risen. He looked across the room at Henry, their eyes clashing. Anger licked his lips. 'I need team players on this squad, not loners, and definitely not people who are close to being nutters. One way or another, I'll get rid of you, Henry . . . and, despite what the Chief said, if it's in my power to prevent you being promoted at the same time, I will, believe me.'

'Oh, I believe you,' Henry whispered. But there was something else lurking behind Anger's glinting eyes, something that told Henry that not the whole truth had been spoken. Dave Anger's resentment towards Henry was far more fundamental than disliking Henry just because he might have been a loner or a nutter, neither of which accusations Henry would have accepted anyway. He certainly wasn't a loner.

Anger left. A few moments later, Debbie came back, hesitance in her step.

'Everything OK?' she asked.

'Yeah, just a bit of mutual appreciation,' he smiled, making her chuckle. 'Right, time for business.'

To be an effective SIO managing a murder investigation requires the juggling skills of a circus performer. There are so many things to think about and it is easy to forget important details in the morass of tasks and information which come in. He knew that his initial priority was to get as much from the crime scene as possible, as well as tracking down George Uren.

Despite his personal conflict with Jane Roscoe, he knew the crime scene was in safe hands. She would deal with it effectively. That left him to think about Uren and how best to track down and nail the bastard, because if this was done, it could very well be a quickly-solved murder investigation with a lot of kudos coming his way, something he was not unaware of.

Problem was, he didn't know where the hell Uren was.

Henry picked up a copy of Lancashire Constabulary's intelligence bulletin, known as 'The Informer'. He looked at the black and white photograph and into the hard eyes of George Uren and then the bold headline underneath: 'Dangerous High Risk Sex Offender at Large'. The text went on to say that some eighteen months previously, Uren was released on licence from Wymott Prison, near Leyland, to a probation hostel in Accrington. Uren had been sentenced to four years imprisonment for the rape of a six-year-old girl when he had been lodging with the girl's family. 'Uren,' it went on, 'has many convictions across the board and has warning markers for weapons and violence and drugs. He is extremely violent, especially towards police officers, and has previously stabbed an arresting officer in the chest.' In large, black letters were the words, 'HE SHOULD BE APPROACHED WITH EXTREME CAUTION.'

After a month at the hostel, he was reported missing and was therefore in breach of his curfew and consequently the conditions of his licence, and was subject to a prison recall.

It went on to describe his clothing and the man himself: six foot two, thirty-eight years old, usually clean-shaven but with a ponytail, with a dagger tattooed on his right forearm and the word 'CUNT' across the knuckles of his left hand.

He had not been seen since he absconded from the hostel.

Further warnings detailed that Uren, as well as being a threat to police officers, had also harassed police officers and their families following a previous investigation. He was on the sex offenders register for life.

Henry put the bulletin down and looked at Debbie Black. It had just turned eight a.m. and he felt, once again, as though he had been up for days. He picked up the sausage sandwich Debbie had brought him from the canteen and took a bite of what, at that moment, was the best meal he'd ever tasted in his life. He washed it down with strong, wonderful tea and energy surged through him, better than a shot of methadone.

'We were just scraping the barrel with this one,' he admitted, tapping Uren's face with his index finger. 'Nothing's been heard of him for months and it was assumed he'd gone south, or abroad or something. Maybe he had ... but then a sex offender was arrested a few days ago on an unrelated matter and during an Intel gathering interview, he mentioned he thought he'd seen Uren in Fleetwood recently, in a pub. That's why we were in town last night ... you look puzzled.'

Debbie's brow was deeply furrowed. She sighed. 'You said you'd never had any dealings with him before?' Henry nodded, bit into his sarnie. 'How did he know to run you down?'

'I've been thinking about that one ... maybe I've had dealings with the guy in the passenger seat.' Henry wrapped his hand around his chin, his palm covering his mouth, munching food thoughtfully.

'At least it's a bloody good start to the job. You know who the prime suspect is, which is always a starter for ten.'

'Yeah, I just need to corner the bastard now.' He finished the sandwich, folding it without manners into his mouth, smiling at Debbie as he did so. She, on the other hand, bit delicately into the one slice of wheat-germ toast she'd bought for herself.

They grinned at each other.

Henry very quickly established an intelligence cell, a grand phrase for a lone detective constable heaved from the local Intel department, to start rooting into Uren's background, to go through everything they could find on him from all agencies, and to start to piece together a crazy pathway that might lead to his door. At nine thirty a.m. he had managed to recall all the detectives who had been working with him the night before, scouring Fleetwood's pubs, and had already briefed them to follow up some lines of enquiry as regards Uren's burnt-out car.

Things had started to tick over, but Henry did not want to lose any momentum. He had a briefing booked for eleven a.m. for the murder team and uniformed officers and had arranged the post mortem for two p.m. Via the press office, he had already issued a holding statement to the media.

The scientific people were at the scene and some local uniforms had been commandeered to begin some house-to-house legwork near the docks just to get the ball rolling. They were knocking on warehouse and factory doors, as well as boarding some yachts in the marina. Possibly clutching at straws, but Henry knew there was rarely a crime committed that went unwitnessed.

By midday, a small team of investigators had been given the scent and unleashed. A Home Office Large and Major Enquiry (HOLMES) team and appropriate admin supported them.

A murder enquiry was well and truly under way. Henry's rudely-christened operation had got a new dimension. He wondered how much time he'd be given to solve it. Several weeks ago he'd been warned he only had a month to get a result and he'd failed. Now a murder had come in which may or may not be connected ... one thing he knew for sure was that Dave Anger was hovering for the kill.

Three

Henry Christie regarded his reflection in the mirror of the gents' toilet of the public mortuary in the grounds of Lancaster Royal Infirmary. His injuries – the combination of the whack on his eye and the painful glancing blow he'd taken on the thigh from Uren's car, together with the long day he'd just had, made him look grey and not a little frail. He splashed some water on his face, though it didn't do much to revive him, and wiped himself dry with a paper towel.

His thumped eye had gone a vivid shade of purple, though the swelling had subsided and he could more or less see through it now. His 'gammy' leg, as he now called it, was sore and aching; he was actually wondering whether he should start using a walking stick, which could maybe become a pretentious trademark. After all, all great detectives had something quirky which defined them.

'Great detective my arse,' he mumbled at his reflection and necked a couple of the strong painkillers the hospital had doled out to him.

Behind him, the door to the gents' opened and the Home Office pathologist entered, still in a bloodied-up apron from having just completed a gruelling three-hour post mortem examination on the body found in the back of the burned-out car. He was called Baines, a stick of a man with ears like a trophy. Henry had known him for longer than he cared to remember. He was a down-to-earth soul, and he and Henry had often retired to sleazy public houses after many a post mortem to ogle womenfolk and, occasionally, to discuss the findings of the examinations. Usually Baines was jovial, often ribbing Henry about his frequently disastrous love life; today, though, he was sombre. The nature of the PM he'd just performed had efficiently damped down all sense of fun.

'Grim one, that,' Baines said, fumbling underneath his apron and lining up on a urinal.

'Yeah,' agreed Henry, also affected. On the whole, PMs did not tend to bother him greatly. Today's, however, had been deeply unpleasant. 'So you're sure?' Henry ventured.

'Oh yeah.' Baines was now peeing.

'She was dead before the car was set on fire?'

'Stabbed repeatedly, then burned when the car was set alight.' He finished, crossed to the sink, started to rinse his hands. 'Murdered in situ, I would say. The angles of the wounds and the position she was found in corroborate that. I think we can get a good idea of the type of knife used, though. Probably a five- or six-inch bladed one, with a straight edge and a serrated edge. Kitchen knife.'

'Bastards,' Henry spat, vividly recalling the recently-completed PM. Henry believed that as SIO, he had a responsibility to attend post mortems of victims whenever possible. He had been present when the undertakers had carefully lifted the body out of the burned-out car in Fleetwood, placed it in a body bag, then driven all the way to the morgue at Lancaster. This was for reasons of jurisdiction, as the north Lancashire coroner covered Fleetwood, and therefore the PM had to take place in his area. It was a long journey and Henry had followed the undertaker's van in his car, having picked it up from home. Professor Baines had spent some time at the scene in order to acquaint himself with the crime, and to offer advice, but he was ready and waiting at Lancaster when the van arrived and reversed up to the double access doors. The body was slid on to a gurney and wheeled into the well-lit examination room where, with little formality, the PM began.

Some details were quickly established: the body was that of a young girl, aged somewhere between eight and eleven years; she was naked and had been trussed up, hands bound behind her, feet tied at the ankles, another piece of what looked like clothes line tied between the feet and ankles. Henry could only begin to imagine the sheer terror she must have gone through. It wasn't a great leap of the imagination to guess she had been abducted earlier the same day, Friday. But from where? No young girl had been reported missing in Lancashire, nor in any of the neighbouring forces in the northwest. A simple telephone call to each control room had quickly established that one. So it was a matter of waiting. Henry had already arranged for messages to be sent with urgency to all forces in the country, giving brief details of the facts, asking for immediate responses if any of their mispers possibly fitted the bill. He had arranged for that to happen whilst the PM was taking place, but so far, to the best of his knowledge, no one had yet got back.

In the meantime, his other priority had not changed: find George Uren. Something that was proving difficult.

'God, I wish I wasn't so knackered, beaten up and run down,' Henry said to Baines as they left the toilets. 'Literally run down.'

'What is it? Too much playing away?' the pathologist teased, his mood lightening a little. 'Is the rather delicious DS Black your new piece of totty? Though I must say, she looks like she's been round the block a time or two.'

. 'You really need to get out more,' Henry said with a shake of the head.

'You provide me with all the entertainment I need,' Baines laughed.

They walked through the room commonly called the kitchen, mainly because of the huge chiller cabinet set against one wall with dozens of doors in it, set at the perfect temperature to keep a dead body fresh and fragrant. Cards with names scribbled on, slotted into the holders on the doors, declared whether there was a body on the roller behind the door. The place looked pretty full to Henry.

They crossed the tiled floor to the double doors and stepped out of the rear of the mortuary into the cool Saturday evening. Debbie Black, who had driven up to Lancaster in a firm's car, stood on the grass verge, smoking. Henry winced slightly at the sight.

Baines elbowed him and hissed in his ear, 'Know what they say about a woman who smokes?'

Henry stopped. 'No, go on, surprise me.'

'Fellatio, your todger's happiest pastime.' Baines winked lewdly.

'Just fuck off,' Henry said tiredly, but not nastily. 'I actually don't shag every woman I work with, y'know, even though I'm regularly accused of it.'

'Not what I've heard.'

They continued to walk towards Debbie, who blew smoke in languid rings into the atmosphere.

'Jesus, smoke rings, too!' Baines gasped. 'You lucky bastard.'

Henry shook his head. 'You're incorrigible.'

'Great word,' said Baines. 'Underused.'

'Hi, guys,' Debbie said, stamping out her cigarette whilst exhaling her last lungful and wafting away the smoke with distaste. 'I only smoke after PMs . . . I can't stand the smell of them. Keep a packet of fags on standby, just in case.'

Henry nodded understandingly, although he had never known the desire to resort to cancer sticks. His stress default had usually been booze in the form of Stella Artois and Jack Daniel's.

Debbie looked distraught, as though it was more than the whiff of death that was troubling her.

'You OK?' Henry asked.

'No, no, not really.' She was shaking her head, eyes filling with moisture. 'It's just that . . .' She looked up to the heavens, seeming annoyed with herself for showing emotion. 'I know I shouldn't let it bother me . . . it's just what you said, Henry, when you described what happened when you clocked Uren.' He looked puzzled. 'You know,' she prompted. 'That poor girl was probably tied up in the back of his car, wasn't she? And those two bastards had stopped for fish and chips. They had her tied up alive and they stopped for fuckin' chips,' she said angrily. 'Sorry, sorry,' she said, drawing her hands over her face. She composed herself, took a few deep breaths, then regarded Henry levelly. 'I want to be on the murder team, Henry. I want to have a chance at collaring Uren and I won't accept anything less.'

'What've you got?' Henry asked the question of the single person who formed the intelligence cell in the MIR. He didn't particularly like the way the DC looked back at him, because he sensed the answer in his expression: nothing.

'Er, not much,' mumbled the detective constable. His name was Jerry Tope and his nickname was 'Bung', short for 'bungalow' because, as legend had it, he had nothing 'up top'. He was the DC Henry had snaffled from the local Intel unit.

'How much more than when I left?'

The DC blinked nervously.

'That much, eh?' Henry said, his mouth set.

'Er, just really the stuff that's already on the system.' Tope held up a fairly heavy file. 'Downloaded.'

'Right,' clicked Henry. 'So basically, since Uren was released and then did a runner from the hostel, we've nothing on him, except a snippet from an interview?'

The DC looked forlorn.

'In that case, I want everything that we do know to be turned into an action. I want all known associates visited, all previous addresses visited, all known haunts visited, however out of date any of them might seem to be. I also want all known sex offenders in the area visited and spoken to . . .' Henry squinted thoughtfully, marshalling his dendrites. 'Anything back on the burned-out car yet?'

'No . . . sorry, yes . . . no current keeper.'

'We have the name of the previous keepers?'

'Yeah.'

'Get that actioned, too,' he snapped. 'And . . . find out who he was in prison with, who he was at the hostel in Accrington with – inmates and staff – OK?'

The Intel cell nodded.

Henry said, even though it sounded rather corny, 'No stone unturned, because I've got a very bad feeling about this, the more I think about it.'

What he did not share with Tope were his thoughts on what exactly gave him such a bad feeling, something he was keeping to himself at the moment . . . not that it was rocket science, but something that had occurred to him after Debbie Black's heartfelt remark about fish and chips; if Henry had interrupted Uren and his friend before they had a chance to do whatever they were going to do to the unfortunate girl, then it was always possible they might still be angry, believing they hadn't achieved their goal. They might just be in the frame of mind to continue where they'd left off – and abduct another.

One thing was certain: Henry was now heading a hot, fast-moving investigation and at that precise moment, feeling tired and jaded, hurt and injured, just wanting eight hours uninter-rupted sleep, he did not feel confident of pulling it off.

Henry raised his eyebrows at DC Tope, who was regarding him unsurely.

'So what you waiting for?' he demanded.

Tope's head dropped and his fingers moved to the keyboard

of the computer in front of him. Henry spun and strutted across the MIR – as much as he could strut with a gammy leg – and as he exited through the door he was pretty sure he heard the word 'git' waft from Tope's mouth. He stopped at the door and, in the fashion of all good TV drama, turned to look, about to say something profound and life changing. However, words failed him, so he just left and made his way back to the office he had been allocated on his redeployment with FMIT.

It wasn't such a bad office really. It was out of the way, which was always a plus point. It was small, with a long narrow window running from floor to ceiling, overlooking Bonny Street and not much else. Daily he was now faced with a massive model of a shark stuck on the wall at the rear of Sea World. It had blood on its fangs and small piggy eyes and looked ferocious. He had named it Dave, after Dave Anger, his boss, and greeted it every day with a nod and a wave. The office was desperately cold, though – always – and he had acquired a plug-in electric radiator from someone else's office, which did the job up to a point. He often felt that his front half was red hot, but his back was frozen, even on the best of days. He had a desk, a computer with a will of its own, a swivelling chair and just enough room for two plastic chairs opposite the desk, for those cosy chats that chief inspectors often found themselves having, usually with themselves.

He sat behind the desk and tilted the chair back until it whacked the wall, then raised his sore leg on to the desk, giving it some relief.

Yes, the office was just about functional, but nowhere near as comfy and spacious as the one he'd been evicted from at HQ. The one with the view of the tennis courts, rugby field, trees and grass. Now all he had was a Blackpool back street to admire. And a shark.

It was eight thirty p.m. A debrief was planned for nine p.m., then there would be another briefing in the morning at eight a.m. Sunday would be a good day for working, getting progress made.

He wondered if he would be able to pull this one off quickly and if he couldn't, what would his future look like.

Dave Anger, who he had now renamed Sharky, would see to it that it would be bleak and tragic . . . Henry was visualizing feeding his boss into the mouth of a Great White shark when the office door opened, clattering against the plastic chairs. Debbie Black came in, a terrible expression on her face.

'I've just had a horrendous thought,' she blurted.

'I know,' Henry said, reading her.

'They're going to do it again, and they're going to do it soon, and if we don't catch them, another young girl is going to die.'

'I know,' Henry said again. 'I know, I know, I know.'

In a nutshell, nothing was achieved that day apart from on the scientific front. Uren had gone to ground and could not be found and all other leads were dead ends – for the moment. But then again, unless someone struck lucky in those first few hours, there weren't even enough detectives to spin a drum. It was clear to Henry that the murder squad would have to be seriously enlarged by Monday at the latest.

His tired detectives made their reports at the debrief in the MIR, including Jane Roscoe, and he thanked all of them genuinely. As knackered as they were, they remained keen and eager.

He sent them home at ten p.m. They were all parched and Henry overheard some mutterings about going across the road for a pint, a thought that tempted him. He gathered up his papers, aware that the room had not completely emptied. Jane Roscoe lounged by the door, looking across at him.

A heart sinking in a chest can be a sickening thing.

'Hi Jane.' He walked towards her. 'Thanks for the work you did at the scene.'

She shrugged an acceptance of the remark. 'You going home?'

He nodded. 'I need a good, long kip.' He paused by her so they were almost shoulder-to-shoulder at the doorway. 'You OK being the crime scene manager for the time being?'

'Whatever.' She sounded like a grumpy teenager.

A beat passed. Henry gave her a sad smile, then walked on by, heading back to his office. Even though he wondered how deep she was into Dave Anger's pockets, his heart was still thumping and a quick sluice of adrenalin had done a rush into his blood as he had passed close to her. He was past knowing how to deal with the situation he and Jane were caught up in. An affair over, feelings still running strong on her part, the work situation.

At the door to his cubby-hole he said, 'Oh fuck, what a mess,' then tried to put her out of his mind, or at least partition her away for the time being, and thought, *Bring on the plasma screen TV.*

A weak man versus a public house. Every time, hands down, the pub wins, as it did that Saturday night as Henry left the police station. Despite his weariness and resolve to go home, his head was still spinning and the lure of a cold beer from a well-cared-for tap was too much to resist. Just the one, he promised himself whilst crossing Bonny Street to the Pump and Truncheon less than thirty feet away from the building. One long, chilled pint of Stella Artois would be the thing he needed to get that all-important eight hours sleep.

Ten thirty p.m., and the place was full to bursting, with good rock music blaring out, unlike the junk he'd been subjected to the night before. With his injured leg making progress twice as hard, Henry eased his way through the throng, nodding at one or two people and edging his way to the bar. On his journey he noticed a gaggle of his jacks huddled in one corner of the bar, engrossed in a real debrief.

It took a while to get served, but his persistence in the face of adversity paid off when the barmaid pushed his golden drink toward him and he crossed her palm with the appropriate amount of brass and silver. He took the pint, turned, intending to lean on the bar, but came face to face with Debbie Black, who was standing right behind him, half a pint in one hand, cigarette dangling from the fingers of her other. He hadn't clocked her on entry.

She gave him a half-cocked smile which he found rather attractive.

'Boss,' she said. 'Am I on the team?'

'I'll swing it.' He sipped his lager, then took a deep draft. It tasted amazingly wonderful, feeling like it was shooting through his lungs and stomach and every capillary. 'Thought you only smoked at post mortems?'

'I lied.' She took a deep draw, held it in for what were obviously a few sweet moments, then exhaled upwards through pursed lips, reminding Henry of the pathologist's observations of a smoking woman. She reached past Henry, deliberately closing in on him, and stubbed the cigarette out in an ashtray on the bar. To Henry, admittedly not a smoker, it seemed to take rather longer than normal to extinguish a cigarette, but he wasn't complaining. Even though he was wearing his wind-jammer, he could feel Debbie's generous curves up against him. He swallowed. She moved back, but remained well within his space, her eyes roving all over his face, completely taking him in.

Henry's heart was pounding again, blood pressure rising.

She smiled in a way he did not understand and stepped further back, having done exactly what she had intended to do to him.

'Can we talk?'

'Sure,' he said.

'It's quiet at the far end of the room.' She turned, he followed at a limp, though for some reason his leg didn't seem to be hurting him half as much now.

Squashed down snugly on a bench seat in one corner of the bar next to each other, they could converse without having to shout too loudly.

'Think we'll get him?' she asked, her lips close to his ear.

'For sure.'

'I want to be part of it.'

'You will be.'

'He deserves stringing up, the molesting, murdering bastard.'

Henry nodded in agreement, though the words jarred in his ear.

'Really got to me, that PM.'

'Nothing to be ashamed of. They often do get to you. You're only human,' Henry said with empathy.

'Did it get to you? It didn't seem to.'

'They all do,' he admitted. 'Nowadays more than ever. Must be an age thing.'

'And just how old are you?'

Henry gave her a sidelong and told her. She raised an eyebrow in surprise and said, 'You don't look it.'

He guffawed at the compliment and, flattered, took a red-faced swig of his Stella.

The street outside the pub was busy with foot traffic, typical of a Saturday night in Blackpool. Music from bars drifted in the wind which whipped down the gap between the buildings.

It was not a well-lit street, though, and there were plenty of places in the shadows in which a person could secrete themselves.

A dark figure stood unseen in a doorway which reeked of stale urine.

The figure waited patiently.

When last orders were called, Henry had just reached the bottom of his beer glass, amazed at his record: that must have been one of the longest lasting pints he had ever drunk.

'Can I buy you another?'

'No, thanks. I need to get home,' he said and made to stand up.

'Are you sure?'

'No – honestly. I'm injured, old and knackered, and I need my bed.'

Debbie smiled and stood up with him. 'I'll walk up to the car park with you.'

With a wave at the other detectives, who seemed to have settled in for a session, he and Debbie left the pub, walking quickly across the street and into the police garage using a swipe card to gain entry.

The figure in the doorway stepped back into deeper blackness and watched the two of them enter the police building.

The person's breathing became shallow and juddery at the sight of Henry Christie, a man loathed beyond anything ever thought possible; a man who had ruined more than one life and who, the person in the shadow had decided, would suffer as a consequence.

They rode up a floor in the lift, then walked out of the police station and across the mezzanine which led to the level in the multi-storey car park on which the police had secure parking. Henry's leg was back to hurting like hell, probably, he guessed, due to tiredness more than anything. He was aching for sleep. They trotted down the concrete steps and through the secure gate on to the police-only parking level.

Henry's car was the nearest, his trusty Mondeo. He clicked the remote and heard the thud of the doors unlocking.

They stopped walking.

'Well, see you tomorrow, bright and breezy,' Henry said, turning to Debbie. She did not respond verbally. Instead she looked up at him with one of those expressions which sent a shimmer of anticipation through him, like a bolt of electricity. There was a moment of – literally – charged silence, then she stepped close, face to face, only inches away. For the third time that evening, his heart started to beat faster than resting pace without the inconvenience of physical exercise. He hoped he didn't have any clogged arteries.

'Thanks for letting me on to the team.' She sounded husky.

''S OK.' His throat was dry.

'I appreciate it.' She moved closer. Her arms slid up around his neck. She rose on tiptoe, paused for the briefest of moments – for effect – before planting her lips on to his.

For a second, Henry wanted to struggle and push her away; it was only a second, because her lips tasted good, the smokiness of her breath somehow giving her a vague taste of liquorice. One of his hands encircled her and pulled her into him until the kiss ended naturally and she dropped back on to the flats of her feet.

'I've wanted to do that for almost fifteen years,' she said hoarsely. 'Believe it or not, I've never kissed another cop before.'

'Was it worth it?'

She nodded, lips slightly parted. 'You bet. Want to do it again?'

Henry swallowed, some moisture back in his throat, making what should have been an easy decision quite hard. 'I don't think so, but thanks, it was nice.'

'OK,' she whispered, 'I understand.'

'Right . . . er . . . goodnight.'

She touched his jacket gently, gave him a look which he translated into something very hot. She spun and walked slowly across to her car, hips swaying gently, knowing Henry was ogling her. Henry watched her gradually disappear into the shadows before breathing out and climbing into the Mondeo. His mind rattled madly. He needed another drink now. 'Get home, get a JD with ice, get to bed and forget this shit,' he said to himself, inserting his key into the ignition and starting up. He drove out of the space – the one now reserved solely for him – and within less than a few feet of motion, he knew something was wrong. He stopped, got out, checked the tyres.

The rear nearside was as flat as an iron.

The words which emanated from his mouth were not pretty nor lyrical.

On the other side of the car park he heard Debbie's car fire up. He stood uselessly by his car as she drove slowly towards him and stopped. Her electric window descended.

'Changed your mind?' she asked coquettishly.

'Flat tyre.' He indicated the offending Firestone.

'That's a bugger,' she grinned.

'Yeah. Better get on with changing it.' He headed to the boot of the Mondeo, opened it, picked his way through assorted clothing, magazines, Wellington boots, hoping like mad the spare wasn't flat, too. He could not even recall the last time he'd checked it.

'Need any help?' Debbie called.

Henry replied from the depths of the spare wheel well. 'No, I'll be fine, thanks.'

She drove off without another word.

Twenty sweaty, swear-laden minutes later, Henry was driving down the ramps of the car park on to Richardson Street. His hands were black with oil and grime, his face looked as if he had tried to camouflage himself. His annoyance levels were at their highest and as he sped out he almost flattened the lone pedestrian crossing through his headlights, making the poor soul break into a short dash to save himself. Henry did not stop, did not really register the person other than to grumble an obscenity in their direction. He tore away, desperate to get home. Annoyed that he had weakened enough to go to the pub, annoyed – but curious – about the kiss, seething about the flat tyre and aware that the chain of events he'd been foolish enough to put into motion now compromised his sleep time. Tomorrow would be one hell of a difficult day and he needed to be on top form to deal with it. Now he knew he wouldn't be.

The pedestrian who had almost become a casualty stood and watched Henry speed away car with a grim smile of satisfaction.

SUNDAY

Four

Before he knew what he was doing, Henry had answered the bedside phone and had it to his ear and was in conversation with the FIM – the Force Incident Manager – who was based in the control room headquarters.

'What? Whoa,' Henry garbled when he realized he had taken part in a dialogue that didn't make sense to him. 'Sorry, Andy, can we start again? My brain is befuddled and I've taken in nothing you've said to me.'

'OK, boss, no probs,' the inspector said patiently. He was accustomed to contacting people at godforsaken hours of the day and conversing with idiots.

'What time is it, first?'

'Six thirty.'

Quick calculation: six hours sleep, well, six hours in bed, two hours tossing about and traipsing endlessly to the bathroom (note: get prostate checked) and four hours in a middling dream-filled sleep which was unsatisfactory to say the least. He cringed.

'OK, go on.'

'You wanted to know asap about any response to your message switch to all forces regarding the body in the car.'

Suddenly Henry was fully awake and operating. He waited for the FIM to continue.

'North Yorkshire Police have responded. A young girl was snatched in Harrogate Friday evening. Nine years old. Not been found yet. Disappeared between her home and her grandmother's about quarter of a mile away. They're very concerned.'

'Right . . . we're due for a briefing at eight this morning, but do me a favour and turn out DI Roscoe and DS Debbie Black. Ask them to meet me at the MIR at Blackpool as soon as. Send a copy of the message from North Yorks to the MIR, too, will you?'

'Will do.'

'And thanks for letting me know.'

Henry got dressed in the walk-in wardrobe, spinning danger-ously around as he pulled on his M&S Y-fronts and socks, trying not to disturb Kate too much and probably not succeeding terribly well. He crashed out of the wardrobe to find her up on one elbow staring crossly at him.

'Sorry,' he said, bending to kiss her. 'Could be a long one, this.'

'I gathered. Just keep in touch, OK?'

'Yep.' He snuck out of the bedroom and down the stairs. He felt his face. He had showered when he got in from changing the tyre and shaved at the same time, as he had thought some-thing like this might happen. He didn't want to be rushing round so he had prepared himself for the eventuality, like the good boy scout he had never been. If only he could have got some decent sleep, the plan would have worked quite well. As it was, he was well groomed but feeling no better than before, and his leg still hurt and his eye throbbed. Before leaving the house he helped himself to two Anadin Ultra capsules and pocketed the rest of the packet now that his hospital supply had been consumed. Stocked up for the day with pain relief.

Stepping out of the front door gave him a flashback to all those years ago when he was a sprog in the job, when work seemed to be an endless round of early shifts and night duty; one way or another he had been awake at some horrendous time of day. He was glad those days were long gone and he genuinely felt sorry for some of his contemporaries, who after twenty-five-plus years of coppering were still PCs working shifts. Poor bastards. Most people he had joined with had moved away from that, but there were still some sad ones left who looked ill, drawn and desperate to retire.

He breathed in deeply at his second early start on the trot, and walked across to his car on the drive, parked next to Kate's Toyota Yaris. He sat in the driver's seat of the Mondeo, wondering how he was going to get time to get to a tyre repair place when, just as he was about to insert his key, something made him sit up straight, furrow his brow. Something he'd seen. But he wasn't quite sure what.

After a moment of cogitation, he got out and inspected the car and saw it.

It began at the headlight cluster on the front wing and finished at the backlight cluster. One long, continuous line: a deep gouge from front to back. He bent down and looked closely at it, touching it.

It was deep. Not superficial. All the way through each layer of paint to the metal below. Probably made by a screwdriver or a key.

He stood upright, hands on hips, speechless. He walked round and checked the rest of the car, but that was the only scratch.

'Bastards,' he hissed angrily. 'Who the . . . ?' Actually, he immediately had a very good idea; not necessarily who had committed the damage, but why it had been done. The corruption investigation in GMP. The police car he'd used during the investigation had been damaged a few times during the course of his time there as he unearthed a web of criminality and upset a lot of nasty people. Obviously the game was now being carried on to his home turf.

A cold, nervous shiver ran through him.

A serious and worrying development, maybe having implications for his family.

Henry wracked his brain, wondering if he had missed seeing the damage last night during the wheel change. It could be that it had happened elsewhere, not on his drive at home. It was possible he'd missed it last night . . . and with that thought of reassurance, he pulled away from home and headed to work, but only after he'd got down on his hands and knees and checked the underside of the car for a bomb.

Sunday is never a good day to get food in a police station, as canteen facilities are usually nine to five weekdays and Saturdays. Henry stopped off at a little café he knew of old in South Shore and ran in for a bacon sarnie and hot tea in a large plastic cup, which he then drove to the nick with. He hurried to the MIR, where he devoured his breakfast feast, scoffing the last mouthful as the two bleary-eyed female detectives slobbed sleepily into the room.

'Progress?' Jane asked, rubbing her eyes.

He held up a copy of the message from the FIM which he had printed off. 'Young girl missing from North Yorks . . . doesn't look good.' Jane took the paper and scanned through the message. 'I'd like you both to go over to Harrogate and do the necessary with the police and the family over there. We need to see if we can get a DNA match with our body. We'll fast track everything.'

'I thought I was crime scene manager,' Jane whined. 'They don't go gallivanting around.'

'They do if the SIO says they do,' Henry retorted coldly, but seeing her stiffen, he relented. 'We won't get a full team on to this tomorrow and I'd like to get as much as poss done today. I don't want any feet dragging on this one . . . and it's a trip out, isn't it? Harrogate's lovely.'

Jane did not reply.

Debbie looked at him, a smile playing on her full lips, the lips Henry had kissed not many hours previously.

'Do we get chance of breakfast before we go?' Jane asked sourly.

'There's a couple of Little Chefs on the A59,' he said unhelpfully. 'Get an all day breakfast.'

'Right,' she said haughtily, getting the message. She turned to Debbie and Henry could feel the friction between the two of them, something he could not understand. But then again, the older and wiser he got, the less he seemed able to get to his head around women anyway. 'You ready to go?' Jane said.

Debbie nodded and they left Henry, a lone figure amongst the blank computer screens.

Time to tell Sharky, aka Dave Anger, about the new development – if he didn't already know, Henry thought cynically.

Most of the morning was procedure-driven, ensuring that the staff he had were briefed and tasked and that everything that should be in place for a murder enquiry would be by Monday. He was under no illusions about the job he had to do, being the leader of the team, providing the investigative focus, co-ordinating and motivating the team, being accountable for every facet of the enquiry whilst managing a whole host of resources to maximum effect. There was no place for a loner in such a set-up, though the use of initiative was always encouraged.

He knew it was absolutely necessary to go through all the correct procedures even though he was confident that the arrest of George Uren was not far away. However, Henry still found that when he got five minutes breathing space he retreated to his office and did some doodling on a pad. He wrote: '*Why* + *when* + *where* + *how* = *who*?' Standard SIO thinking. It was pretty obvious that Uren and A. N. Other constituted the 'who' of the equation, but Henry was certain that all the other bits would need to be addressed in depth, particularly the 'why?', even after Uren had been locked up.

There was also something else he did not want to forget, and that was the fact that he was originally heading an investigation into a series of sexual assaults on young children and the discovery of the body in the boot had spun that off at a tangent. He knew he had to bear this in mind and keep his thinking open. It would be a tragedy if he pinned his hopes on George Uren to be the offender for those offences and then find out he was wrong. If the two strands came together and Uren confessed to these crimes, that would be great, but Henry wasn't banking on it.

There was something altogether more sinister and brutal about the death in the car. He knew that sex offenders usually committed increasingly terrible offences, but was this one step too far? Or was it just a natural progression? Who could tell? The last offence committed in the series of abductions had been nasty, almost fatal, so maybe this was the next phase. The use of incendiaries to set fire to the car was strange, too. How many people used incendiaries? If nothing else, it was such an unusual MO that if they were used in other crimes, a link could be quickly established, hopefully.

He sat back, fingers interlinked behind his head, looking at the shark in the wall – almost a metaphor for the dangerous streets of Blackpool. He was feeling frustrated now. This had become one of those early investigation lulls when lots of things were happening, but nothing seemed to be going on. It was a time of waiting. The two women should have reached North Yorkshire by now, breakfasts taken into consideration, and soon they would have the means to make a scientific match, or otherwise, with the missing girl; a few pairs of detectives were visiting addresses and associates linked to Uren; the crime scene investigation was still on-going; Intel was being worked on . . . in fact, everything that should be happening was happening with the resources at his disposal, and even more would be happening come tomorrow. It just felt like nothing was going on. He was sitting on his backside, making sure the I's were dotted, T's crossed, doodling with ideas and twiddling his thumbs. Or, as a much-hated police driving instructor on his advanced course once accused him, when he'd nearly totalled the car, 'Your finger's up your bum and your brain's in neutral, PC Christie. You're in a fuckin' world of your own.' Despite the compliment and near collision, Henry had managed to pass the course. Just.

But actually, inactivity was not Henry's strongpoint. It was unnatural to him. He enjoyed doing, not doodling, which is why he heaved himself out of his chair and strode purposefully to the MIR. He had realized that today would be his last opportunity to get out and about with this investigation. Once all the troops arrived tomorrow, he would be the office-bound strategist. Just for today, though, he was free to do some digging for himself instead of delegating others.

As he walked down the corridor he took off his jacket and slung his covert harness over his shoulders, which held his rigid handcuffs, ASP baton and CS gas canister underneath his left armpit, then shrugged his jacket back on.

With the ultimate and exact science of hindsight, he would often wonder if it would have been the better option to have stayed in the office, drinking tea and pen-pushing, thinking strategy.

It would certainly have been the safer option.

DC Jerry Tope, Henry's impressive intelligence cell, had actually done a good job of going through George Uren's file and turning the information gleaned into actions for allocation, dropping the completed, triplicate, handwritten forms into the appropriate tray for distribution following Monday morning's briefing.

Henry picked up the sheets and leafed through them, aware that Tope was eyeing him warily from his desk nearby. He smiled winningly at the DC and said, 'You've done a good job here.' Tope relaxed visibly, almost heaving a sigh of relief. 'Have you started working on timelines yet?' he then asked, to keep him on his toes.

'Er . . . er . . . just about to start,' Tope said hurriedly, brushing his hair back nervously and riffling through the papers on his desk.

Henry winked at him. 'Good man.'

He took the sheaf of actions – which had yet to be entered on the HOLMES system – and wandered over to a spare seat. He began to read them carefully. Truth was, he should have simply selected the top one and not gone through them to try and pick out a juicy one. From tomorrow, all the actions would be prioritized by the Allocator, but here and now he had the pick of the litter.

It was true to say that ninety-nine per cent of the actions were dull and mundane. Essential, but boring, with no real chance of leading directly to a killer, although this is what every detective would hope for. They were all pieces of a jigsaw, and those in Henry's mitts were no exception. Most were just tedious pieces of sky, but a few were interesting and might just lead somewhere significant. There were four that looked a bit tasty. Henry discarded one, then eeny-meenied the other three, leaving one. Oddly enough it was the one he wanted to do anyway.

The actions were on triple carbonated paper. He wrote 'DCI Christie dealing', timed and dated it, tore off the top sheet for himself and dropped the remaining copies on to the Allocator's desk. He returned the others to DC Tope. He picked up his PR from his office and clutching his job, started making his way to his car.

Reaching the lift just before the doors slid shut, he stepped in to find himself standing next to an old protégé, a detective sergeant called Rik Dean. Rik had once been a customs officer and had joined the police late, mid-twenties, but had brought with him an instinct for sniffing out thieves and bad people. His gravitation on to CID and subsequent promotion had not surprised Henry, who had always backed Rik, and not just because he was a good thief-taker. He was also a ruthless lady-killer, his exploits well known, but for some reason he was rarely in trouble over his conquests. Unlike Henry.

Henry had specifically asked that Rik be released to join the murder squad for the big push tomorrow.

'Henry,' Rik said, 'got your message about tomorrow. The DI's happy to release me for the murder team . . . well, when I say happy, he doesn't want me to go but knows he doesn't have a choice.'

'Good . . . in that case, how are you fixed to join me a day early? I could do with some company.' He shook the action

at him. 'I'm going over to Accrington to knock on a door
. . . if you could make it . . .' Henry gave a 'whatever' gesture
with his shoulders. The lift reached level One, doors, as ever,
sliding sluggishly open as though they resented doing the job.
Henry stepped across the threshold to prevent them closing.
He could see Rik was tempted. 'Could be a juicy one,' Henry
said tantalizingly.

'I'll have to clear it with the boss.'

'Tell you what. I need to nip out to have a tyre repaired.
I'll give you a shout when I'm clear . . . that should give you
enough time to get an answer one way or the other.'

'Done,' Rik said.

Henry left Rik in the lift and made his way across the mezzanine to the car park.

Before getting into the Mondeo he checked it for damage
again. There was nothing further. He looked at the new go-
faster stripe down the side and felt a tremor of anger, tinged
with an unsettling feeling. He had to assume the damage had
been done on his drive at home; anything else was just wishful
thinking. It couldn't have been done on the secure car park,
could it? If it had happened outside his house, it meant that,
unless it was just a random act of vandalism, someone who
did not like him very much knew where he lived. To Henry,
that constituted a threat to his family. Unless . . . unless the
culprit was that neighbour he'd fallen out with who had allowed
his poodle to shit on Henry's front lawn. Whilst a person's
reaction could never be second-guessed, the incident had
happened months ago. Maybe there had been a festering resentment as Henry's response to the fouling had hardly been
restrained: delivering the offending faeces back on to the
neighbour's front door step could have been a tad too far. Even
so, his car had been scratched and he was extremely annoyed.

He drove out of the garage and up to the nearest tyre repair
garage he could think of, which was, fortunately, not too busy.
Within five minutes he was being attended to and his flat was
being examined.

Henry stood, hands in pockets, breathing in the Blackpool
air. It was a good day. Clean, almost warm, lots of blue sky,
some sun even.

'Excuse me, sir.'

Turning, Henry saw the young lad who was dealing with

the puncture. Being addressed as 'sir' by anyone other than someone of lower rank in force was a peculiar sensation. Especially by a spotty teenager in overalls who would probably be out on the lash later, happy to spit at patrolling cops and getting girls pissed on alcopops . . . or was he being a bit harsh on the poor lad? He held up the tyre, which had been taken off the wheel hub.

'Can't repair this.'

Pound signs clattered across Henry's brain. 'And why not?'

'Bit more than a puncture.'

'How do you mean?'

'Someone's stuck a knife, or a screwdriver or summat in it in several places. The inner steel belt is damaged. Looks like a big screwdriver, actually. See.' He showed Henry just what he meant. 'Someone got it in for you, sir?'

'It's beginning to look that way,' Henry said darkly.

Five

It came in black, like a thundercloud, hanging over Henry's brain, fuelling a deeply unsettled mindset as he drove across Lancashire from west to east. Not only was it the seventy-five pounds it had cost him to replace the tyre ('Surely you would like one that matches the rest?'), it was the fact he felt he was being stalked. Maybe they could have been unrelated incidents – the scrape down the car, the damage to the tyre – just co-incidences, perhaps, but he did not see that as being the case. A queasy sensation of vulnerability crept over him.

'If I'd known you were going to be a boring old fart, I'd've stayed in Blackpool,' Rik Dean remarked as, so far, apart from the occasional grunt, Henry had not spoken. He'd been deeply engrossed in running through the suspect list in his head, but try as he might, he could not begin to accept he was a target for anyone other than some aggrieved cop, relative or friend of a cop from Manchester. He had put a lot of noses out of joint, shaken some reputations, angered many. He was not popular over the border.

'Sorry, pal,' he said, breaking out of his reverie.

'Something troubling you?'

'Nah, nothing.'

'Women problems?'

Henry chuckled. 'Always have women problems.'

Rik Dean sighed. '*Moi aussi.*'

'Oh?' Henry said, suddenly interested in the scandal of someone else's life. 'And who is your most recent conquest?'

'It would be ungentlemanly to reveal a name,' Rik said mysteriously. 'Other than to say she's in the job and she's a bit jangled. Went a bit far one night, now I can't get rid. She keeps wittering on about love . . . wouldn't mind, but she's hitched, though separated.'

'Dangerous.'

'You said it. And all that baggage – ugh!' He shivered

Henry's mood had brightened a little as he hit the M65, continuing a journey that was all motorway.

'So what are we looking at?' Rik asked, refocusing on the job.

'George Uren was released from prison to a probation hostel in Accrington eighteen months ago. He did a bunk from there and hasn't been seen since. Bit of a long shot, but the staff there should remember him and you never know.'

'Why did you need a sidekick? It's not exactly a two-man job.'

Henry looked coldly at him. 'I get scared on my own.'

Dean laughed.

Fifteen minutes later they pulled off the motorway and drove down the dual carriageway into Accrington town centre. The place had changed considerably over the years since Henry had spent time there. He had done a lot of teenage drinking, carousing and courting around Accrington, and had loved the place at the time. He'd touched base with it on and off during his police career and seen it evolve, seen the population become much more multicultural, and grown to dislike it. Very different from the town he had known as a youth, now with multi-storey car parks, big shopping centres, car-free zones and blue disc parking – what was all that about, he often wondered.

Although much had changed, the basic layout of the place hadn't, and Henry threaded his way easily across town on to Manchester Road, where the hostel was situated. He drove past the police station, an old building, connected to the magistrates court, which should have been flattened years ago. As cop shops went, Accrington was pretty much the pits. Whilst acknowledging that some officers might have warm feelings for the building, Henry wasn't one of them.

Less than half a mile further, he pulled up outside a large double-fronted house on Manchester Road which had once been a palace, could have easily belonged to a mill owner in days gone by. Now it was a bail hostel, badly maintained and, no doubt, deeply unpopular with its neighbours. It was one of those not-in-my-back-yard things, and Henry felt a great deal of sympathy for people who suddenly found such an institution on their doorsteps – and often inmates from that institution in their front rooms. Pinching the telly.

'Here we are,' he announced.

Both detectives looked at the building, once a spacious home, now probably divided up into a dozen pokey bed sits in which a dozen criminals resided, supervised by the Probation Service.

'Let's do it,' Rik said.

They climbed out and walked up the flagged garden, up a set of concrete steps to the front door. Henry pressed the bell which rang somewhere deep inside. They waited.

'I never asked how you got that eye,' Rik said, nodding at Henry's still-swollen, beautifully-coloured shiner.

'Hit in the face by an irate woman,' he said mock-proudly.

'Hm.' It was a doubtful sound.

Footsteps approached from within.

'Bets?' Henry said quickly.

'Er, big, overweight guy, been living in his shirt for a week, BO to die for.'

'Dominatrix. Leather clad. Whip in hand. Eats a lot of pies,' Henry said, and shut up as the big door opened to reveal someone who proved them both wrong.

She led the two detectives along the ground floor hallway to a couple of rooms at the back of the house, one an office, the other a room for staff to chill out in. She motioned them into the latter, then disappeared, leaving them alone.

'Both wrong,' Rik hissed

'Only by a mile.'

'She's very . . .' Rik began, but stopped abruptly as she came back in. His whole manner changed to one which Henry would have described as 'fawning'. 'Hi,' Rik said. Every feature on his face lifted and his smile put the sun to shame.

Her expression was disdainful. She gave Rik a withering look and turned to Henry, her face set hard, which he thought was a shame, because she was extremely pretty. Though she was dressed in a severe, businesslike way in a grey trouser suit which did nothing for her, it was screamingly obvious to the two testosterone-filled males that underneath the outer coating there was a curvaceous, wonderful body. Her hair was scraped tightly back and clipped at the back of her head, but that accentuated the delicate features of her face, which were slightly offset by a crooked nose that made her outstanding. She was dressed for work, for practicality, and Henry could see that, scrubbed up and ready to rock, she would be stunning.

'I'm sorry,' she said. 'I didn't catch your name.'

'Henry Christie . . . DCI Henry Christie.'

'And where are you from?'

'The Force Major Investigation Team, based in Blackpool . . . er, sorry, I didn't catch yours, either.'

'Jackie Harcourt.'

'And you are?'

'The manager of this facility,' she said haughtily. 'And it's obvious you haven't liaised with your local colleagues, because police visits here are strictly by prior appointment and only when absolutely necessary. So,' she sighed, 'I'll have to ask you to leave and make an appointment. I apologize for even asking you in.'

'We've come a long way, Jackie. I'm Rik Dean, by the way . . . Detective Sergeant Rik Dean.' He sounded like James Bond. He flashed his warrant card.

Her eyelids closed and opened slowly. She looked down her imperfect nose at him. 'I'm sorry you've had a wasted journey, but the fact is that police officers on the premises upset the residents. We are trying to create a positive atmosphere here, working to try and rehabilitate offenders, provide a secure environment in which they can thrive . . . So.' She made a 'shooing' gesture, waving her fingers away.

'What about inter-agency cooperation?' Rik blurted, getting mad.

'And what about procedures?'

'You don't even know why we're here, do you?'

'No, I don't . . .'

Henry could see Rik bristling in front of him. 'Look,' he interjected, hoping to pacify things. 'I know we've jumped the gun by turning up unannounced and I'm sorry about that, but if you'd just hear us out, maybe you'd make an exception in this case?' He knew he had a habit of not phoning ahead, but he always liked to catch people on the hop, especially during a murder investigation, even if sometimes time was wasted. He gave her his best lopsided, boyish grin, which he knew was wearing thin at his time of life, but he believed there was still a few miles left in it.

Jackie Harcourt regarded him thoughtfully and for a tiny

moment, Henry thought he had lost. But then her lips pursed, the shoulders dropped and victory was his. 'Come into the office. I'll give you a couple of minutes.'

'Thanks, appreciate it.'

There was a male member of staff sitting behind a desk.

'Can you give us a few minutes, Guy?' Jackie Harcourt asked him pleasantly.

He scowled, but responded to the request without a murmur, collecting his papers and leaving them to their business.

'OK, so which one is it?' she asked. 'Which one of my little angels had been doing wrong?'

'Actually it's not about one of your present residents. It's about one who should be a resident, but isn't,' Henry explained none too clearly, though Ms Harcourt immediately understood.

'An absconder? Which one? Carl Meanthorpe? Danny Livers?'

'I take it they're recent absconders?'

She nodded.

'Neither,' Henry said and saw Ms Harcourt's lips pop open and a cloud quickly scud across her face; he saw something in her eyes which made him watch even more closely when he said, 'George Uren.'

Her lips came together, tight. She blinked and swallowed, then coughed nervously. Her composure, for a brief but telling moment, had been lost. It was quickly regained. She said, 'Ah, him. What do you want to know?'

'Anything you got, love,' Rik slid in, getting her back up again.

'I'm afraid there's not much I can tell you. He was released from prison on licence, conditions to stay here until he settled back into society, received counselling, got himself a job . . . that sort of thing. He didn't stay long.'

'Have you got a file on him?' Henry asked.

'It's confidential, can't let you see it.'

Henry noticed her hand was dithering as she ran it across her face. His eyes narrowed thoughtfully, but before he could speak, Rik intervened like a panzer tank again.

'We need to see it, love, and if you won't show it to us, we'll just get a court order.'

'Rik,' Henry snapped. 'Just fuck off, will you?' Actually he did not say it, but was very tempted. Instead he said, 'Jackie . . . we're investigating the murder of a young girl and we have

70

reason to believe Uren was involved. Unfortunately we can't find him. By coming here we hoped to generate some leads which might take us to him. I know it's an imposition.'

'I don't know where he is,' Ms Harcourt said.

'I appreciate that, but maybe you know who he knocked about with, any residents past or present who might know anything about him, anything really that might be of use.'

'OK, OK,' she sighed. 'I'll get his file, but this is strictly against policy. All client information is confidential.'

'I understand,' Henry said, 'but please trust us. This is a very fast-moving investigation and the quicker this man is caught, the safer the streets will be . . . and that's not just rhetoric. It's God's honest truth.'

The file was fairly thin, containing details of Uren, his background, conditions of release and then a log of his time at the hostel which ran for a couple of pages, then ended abruptly on his unauthorized departure. Henry slam-read it, his eyes taking it in quickly, realizing that it did not actually tell him very much. He sniffed as he finished it and passed it over to Rik who started to peruse it. Henry regarded the hostel manager.

'There's a visitor referred to . . . who was that, do you know?'

She shook her head. Henry could tell her teeth were clamped tightly shut. He watched the muscles in her jaw pump as she tensed them. 'He only came the once, a sort of rat-faced man, but he didn't spend much time here. He and Uren spoke in the residents' lounge for a few minutes, then he left. I don't remember much about him. It was eighteen months ago.'

'Yeah, yeah . . . so what sort of resident was Uren?'

'Nasty, unpleasant,' she said with feeling. 'Glad to see the back of him, to be honest.'

'Are there any people here now who were resident when Uren was here?'

'We have an ever-changing clientele, but old Walter Pollack was here, still is and probably will be this time next year. He's institutionalized.'

'Did he have any dealings with Uren?'

'Not specially, I don't think.'

'Is he in now?'

'Yes, but . . .'

'We'd like to chat to him, please,' Henry said firmly. Ms

71

Harcourt backed off, still flustered underneath her smooth veneer. Henry could not make out what was troubling her, but something was bubbling.

'He's in his room – upstairs, number three.'

Rik, who'd had his head in the Uren's file, looked up and snapped shut the ring-binder. 'Bugger all in here,' he announced, words which drew an expression of condemnation from Ms Harcourt.

'What's Pollack in for?' Henry asked.

'He feels up little boys.'

He was sixty-four years old, thin and wiry, had the hook nose and eyes of a predator, which is exactly what Walter Pollack was. Henry recognized a dangerous individual when he saw one and Pollack was one of those horrendously dangerous people who pick on the young – and destroy them. Ms Harcourt had been obliging enough to show the two detectives his file, including his list of previous convictions. They stretched back over thirty years, many with a common theme: indecent assaults on young boys, gross indecency with some, and stealing to subsidize his lifestyle. Pollack was obviously a lost cause, his perversions not mellowing with age, and the best thing society could think to do with him was keep an eye on him until he slipped away and re-offended, and then jail him again. It was something Henry would have bet his last week's lottery winnings on happening, all ten pounds of it.

His room was neat and tidy with a metal-framed bed, wardrobe, sink and desk, reminding Henry of the rooms at the police training centre at Hutton where he'd spent many a sleepless night over the years. Pollack was sitting at his desk, smoking, emptying his lungs out of the open window overlooking Manchester Road.

Pollack's head turned slowly as the detectives entered, Ms Harcourt in their wake.

'Walter, these men are—' she began.

'—the filth,' Pollack finished for her, a sneer of contempt on his face. He stumped out his cancer stick and coughed, a rasping harsh noise which sounded as though a lot of fluid was gurgling around inside his chest. Henry hoped it was nothing minor. 'I clocked you walking in and made you straight off. I've done fuck all.'

'Never said you had,' Rik retorted.

'They want to ask you about George Uren, Walter,' Ms Harcourt said over Henry's shoulder.

'Why, what's he done?' There was smirk on Pollack's face.

'We just need to talk to him. You don't need to know what he's done,' Rik said.

'It's that Fleetwood job, isn't it?' he guessed correctly. He tapped his ear. 'Radio Lancashire.'

Henry regarded the man's face. Wrinkled with age, grey hair, bald on top, permanent curl on his lips and piercing cold eyes. Paedophilia had never been Henry's field of expertise, though he had dealt with a few offenders, mainly via murder enquiries. He had found that he had always despised the offenders he came across, usually men, probably because he always had to fight against the images of his own children and the thought of what he would do to anyone who hurt them. He detested Pollack immediately and his right hand balled into a fist at his side.

Pollack saw the movement, smiled. 'Want to hit me? All cops do.' He raised his wiry eyebrows. 'Except for the ones who molest kids like I do.'

Henry did the quickest count to ten ever, still felt like kicking the living shit out of this old paedophile, but got a grip, relaxed . . . c'mon . . . relax . . . 'Have you got any idea where George Uren is?'

'Why should I know?'

'You were here when he was,' Henry said. 'Presumably you talked to him.'

'Not specially. I practise talking to the little people . . . that's my speciality.'

Rik Dean reacted instantaneously. Before Henry could stop him, he'd blurted the words, 'Sick bastard!', crossed the room with one stride, heaved Pollack out of his chair and pinned him up against the wall by the open window. His face was centimetres away from Pollack's. 'I'm going to throw you out of this window, you perverted git.'

Pollack's expression remained unchanged, as though this was something that always happened to him.

'You let that man go!' Ms Harcourt screamed. 'And you get off these premises now.' She pushed Henry out of her way and tried to drag Rik off Pollack.

Dean was a strong, burly man, and he did not flinch. Instead, he almost shrugged Ms Harcourt off and slammed Pollack against the wall once more, inducing a further scream from her: 'Get off him! I knew this was a mistake, letting you two in here.'

'Rik, put him down,' Henry said.

'Yeah, you're right. I don't know where this piece of shit's been, do I?' He released Pollack with a flick and stepped away. Pollack sniggered, unshaken by the event. He brushed himself down disdainfully. Hard-faced bastard, Henry thought. Love to meet you in a back alley.

'Come on.' Henry touched Rik's shoulder.

Rik's teeth were grinding, his whole being coiled up tight. He gave Pollack a last look which would have killed him if there had been any justice, then strutted out of the room. Henry also shot Pollack a last glance.

'Expect a complaint of assault and police brutality,' Pollack said coolly. He sat down and tapped a cigarette out of the packet on the desk top, placed it between his curdled lips. Henry reached out, snatched the cigarette and ground it to pulp in the palm of his hand, allowing its content to flake on to Pollack's lap. He leaned in close.

'Don't,' he whispered, 'or I'll revisit.' He winked and left it at that, easing past the trembling Ms Harcourt.

By the time Henry got to the front door of the hostel, Rik had already reached the car. He waited for Ms Harcourt, who came down the stairs and walked angrily toward him.

'I'll be reporting this,' she said.

Henry shrugged. 'Sorry,' he said. 'Didn't go the way I'd intended.'

She held Henry's eyes for a few moments, some internal wrangling going on behind her eyes. Then she relented slightly. 'I'll see what Pollack wants to do.'

'He won't do anything.'

'How can you be sure?'

'Because if he does, he'll get investigated. I'll get a surveillance team on him and I guarantee he'll re-offend – and he knows that.'

'Are you saying I'm not doing my job?'

'I'm saying he'll never change.'

Henry was about to leave it at that when Ms Harcourt said,

'Just hang on there a sec.' She spun away down the hallway, disappeared into the staff rooms and was back a minute later, a piece of paper in hand. She waved the paper. 'Look,' she said unsurely, 'don't think I don't want George Uren caught. I do. He's an evil man ... This is the name and address of a previous occupant who did spend some time with him. He's moved on to the coast now and this is the address we have on file here. It may not be current. If it isn't, he should have registered with the Probation Service on the Fylde. He might know where Uren is.'

'Thanks.' Henry took the paper.

'I heard what you whispered to him up there,' Ms Harcourt said. 'That sort of thing can be very scary, the threat to return.'

'And? I meant it.'

'That's what makes it scary.' She looked into Henry's eyes. He saw fear there, terror maybe. Henry was puzzled, but did not have time to pursue it because his mobile phone rang. He gave her a business card and Ms Harcourt opened the door for him to leave.

He answered the phone as he trotted down the front steps of the hostel. It was Debbie Black calling from Harrogate. 'Got anything?' Henry asked, doubling into the driver's seat of the Mondeo.

'Could have,' she replied. 'Obviously we can't be a hundred per cent, but the young girl went missing last night from an estate on the outskirts of Harrogate. Would be about the right age and height as the dead girl in the Astra. Won't know for sure until we get the forensic matches back, but I have a feeling about it.'

'Where are you up to with it?' Henry slotted the key into the ignition, fired up the engine.

'Just off to the parents with the SIO. We've brought some DNA kits, so we'll take swabs and also turn out the family dentist for those records, too.'

'Good stuff,' Henry said, raising an eyebrow at a po-faced Rik Dean, who was still smarting from his recent encounter. 'Get the kits back over here and we'll fast-track them tomorrow.'

'Yeah, no probs with that.'

'How are they treating you out in the sticks?'

'Excellent.'

'Good – and how's Jane?'

'Being a first-class bitch as ever.'

Debbie cut the connection, leaving Henry with a dead phone at his ear and a twisted grin on his face. 'Could be some progress,' he said to Rik.

'Was that Debbie Black?' Henry nodded. 'Hm,' Rik grunted.

Henry turned squarely to the DS and looked disappointedly at the grim-faced officer. 'Two things: first off, I thought you were a wow with the chicks?'

Rik shrugged. 'Sometimes things just don't gel . . . not that I wouldn't give her one, all things being equal. Actually, she was pretty bloody tasty. And secondly?'

'Your temper could get you in the shit. I always thought you were a pretty placid sorta chap.'

'Got it wrong on two counts, then, haven't you, boss? The temper's an experience thing,' he explained. 'The more experience I have, the less patience I have for crims, pervs in particular.'

'Hm, going by that logic, my temper should be just about at ground zero.'

'From what I've heard, it is.'

The two men eyed each other for a moment, then Henry waggled the note Ms Harcourt had given him, the Ms Harcourt he could not quite figure out. 'She relented a bit – gave me this name and address as one of the previous inmates who knew Uren and may know where he is now.'

'How did you manage that?' asked an astonished detective sergeant.

'Boyish charm . . . crumbled under my aura of male sexuality . . . a combination of things.'

'Hardly,' Rik muttered, snatching the note. 'Bloody hell!' he blurted on reading the name. 'Percy Pearson – Percy Pearson the perverted person from Preston – now living on us, that is. He was locked up on sus of gross indecency last week sometime . . . luring boys into public toilets, then introducing them to the delights of his donger. Enticed one kid back to his flat, I think.'

'Oh,' said Henry, not quite slapping his forehead. The penny had not dropped when he had read the name. Now it had. 'He's the one who said where Uren might be in the first place. We were in Fleetwood because of something he'd said during an Intel interview. Could've saved us an eighty-mile round trip if I'd remembered.' He pulled an agonized face, annoyed.

'You wouldn't have had the pleasure of the frigid Ms Harcourt, though.'

Henry pulled away from the kerb. 'I don't think I'll ever have that pleasure,' he admitted sadly, 'but something tells me that behind that chilly veneer she isn't frigid.'

Rik gave a wistful, 'Mm, quite fancied her, actually.'

The return journey across the county was tedious. They joined queues of the great unwashed masses heading into Blackpool. It only dawned on Henry he would have been better going back by another route than the motorway when he hit a tailback of slow-moving traffic as he left the M6 and joined the M55. He began to zigzag through the crawling morass, but to no real avail. Progress was tortoise-like at best. The section of the journey which would normally take about fifteen minutes took almost an hour on a day that was becoming hotter and hotter, and every driver seemed fractious.

Rik Dean chuckled when Henry middle-fingered a guy and his family who unintentionally cut him up in their people-carrier. 'You were right about your temper,' he laughed. 'Mr Road Rage personified.'

Henry uttered a 'Harrumph!' and his mouth tightened as another car veered across his bows, causing him to brake hard. He said nothing more, bottled up his frustration and decided to ease off, get back in one piece.

There were definitely no crowds of day-trippers on Shoreside, Blackpool's largest council estate, one of the most deprived areas in the country. A place where unemployment ran to a staggering percentage and drugs and crime all but dominated an estate where kids ran riot and the cops trod very carefully. Whole avenues of houses were boarded up, abandoned by tenants who had lost all hope; rows of shops that had once provided essential local services had been destroyed and burned down, with the exception of one which, steel-grilled and CCTV-protected, somehow continued to trade.

'Fuckin' dump,' Rik commented as Henry drove on to the estate.

Henry made no response. On and off for many years he had policed Shoreside and seen some terrible things. He knew, however, that the blight was caused by just a few individuals who brought misery to the majority, who were decent, law-abiding folk wanting peaceful lives.

'Sink-hole,' Rik added, his eyes roving.

'Made your point,' Henry said bluntly. 'You've become very cynical.'

'Haven't you?'

Henry considered the question, brow furrowed. 'Possibly,' he said in an unconvincing way.

'So you haven't become cynical?' Rik peered at him.

'I'd like to think I haven't.'

Before he could continue, Rik said, 'We police the shits of the world who are all out to lie and cheat and hurt you; all they're concerned about is themselves and a fast buck; we get treated like shit by the organization, we deal with the dross of society and you say you're not cynical. I mean, you're on the bloody murder squad, Henry . . .' His voice trailed off hopelessly.

Henry remained silent.

'I mean – look.' Rik pointed to a group of youths lounging indolently at the roadside. One of them stuck a middle finger up as the car drove past. Rik shook his head sadly. 'Shits.'

Henry had had enough introspection, because he was feeling strangely uncomfortable with Rik's allegation. Something inside was telling him that being a cynic was a 'bad thing', and he was agreeing with it, even though the evidence which pointed to him being the biggest cynic of all time was overwhelming. 'What's the address again?'

Rik gave him a sardonic sidelong glance, then read it out from the note, realizing the conversation had come to a grinding halt.

Henry drove through Shoreside, the progress of the car monitored by many pairs of suspicious eyes. Henry felt a shiver of menace. He knew the estate had become an increasingly dangerous and intimidating place for cops, or anyone from the authorities. Although some government money had been tossed at it, it was to no avail. Henry believed the local authority saw it as a lost cause and would have loved to ring fence it, which saddened him. Even the police seemed to keep it at arms' length, though they would deny this. Henry knew the post of community beat officer was vacant and had been for a few months. No one wanted it.

'Psycho Alley,' Rik said.

'What?'

He repeated the words. 'That's what they call that rat run these days,' he said, pointing to a high-walled ginnel which ran between two sets of council flats. It threaded from one side of the estate to a pub on the outer edge where many locals drank, and a row of shops which were not on the estate. It was actually called Song Thrush Walk.

'Why Psycho Alley?'

'The place where sane persons fear to tread,' Rik said spookily. 'Not unless you want to be raped, robbed or battered.'

'Go on,' Henry urged.

'Two old biddies robbed and beaten; three assaults and one indecent assault in the space of six weeks ... hence it being christened Psycho Alley. All the street lighting has been smashed, and even on a good day it's a menacing walk.'

Having been based at HQ until recently, Henry often missed out on local crime hotspots and he had never heard of the problems here. 'What's being done about it?'

Rik shrugged as if to say, 'Who knows?'

'It's a problem to be solved, isn't it?'

Rik guffawed. 'Problem solving. Our policing panacea? We're so fucking busy, Henry, we don't have time to solve problems. All we do is respond, respond, respond. Every bugger is driven by the brick around their necks,' – he was referring to the personal radio – 'or just by sheer volume of work. Do you know,' he began to rant, 'there are over five thousand crimans outstanding for Lancs PCs?' Crimans were the follow-up enquiries doled out by supervisors to their officers. It was a statistic Henry did know. 'We're running round like blue-arsed flies, chasing our tails all the time. It's horrendous. We don't have time to solve bloody problems!'

'Finished?' Henry said, unimpressed.

'Finished.'

'Now where's that house? Down here somewhere.'

Henry drove into a cul-de-sac with three-storey blocks of flats on either side of the road, one of which contained the flat Percy Pearson lived in.

Peering through the windscreen, Rik pointed. 'That one up there.'

Henry pulled into the kerb, looking up at the block, which

made his mouth turn down at the corners. The sort of place he had been into, it felt, a zillion times. One of those 1970s experiments in housing which looked good on the plans, but when built turned into a social nightmare. A crumbling concrete balcony ran along the front doors of all the first and second floor flats, and one or two kids leering over were already interested in the appearance of an unknown car in the area. Henry was uncomfortable at leaving the Mondeo which had been the victim of enough damage recently, thank you.

Wondering whether it would be on bricks when he returned, he did leave it and walked toward the flats, up the stairwell which ran up the gable end. He was not surprised to step over what he had to step over on the way up, and this made him think that not being surprised by anything any more equated to cynicism. Or was it pragmatism? Some sort of 'ism' anyway.

All the while next to him, Rik Dean chunnered away about druggies and shits and no-hopers and low-class denizens of the jungle in general. He was having a bad day. It was about to get worse.

The pair emerged on to the balcony which clung to the upper floor, pausing to check on the car, which had attracted the attention of two snotty kids who were standing close to it, rather like a newly-born antelope found by ravenous wolves. They looked fearlessly up at the two detectives.

'Don't even think about it,' Henry called through hands cupped like a loudspeaker.

Both kids shouted something back and stuck their fingers up at him, but sauntered away. Henry watched them a while longer until he was satisfied they'd gone for good.

The detectives walked along the balcony until they reached Pearson's front door, which had been repaired by boards and had graffiti sprayed across it. Henry looked for anti-paedophile slogans, but saw none. Rik banged on the door, hard and clear: a copper's knock. He caught Henry's eye, then thrust his hands into his pockets. There was no response, so he kicked the door instead with his toe cap, then bent down and tried to peer through the letterbox. He found he could not push up the flap. He rapped on the door again, put his ear to the wood and listened. Henry raised eyebrows at him.

'I think I heard something . . .' Rik stood back, knocked again, but not so dramatically. Just another door to add to the hundreds he'd knocked on in his career. He waited for a reply with a certain amount of diffidence.

Henry folded his arms patiently and glanced toward his car. Still OK.

There was a shuffle behind the door. The security chain was either slid back or slipped into place. Then it opened, and the chain was on: a face peered through the four-inch gap. 'Yes?'

'Afternoon, Percy, I think you know me.' Just in case he didn't, Rik extended his arm and thrust his warrant card into Pearson's face.

Pearson didn't even look, but a big, frightened eye – the only one they could see – flicked from one detective to the other.

'DS Rik Dean from Blackpool nick, as you know. This is DCI Christie from the Force Major Incident Team.' Rik wasn't having any misunderstandings here, even though he knew Pearson did know him.

'Well I don't know what you want with me. I was locked up last week and now I'm on conditional bail, which I haven't broken.' It was a very whiny voice.

'I know, I know,' Rik cooed reassuringly. 'We're not saying you have done anything, but we'd like to have a chat with you all the same.' His hands spread wide in an open gesture. 'You might be able to help us.'

'I doubt it,' Pearson said, 'and if you haven't got a warrant, you're not coming in here.'

He was about to slam the door. Rik managed to step in and wedge his shoulder against it, preventing it from closing. Henry came in behind his colleague and over Rik's shoulder said, 'Red rag to a bull, Mr Pearson. You chose to say some very poor words, because when we get told we need a warrant, that makes us very sus indeed, usually meaning that we don't bother getting one, we just come in anyway.'

'I'm hiding nothing,' he protested.

'Open the door then, and let us in,' Henry said reasonably.

'OK, OK, but you need to step back.'

'And if you lock us out,' Rik warned, 'we'll kick the door in and think of a reason after, got that?'

Pearson nodded. Rik and Henry took a step back. The door closed. For a moment they thought they were going to have to make good their promise about forcing an entry, but then the chain slid back and the door opened slowly. A wary sex offender said, 'Come in,' and led them through to the living room. It was a bare, basic place. Cheap furniture, big TV, DVD and video, and a computer in the corner, which attracted Henry's attention.

'You lot've got my hard drive,' Pearson said.

Henry looked at him properly for the first time. Saw a middle-aged man with pockmarks cratering his face and a look in his eyes which showed fear. Pearson was breathing shallowly, and Henry could have sworn he heard the man's heart beating.

'No need to be nervous,' Henry told him with a wicked smile, making him even more tense. There was something wrong, Henry sensed. His eyes narrowed. 'Just want a chat, Percy, that's all.'

'D'you want to sit?'

'I'll stand,' Henry said, not wishing to lose any advantage. 'Move around a bit, if you don't mind.'

'Me too,' said Rik, also sensing Pearson's unease. The detectives circled like hawks.

'What d'you want?'

Maybe it was simply the fact that two cops had arrived unannounced and were invading his space that made Pearson nervous; the fact that it was hugely apparent they immediately disliked him and that here he was, alone with two big guys who might want to do him damage. Maybe that's why he's all jittery, Henry thought.

'I believe you're on the sex offenders register,' Henry put to him. Pearson blinked, swallowed, looked pale, nodded. 'How long for?'

'Life,' he whispered. 'But I've signed on and done everything I'm supposed to do.'

'That's good, even though you still are committing offences,' Henry pointed out, happy to continue to make Pearson squirm, even though he knew he was being a bit naughty.

'Allegedly,' he retorted primly. Then, 'What *do* you want?'

'You were in a probation hostel in Accrington,' Rik said.

'Which you already know . . . look, what is this?'

'You were there with a guy called George Uren.'

Pearson's mouth closed tightly. 'And?'

'We want to know where he lives,' Henry said.

'I already told you lot last week. I've seen him knocking

about in Fleetwood, but I don't know where he lives. God, I wish I'd never opened my trap.'

'According to the hostel records, you were pretty pally with him.'

'Hm! That bitch Harcourt tell you that? Well she's wrong. He was a bloke I talked to, that's all. Nothing more.'

'Sharing experiences?' Rik cut in with a sneer. Pearson's eyes turned to Rik. He licked his lips.

'We talked . . . that's all. He wasn't a man I particularly liked, OK?'

Suddenly, the heads of all three men turned to a door off the living room which Henry guessed led to the bedroom. Was it a scratching noise?

'Someone in there?' Rik demanded. 'You not alone?'

Henry focused closely on Pearson, himself now tense, wondering if they'd stumbled on to something. There was a faint meow. Pearson crossed the room with an angry look on his face and opened the door six inches, allowing a tiny kitten to tumble through the gap. Pearson lifted it up in the palm of his hand and closed the door. The expression on his face morphed into one of triumph tinged with . . . Henry attempted to work it out, then got it: relief.

'Just my cat, Nigel.'

'So, nothing more than a passing acquaintance with Uren, then?' Henry said, resuming the conversation.

'Exactly. He is not the sort of person I wish to be associated with.'

'Why not?' Rik queried.

'Erm . . .'

Henry's head jerked toward the bedroom again, his whole concentration on it, a tingle of static crackling through him as his senses clicked into overdrive. He was certain he'd heard something else, not just a cat. His head revolved slowly to regard Pearson. 'Who's in that room?' he asked quietly.

'Nobody,' he snapped defensively.

The cold, hard eyes of the detectives picked up Pearson in their glare, deeply suspicious.

'Another cat?' Henry said. Pearson's mouth stayed clamped shut. 'Have you anything to hide, Percy?'

'No.' It was just a whisper of denial, no strength in it.

'Then you won't mind if we have a glance,' Rik said, taking

a step to the door. Cat still in hand, Pearson made a sudden move toward him. Rik came up sharp. 'Yes?' he said. Pearson stopped, his countenance desperate with indecision.

'You need a warrant.'

'Like hell,' Rik said. 'I need fuck all.' His hand reached the door handle and rested on it, then pushed it down and pushed the door which swung open on its hinges, revealing a dimly-lit bedroom beyond, a double bed up against the back wall and an indistinguishable shape upon it, under the duvet.

The detectives shared a quick glance, then Henry looked at Pearson whose shoulders dropped in a gesture of defeat. 'You fibbed.'

Rik took a step into the bedroom, his broad frame filling the doorway, his back now to both Henry and Pearson.

Pearson moved with sudden violence, catching both men off guard. His right hand, the one holding the kitten, swung in Henry's direction and with all his might he hurled the poor feline at him, a tiny bundle of fur and claws flying across the room and slamming into Henry's face, a squeal emitting from both man and beast with the shock.

Then Pearson lunged at Rik's back, his right arm raised.

Henry scrabbled the kitten away, sending it sprawling into the safety of the settee; at the same time he saw a flash of silver in Pearson's raised hand and immediately realized it was a knife – where the hell had it come from? – and it was plunging toward Rik's unprotected back.

A primitive roar of unintelligible sound uttered from Henry's throat as he tried to warn his colleague, whilst at the same time he dove at Pearson. But even then, in that nanosecond, he knew Pearson had the advantage. He was close to Rik. Henry was too far away. And Henry knew he could not stop the arc of the blade, which he now saw clearly was thin, narrow, about seven inches long. A knife which could easily kill.

At the last moment, Rik twisted, but the knife was thrust into his shoulder, drawing a gurgling, inhuman scream.

In the surreal way in which incidents like this unravel in the gap between vision and thought, it all slowed down to an agonizing speed and clarity as Henry saw the tip of the blade touch Rik's shoulder, enter through the fabric of his jacket and disappear a millimetre at a time into his flesh.

Then real time clicked back in.

Rik bellowed in agony and stumbled down to his knees.

Pearson shrieked with rage.

Henry Christie yelled as he went for Pearson, contorting toward him and looping his left arm across Pearson's chest, but not in time to prevent him from going for Rik again, this time angling the knife into his neck and forcing it into the unprotected flesh just below his ear. Rik screamed again, fell, clutching the wound which spurted a fountain of crimson, causing Henry to think, 'Shit, he's hit his jugular!'

Henry managed to wrap his left arm across Pearson's chest and yank him backwards, frighteningly aware that the knife was now searing toward his own face. Henry's only thought was to overbalance Pearson and dodge the blade at the same time. He was bigger, heavier and stronger than the out-of-shape offender, and he used this to his full advantage, pulling him backwards and sticking out a leg, over which he dropped Pearson who, realizing he was falling, tried to keep upright, failed, and let out a yell as Henry slam-dunked him to the floor.

All the while, Rik's predicament was there in his mind.

He knew he would have to deal quickly, efficiently and ruthlessly with Pearson.

As the man hit the carpet, Henry reached out and grabbed his right wrist, then dropped his full weight on to the guy, landing across him and pinning him down. Henry's other hand went for the wrist too, and he bashed the knife hand down on the floor repeatedly. The grip gave almost immediately and the knife rolled away just out of reach. At that exact point, Henry knew he now had the power . . . particularly as Pearson simply went weak and lost the will to fight. He began to sob.

'Oh God, I'm sorry, I'm sorry . . . I didn't mean . . .' he blubbed.

Henry kept him held down as he readjusted his own position, straddling his chest, trying to control his own breathing and temper – two things which did not happen. He glared down and bunched the fist of his right hand, nostrils flaring, shaking angrily. Then he had a thought and checked himself.

Instead of punching him, he slapped Pearson hard across the face, employing the technique he had learned from his recent defensive tactics training, then slapped the other way, then the other, and kept going until his anger had dissipated.

It was satisfying to see Pearson's face swell and hear him whimper.

Then he spun him over on to his front, dragged his arms behind his back and cuffed him tight so the ratchets ate into his flesh, right on the wrist bone.

He stood up, kicked the knife away, growling, 'Do not fucking move,' and turned his attention to Rik, who was lying across the threshold of the bedroom, clutching his neck and shaking uncontrollably as though he was being jabbed with a cattle prod. Blood pumped through his fingers. Lots of it.

'Jesus, Henry, Jesus . . .' he gasped. 'Oh, God, I'm gonna die.'

'Are you fuck,' Henry said reassuringly, wondering when he'd last seen so much blood flowing; not in a long time. It was everywhere. 'Come on,' he said, bending over Rik. 'You need to get up and sit on a chair, keep the wounds high up for a start, OK?' Rik tried to respond, his mouth opening and closing like a fish, eyelids fluttering like a doll's as he went into the first stage of shock. Henry panicked internally, but outside stayed calm, forceful. 'I'm going to help you get up and sit down, OK? Then we'll sort out the wound.'

'Whatever.' For a second, Rik took his hand from the cut and a fresh spurt of bright blood shot out across Henry's trousers.

Henry instinctively squirmed away, then overcoming his squeamishness said, 'Get your hand back over that wound and keep pressing.'

Rik nodded, no colour, only deathly grey in his face. He put his blood-soaked hands back on to his neck, clamping them there. Henry quickly searched around for something else to put on the wound, his eyes settling on a grubby tea towel thrown over the side of a chair. He grabbed it, folded it and eased it under Rik's hands. 'Keep that there. Hold it on tight. You'll be OK, promise. Now come on.'

He eased Rik into a sitting position, then gradually up on to his knees, then up on to wobbly feet before steering him into an armchair. All the while, the blood flowed incessantly, filling the towel, drenching it, and Rik's condition deteriorated.

Then Henry got on to the radio, and moments later comms at Blackpool had contacted the ambulance and other patrols were en route to assist.

After that he gave Pearson a cursory check. He was still secure, lying there uttering blubbering sobs, watching Henry nervously. His attention returned to Rik. He found some more towels in the kitchen, folded them and placed them on top of the one already there and pushed Rik's hands back on. 'Pressure, keep pushing.' He sat on the chair arm.

Rik shivered.

Henry checked his watch: two minutes since he'd called in.

Time crawled with unbelievable slowness in situations like these. He'd experienced it many times before, but took comfort because he knew his colleagues would be tear-arsing to the scene, putting their own lives in danger, and the paramedics would be doing the same because they were as mad as cops.

'Henry,' Rik rasped worryingly, blood bubbling from his lips. 'I'm gonna die.'

'Are you fuck,' Henry repeated, aware his bedside manner wasn't what could be called overtly caring, but he knew it was pitched right for Rik. The new towels were filling with blood. It looked like the jugular had been severed as Henry suspected.

'Why . . . why . . .' Rik continued, 'why attack me?'

Henry got to his feet and walked to the bedroom.

A strained, 'No,' came from Pearson's lips.

Henry gave him a sneer and stepped into the dimly lit bedroom. In the distance his ears caught the welcome sound of sirens approaching. There was the aroma of sandalwood from a number of candles dotted around the room. The curtains were drawn, almost no light chinking through them and though there was light from behind, it was not easy to see.

He paused one foot beyond the threshold, his instinct as a detective telling him this could be a crime scene.

Henry flicked on the light using the switch by the door. Even that wasn't much of a light, just a low wattage bulb. Henry's eyes adjusted and saw the shape in the bed underneath the crumpled duvet. He drew back the cover and revealed the reason why Pearson had reacted with such astounding violence.

At his feet, Nigel the kitten rubbed its head on his ankles, purring loudly, having recovered from its subsonic flight.

Six

After the slowness of those minutes when Henry was waiting for the arrival of assistance and relief, three hours later found the world revolving very rapidly indeed, threatening to spin him off into the stratosphere.

Rik Dean had been dragged off to hospital, tended by a couple of cool-dude paramedics who made Henry insanely jealous by their calm approach. The initial prognosis was good, confirmed subsequently by the A & E doctor: Rik was going to be OK. He needed emergency surgery to stitch up the jugular and the wounds, but he hadn't lost as much blood as Henry had feared. It just looked bad.

The two detectives sent to Harrogate had returned, both slightly weepy and emotionally drained after having to deal with a family whose daughter had disappeared and could be dead. They had brought back the DNA swabs, everything packaged and secured precisely, and some dental X-rays. A comparison would be done first thing Monday by the forensic lab. Henry sensed the brittleness of the women, but they refused to go home when ordered.

Percy Pearson was in custody, but Henry doubted whether he actually had any link to the murder investigation he was running, although his knife would come under careful scrutiny by forensics, also in the morning.

And to top it all, the custody office at Blackpool central was full to bursting following a weekend of drunken debauchery.

His head hurt.

He needed to get changed out of his blood-splattered clothing. He kept a spare pair of trousers and a shirt in the office, and he gladly did a runner through the barred gate of the custody office and made to the lift after telling the custody sergeant to call him when the duty solicitor got round to Pearson.

Unusually, the lift was there waiting for him, doors akimbo.

88

His only stroke of luck all day, he thought wistfully as he stepped in. Before he could select the button, Debbie Black joined him. She pressed the button for him and once the doors had closed with their usual reluctance, she moved into him. Her hands slid around his neck and before he could say anything she'd dragged his head down and parted his lips with hers, inserting a hot tongue.

It tasted good, warm, wet, sweet, smoky.

He responded by pulling her tight to him and getting his own tongue going. How long was it since he had French kissed? Did they even call it that these days?

They parted seconds before the lift reached its destination, Henry holding his breath. The doors creaked open, but no one was there and they had not reached their floor anyway. The doors closed.

Neither moved this time.

Debbie exhaled a long breath as though she was blowing a smoke ring. 'Fifteen years is a long time to make up.' Her breast rose and fell.

'Aye,' Henry said inadequately, a little twitch of the head accompanying the word.

The lift stopped at the required floor. They stepped into the corridor.

'It's terrible what happened to Rik, isn't it?'

'Aye,' Henry said. They were walking toward his office. 'He'll be OK, though.'

It wasn't a long walk. The corridors in Blackpool nick were all short. Within moments, they were outside his office door, Henry pausing with his hand on it. 'I need to get changed.'

Debbie glanced down at him, taking in the blood on his trousers. Her eyes rose. 'I'd love to get you out of those,' she said wickedly.

Henry swallowed, fighting all his instincts, which were telling him to drag her into the office and let her wreak havoc.

'Nice thought, just a smidgen busy,' he shrugged.

She nodded understandingly. 'Drink after work,' she said, 'whatever time you finish. I need a debrief.' She raised her head and marched off around the corner. Henry pushed open the office door, muttering an obscenity of relief, and was immediately glad he hadn't followed the weak path, because sitting plonk behind his desk was the chief constable, Robert

Fanshaw-Bayley, rifling through his drawers and paperwork, grinning like the cat with the kill.

FB had no shame, showed no embarrassment, just raised his head and greeted Henry, making him think that perhaps he wasn't actually going through his stuff at all, but simply winding Henry up. He was a past master at this. The plump chief's grin turned to one of superiority and he lounged back in Henry's chair, hands clasped behind his head, surveying the lower ranking officer.

'Boss,' Henry acknowledged, closing the door. He stood there hesitantly. 'Can I help you?' FB just shrugged. 'I need to get changed.' Henry indicated his trousers.

'Don't let me stop you.'

The office was so tiny, Henry had no room to manoeuvre and was obliged to drop his pants in front of FB.

'More bloodletting follows you?' FB said.

'So it seems.' He hopped around the very tight space in front of the desk as he pulled up his spare pants. They were reluctant to come up. 'Fortunately he'll be all right.'

'I know – I've been to see him.' FB looked sad. 'He wasn't wearing a stab vest.'

'Doesn't mean you don't get stabbed even if you wear one.' At last the pants came up. 'Even if he'd worn it, he'd have been stabbed in the same place. Ahh . . .' He buttoned them up and they were tight. 'I've got to go and interview the offender,' he said, 'so . . .' he squidged up his face, 'unless you've anything pressing, I need to go back to the custody office.' Henry wasn't about to tell FB that Pearson's solicitor wasn't ready yet, but he did not want to spend any unnecessary time with FB.

'Yeah, I understand that.' FB paused. Henry finished zipping, folded up the bloodied pants and tossed them on to the spare chair, having decided the best course of action would be to have them incinerated. Maybe then claim for a new pair, a thought dismissed when he glanced at FB: getting money out of the organization was not easy.

FB sniffed. 'How's the whole thing going?'

'As this started out as the hunt for a flasher, it's taken a turn for the worse, I'd say.'

'Is this murder part of that original investigation? And where does Pearson fit into it?'

'Not sure on any of those points yet, but at least I know who the probable murderer is and we'll track him down sooner rather than later,' he said confidently.

FB nodded sagely, double chins wobbling. 'I need to warn you about something, though. Dave Anger.'

'I'm pretty well sighted on him.'

'Don't be too sure, Henry,' FB said gravely.

'Why?' His stomach fell.

'Because I'm not sure how much longer I can protect you.'

Henry's eyebrows came together. He knew that, despite everything about their love-hate relationship, he had quite a lot to thank FB for, particularly the posting to FMIT, but he wasn't sure FB was actually protecting him. 'What do you mean?'

'Basically, if you don't get a result on this, wave bye-bye to FMIT. Anger will cane you and there won't be anything I can do about it. At the end of the day, staff selection is down to him, not me.'

Henry groaned. 'I really fell for it, didn't I?' he said, trying to keep bitterness from his voice. 'Conned by the carrot of substantive DCI. I feel like a sprog. I should've said no.'

'And if you had said no, it would've been a good excuse to get rid of you. He's out to drop you, that's all I'm saying. He wants rid, wants a reshuffle, wants new blood, wants his mates on board, and mostly it's not something I can argue against. You need to show him you can get a result and the pressure might ease, but only until the next job comes along.'

'Fuck,' Henry spat, sighing deeply, head shaking. 'I actually thought he'd come round a bit with the GMP job. Obviously not. It goes deep, this, but I just don't know what I've done to upset the twat.'

'That I cannot answer, but it seems deeply personal.'

'I wouldn't mind if I knew the guy, could've upset him somewhere down the line, but he just seems to hate me, end of story.'

'You could put in for a move,' FB suggested.

'Sideways and as a DI?'

'Would that be so bad? Special Branch are on the lookout for DIs.'

'I'll think about it . . . now I need to get going, if you don't mind. Got a murder to solve and all that. Not that it means anything these days.'

'Sure . . . oh and by the way, take a bit of fatherly advice.' FB winked salaciously. 'Keep your cock out of Debbie Black . . . she's a bit of a handful.'

The trousers were too tight, which was not surprising. They had been Henry's 'emergency' pair for the last four years, and this was the first time he'd ever had to use them. It was apparent he had become more rotund over that period. They were also a bit too short, which was strangely uncomfortable. He was certain he had not grown.

Debbie Black and Jane Roscoe were hanging around the custody office, both descending on him when he appeared.

'What's going on now?' Jane wanted to know.

'I'm going to have a preliminary interview with Pearson and then I'm going to hand him over to the local CID to sort out, unless I think he has some involvement in the murder, which I don't. My priority is still to find Uren.'

'Who's second jockey?' Jane asked, meaning who would accompany him in the interview.

'No one.'

'I'll do it,' Jane offered quickly, turning Debbie's face granite-like. Henry said OK, and Debbie looked mortified.

He walked to the custody desk which, for a brief spell, was quiet, with no prisoners waiting. 'Has the duty solicitor got to Pearson yet?' Henry asked the custody sergeant.

'No – for some reason he's decided not to have one, but I will make sure he gets one whether he likes it or not. For the time being, though . . .' The sergeant shrugged and looked meaningfully at Henry. 'You can have him.' He reached under the desk and emerged with a set of sealed interview tapes and associated paperwork, which he dumped in Henry's hands. 'I'll sign him out to you. Interview room two. Just make sure you comply with PACE.'

Pearson sat behind the table in the interview room in his white paper suit. His own clothing had been removed for forensic examination. He looked cowed and pathetic, not like the crazed knifeman he'd recently transformed into a few hours earlier. He could not make eye contact with Henry.

Henry held the sealed tapes in his hands, wanting to speak to Pearson off the record. It was a difficult thing to pull off these days, but Henry reckoned he had about four or five minutes grace. Some of the things he wanted to say, he didn't want recorded. He glanced at Jane, wishing she wasn't here.

Before Henry could start, though, Pearson blurted, 'I hope you're looking after Nigel. If you don't look after him, I'll sue you.'

Henry gave him a cold stare. 'Let me get this straight,' Henry said. 'You are more concerned about the fate of a kitten, which you were only too happy to throw at me, than the predicament you're in? Because, let me lay this right on the line: you are in very serious trouble. Not only have you attempted to murder a police officer—'

'Yeah, yeah – and look at me!' he cut in, pointing to his face which was red and swollen from Henry's slapping. 'I've been assaulted too – by you!'

Henry surveyed the prisoner. 'Not only have you tried to murder a police officer,' he reiterated, 'but a twelve-year-old boy was found bound and gagged in your bedroom, naked, having been brutally buggered, and video-recording equipment was also in the room. I've very quickly skimmed the tape found in the camera and yes, you are in very serious trouble, Mr Pearson.' Henry could not keep the contempt out of his voice or his body language. 'And yes, I slapped you to defend myself and my colleague. I slapped you as hard as I could under the circumstances and I'll quite happily tell that to a court . . . the offender in this case is you, and you need to get that firmly in your brain.'

Their eyes remained locked. Henry's were hard and unyielding; Pearson's were initially defiant, then crumbling.

'He consented,' he pouted. 'He was very mature.'

'Twelve-year-olds can't consent,' Henry corrected him. Pearson went silent. 'And it's all on video.'

Still no response.

Henry allowed the pause to stretch out a while, enjoying the prisoner's discomfort as the consequences of his actions filtered through.

'I'm going to prison, aren't I?'

'I'll say – and for a very long time. You are a danger to young boys and I imagine any judge will relish sending you down.'

Pearson nodded thoughtfully.

'Whatever happens,' Henry persisted, 'you will be going down. That's a fact – no way round it.'

'I think I've got that message.' Pearson began to well up.

'But you can smooth the way.'

Pearson wiped his red, bloodshot eyes. Henry saw the swelling around Pearson's cheekbone was lovely. He was rather proud of it, never having appreciated the value of a good slap, well delivered, other than in the occasional soft-porn he'd watched.

'How?'

'Admit, admit, admit – and help me. Throw yourself on the mercy of the court – and help me.'

'Why should I help you?'

'Because I truly can make sure the court knows how helpful you've been, how remorseful you are, all that sort of thing.'

He eyed Henry with suspicion. 'What sort of help?'

'I need an address.'

Pearson swallowed as though he knew what was coming. 'Whose?'

'You already know. George Uren's.'

'I don't know it,' he said, too quickly.

Henry paused. 'Yes you do.'

Pearson looked down at his knees. 'I can't tell you. It was a mistake to tell you lot I'd seen him around . . . if he ever found out I'd said anything, he'd kill me.'

'Violent, is he?'

'You don't know the half of it.'

'I promise he won't find out and, this is a promise too, if you don't tell me you're looking at the difference between five years or ten years in the pokey. That's what I can do for you.'

'You can't do that!'

''Course I can. I have very good contacts in the judiciary. A trial court judge is in my lodge,' he lied. 'I can make things happen, Percy, but only if you give . . .' Henry's voice trailed away. Using Pearson's first name stuck in his throat. He found it almost impossible to be matey with anyone who abused kids. 'I know you spent time with him in Accy. I know you were his pal.'

'No,' he said. 'I was never his pal. I did what I had to to rub along. He is very violent, he hurts people . . . know what I mean? I don't. I love people and they love me. I treat people right.'

Henry felt Jane squirm next to him. He glanced at her and

saw her face was seething with disgust at what Pearson was claiming.

'He is a very bad man,' Pearson said.

'And I want his address.' Henry persisted. Pearson touched his swollen face gingerly. 'And I want to know who he's running with.'

Pearson gasped, his eyes suddenly filled with terror. He began breathing rapidly and held his hand over his chest. Henry had hit a nerve. 'I don't know that. I don't know who he's with, honest.' His rapid breathing continued as he wound himself up.

'OK, just the address then . . . think of the difference between a five and a ten stretch.'

Pearson gave him what he wanted.

Henry checked his watch, quickly ripped the wrapping off the tapes and inserted them into the recorder. 'Now let's have a quick interview,' he said.

With Pearson back in his cell, Henry, Jane and Debbie stood in one corner of the custody office having a scrum-down.

Henry was excited, something concrete in his hands at last: an address.

'Good bloody result,' Jane said. 'You dealt with him well.'

'I lied . . . because I'll actually do my best to get him fourteen years, not five or ten . . . it's the least he deserves . . . and I don't know anyone in the judiciary, except a few local JPs.'

'And I didn't know you were a mason,' Jane teased.

Henry just winked at her and touched his nose mysteriously. 'Still, good result, but what a creepy bastard.'

Jane shivered in distaste as though she was chewing something sour. 'All that talk about love.'

'One thing's for sure, we're dealing with the grubby end of policing. Give me a good old drug dealer any day.'

'Course of action?' Debbie interrupted, annoyed by the intimate exchange between Jane and Henry.

'Let's get a team together and hit this house.'

MONDAY

Seven

00:05 hours. Fortunately the adrenalin was rushing, and despite the fact he'd been on duty since early morning Sunday, Henry was feeling elated, even though he knew it was a sensation that would be short-lived.

The last two hours had been a flurry of activity and he was now revelling in being at the middle of things, unlike earlier when all he wanted to do was hide his head in a bucket. Such were the vagaries of being a cop. Feelings often contradicted themselves within the blink of an eye, and this was often how officers burned out. Lows, followed by highs, followed by lows, then seeking the next high. It was like being on crack cocaine, only it was legal, and far more addictive.

So for the moment, Henry was loving it, but he realized when it was over he would be exhausted and not in receipt of any overtime payments.

He looked at the faces in the briefing room. A dozen blue-overalled Support Unit officers, all mean-looking with close-cropped hair (even the women), wearing steel-toe-capped boots, everyone eager to go and smash down some doors. They lounged around indolently, sipping free hot drinks from polystyrene cups and helping themselves to mounds of biscuits Henry had managed to source. A dog handler, minus dog, chatted with them, anticipating the use of his dog in a search. Three crime scene investigators in white overalls hovered behind the uniforms and two local jacks leaned against the wall, annoyed they were here so late.

Henry coughed the cough of the person wishing to bring chatter to an end and draw attention to themselves.

'Evening folks,' he said amiably, getting a muted, but fairly friendly response. 'Thanks for coming . . . hopefully tonight we are going to catch ourselves a murderer.'

* * *

By calling in a couple of favours, Henry managed to turn out two members of the surveillance team who lived locally. Following a quick telephone briefing, they pinpointed the address Pearson had divulged and were keeping discreet obs on it.

The house was a four-storey terrace in Blackpool's North Shore, in the streets behind the Imperial Hotel off Dickson Road. It was a substantial building, like thousands of others in town, having been through a series of uses, now split into eight units, or bedsits. Henry had managed to get as much information about it as possible, but in the time available, he struggled to get very much. All he had was what Pearson had given him: Uren lived at that address in one of the flats, but which one he did not know.

A check in the voters register was inconclusive, so up to a point the police would be going in blind – but what was new about that? It just meant a slow, systematic raid, going to each flat in turn as quietly as possible, with a secure cordon around the perimeter so that if Uren was spooked and did a runner, he'd be caught in the net.

As a plan it was flawed, but it was the best he could do.

He RVd with one of the surveillance officers, together with Jane and Debbie, at a pre-arranged point just behind the Imperial Hotel.

'All we can say is that the place is occupied, Henry,' the constable informed him. 'It's obviously split into flats and we haven't seen Uren enter or leave the place. We haven't seen anyone, actually.'

Henry considered the information, still wondering what the best way would be to search the place. He concluded that low key was the answer.

The RV for everyone else was the forecourt of a deserted filling station on Dickson Road, plenty of room on it for the Support Unit personnel carrier, dog van, as well as Henry's, Jane's and Debbie's cars. He looked at the two DIs, thinking that there was nothing like a dynamic operation to keep the grey matter churning. After licking his lips thoughtfully and pulling a few pained expressions, wondering what the hell else he could do, he said, 'I think the best way to go about this is . . .'

* * *

Based on the information from the surveillance guy, Henry and one of the Support Unit constables wearing a civvy jacket over his overalls simply walked up to the address, opened the insecure front door and stepped through a tiled vestibule into the ground floor hallway. It was wide and spacious, two doors off it and stairs leading up to the first floor. Henry could have had an educated guess at the floor plan based on past experience, and been confident at getting it right. The two doors would open into the ground floor flats, and he wondered fleetingly if there was a basement flat, but there didn't seem to be any entrance to it from this level.

'We're inside,' he said into his PR. 'Next pair please, nice and easy.'

Jane Roscoe and another Support Unit officer walked smartly down the street and entered the building.

'OK?' Henry said. They nodded. 'You stay at the foot of the stairs and we'll do these two.' He thumbed at the doors down the hallway. Into his PR he said, 'Everyone in position?'

'Four-eight-five and one-one-three-one at the rear,' came one response.

'Four-oh-nine, eight-one-oh covering the front.'

'Roger,' Henry said, not entirely comfortable with radio jargon even after so many years of coppering. It always felt a bit daft to him. However, it meant that two officers were sat at the front in a car and two were on foot in the back alley, avoiding shit and trash, covering the rear of the premises, all ready to nab anyone doing a runner. In addition, it was Jane's job to cover the stairs while Henry and the constable dealt with the first two flats at ground floor level. Under the circumstances, it was as good as it gets if this was to be as low key as possible.

He knocked on the first door. Hard, loud. His warrant card was at the ready and next to him, the SU constable had a 'door opener' in his hands – basically a solid metal tube with handles – just on the off chance the door needed battering. He could hear muted TV inside and the door opened fairly quickly, secured by a chain.

A woman answered, peering through the crack.

Henry held up his ID and smiled the good smile. 'Sorry to bother you at this time of day, love,' he began apologetically.

* * *

101

Pleased that, so far, his powers of persuasion had not diminished, he was now about to knock on the fifth door, the third flat on the first floor, and had managed to gain entry and search every flat he'd tried without too much of a problem.

The first one had been a lone, single female with a baby, who had been more than happy to have a couple of big blokes nosing around her sparse bedroom; next was a smackhead couple, both of whom Henry had locked up in his dim, distant past. They'd been too spaced out to know what was going on, and would probably wake up later believing it had just been a bad trip. Henry could have busted them, but he didn't have time to be derailed by inconsequence, so he let it go.

He and Jane and their accompanying constables went to the first floor after ensuring that another pair were stationed at the foot of the stairs. It was a bit like a military operation: taking and securing ground, bit by bit. Slow and steady and a bit boring, but Henry struggled to see any other way of doing it, other than by blitzkrieg, which he didn't really want to do because of the lack of planning time.

The first two flats on this level had been a doddle too. Henry marvelled at how easy it was to gain entry to other people's homes. The flash of a card which no one really read. A few persuasive words and, of course, the addition of an evil-looking henchman bearing a mini battering ram did help matters. The first flat on the first floor had been a teenage couple with a foul-smelling baby; the second was another of Henry's old customers, a guy who was a prolific shoplifter in order to feed a drug habit which had spiralled out of control. Entry had been easily gained and a cursory search – with permission – carried out swiftly. Henry was certain that a more detailed search could well have uncovered the guy's stash, but again, Henry did not need that distraction.

Before leaving, as he had done on all his visits, he produced a photo of Uren and asked if the occupant knew him. Up to that point they had all looked very fleetingly at the image and shook their heads. Henry knew not one of them had looked properly – but the guy in the fourth flat said simply, 'He's next door.'

'Cheers,' Henry said, hoping to hide his rush. He'd been beginning to think he was on the road to nowhere.

There was a hushed conflab on the dimly-lit corridor – dimly lit because there were no light bulbs in the sockets.

Two more officers were called in from the street and the two from the bottom of the stairs were summoned up to join Henry and the three already on the first floor, six of them altogether.

'I know you all have, but I'm still checking,' Henry whispered. 'You're all kitted out in body armour, yeah?'

There was an affirmative from everyone. 'Right, I'll knock. If he comes to the door, we grab him, overpower him, ask questions later . . . let's go.'

Henry raised his hand, about to bang it down on the door, but then paused. He glanced round at the officers behind him. 'Change of plan.' He reached for and tried the door handle, turning it slowly and putting his weight against the door, but it was locked. 'Shit,' he mouthed.

He knocked, rapping with his knuckles.

There was no response. He glanced down, saw no light from underneath the door; listened, but there was no sound. He glanced at the constable with him, then down at the weighted door opener. 'Pint of Stella if you open this door in two.'

The constable, clearly experienced in such matters, eyed the door. 'I'll open that door in one,' he proclaimed proudly.

'OK, go for it in one.'

He stepped into position, braced himself, swung the opener back with the easy flow of a grandfather clock pendulum and smashed the flat end of the opener over the Yale lock. Hard, accurate, and in keeping with his promise, the flimsy door clattered open without need for a second blow. The smirking officer stood to one side and allowed Henry to stride into the flat, shouting, 'This is the police!'

It was in darkness.

Henry stood still, awaiting some response perhaps, and at the back of his mind aware that someone was coming down the steps from the third floor, but that fact was just there, of no note, no importance, because Henry could smell smoke in the room.

Jane and his door opening PC were right behind him.

Voices came from the corridor. 'Yeah, no probs,' he heard someone say – still of no consequence to him. 'What's your name?'

'What is it?' Jane whispered.

'Smoke.'

He flicked on his Maglite torch, one he'd bought himself, more powerful, sturdier and better for hitting people than the tiny personal-issue penlight provided by the firm.

He was standing two feet over the threshold, right in the living room of the flat. The torch played over everything in the room. A settee, armchair, TV, DVD, all basic stuff. No sign of anyone in that room, nothing untoward – just the smell of smoke. The beam crossed to the kitchen area.

'Why aren't you going in?' Jane hissed.

'Not happy.'

'Fancy that,' she said sarcastically. 'You never are.'

He fought the urge to retort with a classy 'Fuck off'. Instead he stayed where he was, drawing the torch beam across the room, back over the furniture on to two doors, one to the bathroom, one to the bedroom, he guessed. Still he did not move.

'Something's burning,' he said.

Then in the torchlight he saw wisps of smoke rising from the gap underneath one of the doors – the bedroom.

'Call the fire brigade,' he said over his shoulder to anyone who was listening. 'Just in case. We can always cancel 'em if necessary.'

'Should we put the light on? Might help,' Jane suggested.

'No,' he said. He slid his foot forward and moved further into the room, caution screaming at him. The smoke from under the door increased in volume. Something crackled behind the door. A sound Henry knew well: flames.

'Trumpton on the way,' someone called from behind him.

He still could not get to grips with his reticence to move forward and could feel the impatience of the officers behind him, particularly Jane. The trouble with cops was that they liked the feet-first approach, and in the past – the simple, straightforward world he used to inhabit – that was a pretty acceptable way of working. But no longer. Everything had to be pre-thought because people were out to get cops these days. They made good trophies.

And here he was, entering the flat of a man suspected of murder. The lights in the corridor had been tampered with, something he had not really thought about until now, and not long ago he'd been in a flat when a fellow officer had been stabbed and almost killed by someone who was not suspected of violence towards police. He was feeling very jittery here, because this did not sit well with him and he didn't want any other casualties. Things did just not seem to be right. Could this be more than just a house fire? Shit. He was dithering, and feeling a bit stupid, too. At some stage you had to either go in, or retreat . . . Henry had to do the business, despite his reservations. It was always possible that someone might be on the other side of the door that needed help.

'I want everyone out into the corridor.' He turned. No one had moved. They were lined up behind him like actors in a farce. 'Out,' he ordered, 'and keep away from the door.'

One by one they left, albeit with reluctance, though none questioned him. Once he was sure they were gone, he crossed to the bedroom door and touched it: warm. He bent low, reached for the handle and turned it, knowing the possible consequences of opening the door. He'd seen enough episodes of *London's Burning* to know that fanning the flames with an input of oxygen could result in a fireball.

'Is there a fire extinguisher out there?' he called.

'Not a chance in hell,' came the response.

'OK, here goes,' he yelled.

Then, all caution to the wind, he threw the door open, stood quickly to one side just in case there was a backdraft, knowing in his mind that if there was, he'd be fried, but also believing in the naïve way that human beings do, that he would be quick enough to save himself.

Flames did lick out of the door momentarily, but died back almost immediately. He waited for a second blast – none came – before peering into the room, fully expecting his clothes to be burned off.

It was a bedroom, and the bed itself had been pulled into the centre of the room and was almost encircled in flame which rose from the carpet. The body of a man sprawled untidily across the single, metal-framed camp bed. Henry's torch beam played across the figure from head to toe, finally resting on the man's ghastly face through the flames – the very dead face of George Uren.

'Shit,' he uttered.

Then there was a crack, like a bullet going off, making Henry duck instinctively, and more flames began to rise from beside the body. This was followed by another crack, then flames, then two more until the body was amass with fire, like a funeral pyre.

'Incendiaries,' Henry shouted. This time he threw caution to the wind, pulled the corner of his jacket over his nose and mouth and dived into the room, stepping through the gap in the flames and sweeping the four recently-ignited devices off the bed with his torch. They landed on the floor, breaking up as they hit, flames scattering across the carpet like mini fire-crackers.

'Get in here,' he screamed, then began dancing like a maniac as he attempted to stamp out some of the less nasty-looking flames, 'but don't turn the lights on ... Ow! Ow!' he yelled as the heat penetrated the soles of his Marks & Spencer slip-ons, footwear not designed for walking on hot coals.

Jane and two PCs crowded urgently into the room and began a stamping dance with him, then two more PCs barged in with fire extinguishers they'd sourced from somewhere. 'Out the way, out the way,' they shouted and started using them, spray going everywhere.

Within moments, they had done the trick, amazingly.

'OK, OK,' Henry coughed, smoke now being the problem, lots of it. 'Well done, folks, well done.'

Debbie Black appeared at the door. She reached for a light switch, her forefinger only centimetres away before Henry bellowed 'NO!' at her, possibly louder than he had ever shouted. She froze instantly. 'Don't switch on the lights,' he said through gritted teeth, teetering on the edge. 'Just don't,' he added almost irrationally. Then he calmed down. 'Not until they've been checked, OK ... just fuckin' leave 'em, OK?' He was terrified that the light bulbs could have been tampered with in some way, maybe injected with petrol, primed to explode when the light was switched on. Paranoid, maybe, but he'd taken enough chances for tonight. 'Right,' he went on, 'I want everyone, except Jane, to go out of the flat. Retrace your steps and get out, please.' The two bobbies holding their fire extinguishers looked affronted. 'Thanks for coming to my assistance,' Henry said to them, 'but this is a murder scene.'

To reinforce his words, he shone his torch into George Uren's dead face and then allowed it to linger on the deep, jagged cut under the chin where his throat had been sliced open and a gaping, horrendous gash smiled grimly at him.

Eight

Henry's neck cracked as he raised his chin, rolled his head and tried to ease some of the tension in his shoulder and neck muscles. He gave himself a minor shoulder massage, feeling stiff all over, exhausted all over, and wondered why he did this shitty job.

He was standing on the street outside the block which contained Uren's flat, There was some satisfaction gained by looking at the police and fire brigade activity which had awoken nearly every resident in the vicinity, the old adage 'If I'm awake, you sods can be too' spinning through his brain, though he knew this was just him being cranky.

The whole building and the ones either side had been evacuated just in case there were more devices to be discovered which might not yet have ignited. Two had actually been found underneath Uren's bed, a good find, valuable evidence.

As the building was declared safe, residents were allowed back into their homes, and the CSIs, Scientific Support and the Home Office pathologist began detailed work up at the scene, a place from which Henry had done a runner for a breath of fresh air, and a coffee if he could find one.

A car turned into the street, Henry recognizing it immediately. Anger's Shogun with personalized plates. Henry's heart did a little sag. The car pulled in behind a fire engine and the occupant got out, marching purposefully toward Henry who, for a fleeting moment, thought of diving for cover behind a wall. His indecision meant he was captured. Dave Anger collared him, the man he loved most in life.

'Henry,' Anger called. 'Hot briefing, please – if you'll pardon the pun.'

'Er,' Henry hesitated, looking around.

'There'll do.' Anger pointed to the Support Unit personnel carrier parked away up the street, just the driver on board. He pushed past Henry, who turned into his slipstream like a little puppy and followed. Anger ousted the driver and the duo had the bus to themselves, sitting between riot shields, helmets and assorted kit bags. Henry took a seat by the door, sliding it shut. 'What've you got?' Anger demanded, though he knew quite well what Henry had because he'd been briefed in detail over the phone. However, Henry wasn't going to argue. Didn't have the time and was too tired.

He took a breath. 'Basically, acting on information obtained from Percy Pearson – the guy who stuck a knife in Rik Dean earlier – we came to this address and started working our way through the flats until we eventually found Uren. He was as dead as a dodo, throat cut, knifed in the chest and stomach, though not long dead. He was on a single bed in the middle of the bedroom, surrounded by several incendiary devices, some on the floor, some on the bed itself. Some went off, others didn't – which is good for us. Obviously the plan was to destroy as much evidence as possible by fire, and it nearly worked. As it is, we've got Uren's body almost untouched by the fire, and these incendiary devices.'

'Suspects?' barked Anger.

Henry shrugged. 'Probably the guy who was in the Astra with him . . . maybe . . . dunno yet.'

'And we don't have a clue who he is?' Anger said impatiently.

'Not as yet.'

'So where does this leave the murder investigation into the young girl in the back of the Astra?'

'With one unknown suspect still outstanding and the girl yet to be identified, which we hope to achieve later today based on the DNA swabs obtained from some people in Harrogate.'

'Square One, in other words,' Anger said unfairly.

Henry bristled and held Anger's gaze for a moment. 'The girl's body was discovered in the early hours of Saturday morning, it's now the early hours of Monday morning and we've made significant progress, so, come on, give it to me.' He flicked his fingers as though inciting Anger into a brawl. 'What the fuck have I done? I've asked you before, but now I want to know.'

Anger reached across and opened the carrier door, moving across Henry and dropping out on to the pavement. He leaned back in. 'Just catch that murderer, OK?' He slammed the door shut and strutted away, leaving Henry speechless.

Henry opened the door and slid out, rubbing his eyes. One thing was for sure: once this murder scene had been tied up, he was leaving some bugger else in charge and going home to bed, whether or not there was a murderer still on the loose.

Under the very pressurized circumstances, Henry was amazed he managed to get five hours sleep, a period of time that successfully recharged his batteries. He did continue to ache all over, as though he was coming down with some bug or other; the leg which had been glanced by the Astra was very sore and his face had turned a nasty shade of green underneath his eye. But he wasn't going to let the small matters of serious physical injuries and illnesses deflect him from his tasks.

The briefing at Blackpool central was fairly quick, and even though there was much to do following the discovery of Uren's body, Henry did his best to delegate every task, from attendance at the post mortem (even though he would also be attending it) to crime scene management. Tempting as it was to try and get involved in everything, he knew that he had to take a big step back and, where possible, keep to a management role. His troops were professionals and he knew he had to trust them to complete their tasks. The investigation was becoming too complex for him to get involved in anything other than what an SIO would be expected to do.

When the team had dispersed – a team now larger and more unwieldy that ever, after that morning's influx of new blood – Henry scuttled away to his office where he began to make some notes in order to make sense of where he was at. He wrote out bullet points in no particular order of importance.

- Initial job / flasher / indecent assault / kidnap / Could this be Uren? Or are they unconnected incidents?
- Percy Pearson – how much does he really know?
- Dead girl? Harrogate? Visit parents if ID matches. Shit!
- Uren – keep digging into background / who is his best mate?
- Revisit bail hostel in Accy. Ms Harcourt. Is she hiding something? Why do I think this?
- Rik Dean – keep track with his progress. Welfare issues?

- XXXX – Who was with Uren? Need to find. Priority 1.
- Who uses incendiaries? Unusual MO / Circulate far and wide? FBI? Karl?
- Other abductions in other forces? Circulate.

He took a breather, knowing this would only be the beginning of a list which would ultimately translate into actions – and these were just his own jottings. He would have to sit down with Jane and Debbie – and Dave Anger – and others, to carry out a massive brain dump. There was no way he could even think of not including them in this process, because this was a team thing and he had to be seen to be running the job as head of a team, not as some maverick individual operating on hunches and luck. And the sooner that process began, the better. He picked up his phone and called a few people.

By midday he was at force headquarters at Hutton, four miles south of Preston, entering the FMIT building on the campus. Formerly a residential block for students attending the Training Centre, it had been snaffled and converted into offices for what was the SIO team, now FMIT. He entered and made his way to the first floor, passing his old office and hoping to find Dave Anger in his at the end of the corridor.

Anger's office was empty. He could well have been at lunch either at the Training Centre or at HQ, or in some meeting. Henry paused at the door, slightly deflated. He had been hoping to get Anger to authorize an even bigger pool of detectives for the investigation, something Anger had the power to swing at superintendent level. He needed to get into the ribs of the divisional commanders to release more of their staff, because Henry felt he needed more bodies, pronto.

He lingered at the door, weighing up his next move. His stomach made the decision for him: a sandwich from the canteen accompanied by an Eccles cake probably . . . but first . . . he stepped into Anger's office and sat down at the desk, intending to write a post-it note . . . then his eyes locked on to a couple of family photographs on the desk top.

He reached across. One was a wedding photo in a frame, Anger and his bride; one of those typical 70s shots, all flared trousers, sideburns and hair like a Roman emperor. Anger had looked pretty good in those days, actually, a bit of a stud.

110

Henry looked at the bride and thought she looked familiar, but could not place her. He replaced the photo, swivelled in the chair and looked at another framed photo on the bookshelf behind the desk. This was a class photograph from Bruche, the Regional Police Training Centre, near Warrington, circa August 1978.

Working on that timescale, Henry guessed Anger could possibly have been in the recruit intake just ahead of him. Henry had gone to Bruche as a raw sprog in September 1978. He did not recall Anger from those days, but it was not unusual not to know other people, especially from other forces. In those halcyon days, Bruche had big intakes, hundreds of students coming and going through the doors following the Edmund Davies review of policing which had hiked up police pay and attracted many willing fools to the job, Henry being one. There was about thirty young, impressionable officers in Anger's class photo who wanted to be coppers. Three rows of them and three class instructors in the middle of the front row. 'Q Class'.

Henry chuckled: good, simple days, when being a young cop was great fun.

There were few females in the intakes, unlike the present day. The majority were white, male and overtly heterosexual – and Bruche had been a hotbed of sex; just a few girls to go round – and certainly no gays, at least none who took the risk of being identified.

Henry scanned the faces. He spotted Anger, boyish, smiling, confident and a bit of a looker. There were a couple of Lancashire officers Henry knew, still in the job, one a DI over in Pennine Division who was a big mate of Anger's and who Anger wanted on FMIT. He looked at the other faces and recognized one of the girls, a lass from Merseyside; the name he could not recall, but the body he could. One of three conquests he had made at Bruche, all short-lived flings, but great memories. The one in the photo he recalled seducing – or was it the other way round? – on a disco night; she'd dared him to take her on the bonnet of the commandant's car, and he had not been able to resist. His bum shone brightly in the moonlight that night.

'Bloody hell!' he shivered at the thought. If he'd been caught it would have ended his police career there and then.

He replaced the photo, and smiling broadly, left the FMIT building. Outside, underneath the trees in the grounds of the training centre, he saw a dead squirrel on a grass bank near to an oak tree. Some wag had put a half-smoked cigarette into its mouth, making Henry giggle out loud.

He was still chuckling when his mobile rang, but he checked himself when he looked at the display and saw who was calling him.

'Hi John, how are you?'

'I'm good, Henry.' It was John Briscoe, a forensic submissions officer who must have been calling from a distance of no more than a hundred metres. His office was in the Pavilion Building close by, recently built to house the Serious and Organized Crime Squad and Scientific Support. Briscoe worked for the latter, dealing with all submissions requiring forensic analysis. The DNA swabs taken from the family in Harrogate as well as those from the dead girl had gone through him.

'Got something for me?' Henry asked tentatively.

Briscoe paused. 'I have – we fast tracked the DNA swabs from the murder victim and those taken from the family in Harrogate – and did a dental comparison.'

Henry waited, a curious charge in his guts, knowing what Briscoe was going to say.

'It's a match,' Briscoe confirmed. 'The dead girl is the daughter of the woman in Harrogate. Your victim has been identified.'

'Thanks, John, thanks,' said Henry, glad on the one hand that things were moving on, sad on the other for the family in Harrogate who were about to be devastated.

Henry had no choice in the matter. Visiting the next of kin of victims was a given for an SIO, probably the worst job that had to be done, but maybe the most important. Many SIOs believed that catching the offender was the be-all and end-all of the role, and whilst this was vital, the police relationship with the victim's family was more crucial even than that, and Henry was not about to shirk this responsibility. He briefly toyed with the idea of asking the local DI at Harrogate to do the job, but dismissed this almost instantly. He was the one who had to be the bearer of the news, even though the family were already primed for the worst – and then he had to set up a full incident room in Harrogate. What fun that would be, he though wryly. Cross-border shenanigans between forces were always a nightmare.

His biggest problem was who to take with him on the hundred-and-forty-mile return trip. It had to be either Jane or Debbie, because they had already formed a relationship with the dead girl's family and Henry needed a bridge into their world before he completely and utterly destroyed it forever.

Jane or Debbie? A real conundrum.

He'd had an affair with Jane which had ended acrimoniously – and boy, was she intent on never letting him forget that! He did his best to avoid her as much as possible because he didn't really trust her, as he suspected her to be in league with Shark Man. He actually thought they were having an affair at one point, but now he just believed they were out to get him for their own individual reasons. So a two-hour journey to Harrogate, plus whatever time it took to deal with the family, then a two-hour return did not really appeal, coward that he was.

Nor did the prospect of a substantial time spent with Debbie Black really tickle his fancy. Fortunately he hadn't had an affair with her, but they'd had a smoky clinch or two, which had been awfully nice, and she'd made it clear that she had hots for him, which had been sizzling away for most of her career. But he guessed she was an emotional basket-case. Dangerous territory. And at a time when he was doing his utmost to stay on the straight and narrow, to have a straight-forward life watching his (yet to be acquired) plasma screen TV with wireless surround-sound. Unfortunately, he was often quite weak when it came to the opposite sex and was walking proof of the truth in the old adage 'a standing cock has no conscience'.

Jeez, what a choice. He was almost sweating with the weight of the decision. But it had to be one of them.

In the end he chose Debbie Black. At least there was no baggage there to drag along, and he could hopefully convince her that a kiss didn't automatically equate to sexual inter-course.

When he told them, Jane looked deflated, Debbie elated and somewhat smug. Jane perked up when he said he wanted her to cover Uren's post mortem and take charge whilst he and Debbie were out of force.

By that time it was four p.m. He realized the Harrogate trip would have to be an overnighter, which made him wince slightly. But he was certain he had the moral fibre to ensure it remained completely professional. He arranged to meet Debbie at Blackpool nick at five, giving them both time to collect overnight things and get a member of the admin staff to fix up a couple of hotel rooms in Harrogate.

'Fill me in on the missing girl,' Henry said.

Debbie was driving the careworn CID Vectra Henry had managed to acquire for the journey. Though he had sketchy details in a file on his lap, he wanted her take on things, what she had managed to pick up from her visit to North Yorkshire the day before. They had left the motorway behind and were steaming along the A59 which snaked right across Lancashire and dropped right into Harrogate.

'Jodie Greaves, nine years old, nips out with the intention of going to her grandmother's last Friday teatime about six-ish. The granny lives, what, maybe quarter of a mile from the girl's home, literally around the corner. She never made it. Disappeared en route.'

'Anything to say what actually happened to her?'

'Nothing as of yesterday. The police response was pretty good, so they claim, and I've no reason to doubt that. All the usual Golden Hour tasks done efficiently and effectively. Quite a lot of resources thrown at it, but nothing turned up.'

'Witnesses? Anyone see her between home and shop?'

'None as of yesterday.'

Henry crinkled his mouth as he pondered. 'What's the area like?'

'OK . . . not the wealthiest part of what is a very wealthy town. It's a private housing estate, mainly semis, a few flats; there's a small council estate nearby and some sheltered housing for old folk, which is where the grandmother lives.'

'And the family? What do you make of them? Are they above suspicion?'

'I think so, but you never know,' Debbie shrugged. 'Seem decent enough. Mum and Dad both work. There's an elder brother, twelve, I think.'

'What was he doing?'

'Watching *The Simpsons* on Channel Four.'

'Hm, me too,' Henry said.

They fell silent as she drove through the village of Gisburn which straddled the A59 a few miles east of Clitheroe. They were heading into lovely countryside, an area Henry had a soft spot for.

'Well at least there's one thing,' Henry announced. 'In cases like these it's usually someone close to home, a relative or friend of the family, who's done the dirty deed. Doesn't appear to be here, unless,' he said ominously, 'the person accompanying Uren is said relative or friend, or Uren himself is known to the family . . . something we'll have to explore.'

'Yep,' Debbie agreed. Everything had to be investigated.

He sighed heavily. 'But this sounds more like a stranger . . . snatched at random, or maybe she'd been a target, been stalked before she was snatched . . . George Uren's not gonna tell us, is he?'

'No, but whoever he was with has got a lot of talking to do.'

'Mm, that's interesting,' Henry said, leaning forward in his seat.

Debbie craned her neck to look for something. 'What is?'

'Something to follow up . . . if she was snatched at six, yeah?'

'Yeah.'

'And I spotted Uren somewhere around eleven-ish in Fleetwood . . . what went on during that intervening period? Five missing hours . . . say three at the most to travel back to Lancs.' He shrugged. 'All supposition, I know, but that leaves two hours unaccounted for.' He shrugged again and gazed at the road ahead, his mind working overtime. 'For argument's sake, if she was alive when I first spotted Uren, she would have been tied up in that boot for five hours . . . poor kid.' A surge of anger rolled through him. 'Bastard.' He pulled himself up short of going on a rant, concentrating on trying to formulate questions which would need answering. 'Did Uren snatch her alone? Did he and his unknown mate do it together? Or what? Shit.' He sighed with frustration. 'And why did Uren end up dead?' He tapped his teeth with his thumbnail. 'Will we ever know?'

'It's a real puzzler,' Debbie acknowledged.

'And . . . and . . . if she *was* alive when I saw Uren, which

I suspect she was, because I think we panicked them and they killed her because they'd been clocked, what was going to be her fate?'

Debbie wriggled with an involuntary shiver of disgust. 'Don't,' she said.

'It's something we need to know, because if she was going to be abused, or whatever, where was she going to be taken to? I wouldn't say Uren's flat was the location.'

'Why not?'

'Not practical or safe enough. Taking a kidnapped girl up through a block of flats. I know it's populated by people who look like customers of that bar in *Star Wars*, but I don't think so. Too many people on top of each other for that to go unnoticed. There must be somewhere else, somewhere safe, somewhere secluded, somewhere to do the business without fear of interruption, some prepared place.'

'Reckon?'

'Would you kidnap someone and not have somewhere ready to take them? I wouldn't. Even if I took someone on the spur of the moment, I'd know exactly where I was going to go, because even if the abductee wasn't known, I'd've done my homework beforehand, because I'd know I was going to get someone, sometime.'

They were travelling over a stretch of moorland known as Blubberhouses. A high, winding, narrow section of the A59 which Henry knew well from his police driving courses. It was a location often visited, as it stretched the nerves and abilities of the students to the farthest degree. Henry had more than once thought he was going to meet his maker on this stretch of road.

'You don't kidnap someone without a plan, unless you're a complete nutter . . . and that's what worries me. We interrupted that plan, so as far as I'm concerned, the plan's still running and another victim is required. Just because Uren's dead doesn't mean the plan's been shelved, does it? We need to do everything right here from the word go. We need to milk everything we can from Harrogate, because that might just give us the clues we need to stop another snatch.'

'You paint a bleak picture.'

'It is a bleak picture,' he said seriously. 'And you know what I'll bet is a certainty . . . this road.' He pointed through

116

the windscreen. 'It's more than likely that Jodie Greaves was kidnapped and then driven back across to Lancashire along this road. It's the most direct. So maybe the missing hours could be accounted for along here somewhere.' He raised his eyebrows. 'Another action to be followed up . . . not far now.' He had seen a roadside telling him that Harrogate was twelve miles away. He stopped thinking about the possibilities and focused on getting ready to deal with a family who was about to hear the worst news imaginable.

Delivering the death message. First practised in the sterile environment of a police training centre, then for most recruits probably done for real within weeks of their first posting. Never easy, even when the news is expected, it always tests the compassionate skills of a cop, as well as their resilience.

Henry sniffed. He was staring blankly into the middle distance. Some might say 'away with the fairies', but his thoughts were one hundred per cent with the grieving family of Jodie Greaves. He had a double Jack Daniel's in his hand, two chunks of ice in it, sitting in the bar of an hotel in Harrogate, alone. A grim expression was set on his face as he tried to imagine the monumental task facing the Greaves family. Just to keep going, taking one hour, one day at a time, knowing their treasured daughter had been brutally taken from them, kidnapped, driven for miles in the back of a car, then murdered.

Henry had tried to be gentle, sparing them the horrific detail, but at the same time firm and as truthful as possible. They had to know she was 'dead', not 'passed away', because the use of anything other than the word 'dead' always gave false hope.

And he had to convince them there was no mistake in the identification of Jodie. DNA, he told them, was utterly reliable; the dental records simply confirmed the science. Their daughter had been murdered. Their daughter had been found in the back of a burned-out car on the bleak Lancashire coast at Fleetwood. Murdered.

Then Henry had had to stay with them. To try and be their rock, the only thing they had to cling to, their only hope of justice, the man who would speak for their dead daughter.

His words had not been empty when he reassured them he would catch the killer. It was a solemn promise, one he would not break unless Lancashire Constabulary made him do so.

He and Debbie Black were with the family for three tough hours, together with a local detective inspector, before they could make a withdrawal. The experience drained Henry and though he felt grubby and in need of a shower, the first thing he did when he hit the hotel was find the bar. Debbie went to freshen up, saying she'd be down in half an hour.

The first JD had sailed neat, un-iced, down his throat, doing something that only that old-time sour mash could do. He bared his teeth as it spread through his chest and into his stomach. Number two was much more considered, sipped thoughtfully, as he sat at the quiet bar, ruminating, watching life go by, but not really seeing anything.

Passing that death message had affected him. It had knocked him for six, hit him deep somewhere, made him wonder if he was up to this sort of thing any more.

He fished his mobile phone out of his jacket, called home. Kate was surprised, but pleased to hear from him. He needed to hear her voice, the woman who had supported him through thick and thin over the last twenty years, who had put up with everything he had thrown at her and stayed with him, even through their divorce. She had been amazing, and Henry hated himself for repeatedly letting her down. He knew he could not ever do it again if he wanted any sort of contented life in the future.

'Hi,' he said.

'Hiya handsome, what's up?'

'You're so intuitive. I've only said one word to you, so how do you know if anything's up?'

'I know you only too well.'

'Mm, you do,' he admitted. He held out his empty glass and waggled it at the barman, indicating a refill was required. 'Just been to see the girl's family,' he said. 'It's hit them real hard.'

'And you, by the sounds of it.'

'Er, yeah,' he said, nonplussed with himself. 'Could be because of the girls . . . y'know . . . thinking what life'd be like if—'

'Henry, don't even go there,' Kate cut in. 'It's not a good place to visit.'

'I know, you're right.' He wiped his face with his hand, scrunching his eyelids with his fingers. 'Need to snap out of this,' he said. 'You OK?'

'I'm fine . . . the girls are tucked up in bed, believe it or not . . . my little babies.'

'Even though they're well into their teens and one's nearly twenty,' Henry laughed.

'Always my babies, though,' she said tenderly.

'About bloody time they left home,' Henry joked. 'Costing me a fortune.'

'They can stay forever.'

'Yeah, yeah, they can,' Henry murmured. 'So what are you doing?'

'Reading a trashy book, sipping red wine, nibbling Nobby's nuts.'

'The bastard.'

There was a pause.

'Wish you were here,' Kate said simply.

'Me too . . . when this is sorted, things are going to change,' Henry vowed – but not for the first time.

'Yeah . . . love you to bits,' Kate said.

'Love you, too.'

'Take care.'

Henry ended the call, eyes moist, looking thoughtfully at the phone, thinking about himself, what he had become, wondering if he could change.

He raised his head and glanced toward the bar entrance through which a well-groomed, manicured and very dolled-up Debbie Black slinked. She wore a tight red dress and sheer stockings which glistened in the lights. She had obviously changed her underwear, too, as a push-up bra did a major job on her breasts; Henry looked and failed to see a panty line and guessed that a thong was now in place, or maybe nothing at all. She'd let her auburn hair down, applied copious make-up . . . and Henry gulped. She smiled gorgeously as she approached, walking like a cat, and the eyes of all the people in the bar stayed with her on her journey from door to stool. It was as plain as day that there was only one thing on her mind: Henry Christie and several bouts of depraved sex. Two things, actually.

Strangely, the latter was a thought that crossed his mind, too.

She paraded on in front on him and he caught more than a whiff of perfume.

'Who was that?' she demanded, nodding at his phone.

'Kate.'

'Ah,' she said, slightly cast down. She looked him straight in the eye, hers twinkling with the sparkly drops just applied to them. Her face was serious at first, then it cracked into a depraved grin. 'Still, you're not married, are you, so it won't be adultery.'

What worked for Henry was that Debbie had not eaten that evening, something which did not seem to dawn on her as he imbibed three WKDs in quick succession. Her subsequent visit to the toilet told Henry that she could not hold her drink: in total juxtaposition to the classy entry earlier, Debbie's walk to the loo was a complete mess, her shapely legs seeming to have developed a mind of their own. They wanted to go in completely different directions to the rest of her, like a newborn fawn.

Seeing his chance, Henry immediately presented her with another bottle of WKD on her return. He bought himself a tonic water, ice and lemon, letting her think it had gin in it.

At one point Henry thought, *God, this is sad – getting a woman drunk so I don't have to sleep with her. What is my world coming to?*

She deteriorated rapidly, ably assisted by Henry's plying of alcohol. Her next trip to the toilet resulted in near disaster as she walked into the edge of the bar door, staggered backwards and landed in the lap of an ageing gent who could hardly believe his luck.

Henry apologized to him, heaved her back to her feet and steered her to the lift, into which she teetered, plugging herself into one corner to prevent a further fall.

'You bashtard, Henry,' she slurred. Her previously shimmering eyes were now red and bloodshot, her lipstick smeared. 'You done this on purpose.'

At first Henry thought she had sussed his plan.

'Gettin' me pissed so's you can 'ave yer way wi' mi.' Her head lolled uncontrollably as the lift lurched upwards. Her stomach must have done the same thing. 'Feel sick,' she announced.

'Well hold it back till you're in your room.'

'Jeez, everythin's goin' up,' she slurred.

Their rooms were adjacent on the second floor. Henry hurried her to her door, rooting for her key in her handbag. Once inside, he pushed her into the bathroom, just in time.

She was horribly sick in the toilet, sinking to her knees, retching, the noise amplified by the acoustics of the bowl. It sounded disgusting. She groaned and twisted her disarranged head to look up at him.

'Yev lucked out,' she admitted. 'Can forget that shag, don't feel like a fuck. Head's spinning . . . urgh!' She hurled up again, the stench turning Henry's nose.

'Thank God for that,' he whispered.

In his room, after a room-service club sandwich and chips, he undressed and showered, then raided the fridge bar. He consumed a Glenfiddich miniature with ice whilst he watched TV and thought about how to find Uren's unknown friend, who he believed would be the true key to ending this investigation, a man who had to be captured, whatever the cost.

At one thirty a.m., dozing, eyes getting heavier, his mind planned the day ahead. He exhaled and sank under the duvet, his toes reaching for those cold places. He wished Kate was next to him and as he thought about her, his phone made a noise like an incoming aircraft: a text landing.

He reached for it and read it, smiling. It was from Kate. Good nite. Luv u v much xxx.

'Mm,' he pondered, knowing how close he'd come to being next door with Debbie, phenomenally relieved he wasn't.

Another text landed. Smiling, he read it, expecting another from Kate.

All it said was, Gess who?

He scrolled down the screen to look at the number from which it had been sent, but did not recognize it. He frowned and put the phone down on the bedside cabinet, shrugging. It was not unknown for an occasional rogue text to come in.

But then the plane landed once more.

This time the text read, UR DEAD.

TUESDAY

Nine

Never one to look a gift horse in the mouth, Henry ensured that – as the firm was paying – he had a hearty full English breakfast at the hotel. Normally he ate a rushed bowl of bran flakes, or maybe a croissant, but today in Harrogate he filled his plate to overflowing and tucked in.

He had knocked on Debbie's door to ensure she was still in the land of the living before coming down to eat. There had been a muffled response, and she refused to open the door. Henry let her be, smirking at how his plan not to sleep with her had worked so well.

Whilst filling his face with a chunk of Cumberland sausage, Debbie appeared in the dining room, slumping down opposite him with a groan. She spotted what was on his plate and swallowed. For a moment nothing happened, until she started to sway, eyes bulging.

'Go be sick,' Henry ordered her, folding a forkful of fried bread and dribbling egg into his mouth.

With her complexion rapidly changing to a luminous green, she nodded, pushed herself back up and exited quickly.

They were at Harrogate Police Station at nine thirty a.m., finalizing details of the working arrangements between the police forces. Henry wanted to set up an incident room that day and the local DCI agreed. As the two male detectives talked strategy, Debbie observed from the world of a bad hangover. She was a mess, looked it, was contrite about it.

Henry shook hands with the DCI, hoping that this cross-border working would pan out well for a change. Historically, two or more forces trying to get their acts together with one common aim was a recipe for disaster. He hoped that by getting in early at ground level, most of the problems would be ironed out, but he knew he'd have to suck it and see.

He turned to Debbie. 'How do you feel about staying over here for a day or two as Family Liaison Officer? Or would that cock you up?'

She stared blandly at him, not a single word having penetrated. 'What?' She blinked, making a clicking sound with her tongue in her dry mouth.

For the purposes of full comprehension he repeated the request in slow motion, adding, 'We'll put you up at the same hotel, which is a pretty nice one.'

'Yeah, sure,' she acquiesced, not totally understanding what she'd agreed to.

The local DCI watched the exchange with a smirk.

'Er, what about transport?' she asked, a cog or two starting to turn at last.

'I'll arrange a hire car,' Henry said. He turned back to the DCI. 'Well, that's that, then. I need to get back across the Pennines, so if I can leave Debbie with you, I'll sort out staffing for the incident room from our end.'

'No probs.'

Henry walked out to the CID car in the yard and as he climbed in, Debbie appeared behind him, still looking desperately unwell. He got in, fired up the engine and opened the window.

'Have I made a fool of myself?' she asked, expecting the worst.

'Not at all,' he assured her. 'But get yourself sorted out now and go round to see the Greaves family. You need to get under their skin, because they might know something they think they don't know, if you see what I mean?'

Debbie looked totally perplexed.

'Maybe another hour in bed,' Henry suggested.

'I'm sorry,' she said simply. 'We never got to make love.'

'No, Debs, we didn't, and we never will.'

'Oh God,' she blurted. For a moment Henry thought she was about to become all emotional and blubbery. He was relieved when she retched, covered her mouth and declared, 'Gonna be sick again,' and legged it back into the police station. He reversed out of his spot and began the journey back west.

Henry wondered where Jodie Greaves's abductors had taken her. He, they, whoever, had lifted her from a street in Harrogate, and five hours later they had been in Fleetwood. He was sure they would have used the A59. It made sense. It ran close to where she had been taken, all the way across to Preston; once they reached the outskirts of Preston it was likely they had gone on to the M55, then off on to the A583 into Fleetwood. He knew he had to get a team to work the route, visiting pubs along the way, doing house-to-house on all roadside dwellings. It would take a long time, but it had to be done, even if it was a long shot.

He'd only just reached the outer limit of Harrogate when he mobile rang. Using his hands-free kit, he answered.

'It's me – Dave Anger.'

'Mornin' boss,' Henry said guardedly. He would rather have said something more piquant.

'How's it going across there?'

'OK. The deed's done, the family know; Debbie Black's staying over here for a couple of days, they're setting up an MIR, chucking some resources at it ... everything's going OK.'

'Good. Glad to hear it. Speak when you get back.' Click. The line went dead. Anger and Henry had little to say to each other and there was no chance of small talk, which suited Henry.

He put his foot down as the A59 rose out of Harrogate and on to the moors. It would take about ninety minutes to get back to Preston, maybe another twenty to get back to the coast, two hours tops.

Valuable thinking and planning time.

His phone rang again, the curse of an SIO running a murder. Everybody wanted a piece of you. It was Jane Roscoe.

'Henry – how's it going?'

He filled her in succinctly, then asked, 'How did the PM go?'

'That's what I'm ringing about ... Professor Baines did it ... God, he's weird, but I do like him ... Uren was stabbed to death and had his throat cut, no surprise there ... but we've had the puncture marks analysed and compared to those in Jodie Greaves's body ... it looks like the same knife was used, a slim knife with a serrated edge, the sort found in most kitchens, so yeah, the same knife for both murders ... also did a comparison with the one Percy Pearson stabbed Rik with ... it's not a match . . .' Speaking via the hands-free, she sounded as though she was talking in a barrel. 'The forensic people also looked at the incendiaries. They're the same as the ones used to set alight to Uren's Astra.'

'Thanks for that . . . how did this morning's briefing go?'

'Good, everyone's busy and up for it.'

'Right . . . I should be back mid-afternoon, so I'll see you then.'

For a moment he thought the connection had been broken, but when she spoke again he realized it had simply been a pregnant pause.

'Henry?' Posed as a question, the word sounded dubious.

'Yeah?' His word was suspicious.

'I need to talk to you . . . on a personal matter . . . about us.'

His throat went as dry as Debbie Black's had been. He gritted his teeth. 'We'll make some time when I get back.'

'OK, thanks. See you later.'

Thinking and planning time gone tits-up, he thought wryly. Replaced by worry and panic time. Why, he castigated himself, why have I continually screwed up my life?

He was going to think and plan his worried and panicky answer when his phone rang again. 'Fuck,' he muttered, not realizing he'd pressed the answer key after he'd said the word.

'I don't think that's an appropriate way to greet an old pal, do you?'

The voice was instantly recognizable. The deep, East Coast Yank accent, now watered down with just a smidgen of southern England.

'Hey, Karl, how you doing?' Inadvertently Henry found himself speaking with a mid-Atlantic twang, and also feeling better on hearing his buddy.

'It's good, I'm real good.'

'To what do I owe this pleasure?' Henry said.

Karl Donaldson was an FBI agent, seconded to the legal attaché at the American Embassy in London for about the last eight years. Ever since he and Henry had met whilst Donaldson was investigating American mob connections in the north of England, they had become good friends on a personal level and had found themselves working together on several investigations since. Most recently, they had been together during the murder and corruption enquiry in Manchester. There had been links to a Spaniard named Mendoza who had been under scrutiny by Donaldson, suspected of murdering two FBI under-cover operatives. Henry was aware that Donaldson had been fully tied up with the fallout of this investigation, so he was surprised to hear from him.

'Can you talk?'

'I'm driving across the backbone of England as we speak, but yeah, I've got hands-free and it's nice to hear from someone I actually like.'

'A simple "yep" would have sufficed,' Donaldson laughed. 'So, go on.'

'Even though I'm up to my balls with the Spanish stuff, I still have time to read bulletins and circulations.'

'My, what a professional.'

'Up yours ... and I'm always interested in anything that comes from your neck of the woods, buddy.'

'We like to keep you amused.' Henry could not even begin to imagine the amount of bulletins and reports which landed on Donaldson's desk. A major part of his job was to liaise with the forty-three police forces in England and Wales, as well as dozens of police organizations across Europe, and because of this he was kept in a circulation loop of a wide range of intel-ligence and criminal activity reports. Henry guessed he could only skim read most of what came across, binning the majority of it.

'Incendiary devices,' Donaldson stated.

Henry's interest suddenly perked up. The details of the fire-bombs found on Uren's bedside and those in the car with Jodie Greaves had been circulated far and wide. Details would only have gone out that very morning, so hearing back from anyone so soon was a surprise. 'Incendiary devices,' Henry echoed.

'Your bulletin is only brief, but the description and photo-graph of the devices are interesting ... any chance of more details? A technical description, maybe? More photos?'

'Consider it done ... but why?'

'Maybe nothing. I'll let you know.'

'Come on, you rogue – spill!'

'OK – murder and intrigue, will that suffice?'

'I guess it'll have to,' Henry conceded as he gunned his car down a stretch of coroner's corridor – the middle lane of a three-lane stretch of road – to overtake a slow-moving HGV. 'How's the family?'

'Good, good . . . let me know soon, will ya?' The conversation ended and Henry returned to his thinking, planning, worrying and panicking – only for the phone to announce an incoming text. Despite the danger of reading a text whilst driving, Henry did so.

Having dismissed the ones he'd received last night as mis-sent texts, it was unsettling to read the content of the newest one as he hurtled past another lorry at 70 and sped toward a roundabout. It read: Have u chkd ur brakes?

His first port of call was Blackpool Victoria Hospital, where he went to see Rik Dean, still in intensive care but due to be transferred on to a ward. After a couple of days observation, he expected to be allowed home. Henry found him in good spirits.

'Screwed up your chance of going on the murder squad.'

'Don't, it hurts when I laugh and think all about that lovely overtime.'

'What overtime would that be?' Henry asked wistfully. 'Still, think about the criminal injuries compensation . . . I'll make sure you get it, so long as you split it with me.'

'Deal.'

Henry updated Rik on the investigation, telling him about the jolly to Harrogate and Debbie Black's drunken excess.

Rik shook his head. 'You need to watch her, she's a bit bonkers, I think.'

'You're not the only one who's said that.'

'I should know – I've been there.' Rik groaned as he made himself more comfortable.

'Oh,' Henry said sharply.

'Remember me saying I'd dallied with a hitched but separated colleague?'

Henry did recall this. It was during their discussion on the way to the hostel at Accrington. He nodded.

'It was her – and I wish I hadn't.'

'And I thought you were talking about a man,' Henry teased him, making him laugh again. 'What's her problem?'

'She's on a big manhunt, on the rebound from a crap marriage, wants to get laid by every cop she sees.'

'She told me she'd never kissed a cop before,' he said, affronted.

'My hairy arse!' Rik eased his head back on to the pillows and closed his eyes, clearly in pain despite the drug relief. 'Having said that, she was rather good in a sort of manic way.' His voice drifted off dreamily, all his energy evaporating. Henry realized he was asleep.

He stood up and quietly tiptoed out.

Fourth floor, Blackpool Police Station, Major Incident Room: Twenty minutes later a few chosen members of his team surrounded Henry. Jane Roscoe, DC Jerry Tope the Intel cell, a DS called Jackson, and two local DCs who had been interviewing Percy Pearson. These two were given the floor first, bringing everyone up to date on their progress: Pearson was amenable to interview, had admitted stabbing Rik Dean and the gross indecency and false imprisonment of a boy of twelve. Increasingly it looked as though Pearson operated alone and, although he knew Uren, was not particularly involved with him.

'So in terms of him helping us find Uren's accomplice?' Henry posed the question.

'I think he knows who he is,' one of the DCs responded, 'but he ain't saying anything.'

'OK,' said Henry, accepting what was being said. The two DCs were first-class interviewers and he had to trust their judgement, even though it was hard for him not to go back down to Pearson himself and wring the bastard's neck.

His attention turned to Jerry Tope. 'I want you to keep digging on all associates of Uren, Pearson and Walter Pollack, the old sex offender who's still at the hostel. I want everything on them, way back to their time in prison. Who they shared cells with, who visited them, anything.'

'Sure boss, but I've already done loads,' the DC said.

'Do more.' Henry made a shooing gesture and Tope sloped back to his desk. Henry looked at Jane. 'So the knife that killed Uren matches the one that killed Jodie Greaves and the incendiaries are the same type?'

She nodded.

'And until we find the person who was with Uren, we'll never be anywhere near the truth of what happened that night?'

'Very much doubt it.'

131

Now Henry turned to DS Jackson, who had been given the task of liaising with other forces to check on all similar disappearances of young people. 'Where are you up to, Ralph?'

Jackson picked up the sheet of paper on his knee. 'Good response . . . and quite a few similar disappearances, abductions, whatever you want to call them. Some high profile, some never even made the news. I've concentrated on the ones where the kids haven't turned up, though I've a list of all the others, too. Just working through everything, really.'

'Any missing, not returned, from adjoining forces?'

'Yeah, one girl about a month ago from Rochdale in GMP; one a couple of months ago from Crewe in Cheshire and another one a bit before that from West Yorkshire, Leeds. There are others further afield.'

'OK, stick with the recent ones from the local forces for the moment. Check to see if they could be linked. I don't want to teach you to suck eggs, but look at times, days, dates, localities, anything you can think of. I'll leave it to you, Ralph, but use Jerry Tope as well. Sooner rather than later.'

'OK, boss.' He stood up, sensing he was dismissed and walked back to a free desk.

'How was Harrogate?' Jane asked frostily, doing her famous cat's bum disapproval impression with her pursed lips.

'Interesting.'

'And how did you get on with Debbie?' A cold question.

'Well enough,' he nodded, not being drawn into dodgy territory. 'Anyway, I need to bring the policy book up to date. There's a lot to put in it. I'm going to retire to my telephone box if you don't mind.'

She opened her mouth to say something, but thought better. Henry gave a quick smile, collected his belongings and headed off.

Dogged persistence, routine police work, procedure, careful analysis, problem solving, use of the National Intelligence Model, diligent enquiries, leaving no stone unturned – all good stuff, Henry thought. The way most murder investigations are solved, without a doubt. But when all those things failed, it was always nice to have a stroke of luck, that piece of good fortune that made everything else fall into place . . . that anonymous phone call, the informant who came good, the guy arrested on some other matter who goes, 'Oh, by the way, I also murdered so-and-so.'

'Lady Luck, where the fuck,' Henry muttered, 'are you?'

He put down his pen, having reread the long entry he'd just made in the policy book, clasped his fingers behind his head and swivelled in his chair. The killer shark stared up at him, a cruel glint in the eye.

'Hi, Dave,' he said.

There was a horrible feeling in his gut that despite all the good work going on, the mystery man would remain a mystery unless something broke soon. If his identification dragged on for a long time, it would get harder and harder.

An urgent rap on the door made him spin round. A flustered and breathless Jane Roscoe stood there.

'Have you got your radio on?' she demanded.

'No, should I?'

'There's been an attempted abduction in North Shore.'

Lady Luck, he almost screamed, surging to his feet.

'Come on, let's go,' she said. 'I'll tell you on the way.'

He virtually leapt over his desk and he scurried out behind her, grabbing his switched-off PR as he went. She hurried to the stairs – 'We'll be waiting for the lift forever,' she called over her shoulder – and began to descend them two at a time, Henry right on her heels like an obedient dog. She talked as she went. 'Kid walking home from school . . . car pulls up alongside . . . male occupant tries to drag her inside . . .' She jumped four steps, twisted and hurled herself down the next set. 'Screamed, fought, kicked . . .' She took a breath. 'Got free . . . ran off . . . passer-by got a partial registration number and vehicle colour . . . patrols making their way now . . .' They landed on the ground floor, hurried into the garage. 'I've got some keys,' she said, dangling them for Henry to see. She ran across to a blue Ford Focus and seconds later they hit the street. By this time Henry had managed to switch on and tune in, listening to the deployments from comms.

'Alpha Four, with the complainant,' one officer called up.

'Roger,' the operator replied. 'Alpha Six, current location?'

'Dickson Road, en route to scene.'

'Alpha Nine – dog van – also en route . . . any further details?'

'Alpha Seven, also en route.'

'Patrols stand by,' the comms operator said coolly. Obviously everybody was eager to get there, particularly as there was a possible link to the murder, but it would be a Keystone Kops type mess if they all descended on the scene like wasps round a can of Coke. Jobs like this needed a firm hand, because bobbies, being bobbies, loved to rush to the action, often losing sight of the bigger picture. Which is where supervision came in.

'DCI Christie,' Henry shouted up.

'Go ahead.'

'Current position with the PNC check, please?'

'We're running the partial number through now. Could take a few minutes.'

'Roger – please recirculate all you've got, for my benefit as much as anything, then get a grip on deployment; two patrols to the scene is enough for now. Everyone else to static points and structured patrol, please. You decide who – and also get on to the motorway and let them know what we've got on.'

'Roger, sir.'

'Ahh, power,' Henry cooed, listening to the operator follow his instructions. 'Obviously none of that applies to me. I'll go wherever I want.'

Jane raced the car up the promenade, past the tower, jerking as she changed gear, whizzing past horses and carriages. 'I still need to speak to you,' she said, niftily pulling in front of a double decker.

'Right, shall we sort this first?'

'Alpha Four to Blackpool,' came a welcome interruption over the radio. It was the officer at the scene.

'Go ahead.'

'Some initial details . . . offender described as white male, fifty years, wearing white shorts and tee shirt. Speaks with local accent, maybe five ten, six feet tall. Brown hair cut short, glasses . . . and further to the car, it's grey, could be an Audi . . . might help refine the PNC search.'

'Roger – any direction of travel?'

'Towards the prom from the scene, but that's all I have.'

'Roger . . . all patrols,' the operator said and relayed the details again for the benefit of everyone.

Jane slowed, to Henry's relief. 'What bit do you want to do, boss?' She glanced at him with irony. They were still on the prom, heading north.

'I'm feeling lucky . . . let's keep going for the time being.'

'Think it could be our man?'

'Who knows, but as I said, I feel lucky.'

One hour later there had been no sightings of a possible suspect vehicle. Henry felt dejected, hoping that the breakthrough might have come. He and Jane patrolled as far north as Fleetwood, then criss-crossed their way back, eventually arriving at the home of the young girl who had been approached and almost abducted. He and Jane spent some time with her and her parents, checking the story, soothing them down, before leaving them in the capable hands of a female DC to obtain a statement. More paperwork to add to the growing mountain.

'Still feel lucky?' Jane asked.

'It's a state of mind, positive mental attitude,' he said grandly. 'I'm always feeling lucky.'

'I need to tell you something,' she said worryingly.

The atmosphere in the car altered palpably.

'What would that be?' he said after a nervous pause, totally aware that his own lips were now pursed like a cat's behind. He had a horrible premonition that what he was about to hear was not very pleasant. 'Dave Anger wants to bin me from FMIT? I know that,' he said, trying to take the lead. 'You'd like to see the back of me, too. I know that.'

'Both true,' she agreed.

'But you don't want to tell me those things?'

'No.'

'Fire away, then.'

'I had an argument with my husband. A real humdinger. Said some things I shouldn't have. Hurtful things, y'know?'

'Sorry to hear that.'

'We'd – I'd – probably had too much to drink.'

'It's always the case, isn't it?' Henry's body was turning slowly to ice. It crept up from his feet, up his shins, just about reached his groin and squeezed. A curious sensation. One you get when you know the hammer's about to fall.

'Things haven't really worked out between us,' she exhaled sadly. 'The child thing never happened and sometimes I think that was just a ruse by both of us to save a failing relationship. Y'know, have a kid, save the marriage crap?'

Not deliriously happy about the way this was heading,

Henry's left hand sneaked automatically to the door handle, wondering if he could perhaps eject himself at the next junction and run like hell, never to be seen again. Fight or flight, the latter won hands down.

'I really didn't want to hurt him,' she continued, now on a roll, constantly checking on Henry as she drove. Henry braced himself and pointed urgently through the windscreen.

'Lights!' he said, the word emitting strained from his constricted throat. Not only did he not like what he was hearing, they might be the last words he ever heard unless she concentrated on her driving.

She slammed the brakes on. Henry jerked forwards, his hands slapping the dash, seatbelt ratcheting on.

The screech to a halt did not seem to affect Jane's verbal momentum. 'Oh God, Henry,' she blabbed on, 'it was an awful row, one of those you never want to have. He was mortified.'

'Right.'

'I couldn't stop myself.' She inhaled, then exhaled heavily, a huge sigh, shaking her head. 'I was so wound up. Too much to drink, tired, pissed off, unhappy,' she concluded softly, and looked Henry in the eyes again, peering straight into his soul, terrifying the life out of him with a stare that made him quiver. Here it was again, he thought: emotion. The thing I do not do any more.

'Sorry to hear it,' he said inadequately, then pointed urgently ahead again. Traffic had started to move, and Jane was oblivious to the fact. She was fast becoming a hazard.

'I wish I hadn't said it, honestly I do.'

'Oh?'

'You know what I mean, don't you?'

This time Henry stared at her, waiting for the bombshell. 'No,' he squeaked.

'It just came out.' Henry saw a tear form on the lip of her eye, then tumble down her cheek. 'But I was so unhappy . . . and all because of you,' she accused him.

He scratched his forehead, feeling as inadequate as Stan Laurel.

'I told him about us,' she announced.

'You did what?' he spluttered, though he suspected this was what was coming.

'Told him we had an affair.'

Suddenly he felt emptier than the Gobi desert – and frightened – but before he could respond in any meaningful way, two things happened, one immediately following the other.

They were approaching the roundabout at Gynn Square from the north. Jane slowed, her attention veering from Henry, as she waited for his reaction, and the road ahead, a split of about eighty/twenty in favour of Henry.

'Blackpool to all patrols . . . regarding the earlier incident of attempted abduction, the PNC check run against the partial number plate has come up with one possible match with a grey Audi A4, no current keeper, previously registered to a male from the Manchester area. The full registered number is . . .' The operator reeled off the number. 'A further PNC check reveals that the driver of this vehicle is suspected of indecency offences in the Greater Manchester area. Details of stop-checks to be forwarded to CID in Rochdale.'

'Ooh, could be our man,' Henry said.

'Could be,' Jane said with disinterest.

Henry looked up. 'Slow down, we're coming to a roundabout.'

'I am doing, I am doing,' she cried, and slammed on the brakes.

'And my lord, there it is,' Henry said, pointing to a grey Audi saloon ahead of them, pulling off the roundabout and heading down Dickson Road towards town, one occupant on board. 'Yep, I'm sure it is,' he confirmed, 'before you ask.'

'Shit,' she uttered, and sped after the vehicle.

'DCI Christie to Blackpool,' Henry said into his PR. 'Regarding the circulation, this vehicle is now heading along Dickson Road towards the town centre, just passing the rear of the Imperial Hotel.' He ended the transmission, then said to Jane, 'Come on, speed up, lass.'

She emitted a snarly growl and jammed her foot on the gas.

Henry gave an update: 'Passing Claremont Community Centre.'

The comms operator was deploying patrols to the area.

In a few seconds the car would be in the one-way system which threaded around the old cinema which was now Funny Girls nightclub.

Henry rubbed his hands excitedly. 'Told you I was feeling lucky.'

'After what I've just told you. You must be nuts.'

'Mm, OK, not lucky in that respect.' Once again Jane looked square-on at him. 'Watch the bleeding road,' he yelled.

'Sorry.'

The Audi drove round on to Talbot Road, stopping at the red lights by the bus station, Henry and Jane two cars behind. Henry updated comms whilst peering through the windows of the car ahead in an effort to get a better view of the Audi driver. He was speaking into his PR when he saw that the driver of the Audi was adjusting his rear view mirror. The lights were still on red, one car between them. The Audi driver adjusted his mirror again.

Then, lights still on red, the Audi surged through them.

'He's clocked us,' Henry snapped.

Jane recovered some of her composure, her cop instincts slotting back into place. She pulled out and sped past the car in front, coming up behind the Audi, which swerved through another red light, left into King Street, then a tight right, followed by a right-angled left into Edward Street, shooting past the Post Office into Cedar Square. Without stopping, the Audi screeched across the very congested thoroughfare that was Church Street, angling across into Leopold Grove, the massive Winter Gardens complex on the right.

Henry held tight as Jane, now concentrating on her driving – or so Henry thought – pursued the Audi.

'He's definitely clocked us,' Henry confirmed into his PR, giving comms the details of the chase.

'The pursuit policy must be adhered to,' the operator warned Henry. 'You should back off now.' Which was all very well, but by the time an advanced driver, pursuit trained, in a fully-liveried traffic car appeared on the scene, the Audi would have disappeared.

Henry said, 'Roger,' but to Jane he said, 'Like hell . . . shit!' He ducked instinctively as she swerved across Church Street into Leopold Grove, causing a bus to anchor on and two old biddies to call on all their reserves and leap out of the way, using Zimmerframes for purchase.

'Don't for a moment think you can forget what we were talking about,' Jane said through grating teeth. She held the steering wheel tight, foot to the floor, and cornered into Adelaide Street, right up the Audi's 'chuffer', having no regard for the pursuit policy. This was one suspect who wasn't going to get away because of bureaucracy and Health and Safety.

The Audi was a fast car, sticking to the road well, and pulled away from Jane down the straight stretch which was Adelaide Street.

'Suspect vehicle, fast speed down Adelaide Street,' Henry said understatedly to comms. 'Pursuit policy being adhered to,' he added, lying through all his teeth.

'Roger,' the operator said doubtfully.

Traffic congestion at the next junction with Coronation Street ensured Jane was up behind the Audi again. The driver was all over the place in his seat, head revolving, body jerking as panic swept through him. He went right on to Coronation Street, closely followed by Jane and a cacophony of angry horns from other cars. Then the Audi went left and Henry said, 'Got him!' He had turned into Hounds Hill car park, a multi-storey monstrosity built up over a shopping centre. In 1985, during the Conservative Party Conference, Henry had been positioned on the top floor of this car park, where he spent a week freezing, with a bad tummy, wondering when the IRA were going to strike, as this was the conference the year after the Brighton bombing. 'He's just driven himself into a dead end,' Henry said.

The Audi bounced up the ramp and into the first level of the car park, Jane sticking close as he sped along that level and veered into the tight ramp for level two, tyres screaming in complaint. Jane almost smashed her car by overshooting the turn, anchored on, found reverse with a crunch – 'That's it, get rid of all them nasty cogs,' Henry said, getting a snarl from her – finding first and accelerating up. By this time the Audi had reached the far end and had swung up the ramp for level three.

It was abandoned, door open, driver legging it, when Jane and Henry reached three. Jane screeched to a classic Sweeney-style swerving, rubber-burning stop an inch behind the Audi and Henry was out after the suspect who was fleeing toward the stairwell.

Henry's current level of fitness – low to zero – hit him as he ran, suddenly aware of the extra weight around the middle. Too many crap meals over the last six months had taken their toll. He was breathing heavily within fifty metres, wanting to stop within fifty-one.

But he didn't. He followed the Audi driver into the stairs, glad to see the guy going down in the direction of the shopping mall. Henry flung himself down the concrete steps four at a time, landing awkwardly at the foot of each flight, jarring his knees, but not stopping, using the wall to propel him onwards whilst breathlessly shouting down his PR.

He was catching up with the guy. If there had been another couple of flights down, he would have leapt on his back. Unfortunately the next stop was ground level and the suspect burst through the doors into the shopping centre, running into a crowd of people.

Henry stayed with him, dodging and weaving past happy shoppers, trying to imagine he was back on a rugby pitch. Until, that is, an old woman he was bearing down on panicked, went the same way as him, making him suddenly switch direction, crash into her and send her flying, probably to heaven. He lost his balance, stumbled, shouted, 'Sorry!' and executed a spectacular forward roll from which he recovered brilliantly, but which gave the man on the run an extra five metres.

But there was no way in which Henry was going to be outrun by a suspected child abductor. Personal and professional pride saw to that.

He accelerated, everything pumping, closing the gap.

The suspect ran into the revolving doors which opened out on to the main shopping street. Henry managed to squeeze in the door behind him.

'Got you, you bastard. You're under arrest.'

In the confined, triangular space, the man turned on Henry, pure hatred in his face. A hand emerged with a screwdriver in it, which flashed as it rose in an upward arc towards Henry's guts. He blocked it with his radio and bundled himself up close to the man so there was no room to move. They were face to face, sweat to sweat, eye to eye, breath to breath – and then the door got to its opening and they spilled out on to the street, giving Henry the chance to swing with his radio and smack the guy hard across the head.

They fell in an untidy heap, rolling across the paved street. Henry was vaguely aware of shoppers and screams and legs, but acutely aware that the screwdriver was still in the man's hand: did all these child abusers carry weapons? Before the guy could take advantage of the space, Henry hit him again with the radio, bouncing it off his temple. It had no discernible effect, as once again the screwdriver arced up towards Henry's face. He saw it had a Philips head. He blocked it, the two men parted, both getting to their feet, completely exhausted by the exertion.

'As I said,' Henry panted breathlessly, 'You're under arrest and you need to drop that screwdriver – now!' He finished with a shout. Henry's hand disappeared under his jacket and emerged holding his CS canister. 'I'll CS you if you don't.'

The man considered his options as people gathered. Henry kept focused on him, aware of the build-up of bodies, which could prove advantageous to the suspect. He spoke into his radio, which he'd swapped to his left hand, and gave comms his current position.

Still the man kept hold of the screwdriver and maintained a threatening stance, undecided about his course of action.

Suddenly his face contorted with rage and he leapt at Henry, screwdriver raised. He screamed as he bore down on the detective.

Henry didn't have the time or the inclination to warn him. He simply raised his hand, pointed the CS canister, and pressed. He was always amazed at how weedy and ineffectual the spray looked when it came out. A bit pathetic, really. But the effects were immediate and devastating on the suspect. His scream of anger turned to one of pain as the spray hit him square in the face. The screwdriver went flying and he clawed desperately at his eyes, nose and mouth, which burned fiercely under the acid-like substance.

For good measure, Henry gave him another blast. The suspect went down on to his knees, screaming in agony

Henry rehoused the canister, whipped out his cuffs and got to work on the suspect, careful not to contaminate himself in the process. He grabbed his arms and cuffed him around his back.

'You fucking bastard,' the man cried as he shook his head, desperate to claw at his face and rub his eyes to relieve the pain.

Henry knew that this was the worst thing to do, actually. Henry turned him to face the breeze and told him repeatedly to open his eyes. This was the only way in which the CS would dissipate.

'Try to keep your eyes open . . . keep blinking . . . keep your face to the wind . . . eyes open . . . I know you want to rub them . . . that makes it worse . . . just look into the wind . . .'

Henry was standing by the kneeling man when Jane pounded

on to the scene followed by a lump of hairy-arsed cops, eager to do business.

'Well?'

It was eight p.m. Another long day ... weren't they all, Henry thought ... and now he was face to face with Dave Anger again who, quite rightly, wanted to know where the investigation was up to.

Henry paused for thought.

A girl found dead in a car. The main suspect found murdered. One guy in custody charged with a serious assault on a cop and other serious offences. Another in custody following an attempt abduction. One still outstanding, but a good few days' work in some respects ... yet in others ... His mind flitted to the interactions with Debbie Black, Jane Roscoe's revelations – she'd told her husband! – plus the damage to his car. Henry's brow furrowed on that point. Could those two things be connected? An embittered husband out for revenge? Maybe it wasn't some embittered detective from GMP after all.

And on top of all that, the icing on the cake, was Dave Anger's unremitting downer on Henry.

Henry gave a twitch of the shoulders. 'A lot of things have progressed,' he said in a non-committal way.

'Are you any closer to finding out who killed Jodie Greaves?'

'That depends on the outcome of the interviews with the bloke I arrested this afternoon ... his MO fits in with the original investigation, y'know, the one I was foolish enough to say yes to?' He watched Anger's face as it remained impassive. 'On top of that he was carrying a screwdriver which he tried to use on me, and while it's not a knife with a serrated edge, it shows he uses blades, so we'll just have to see how it pans out.'

'How are the interviews going?'

'At the moment, there's very little. He's refusing to speak, being very awkward. Early days.'

The boss pushed himself to his feet. 'Keep me informed,' he said, clearly unimpressed by the progress. He lumbered out of the office.

Henry sat back, breathed out, still speculating as to why Anger hated him so much. He gave Anger a few minutes to disappear, then picked up his phone and dialled the number of a detective constable called John Walker, who worked on the technical support department. Walker owed Henry a few favours and Henry was leaning on him to pull them in – all in the name of justice, of course. After this he rose from his chair and strolled to the MIR, which was buzzing with activity, albeit fairly muted. People were having 'heads-togethers' in a few locations in the room.

DS Jackson and DC Tope were chatting quietly. Two detectives just back from enquiries were sipping coffee, chatting. Two HOLMES indexers were busy entering data on to the system. Another pair of detectives, the two Henry had tasked with the initial interviews with the Audi driver, were also taking a brew. Henry, surprised to see them, approached.

'Boss,' they said in unison greeting.

'What's happening?'

'Just a break . . . but we're not doing right well. He's clammed up tight, saying nowt.'

'Can we prove today's attempt abduction?'

'I'd say so,' one of the DC's said.

'Do we know where he lives yet?'

'Over in Rochdale. A Section Eighteen search has been authorized, but that's going to take some time.'

Henry squinted, trying to get his head round the best way. He suspected they probably had the man who had committed the series of abductions he had originally been investigating, and maybe he was the missing link in the Jodie Greaves/George Uren scenario. Was he Uren's mystery companion? So many questions, so much to do.

'I think I'll have a word with him,' Henry said.

The two jacks exchanged a worried look. 'Is that wise, boss?' one had the courage to ask. 'After all your fisticuffs with him?'

'One of you can be second jockey,' Henry said as though he hadn't heard the question.

Interview room two again: the scene of many conquests and a few failures. A prisoner had once even picked up the tape-recorder and attacked Henry with it; another had jumped on to the table and kicked Henry in the face. Mostly, though, interviews had been mundane affairs, sometimes easy, often hard and tortuous. But a good interview was usually key to

143

any investigation, the bread and butter of being a detective. That ability to talk to someone and get the truth out of them.

The name of the Audi driver was Bernard Morrison. Mid-forties, divorced, a travelling salesman for a digital TV company, with a string of convictions over the years, all related to indecency.

He fitted Henry's bill nicely. That progression of seriousness which ultimately leads to murder, unless nipped in the bud.

Bernard's bud had not been nipped, though.

His eyes were bloodshot and watery. His nose still dripped from the double tap of CS, though the worst effects had worn off.

Morrison blinked, sniffed, regarded Henry with dislike.

'Recovered?

'Does it look like it?'

'Be thankful I didn't staff you.'

Morrison said nothing.

Henry inserted the tapes and went through the formal procedure of words that prefaced every tape-recorded interview.

He looked at the people in the room – the duty solicitor, the DC who was second jockey, the suspect – and then began by reading out the caution and asking Morrison if he understood it. He nodded reluctantly.

Henry was about to take a big step, but he could not resist doing it. 'I'm investigating two murders, one of a nine-year-old girl and the other of an adult male.'

'So?'

'I'm arresting you on suspicion of the murder of Jodie Greaves and George Uren.' He cautioned Morrison again for good measure and waited for a response.

It was a long pause. Morrison's eyes flitted round the room, blinking repeatedly; he shifted uncomfortably. Nostrils flared as the breath hissed in and out of him. Then he suddenly stopped all this movement, getting a grip of himself.

'I killed them both,' he said simply.

Henry had not realized he had been holding his own breath tight inside his chest until he released it. He tried to remain composed, but his mouth had gone dry and the next words were a struggle.

'Tell me about it,' he said.

WEDNESDAY

Ten

'Why don't you charge him with murder and have done?' Dave Anger said the following morning after the daily briefing. He and Henry were in the MIR, standing apart from the others in the room whilst having their discussion.

'We're not in a position to do that. There's more interviewing to be done,' Henry explained. 'The house search has been inconclusive and hasn't turned up a knife that matches the murder weapon, there's a lot more legwork to do about him. I'll probably need a superintendent's extension on his custody later today, too.' Superintendents had the authority to grant extensions to the custody of a detained person by a further twelve hours on top of the twenty-four hours normally allowed. 'Even if we pull our fingers out – which we are doing – I don't think we'll be in a position to charge before late evening at best.' He checked his watch. It was ten thirty a.m., leaving a good few hours before he needed to approach a super. 'I want to get it as right as it can be before that happens.'

'You'll have to do a lot to convince me to extend,' Anger said gleefully. Superintendents did not dole out extensions lightly, and he was now clearly looking forward to making Henry grovel.

'You're making the assumption I'm going to ask you,' Henry said.

Morrison opened up as neatly as a fly zip. Henry took a step back from the questioning but kept in touch by watching and listening to the interviews taking place via an audio-visual link specially installed and relayed to the MIR. His detectives impressed him. They questioned carefully and slowly, getting to the point and neatly nailing Morrison to the ground as they did.

He blabbed in detail about his abduction attempts, including the rape and near-murder of one of his victims. He was proud to be a predator. He loved stalking children – 'I love kids,' he insisted – at which point Henry would have loved to rush into the room and smash the bastard's head on the interview table. He refrained.

The case against him was building up nicely, he thought, though something was niggling at him, something not quite right, but he couldn't put his finger on it.

'Boss?'

Henry looked up from the policy book he was again working on. It was Jerry Tope, Henry's intelligence cell. Henry sat back.

'Can I come in?'

'Enter my domain,' he said gravely, inviting the DC into his vast, spacious office, making him walk the walk of death from door to desk. Or at least take the three steps required. 'What can I do for you?'

Tope had a sheaf of papers in his mitts. He shook the paper gently at Henry. 'Some of the research you asked me to do.'

'Fire away.'

'Been looking at the abductions from surrounding forces with Ralph Jackson, like you asked.'

'A commendation for you, then.'

Tope gave him a quick glance, then continued. 'We found three over the last eighteen months, three young girls who never turned up. I think Ralph mentioned these to you yesterday.' Henry nodded. 'Now, this is only me putting two and two together,' Tope said nervously.

'Fair dos,' Henry said, placing his pen down, giving his full attention.

'Executive summary first,' the DC said. 'Three girls missing without a trace equals, I believe, three dead girls,' he said solemnly. Henry nodded again. 'All the MOs seem to tie in with the Jodie Greaves murder – girls go missing on Friday evenings, all near motorways or A-class roads – and I think, therefore, we've got three dead girls on us . . . somewhere.' His voice trailed off.

'Carry on,' Henry urged.

'The MO: all abducted from similar locations, all within yards, literally, of main roads which lead into Lancashire.'

'Or in other directions to who knows where,' Henry pointed out.

'Agreed,' Tope conceded. 'But if they have come in this direction, they all fit together ... the locations of the abductions are similar: poor-ish areas, primary schools nearby, sheltered housing for old folk nearby, quick getaway access to roads leading to Lancashire ... and no offences actually committed in Lancs.'

'Whoa, hold up there.' Henry raised a hand. 'What about matey in the traps down below, singing like a soprano?'

The DC pulled a doubtful face. 'I'm an intelligence analyst and I make judgements on what's in front of me. If you ask me, Morrison doesn't fit the pattern.'

'Why not?'

'Trust me, boss, he doesn't.' Henry eyed his junior colleague, who went on, 'I'll lay odds he's not guilty of Jodie Greaves's murder. He's too disorganized, too random, too stupid.'

'He's admitted killing her and George Uren,' Henry insisted defensively.

Another even more doubtful face from the DC, followed by a sigh of confidence. 'There's a good chance he did know Uren. They served time in Wymott about five years ago, but only overlapped briefly. Since then, Morrison hasn't been back to prison and there's nothing in his file,' – he held up his sheaf of papers – 'which Rochdale were good enough to send us, to suggest he's seen Uren since that time. If I had to put a quid on it, I'd say Morrison isn't a killer. In future, he could be, but he hasn't got to that point yet.'

'So you're a psychologist now?'

'Just looking at the escalation of his offences, and, and, there is something else.'

'Astound me,' said a rather pissed-off Henry Christie.

'Morrison comes into Lancashire to commit offences; the three girls, plus Jodie Greaves, were all snatched outside Lancashire, and I'll bet they were brought into the county and murdered.'

'Big hypothesis.'

'That's what we do, isn't it? Test hypotheses?'

'So you don't think he's our killer?'

'Nah. He's the one you were after for our abductions and assaults, I reckon, but not for the murder. From what I've seen of the interviews, he's very detailed about what he's done in Blackpool, less so when it comes to the murders.'

'So why admit it?'

'To please you? Who knows? He's a nutter. I'd be interested to know how much detail he gives about the murders.'

Henry rubbed his temples. 'Let's go and see-hear how they're getting on. Let's get them to ask detailed questions about Jodie Greaves and Uren.'

As they rose to their feet, DC John Walker, the detective on technical support who Henry had contacted for a favour the previous evening, appeared at the office door.

'Your car keys,' Walker said, handing Henry his bunch of keys.

'All done?' Henry said, eyebrows raised.

'And dusted.'

Henry sat looking at the monitor for the audio-visual link to the MIR, an ugly sensation pervading him. He felt quite tired, ill and not a little bit old.

'Shite,' he said under his breath. He folded his arms self-protectively, chewing on his bottom lip, flicking it with his tongue. His eyes watched the monitor, his eyes occasionally glancing at Jane Roscoe and Jerry Tope. Henry's chest was tightening as he listened to the probing questions the interviewing detectives were now putting to Morrison, who squirmed as the verbal shots were fired.

'I swear I killed her and Uren,' he insisted.

'Did you abduct her?'

'Yes.'

'From where?'

'Harrogate.'

'Exactly where in Harrogate?'

A shrug.

'How well do you know Harrogate?'

'Not well.'

'How many times have you been there?'

'Quite a few.'

'Tell me how you get there.'

Morrison paused, stumped. The DC repeated the question, but got no reply.

'Let me ask you again – did you kill Jodie Greaves?'

'Yes.'

'Describe how.'

150

'Stabbed her.'

'Back, front, neck . . . where? How?'

'All over.'

'What about Uren?'

'Same.'

'What else did you do at the scene of Uren's murder?'

'What do you mean?'

'You tell me . . . what else did you do?'

'Don't know what you mean.'

'Did you stab him in the back?'

'Yes.'

'How many times?'

'Ten, maybe.'

'Did you stab him in the eye?'

'Yeah, both.'

'Did you cut his little finger off?'

'Yes.'

'Did you stab him with your screwdriver?'

'Yeah – and the girl too.'

'What complete and utter bollocks,' Henry said. 'You're right, he just wants to please us, the bastard.' He looked coldly at Tope. 'Well spotted,' he acknowledged grudgingly, realizing that his nickname 'Bung' was in no way justified.

The silent scream. Head in hands, elbows on desks, eyes covered. Henry could not stop shaking his head in disbelief. He sat up, thumped the desk and steadied himself.

He'd been so sure that he had tunnel-visioned himself, but when the facts were examined, there was no way in which Morrison could be the killer he was after. Oh yes, there was a lot of work still to do on him. He was a very bad man, a danger to the public, and the case against him had to be built very carefully. He had to go to prison for a very long time and all the offences he could possibly have committed must be investigated and pinned on him. There would be many more than the ones in Lancashire, Henry was sure. But not Jodie Greaves's murder, nor George Uren's. Morrison had now given up that pretence under questioning, but could not even begin to explain why he had admitted to the murders in the first place, other than to say, 'I want to kill someone.'

A noise at the office door made Henry look up: Dave Anger

stood there smirking. He didn't say a word, but pushed himself away from the door and walked off.

'Fuck you,' Henry said. Quietly. His attention turned to the paperwork, but he could not concentrate on it.

'Can I enter the dragon's lair?' Jane Roscoe said. She was holding two mugs of steaming coffee.

'Only if they contain shots of JD's finest.'

'Kenco unleaded, I'm afraid,' she said, meaning the coffee was decaffeinated.

'That'll do.'

She came in, closed the door with her toe, sat down opposite and passed a mug to Henry. He took it gratefully, smiled. They regarded each other over the rims of the mugs. A flash of memory: Henry saw them making love, could feel how good it had been, but how it had to end.

'Cheers.' He raised the mug, more to the memory than anything.

She placed her mug on her lap, wrapping her hands around it, leaning forward on the chair. 'You must think you'll never get rid of me,' she said. 'The bane of your existence.'

'It has crossed my mind. But still, you reap what you sow.

'And you certainly sowed some seed,' Jane smiled. Maybe she was recalling some of the things Henry had just seen in his mind's eye. She sat back. 'Look . . . I can't deny I have feelings for you, probably always will have. You saved my life for a start, but that's not the only reason I fell in love with you, the knight in shining armour stuff, and when you dumped me I was devastated and angry. Still am a bit, but,' she gave a movement of her shoulders, 'it's over and won't be resurrected.' She closed her eyes and slowly opened them again, as if drawing a line under something. 'That's why my behaviour towards you varies so much. Anyway, fact remains I told my husband. Things aren't going well for us, the baby never came – thankfully, I suppose – we drifted apart, started arguing . . . the story of a million crap marriages, I guess. But blab I did.'

'How badly did he take it?'

'On a scale of one to ten – ten plus. He made all sorts of childish threats.'

'Such as?'

She hesitated awkwardly. 'Threatened to kill you, threatened to tell Kate, threatened to cut your brake pipes, threatened to go to the chief constable . . . run of the mill stuff.'

'Think he's capable of doing these things?'

'No . . . maybe . . . no,' she decided finally, but not with a great deal of conviction. 'He's a gentle man, really,' she said whimsically.

'Worms turn,' Henry said. 'I've already had my car damaged.'

'You're joking.'

'And I've received some threatening texts.' Henry fished out his mobile and handed it to Kate. 'One of which relates to brake pipes.'

She looked at the texts, mouth dropping open. 'It's not his number,' she said as she tabbed through the screens. Henry shot her a withering glance. 'I know, I know,' she admitted, handing the phone back. 'Anyone can buy a new SIM card. Nice little message from Kate, though . . . sorry, couldn't resist.'

Henry coloured up, but decided to ignore it. 'Could it be him, you think?'

'Dunno. He has been out of the house a lot at strange times, and so have I, I suppose.' She screwed her face up. 'I don't see him doing things like that, really, but he was furious when he made the threats.'

'More furious than you'd ever seen him?'

That stumped her, because the answer was yes. Her foot started to shake.

'Bloody hell,' said Henry, visions of his new, steady life being torn apart by a past indiscretion. He had managed to keep the affair secret from Kate, though he suspected she had an inkling about it, but if Mr Bloody Roscoe went and told her, he would have trouble keeping Kate from throwing him out on his ear. He rubbed his neck and groaned, feeling his bones scrape.

'You still under one roof?' Henry asked.

'For the time being.'

'Reconciliation?'

She shook her head with certainty.

'OK. Way forward?'

She shrugged. 'See how it pans out?'

'Oh . . . my . . . God,' he uttered desperately. 'Let's see if he tells Kate and then murders me. Hm.' He put a thoughtful finger to his lips. 'Let me think about that one.'

'Not much else we can do. The cat's out of the bag and if he chooses to make a stink about it, we'll have to deal with it then.'

'Fantastic,' Henry said dryly. The phone on his desk rang. He scooped it up before the second ring and announced himself, then went quiet and sat upright as he listened. Finally he said, 'I'll be there in . . .' He checked his watch. 'Twenty minutes.' He replaced the phone and stood up. 'Gotta go,' he said urgently, flustered, searching for his car keys which were right in front of him on the desk.

'What is it?' Jane asked, face creased with concern.

'My mum's been burgled.'

Eleven

Janet Christie, eighty-six years old, lived alone on a warden-controlled old people's complex on the outskirts of Poulton-le-Fylde. She had a comfortable one-bedroom bungalow with all the mod cons for an easy life. Frank, her husband, Henry's father, had died ten years earlier, having left her with serious money from property and pensions and she did not want for anything, except better health, better memory and a son who visited her more regularly.

Henry had watched her slow deterioration since his dad had died. It had been her decision to go into sheltered housing, having sold the mortgage-free marital home, because she did not want to be a burden. At first the decision had been ludicrous to Henry, but as the years passed, he'd seen the sense. She had anticipated the future, but he had not. Now she needed a cane for support and it was a struggle for her to even make her own meals. She had not reached her dotage, but it was on the horizon, yet she remained fiercely independent and fought the prospect of the next big move in her life . . . to an old people's home.

The journey to her house was not without risk for Henry. He arrived five minutes earlier than promised.

A car was parked outside and Henry found a local DC inside talking loudly to his mother. Henry knew the detective well, having worked with her over the years. She looked at the DCI and gave him a worried smile.

'Henry!' his mother said, obvious relief flooding through her

'Hiya, Mum, what's been going on?' He scooped down and pecked her cheek.

'Been bloody robbed . . . uuhh!' she shivered. It was at that exact moment Henry saw how shaken and vulnerable she was. Her old, watery eyes turned up to him, edged with cataracts, and a tear rolled down her cheek. 'Need a hug,' she blubbed.

Henry gasped quietly, swooped down and wrapped his arms

around her, feeling guilty he had allowed this to happen. He even began to fill up himself and get a wobbly chin. 'It's all right, mum,' he said brightly, 'I'm here . . . it's OK.' He twisted his head to the detective and said, 'Can you give us a minute?'

They were in the tiny but well-appointed kitchen, each with a cup of tea and a biscuit, leaning against cabinets. Henry's mother was in the living room, chatting happily now to her friend who had called round; a friend who was a mere slip of a thing at eighty and who did quite a lot for her. This gave Henry and the local detective time to speak.

'I idealistically thought that a warden-managed complex would make this sort of crime more difficult,' Henry said. He had to admit that he was pretty much out of touch with this level of criminality, and it had come as quite a shock to him that his own mum could be the victim of such a callous individual.

The detective was called Sheena Waters and had been posted to this area for a good number of years. 'It's an epidemic, distraction burglary,' she said. 'I'm investigating four others on this complex and about ten others in the area. They're all much the same MO, same offender, I think: targeting old people, mainly women, using a variety of scams to gain entry and steal.'

'What happened here?'

'Electricity board checking pipes.'

'She fell for that?'

'It all happens quite quickly, and for an eighty-odd-year-old it's pretty unstoppable. They don't really know what's happening until it's too late. Preying on vulnerable people is easy.'

Henry's mouth twisted with revulsion.

'I think I'm dealing with someone who makes a living from this type of crime, someone who's chosen the location very carefully; there's lots of older people round here, the main road in and out is easily accessible . . .' Sheena stopped, seeing her words weren't really penetrating. 'Henry, it's not your fault,' she said kind-heartedly. The expression on his face informed her he was feeling differently.

He sipped his tea – Yorkshire tea, the kind his mother swore on, even though she'd been born in Rochdale – and pulled himself together.

'It's not the first time, though,' Sheena said tentatively.

Henry closed his eyes in despair. 'What?'

'She's been burgled before, same MO, but didn't report it.'

'What?' His incredulity was tangible.

'It often happens. Embarrassment, plus the offender threatened her.'

'Threatened her?'

Sheena nodded. 'She only told me just before you came, by the way.'

Henry felt queasy. 'What's the description of the offender?'

'Male, white, twenty-five to forty years, black hair, five foot six inches tall, slim build, local accent.'

Henry rubbed his face. 'What did he take?'

'The two thousand pounds under her mattress.'

'What?' he said, horror-struck. 'Money under the bloody mattress? She keeps money under the bloody mattress? The stupid bloody woman.'

'DC Waters receiving?' Sheena's PR blared out.

'Go ahead.'

'ANPR hit you might be interested in.'

'Go ahead.'

Henry mee-mawed he was going back into the living room, leaving Sheena in the kitchen. He found his mother and friend devouring cake – Yorkshire Brack – to accompany their cups of tea. She seemed more relaxed now, but gave Henry a weak smile. Before he could speak, Sheena swung through the door behind him.

'Henry,' she hissed and beckoned him back to the kitchen, out of earshot of two people who couldn't hardly hear a rock concert between them. 'Traffic have an ANPR site set up on the 583 into Blackpool,' she said quickly. ANPR stood for Automatic Number Plate Recognition, and was a superb computerized system of recording and checking vehicle registration numbers by the thousand. It was linked to PNC, the DVLA and other intelligence systems and was a tool often used for crime or traffic operations with great success. 'They've had a hit which resulted in a motor being pulled and someone being locked up on suspicion of this job.' Sheena pointed to the floor, meaning the burglary which had been committed at his mother's. 'He's presently in custody at Blackpool.'

As ever, the custody office was heaving. Henry had never known it to be anything other. In excess of twelve thousand prisoners were processed through its doors each year, a phenomenal amount of human flesh being put through the sausage machine and spat out at the other side into the monster that was the criminal justice system.

Henry and Sheena eased their way through the horde, up to the custody desk, Henry's eyes roving over the whiteboard on which the names of all detainees were posted for ease of reference. One name stood out, marked up as arrested on suspicion of burglary. Troy Costain. On their journey into Blackpool, he and Sheena hadn't been told the name of the person who'd been arrested, and Henry hoped this wasn't the person who had burgled his mother.

Sheena spoke to the world-weary-seen-it-all-don't-give-a-flying-fuck custody sergeant. 'Someone just been lodged on suspicion of burglary as the result of an ANPR check?'

The sergeant looked up from his thick binder of custody records. Eighteen people were presently in the cells, and he thought he was having a quiet day. He lifted his pince-nez and squinted at Sheena and Henry. He knew both well. 'Doctor's room, just being stripped for forensic.'

'Who is it?' Henry asked.

'One of the Costain clan from Shoreside.' It was the one Henry had seen on the whiteboard.

Henry swallowed. He edged up to the sergeant. 'Put me down for supervising the forensic stuff.'

The sergeant eyed him, slightly puzzled. 'Why?'

'He burgled my mum's house – whilst she was in.'

The sergeant nodded. 'Don't drop me in it, Henry.'

'I won't.'

Henry twisted away from the desk and, Sheena trailing behind him and giving the custody officer one of those 'What the hell's happening?' looks, they made their way down the corridor to the doctor's room, a place reserved for the police surgeon to assess any prisoner requesting treatment. It was also the room in which the breathalyzer machine was located.

Inside, the prisoner was stepping into a paper suit. His clothing had been bagged up appropriately. Two uniformed traffic cops were supervising.

'There's no effin' way you can put me in a cell. I'm claustrophobic, and I promise you, I'll kick off big-style.'

The constables blinked with disinterest. Then the prisoner

turned and saw Henry. For the second time that day, someone breathed a sigh of relief at the sight of him coming through a door. The prisoner opened his mouth, about to say something, but Henry gave a minute signal with his index finger to silence him.

'You guys finished bagging up?' Henry asked.

'Yeah, boss.' They picked up the parcels containing the prisoner's seized clothing.

'You've done a good job.' Henry stood back, indicating they should leave, which they did. He closed the door behind them, softly and firmly, leaving himself, Sheena and the detainee in the room.

'Thank fuck you've turned up,' the prisoner whined. 'They were gonna put me in a cell. I'd go ape, you know that.'

Henry eyed the felon up and down, unable to hide his look of utter disgust.

Troy Costain, hard man from Shoreside estate on the outskirts of Blackpool. One of the ever-multiplying Costain clan, which ruled the estate through violence, burglary, intimidation and drugs, as well as populating houses with an array of illegitimate kids, rather like cuckoos. The Costains claimed to be descended from Romany gypsies, that they had blood running through their veins which could be traced back proudly through generations and that their behaviour – believing in the righteousness of theft and the fist – was part of their wild and legitimate legacy.

Troy was the eldest son. He pretty much ruled the roost, as old man Costain now spent most of his time in Spain. What no one knew was, though, was that he had been one of Henry's top informants for many years, and, because of that, Henry had turned a blind eye to his nefarious activities. Recently, however, Troy had been trying Henry's patience to the nth degree.

He had become Henry's grass when Henry had arrested him years earlier and discovered that the hard man Troy purported to be became a weak, pathetic little shit when introduced to the inside of a cell. Confined spaces sent him batty. A chink in his armour which Henry had ruthlessly shoved a metaphorical knife through during the intervening years.

As Henry looked at him today, though, he knew that their 'special relationship' was at an end.

'What've you been up to, Troy?' Henry asked calmly.

'Nowt, really. Just a bit of a scam.' He glanced worriedly at Sheena, then back at Henry. 'Can we get rid of the totty,' he said conspiratorially, edging up to Henry.

Troy did not see it coming. Henry was hardly aware of it, either. It was just a reaction.

He punched Troy in the lower stomach with a fist bunched hard as iron. Then, he slapped him across the face, open-handed and sent him spiralling across the room, falling across the doctor's examination table, with Henry right with him. He grabbed Costain by the throat and smashed him against a steel cabinet, making an awful din, but one which Henry knew could not be heard outside the room.

Troy slumped down, clutching his gut, gasping for breath. 'What the fuck was that for?'

Henry towered over him, shaking with rage.

'Tell me again what you've been up to, Troy.'

'Henry, man, what is this? Jesus Christ, I've only been rippin' off old biddies, everybody's doin' it,' he wailed.

Sheena laid a hand on Henry's shoulder. She had witnessed the assault from behind and could see Henry trembling with fury. Her touch stopped Henry from launching a full-scale battering, which was what he desperately wanted to do. Beat the evil bastard to a pulp. The last time Henry had completely lost his rag in the cells it had cost a young man a testicle and caused Henry endless grief. He stepped back, removing the red visor that had clicked down over his eyes. He was astonished at how entirely furious he was, how his anger was driven by the thought of someone violating the home and property of his mother.

He caught his breath, then knelt down next to Costain, who was looking at him with the surprise of a beaten puppy. 'I want you to admit all the offences you've committed, Troy, do you understand?' Costain nodded, wanting to please Henry there and then, discretion being the better part of valour and all that. 'Stand up and let me take you to the cells. You need to be punished for what you've done.'

'Henry, you know what the cells'll do to me.'

'Yes.' A beat. 'I do.'

'No fucking way, you bastard.' And Costain did exactly what Henry wanted him to do as the prospect of being locked up blinded him to everything else. He went for Henry, using his legs like a sprinter, driving himself into Henry's chest, arms flailing, punches landing on Henry's upper body.

Henry stumbled backwards awkwardly, riding the blows with a bleak smile, before easily brushing off the attack, grabbing Costain by the throat and waltzing him across the room like a farmer strangling a chicken and slammed him across the breathalyzer machine, holding him down, the grip tightening on his neck. Both their eyes bulged.

Henry was enjoying the sensation, but after a few moments he let go, spun Costain round, put an arm around Costain's neck and bent him double.

'OK, I'm going to walk you nice and easy out of here down to the cells, Troy, and if you so much as tremble wrong, I'll make you do the funky chicken, OK?'

'OK,' he wheezed.

'Open the door,' Henry growled at Sheena, who was shocked and speechless by Henry's display, having seen a side of him she did not know existed. She did as instructed, meek obedience, awe and fear in her face. Henry gave her a wink as he marched Costain out of the door, but it did not reassure her.

'Which cell?' he asked the custody sergeant.

'Trap four.'

Henry led him down the cell corridor, turned into cell four and pushed him in, sending him stumbling against the bench. Costain rubbed his throat and turned to Henry. 'Fuck's this about, Henry, fuck's this about?'

'I'll tell you what it's about, Troy, mate,' Henry said through clenched teeth. 'It's about you trespassing, you preying on people who can't defend themselves. You being much, much worse than I ever thought you could be.' With that, Henry slammed the heavy metal cell door shut with a reverberating crash.

Immediately Costain started to scream and pound and kick on the door from the inside. Henry listened to it for a moment, then turned away and stalked down the corridor.

Tea and a piece of cake, just like his mother was having; just the things Henry needed at that time of day to calm him down. At first, as he drank the tea, his hand dithered. After a few sips and some coffee walnut cake, he began to mellow out, to feel a certain serenity. At last he exhaled the last breath of tension, and the veins stopped pounding in his head.

He and Sheena were in the canteen on the eighth floor of the police station. She had said little, but had herded him up in the lift, sat him down and made him chill out.

'I thought you were going to kill him.'

'As Clint once said, "Killing's too good for him".' He smiled again to try and reassure her, but his boyish grin wasn't working on her. She was clearly upset and unsettled by Henry's attack on a prisoner. 'It's probably a good job you put a hand on my shoulder when you did, though,' he conceded. 'He's a bit too smackable.'

'Mm,' she said doubtfully.

'Reckon he's a possible for your other jobs?'

'Fits the description well enough.'

'He'll have done them.'

'I take it you know him of old . . . I sensed a certain history there?'

'We go back a long way,' was all Henry would say. That Costain was an informant was not known for sure by anyone else, nor was Costain even in the new informant handling system. Henry was handling him the old, unethical way, totally against modern procedure. Not that he would be doing that any more. He'd protected him for too long and now Troy had overstepped the mark. Time to jettison him.

'I'd better get down and start interviewing him,' Sheena said, standing up. She vacillated. 'Look, Henry, if he makes a complaint or this gets asked about, I don't think I'll be able to cover for you,' she said anxiously, unable to look Henry in the eye. 'I've got my job to think about, y'know.'

'I know, don't worry. I wouldn't expect you to do anything but do the right thing. It's fine. But he won't rock the boat. Thanks for looking after my mother.'

'Pleasure.'

Henry watched her walk out of the canteen, then sat back and finished his tea and cake alone, two blissful flavours combining to de-stress him.

'Time to get back to a murder enquiry,' he announced to himself.

Twelve

Henry was alone. He stood in the major incident room and surveyed the walls. On them were photographs of the burned-out Astra, the body of Jodie Greaves inside the boot; George Uren's dead body was also displayed up there, his neck gaping with that dreadful wound. Charts abounded: timelines, 'family' connection trees, flip charts with 'to do' lists on them, staff availability and commitments. Henry mooched around, his brain taking in everything, ticking over, trying to get back on track.

Thinking the case had been solved with Morrison's false confession, the incident with his mother and the Jane Roscoe fiasco had all managed to knock him off track, make him take his eye off the ball.

His mother's burglary had triggered something in his cogitations, but the importance of it was eluding him. He wasn't sure if it was a valuable thought, but it was annoying him that he could not draw it up to daylight from the depths of his grey matter.

His hands were thrust deep in his pockets.

He was alone in the room because it was six thirty p.m. and everyone had gone for food. The room would start to refill in about ten minutes. He sat down at one of the desks, thinking hard.

'C'mon, dumb-ass,' he chided himself. 'Think.' He reached over and picked up the Intel file on Uren, skimming through its contents. He paused at the section devoted to Uren's finances. It detailed his National Insurance number and that he drew meagre unemployment benefit. A paltry figure, Henry thought, hardly enough to sustain anyone. So how could he afford to run a fairly new Vauxhall Astra? Uren's bank accounts had been discovered and there was little in them. Yet if he was travelling and was responsible for the other abductions in other forces, and maybe beyond, he needed cash to operate.

'Show me the money,' Henry muttered to himself.

Uren travelled and committed crime, so therefore he was a travelling crim, but the offences he was suspected of committing were not cash generators. Abducting kids did not make money. But he needed cash to operate.

Henry sat back and wondered if he had the answer.

Quickly walking back to his office, he picked up the Intel reports that Jerry Tope had dumped on his desk when he'd hypothesized that Morrison was not the man they were after. The reports detailed the three other abductions from surrounding forces, including MO, locations, times and dates.

'I bloody wonder,' Henry said – again to himself. He was doing too much of that lately, chatting alone. Not good. The first sign of madness.

His mobile rang: 'Jumpin' Jack Flash', the ring tone the chief constable had once told him to get rid of as it was unprofessional. Because of that, Henry had kept it. It was Debbie Black.

'How goes it?'

'Not good. Family distraught, getting worse by the minute. Even so, I need to get home for a day or two, if that's OK? The incident room is up and running here, as you know, so I could do with a breather, please. Need to get my washing done.'

'Yeah, no problem . . . just one thing I could do with you to have a look at first, if you don't mind.'

'Go on,' she said unenthusiastically.

'The location Jodie was taken from? Is there any sheltered housing, old people's accommodation, anything like that nearby?'

'If you remember,' she said in a rather pedantic way, 'Jodie was actually on her way to see her granny, who lives in an old people's complex nearby.'

Henry did remember, after being reminded, that is. He resisted the temptation to say, 'I've got a lot on my plate,' but bluffed by saying, 'Right, yeah, I recall.' Debbie's silence at the other end let him know she wasn't taken in. 'This is a bit of a long shot, but could you make some enquiries with the police over there, just see what other crimes have been reported in the area, say up to two weeks before Jodie was taken . . . I suppose I'm looking for burglaries, bogus official-type offences, distractions.'

'Henry, I'm completely goosed. I've been living out of a

164

suitcase over here, in a hotel room, all at short notice, I might add.' She sounded harrassed. 'I've got a hire car, but I've had enough and need a bit of a break. I need to get home and sink into my own bath, y'know?'

Henry bit his tongue, fighting back the urge to tell her she was also being paid well enough for her time and that she was a cop twenty-four hours a day, blah, blah, blah. He didn't. 'I know it's hard, but if you could just do that for me, then come back and we'll reassess everything. How's that sound?'

'Urgh,' she said sullenly.

'If you can make it back before closing, we could have a drink,' he volunteered, then winced. Why the hell he'd said it, he didn't know. She would surely see it as a come-on.

'I'll hold you to that,' she said, suddenly sounding eager. 'We have unfinished business, don't we?' she added, sultry now.

Henry hung up, doing a silent scream again. Mr Self-Destruct was at it again, the man who could not say no. He growled at himself and picked up the Intel reports again, sure there was something else he was missing. Before he could concentrate, his desk phone rang, making him jump.

'Henry, it's me, Jane. I'm in comms on the seventh floor.' Her voice was urgent. 'A report's just come in . . . a young girl's gone missing on Shoreside. There's something about it. I'm not happy.'

Kerry Figgis, nine years old,' Jane Roscoe said, reading out loud from the report on the monitor of the computer screen in comms. 'Mother sent her to the shop at six o'clock and she never returned.'

Henry automatically checked the wall clock: six fifty-three p.m. Missing for almost an hour now, the report having come into the police at six forty-five. A uniformed patrol was at the family house and another mobile patrol was combing the streets. Henry swallowed, a trickle of seat beaded from his hairline down his temple. He tugged at his collar. He was torn. As senior officer it was incumbent on him to keep an overview of what was unfolding, but as a hands-on cop he wanted to be at the scene, directing people, pointing this way and that.

Jane was eyeing him, sensing his tension. 'Could be nothing,' she said. 'We deal with thousands of mispers each year. Most turn up unscathed.'

'Not all go missing when we're hunting for a child murderer, though,' he said.

'Might be no connection whatsoever.'

'Well, until we know different, we'll treat it as though it's the next victim, although, again, it doesn't fit the pattern. But then again, where is it written down that crims have to stick to patterns?'

'It isn't, though they often do.'

'And, remember – we interrupted something when we spotted Uren and his pal in Fleetwood; if Morrison isn't the mystery guy, and it looks like he isn't, then we have to assume that whoever he is, is still out there, still on the prowl. Maybe we've made him act outside his normal pattern?'

Jane understood. There was no egg-on-face to run an MFH enquiry as though it was a murder. Better safe than stupid. 'What do you want to do?'

'All the bread-and-butter stuff. Make sure the bobby on the scene does the initial house search and get a real story from the parents or whoever's in charge. Take it from there.'

'Alpha Six to Blackpool,' the voice of the first officer at the scene called up.

'Go ahead,' The radio operator dealing with the incident was sitting close to Henry and Jane, earphones on. The two detectives could hear the conversation through their own PRs.

'Done a quick search of the house, no trace of the misper. Got a description if you want to circulate?'

'OK, go ahead – you're on talk-through,' meaning the officer could be heard by all other patrols on that frequency.

He began to relay the description of Kerry Figgis over the airwaves. Henry listened, nostrils flaring. In his uniformed days he had reported dozens of kids missing, and most had turned up just as he was circulating their details. Without exception, they had all come home or been found sooner or later. He'd even found one hiding in a wardrobe, another in a garden shed, just to wind up the parents, which was why an initial house search was essential.

'DCI Christie to Alpha Six,' Henry said when the officer had completed the transmission, using his PR. 'Can you talk?'

'Yes.' Meaning he could not be overheard by the family.

'Quick situation report, please.'

'OK, boss. Kerry left home at six from the house on Cloister Parade to go to the shop next to the pub on Preston Road.'

'By what route?'

'Down the Parade, up through Song Thrush Walk and out on to Preston Road.'

'Is it a route she's done before?'

'Yeah, lots of times, apparently.'

'How long should it take for her to get to the shop?'

'Three minutes, maximum.'

'Did she get there?'

'No.'

'OK – first impressions?'

'Genuine,' he said firmly. 'She's never been missing before, family say there's been no falling-out or disagreements . . . I'm concerned at this moment in time.'

'Thanks for that,' Henry said.

'Alpha Nine to Blackpool,' another patrol called up. 'I'm at the shop now and they know this girl well. Just to confirm, she hasn't been in, not today anyway.'

'OK, could she be with friends?'

'Just starting that enquiry now.'

'Shit,' Henry said, but not down the radio. Panic welled up, but he controlled it, looking thoughtfully at Jane Roscoe. 'Song Thrush Walk,' he said quietly. 'AKA Psycho Alley . . . bugger.' He made a decision. 'Whether or not this is linked to our job or not, we do this properly because I'm not taking any chances. Get all available resources to the area, road-policing unit, dogs, ARV's, Support Unit and whoever else is knocking about. I want some initial hasty searches and I want the patrol inspector to get his or her arse down there, get an RV point sorted and this all coordinated.' He was almost breathless, counting off the things on his fingers. 'You stay in here, Jane . . . I'm going to speak to the family.'

'No surprise there,' she muttered.

'I'll feel better on the ground, at least initially.' They regarded each other. 'Have I missed anything?'

In the gap between question and response, the radio blared again.

'Alpha Nine to Blackpool – urgent!'

'Go ahead,' the comms operator replied.

'Got a witness who saw a young girl getting into a car on

the Preston Road side of Song Thrush Walk, on the car park behind the shops . . . from the description of the girl, it sound like our misper.'

Henry Christie did not want to make any more assumptions. Without exception, they always came round like an angry alligator and bit your arse – rather like his blind, but short-lived, belief that Morrison was the killer he was after. Which was why, as he sat in the living room of the Figgis household, he was not going to immediately decide that George Uren's mystery partner and probable murderer was responsible for what appeared to be the disappearance of Kerry Figgis.

In most cases, it was someone close to the victim anyway; a friend, relative, work colleague, who was responsible for the crime. As much as TV drama, films and the factual news liked to sensationalize, most abductions and murders were committed by someone in this category, not a super serial killer. Most murders were grubby, unspectacular, sordid, brutal affairs committed by half-wits and doom-brains, not by masterminds.

Which was good in one respect because Henry usually felt intellectually superior to the majority of people he locked up.

He looked at the room. It was comfortably, if cheaply, kitted out, with mainly self-assembly furniture, all of which was chipped and knocked. The three-piece suite was tatty, worn and looked very comfy. The pictures on the walls were inexpensive but reasonably tasteful prints bought from DIY superstores.

Henry had never come across the Figgis clan before, so that was a positive for him as he sat there, trying not to stereotype another family existing on a council estate.

He was sitting on an armchair next to Kerry's mother, who was sunk into the settee. She had short, blonde, spiky hair, studs through her nose and left eyebrow, and a lot of empty holes in her pierced ear lobes. She was caked with a layer of badly-applied make-up, which had run into little rivers as her tears fell down her cheeks. She had sobbed uncontrollably since his arrival, and had chain-smoked through it all. Other members of the clan were doing the same thing, and the air in the room was thick with an unmoving cloud, making Henry fully appreciate the dangers of passive smoking.

She was called Tina, and she was twenty-six years old. Next to her on the settee, holding her with dramatic tightness, was

Callum Rourke, the boyfriend. From the huge craters and pimples on his face, Henry guessed he was about nineteen. The missing girl's grandmother, Tina's mother, a woman with a harsh cheese-grater voice, aged about forty, sat in the armchair opposite Henry. She must have had Tina when she was about fourteen, Henry thought bleakly. She was wearing a far-too-short denim skirt, which rode up to reveal an overweight expanse of chubby thigh which she was not trying to hide.

Tina glanced at Henry. Not much had been said for a few moments, but now that gap of silence was filled with a roar of anguish as she stood up, her thin body juddering with sobs. She pushed Callum out of the way as he stood up with her, and rushed to the door, exiting and running upstairs, howling as she went.

Callum made to follow. Henry was up quick, stopping him with a hand to the chest. He looked at the grandmother and with a twitch of the head, gestured for her to go and see to Tina.

'I'd like a word with you, Callum,' he explained and encouraged the woman to go with another jerk of the head. 'Sit down, mate,' Henry said when she got the message and went.

He was no more than a spotty beanpole of a lad, not someone who looked capable of being the guardian of a nine-year-old kid. He sank back into the settee slowly at Henry's request.

'You're the love interest?'

'Yep – you know that.' There was a big, yellow-topped pimple on the young man's chin, fit and ready to erupt.

'So what's the crack? You here all the time? You look after Kerry?'

'I live here, yeah – ever since the shit who says he's Kelly's father left 'em in the lurch,' he spouted defensively.

'You work then?'

'All the hours God sends. Down at Tesco.'

'When did you last see Kerry?'

'When she went out to the shop. We were havin' tea and we needed some bread, so Tina sent her.'

'When I got here, you weren't here,' Henry said. 'Where'd you been?'

'Lookin' for Kerry.' He gave a short laugh. 'You fuckin' think I did it, don't you?'

'Did what?'

He shrugged. 'Whatever happened to her . . . I dunno.'

'Did you?'

He slumped back, shaking his head. 'You're all the friggin' same, you set o' twats. Well, I'll tell you.' He sat upright, tense, and pointed at Henry, angry. 'I love Tina, she's my world, and I love little Kelly. We've made a go of things since shit-face pissed off and left her, and I wouldn't hurt a hair on that little girl's body, or God strike me down.' His speech was impassioned, impressive. A tear formed in his eye, and the cynical Henry thought, 'Doth he protest too much, or would I think that anyway – or am I just being cynical, even though I know I'm not cynical?'

'OK,' Henry said, easing off, 'but get yourself ready to be questioned closely, because if Kerry doesn't turn up alive and well, you'll be in our sights just so we can eliminate you from the enquiry.'

Callum nodded glumly, accepting the inevitable. 'You'd better look at Kerry's dad, though . . . he was always makin' threats about no one else could be her dad, how he'd kill her rather than have someone else being her dad, even though he was the one who buggered off.'

'We will,' Henry promised. 'No stone unturned.'

He did a walk through of the route Kerry would have normally taken from home to the shop. The evening had gone cold and his suit provided him with no real protection from the chill of Blackpool.

Kerry's house was on Cloister Parade. He stepped out of the front door, down the garden path and along the Parade. Fifty metres later he turned into Song Thrush Walk, otherwise known as Psycho Alley. Suddenly, from the brightly-lit Parade, Song Thrush Walk was all darkness, no lighting whatsoever, even though there were lampposts. He looked up. Smashed lenses told the story. He walked on, high walls either side of an alley about eight feet wide. His foot scuffed a bottle, he felt broken glass underfoot, crunching as he walked, like stepping on garden snails. The alley dog-legged, first right, then left, then twenty metres further opened out on the car park at the rear of what used to be a row of shops – a chippie, a hairdresser and a convenience store and beyond them the pub on Preston Road. Only a heavily-defended convenience store now existed in the row, the other businesses boarded up and empty. The car park was unlit and, emerging into it from the walk did not make you feel secure. There was a burned-out car, lots of fly-tipping – a discarded three-piece suite and a large mattress – and signs of substance, drug and alcohol abuse, discarded needles, bottles, cans and glue tins.

Henry shook his head.

A young girl coming through the alley to go to the shop. The Figgis family needed berating for sending her alone. It was no wonder the alley was the scene of assaults and muggings. It was ripe for them, a bad place where bad things happened. He resolved to get something done about it as he walked across the car park.

He stopped in the middle, the spot where, allegedly, Kerry had been seen getting into a car. What did that mean? 'Getting into?' Willingly? Unwillingly? He needed the witness to be spoken to in some detail. He considered it was his job to do that, but realized he would have to delegate it to someone else, but someone he trusted. There was only so much he could do personally.

It was the fundamental question, though.

Willingly, unwillingly?

Someone she knew? Or a stranger?

Henry carried on towards the shop, nostrils flaring.

Eleven forty-five p.m.

'What've we not done?' The question was thrown out to Jane Roscoe and the other detectives and uniformed officers crammed into the MIR. There was a distinct hum of body odour and everyone looked creased and worn out. It was Henry who had barked the question, asking it in a defiant way which almost dared anyone to suggest that something had not been covered or at least considered. 'To say that we've got an abduction on our hands, a nine-year-old girl missing, what have we not done that we should have done in the last five hours?'

The sea of tired blank faces told its own story. Henry experienced a slight tinge of regret for the challenging way he'd posed the question. Anyone who came up with something now would expect to be treated with hostility, and he realized he would have to be careful. Just because he was knackered and under pressure did not mean he had to alienate the people he depended on, people who had been run ragged for the whole of the evening. They were all as exhausted as he, all as dedicated and professional. He needed to keep them on board. He tried to soften his tension-raged face, opened his arms and said, 'Any ideas warmly welcomed.'

Nothing.

He checked his watch: ten to midnight. 'OK folks, back for a seven-thirty a.m. briefing.'

'Why not seven?' someone chirped.

'I'm already breaking working-time regs by asking you to come back at half-seven. But if anyone wishes to trap at seven, I'll be here.' From the nods and the looks on the faces, he knew that to a man and woman they would all be back. A missing girl, added to everything else that had happened since Friday, meant that everyone in that room thought it obscene to be even going home, let alone going to bed. The reality of it was that there was little to be done at that time. Every possible lead in terms of friends, relatives, acquaintances had been followed up. They hadn't yet traced Kerry's true father, which was a bit unsettling. Searches had been done, would be redone in the cold light of dawn. The night duty inspector was staying in touch with the family and all night patrols had been briefed . . . and Henry was feeling nauseous because he feared the worst. Kerry Figgis was probably dead now, and he felt a fraud too for even thinking about going home.

The team sauntered reluctantly out, leaving Henry and Jane in the MIR.

'Need a drink,' Jane declared.

'Me too, but not alcohol.' He stretched, bones cracking. He touched his injured eye, now a rather putrid shade of yellow, and rubbed his sore leg, injured by Uren's car so, so long ago. 'Definitely not alcohol. I'm knackered and if anything happens overnight, I want to be at least half-compos to deal.'

'Mineral water, then,' Jane announced. 'Down at the King's Arms. They've got a late licence.'

'OK, see you down there. Just need to check my e-mails first.'

'And call in?'

'And call in,' he confirmed. They stared uncomfortably at each other, Jane bristling that Henry wanted to call home and speak to Kate.

'So why does it still bother me?' she said. She shrugged. 'See you in the pub . . . don't be long.'

THURSDAY

Thirteen

He called Kate using the work phone on his desk. She sounded sleepy but concerned, and promised to keep the bed warm for him. A pleasant thought which made him fleetingly consider cancelling the mineral water with Jane.

He spun in his chair and glanced at the shark. A dark figure hovered in a doorway below the model, but Henry thought nothing of it. Doorways in Blackpool abounded with dark figures. He sighed and forced himself to his feet, everything aching, everything weary, everything needing a warm bed and lots of sleep.

He wended his way down through the police station using the stairs. He crossed New Bonny Street and headed towards the King's Arms, unaware his progress was being monitored by the figure in the shadows. Henry had completely forgotten he was there.

In the pub he found Jane at a table clutching something that looked remarkably like a gin and tonic and munching from a 'Big Eat' bag of crisps, which was torn apart on the table. He sat opposite – after nodding to a couple of other detectives at the bar – and lifted the long, cool, iced mineral water Jane had bought him. He said cheers and had a sip. It was nice, but it wasn't Stella.

'Contact made?' she asked coolly.

'Contact made,' he confirmed.

She looked sad and a little frustrated, but said nothing. Carefully she selected a large, corrugated crisp, and folded it into her mouth, chomping meaningfully into it.

'So, have we done everything?'

'Yes we have,' she said. 'You feeling a bit vulnerable?'

'A wee bit.'

'Don't worry, you've done good – but what about tomorrow?'

'Find the missing dad for a start, interview Mum properly, and spotty Callum . . . keep looking.' He sounded a little hopeless.

'Think she's dead?'

'My gut feeling . . .' He paused. 'Hm, gut feeling: I know she is.'

'Uren's mate?'

'Doesn't fit the pattern as such, but it could be. Could be Daddy, could be anybody, could be Callum. Keeping an open mind. Need to get the press on board big-style.' He took another ice-against-the-teeth drink of water. 'One dead girl, another abducted, similarities with other missing girls, inter-force working . . . it's going to be a feeding frenzy, and I don't want anything going wrong, like Soham,' he said. He was referring to the abduction and murder of two young girls a couple of years before, which exposed police procedures and information-sharing protocols as a joke. 'All interested parties need to get together tomorrow, and we need to start talking.'

He sat back, the enormity of the task daunting him, making him wonder if he was up to it. There was going to have to be a lot of political game-playing from now on and the spotlight would be firmly burning his eyeballs out.

Tearing his eyes from the pub ceiling, he found Jane staring at him. He instinctively knew the subject was about to be changed. Call it a hunch. There seemed to be no escaping past misdemeanours. He was beginning to feel some sympathy for felons who were tarred for life by a moment of madness.

'Go on,' he said suspiciously.

'Nah, nothing really.'

'Go on,' he ordered her this time.

'I was just wondering how many people would send you texts and damage your car. I'll bet there's more than just my husband. Correction, my ex-husband-to-be.'

'You've made that decision then?'

'Oh yeah,' she said passionately

'I'm sorry.'

'One of those things.' She shrugged stoically. 'Even if you hadn't come along, him and me would've ended up in this position at some stage, I guess. Me and you were just a symptom of an underlying problem . . . so don't avoid the question. You're too good at that, deflecting attention. How many people have you driven to hate you so much?'

He contemplated this, then blew out his cheeks. 'Lots of villains, of course, but I don't mind that so much. Anyone who

176

hates me because I'm a cop doesn't bother me, goes with the territory, but I get unsettled when I think someone hates me on a personal level.' He screwed up his face. 'Does that make sense?'

'You don't really want anyone to dislike you, do you?' she observed. 'You're not terribly good at relationships, are you?' She smiled sadly.

'They frighten me,' he admitted, wishing he had a double JD in his hand instead of a poxy mineral water.

His mobile rang, attracting stares of derision from other punters because of the ring tone.

'Henry Christie.'

'It's me, Debbie, sorry I'm late calling, but I'm only just back from Harrogate.'

'No probs.' He 'phewed' inwardly, having completely forgotten about her and his promise of a drink. 'Did you do that job for me?'

'Yeah, and guess what? Jodie's grandmother was a victim of a bogus official earlier in the week and there were three other jobs in the same area, but no one was locked up. The evidence points to travelling criminals.'

'Right, thanks, that's really good stuff,' he said enthusiastically. 'How much went from the burglaries?'

'Not sure, about two grand in total, I think.'

'How many offenders?'

'Two white males on each job.'

'OK, good stuff, Debbie. Look, there's a briefing at seven, because there's been another kid gone missing over here. If you want a lie-in, that's OK, but I could do with seeing you. I might need you to go back to Harrogate, I'm afraid.'

'Anything to keep me at arm's length.'

'Not at all. I want someone there I can trust to help catch a killer.'

There was a burst of laughter from the other detectives at the bar.

'Where are you, Henry? I thought you were at home. You're in a pub, aren't you? Can I come?'

'I'm off home now,' he said. 'See you in the morning.'

He ended the call and folded his mobile into the palm of his hand.

'The lovely Debbie,' Jane said with a distinct snippiness.

'So did you shag her in Harrogate? She's deffo got the hots for you, but she's a bit mental, you know.'

'Answer – no. And so I've heard.' He paused, waiting for Jane to come back at him, but she remained mute. His mouth twisted thoughtfully, his mind back to the more serious matters at hand. 'I'm just going to go back into the nick to see if Troy Costain's awake. I'd like an informal chat with him.'

'I'll come with you,' Jane said, 'to protect you from yourself.'

'No need – and I won't give him a crack, even though I still want to murder the little shit.'

They finished their drinks and left the still-busy pub. The wind was whipping up and they huddled into their coats as they walked back to the station, entering through the door into the police car park, separating at the lift and stairwell, pausing to say goodnight. Their eyes caught for a spell, then Jane turned quickly away and ran upstairs. Henry walked down the corridor to the custody office.

Half past midnight mid-week, and a stream of prisoners was coming through the doors. Henry pushed through, ecstatic that his time in the custody office was long since over. After a quick chat with the night custody officer who, against all regulations, gave him the cell keys, Henry entered the cell complex, which was a series of cells built around an internal, barred-roof courtyard used to let prisoners exercise and smoke.

Cell four. Henry peered through the peephole.

Troy Costain sat huddled in a shaking ball on the wooden bed, rocking, his arms wrapped around his drawn-up knees. A pitiful moan came from somewhere deep inside him. Henry felt no sympathy. The old adage, 'If you can't do the time, don't do the crime,' came to mind. Although he had used Troy ruthlessly over the years, Henry had always kept him out of custody, protected him, even though their relationship had never been smooth. Troy deeply resented the power Henry exercised over him. But now Henry felt no longer able to do look after him, not with visions of his mother skipping through his mind. As far as he was concerned, Troy was on his own now.

He opened the door. Troy raised his head. He looked dreadful, not least because of the swelling of his face from Henry's earlier battering. Again, Henry experienced no regret at that. A punch in the plexus was the least Troy deserved.

178

'Get me out of here, Henry,' he whimpered.

'Not a chance.'

'I can't stand it, it's fuckin' killin' me.'

'Good. I like to see you suffer.'

He spread his hands. 'Why, what the fuck have I done? What's making you treat me like this?' He looked at the non-responsive Henry Christie and it suddenly struck him. 'Oh, fuck, oh my good fuck! I did your mother, didn't I?'

They were in the exercise yard. Henry had given Costain one of the cigarettes he always kept on him for such occasions. The non-smoking regulations in cells and interview rooms was strictly enforced, and prisoners were lucky if they were allowed to smoke anywhere these days, not something which enhanced cop-prisoner relationships. It was cold, the wind swirling in through the metal bars which formed the secure roof of the yard. Dark clouds scudded across the night sky, rain threatened.

Costain leaned against the wall, deeply inhaling the smoke from the cigarette, relieved to be out of his cell.

'I'd never have knowingly done it, Henry, not if I'd known . . . never . . . you've got to believe me, mate.'

'Don't "mate" me.'

'Sorry.'

'If it wasn't my mum, it would've been somebody else's.'

'Aye, suppose.'

'You are seriously in my debt now, you know?'

'Yeah, yeah, anything.' He sucked the cigarette down to the filter, tossed it down and scrubbed it out, then exhaled the lungful of smoke into the air. 'Can I have another, Henry?'

Henry shuffled the packet out of his jacket pocket and let Costain take one. He was already trying to work out the best way of getting the most out of the rueful Costain one last time.

'Callum Rourke,' Henry said.

'What about him?'

'What do you know about him?'

'Shacked up with that bird on the Parade. I sell him a bit of smack, but I don't know much about him really.' He lit the new, slightly crumpled cigarette with Henry's lighter (also carried for on-the-hoof interviews), cupping the flame against the wind. Another deep intake, followed by a long, pleasurable emptying of the lungs. 'Lucky bastard, actually. I've always fancied shaggin' her . . . anyway, why should I tell you what I know, you've been treating me like shit, Henry. I could complain against you for assault. You're only being nice now 'cos you want something.'

'OK.' Henry snatched the fag from Costain's fingers. 'Back to your cell.'

'No, man, no.' He held up his hands in surrender. 'Stay cool, c'mon . . . gimme the stick back.'

Henry slowly handed it back to him. 'All right, Troy, you're right. I do want something from you – and I'll do you a very big favour, if you agree to do it.'

'What's the favour?'

'I'll release you now on Part Four bail. You'll have to come back and be interviewed, but at least it'll keep you out of the cells for tonight.'

'You can do that?'

'I'm a DCI – I can do anything.'

'But what do you want from me?'

Henry knew he would have some major explaining to do, but a deal was a deal, and he bailed Troy Costain to come back to the station in a week, then led the claustrophobic felon out through the police car park and pushed him out on to New Bonny Street.

'You're makin' me walk home from here?' he whinged. 'What about my car? You've bloody snaffled that from me. Can I have it back?'

'Seized for evidence – now fuck off.'

'I'm going, I'm going.'

Henry stood at the door and watched the young man saunter away in the hard-man, balls-of-the-feet walk they all seemed to use, wondering if he'd done the right thing. Even though he thought that justice would be served, he would rather have seen Costain locked up for what he had done to his mother. He comforted himself with the thought that when Troy eventually came to court, he'd probably end up being sent down for a few months.

As he closed the door, his mobile phone rang. He answered it, noticing that the caller display screen said 'Number withheld'.

'Henry Christie . . .'

There was no response.

'Hello, can I help . . . ?'

A gasp came down the line, then the sound of a female sobbing, but no words were spoken.

'Hello . . . who is this, please?'

The line suddenly went dead. He stared at his phone with mystification. So now women were calling him up just to cry, he thought, but put it down to another of those rogue calls, a wrong number or a misdial. He seemed to be getting an awful lot of them these days. Perhaps he was just unlucky.

Before he could put his phone away, a text landed.

Watch ur bak, it said.

Henry froze and swallowed. He tabbed on to the display which showed the number the text had come from – and saw it was the same one from which the previous texts had emanated. He chose the call option and pressed the green phone icon on his keypad.

The number rang out, but no one answered. When the call cut through to the 'Orange ansaphone', he cut the connection, holding his phone in his hand, staring accusingly at it. How did people make threats before the advent of the text message, he thought. By phone or by letter or in person . . . three ways in which he would have preferred to be threatened.

Who was sending these texts? There had been too many now for it to be a mistake, surely.

And who was damaging his car?

He had a feeling he would find out soon, one way or the other.

He walked back through the garage, up the stairs to the first floor and left the police station from the door of the old enquiry desk and walked across to the multi-storey car park. He paused at the door, searching his pockets for the swipe card which would let him through.

A creeping sensation snaked down his spine, one of those feelings that tell you you're not alone.

He spun.

A dark figure – a man – stood behind him, a balaclava pulled over his face and a baseball bat in his hands which was arcing through the air towards the side of Henry's head.

His mind instantly computed what such a blow would do

to him were it to connect. He reacted by throwing himself at the figure, basically rugby-tackling, driving his shoulder into the man's lower intestine underneath the sweep of the bat which swung harmlessly through the air.

Henry rolled on top of the figure, grappling with him. The bat came out of his hands and clattered away across the concrete, and both men fought desperately across the hard ground. Henry punched hard, trying to hit any part of him, but with no great effect. He'd been so surprised by the attack that he hadn't quite got a mental or physical grip of what was happening. He did a sideways roll and tried to get to his feet, feeling his knees crack, but as he got up his legs were hacked from under him and he went down again on to the palms of his hands.

The hooded figure got up, turned and kicked Henry's hands from under him, then started to boot Henry around the face and upper body. Henry grabbed a foot, hung on grimly, twisting it sideways and knocking the assailant off balance. The man fell and Henry clambered to his knees and sprung at him. He missed as the man rolled away and, in a flowing move, picked up the baseball bat and tore away across the mezzanine. He was down the steps which dropped on to New Bonny Street before Henry could recover.

Breathless and slightly battered, but in much better condition than he might have been had he not reacted so quickly, Henry loped after him without much enthusiasm, reaching the top of the steps only to see the man legging it towards the town centre.

Henry watched, trying to steady his breathing, his lower jaw jutting out.

'Bastard,' he panted. A quick physical check revealed nothing untoward. He'd banged his sore leg, grazed his palms on the ground and banged the knee on his right leg, but apart from that he was unscathed, though there was a tear in his trouser leg. 'Who the hell were you?' he wheezed.

Fourteen

He was back in his miniature office by six thirty a.m., attempting to stay awake by means of strong black coffee and to keep focused by making lists. Unfortunately the lists were all over the place, no sequence to them, no structure. There was just so much to be done.

The priority was to keep the momentum going with the Kerry Figgis disappearance. She'd been missing twelve hours and he was gravely concerned about the situation, so finding her was his number one priority. What he didn't like to add was 'dead or alive'. He'd decided that he would spend the morning fighting for more resources, and if he didn't have a hundred cops working on it by lunchtime, he would chuck himself off the tower.

Jane strolled in at six thirty-five, shocked by Henry's appearance.

'Jesus!' she gasped.

'Where was your hubby last night?' he asked accusingly.

'I don't know . . . what the hell . . . ?'

'I got jumped,' he said and explained his encounter, which had, in the cold light of day, resulted in scratches on his forehead to add to the still-discoloured black eye. He didn't mention the hidden scrapes and scratches underneath his clothing which he had discovered when naked.

'I can't see him doing something like that,' Jane said, but not too convincingly. 'But he wasn't home when I got in, admittedly.'

'Well, whoever it was got away . . .' His voice trailed off. 'I am so pissed off with being the target for mad people . . . but today is about Kerry Figgis and Jodie Greaves and all the other young girls who have gone missing in the region in similar circumstances. I want to start catching bad men today.'

Jane nodded, though she was clearly affected by Henry's assault.

'Listen hard, because I'll only say this once.' He picked up his notes and apologized. 'No particular order to this, just a melting pot of ideas at the moment, others welcome, but here goes . . .'

The motley crew of world-weary detectives who paraded on at seven were briefed, tasked and duly dispatched.

Next were the Support Unit officers, who came in at eight. They were tasked to search the route Kerry Figgis had taken from home, through Song Thrush Walk and to the car park behind the convenience store; they were also asked to start house-to-house enquiries. By eight fifteen they were out. Henry was eager to get bodies out on the streets.

His next heads-down was with Jane in his office, together with Jerry Tope.

Just as he was about to launch into his discussion, his mobile phone rang. He almost ignored it because there was no caller ID, but habit more than anything made him thumb the green phone icon.

'Hello . . .' He glanced round at the people in the office and shook his head, irritated because there was no response from the phone. 'Henry Christie here.' Then he could hear breathing, then the choking sob of a woman, then the line went dead. He placed the phone down on his desk, troubled by the call, the second of its nature. 'Strange,' he said. 'Right . . . let's get our heads round this: Jodie Greaves dead in a car after being abducted from Harrogate; George Uren, who we are sure was one of the kidnappers, is murdered with the same weapon that killed Jodie. He may have killed her, let's not forget that. The car was set alight, as was Uren's body, using incendiaries. Was he murdered by his accomplice? That's rhetorical, by the way,' he said to Jerry Tope who had opened his mouth to utter some- thing. 'We're sure Morrison isn't the man we're looking for, thanks to your analysis, Jerry.' He took a breath. 'The circum- stances of Jodie's abduction fit with the disappearance of at least three other girls in the region, yeah? You can nod, or murmur if you concur,' he said to the lifeless couple. Jane and Jerry nodded. 'Good, I like yes-men and -women. Bottom line, we have a cross-border investigation to start to manage, which includes us and four forces. That needs to get off the ground today. We've also got the addition of Kerry Figgis, snatched on us last night, which doesn't fit the pattern . . . but you never know.' He took a deep breath. 'Good enough summary?'

'Yep, if a bit simplistic,' Jane said.

'I like simplistic,' he said defensively. He looked at Tope. 'Contact the relevant Intel officers in the forces where the other missing girls have disappeared from – which I know you already have done – but this time get a summary of all the crime committed in the two-week period leading up to the date of these abductions, OK?'

'What am I looking for?'

'Patterns. That's what you do, isn't it?'

'Gotcha.'

'And, I want to know how Uren made his living. He was on benefit, but it wasn't enough to sustain his lifestyle. See if you can find more.'

'Will do.'

Henry sat back. 'OK, then – at the risk of repeating myself, this is the strategic hypothesis driving this investigation as of today, bearing in mind it could change at any time: we are investigating the possibility that the four girls who have gone missing from surrounding forces have all been taken by the same person or persons, who could well be living in Lancashire. George Uren is one of those people, now deceased. His companion is the man we are now trying to urgently trace.'

'It's sounding good, Henry. Did you swallow a dictionary?' Jane teased.

He gave her a stern glance. 'And I continue: whilst the disappearance of Kerry Figgis does not totally fit in with this series of crimes, we believe it may be connected, though we are keeping an open mind about that. And that's my hypothesis, for what it's worth – and that's what we're sticking to at the moment.'

Jane looked slyly at him, 'You couldn't be rehearsing for the press conference later this morning, could you?'

Henry gave her his best expression of innocence. 'As if – but most of what I've said isn't for their consumption, especially speculation about series crimes. The last thing they need is to get hold of the possibility we might have a serial killer at large. They'd run us ragged with it.'

There is a feeling of realization, a palpable sensation, that comes over people when it suddenly dawns on them that they are being set up. It is a feeling of creeping dread. It doesn't always come quickly, indeed, it's usually the opposite, but when it arrives it's accompanied by a churning and twisting of the pit of the stomach.

The exact feeling Henry experienced at ten thirteen that morning: thirteen minutes into the press briefing.

Up to that point, things had gone well enough. They rarely go as planned, but that's the way it is with the media, and Henry accepted that. But other forces were at work that morning.

All disciplines of the media had been wheeled into the tiny press room at Blackpool nick, and Henry had taken up position behind a lectern on a raised dais at one end of the room. He was reading from a statement he had prepared that morning, which was designed to keep the hounds at bay – tell them not very much, but get them on side at the same time. It had seemed to be going pretty well and they were all up for it – until the guy from the local rag, a short-arsed individual called Eddie Skirvin, who described himself as crime correspondent (as well as cookery, travel and anything-else-he-was-chucked-at correspondent), raised his hand languidly.

Suspecting nothing, Henry nodded at him. He knew the guy had his knives into the police and had a lot of sport with them, but as he permitted him to speak, he had no reason to think anything was other than well.

'DCI Christie,' he said, sort of chewing the name. 'Temporary DCI Christie,' he smugly corrected himself in a way which made Henry's eyes squint and set off a distant alarm bell. 'It's actually true to say that Blackpool is now in the grip of fear of a homicidal, child-killing maniac – wouldn't you say?'

Taken aback, Henry said, 'No, I wouldn't.'

'Parents are actually in fear of letting their kids out on the streets now, aren't they?'

Henry stiffened. His fingers tightened on the edge of the lectern. He had never really enjoyed dealing with the media, despite going on the course. 'No, I wouldn't say that.'

'Oh, really?' Skirvin said, raising his eyebrows. He paused, then posed and pounced at the same time. 'It's true to say that you've been running an investigation into the abduction and attempted abductions of a number of young children, haven't you?'

Henry nodded dourly. Where was this going?'

'I believe it was a number of months before the police even connected the incidents . . . by which time a number of young-sters had either been abducted, assaulted, or attempts had been made on them. And all the while, the people of this town were kept in the dark about this. Is that true?'

'It's not always easy to make connections,' Henry started to explain.

'A monkey could have put two and two together and made that connection,' the journalist said. A roomful of media bods tittered, enjoying the floorshow. 'The press were not told about these incidents and we could have done a valuable commu-nity service by letting the townsfolk know about the dangers to their children.'

Henry started to splutter.

'And now,' he ploughed on, 'within the space of a few days, one girl is dead, another is missing and the police fear for her safety. Yes, I would go as far as to say the town is now in the grip of fear.'

'The fear of crime is often worse than the reality,' Henry said stupidly, realizing immediately he had said the wrong thing. This room was hot now. He was sweating.

Skirvin made an expression of mock horror, as though he could not believe what he was hearing. 'Is that something you'd like to repeat to a grieving family and an extremely anxious one, Temporary DCI Christie? The fear of crime around here exists because crime happens and people suffer. Serious crime happens. Violent crime happens . . . and I'd like to know what you're doing about it, as would my colleagues.'

There was a murmur of agreement from the assembly.

Henry scratched his head, tugged his tight collar and fixed the journalist with a defiant stare designed to burn him all the way to hell. 'With regards to the series of incidents concerning approaches made to young children, there is now a man in custody for these offences. He will be appearing at court today.' He really then wanted to add, 'Nah-nah-ne-nah-nah,' and pull out his tongue.

'And the dead girl and the missing girl, Kerry Figgis?' the journalist harried Henry. 'Are they connected?'

'It's too early to say for sure,' Henry said evenly. He was thinking, *You've been fed stuff, you bastard.* 'My analysts are looking at the possibility as a matter of routine.'

'And what about the three girls abducted in surrounding forces?'

Henry blinked and tried to keep surprise out of his face. At the back of the room he saw the time on the clock: ten thirteen. 'What about them?' Henry said.

'What I want to know is – is there a serial killer at large who is operating from inside Lancashire? Is that the hypothesis you're working to, one which you'd rather keep from the press?'

'That's not something I can answer. We always look at the possibility that crimes are connected, maybe committed by the same people, but as yet there is nothing to connect the crimes which I believe you are referring to.' Oh God, this was poor bullshit, he thought, a rage creasing through him like a great fire. Bitch, he thought, as he speculated at who could have told Skirvin about the other incidents in surrounding forces. 'Now, ladies and gentlemen, if you'll be so kind, this briefing has concluded.

'Actually, actually,' the offensive little journalist stood up. 'Just one last question, temporary DCI Christie.'

Henry's shoulders dropped. Bad body language.

'Do you actually think you are the best officer available to deal with such a complex, emotionally charged investigation? After all, you do have a history of, how shall I put it?' He feigned a wince. 'Stress?'

'How can it be?' Henry was shaking from head to toe following the encounter with Eddie Skirvin. He paced up and down his office, three steps one way, three steps back. 'How can it be,' his index finger pointed angrily, 'that within minutes, almost, of me using the word hypothesis, a journalist throws it back at me? And how did he know we didn't connect the earlier abductions? That never went to press as such.'

He knew he looked dreadful, but didn't care. He wanted to come across as the baddest, nastiest thing Jane Roscoe had ever encountered in her life. She was sitting in his office, her legs drawn up tight to the chair to allow Henry the room to rant and rave. Now he stopped and towered over her, fuelled by anger, probably about to lose it.

'Honestly, Henry, I don't know,' she said croakily, intimidated. 'I didn't tell him, didn't tell anyone.' Henry glared disbelievingly at her. 'I didn't, honestly.'

'There's only you and Jerry Tope who knows what I'm thinking.' His teeth ground loudly. He pushed past her legs and she drew them further back. 'Must be him, then. I'll sort the little shit out,' he growled and spun out of the office. He had been gone a few seconds when an almost audible thump landed in Jane Roscoe's stomach. She gave chase.

Henry was well ahead of her. He had reached the MIR and was striding across to Jerry Tope, now having lost his rag completely. 'You!' he bellowed across the busy room, full of detectives, uniforms and police staff. Work stopped instantly, everyone turned and shut up. 'You!' he shouted again and the meek DC realized it was he who was being singled out. He sat up, shock on his face, and pointed at himself.

'Me?'

'Yes – you,' Henry reiterated for the third time and used a phrase heard in countless police dramas, something he had never uttered in his life before. 'My office – now!' Even in the mist of his red rage, there was something naff about saying it, but he couldn't think of anything else.

'But . . . I . . . I'm . . .' stuttered the DC.

'I don't effin' care what you are,' Henry said. 'Get into my office, you little snitch.'

'Yes, boss.'

'Henry!'

He turned as Jane ran in behind him, his head twisting, his expression contorted, lips a-snarl like a werewolf. 'What?' he barked.

'It's not him,' she panted. Her shoulders fell. 'It's not him.'

They were back in the office, door closed, Henry leaning on it to ensure they were not disturbed. Jane was sitting demurely in a chair on the 'public' side of the desk, knees together, hands clasped on her lap, shoulders hunched. Her tongue was visible, the tip of it touching her top lip. Her eyes were closed.

'Do tell,' Henry invited.

'After our conflab this morning,' she said after a pause, 'you know?'

'I know the one.'

'I did speak to someone about what had been said,' she confessed, tugging down the hem of her skirt. She paused again.

'I'm waiting.'

'Dave Anger wanted an update.'

Not for the first time that morning, Henry's teeth ground together. 'Dave Anger?'

'He, er . . .' Jane's body language – shrugs, little jerky hand gestures, tight facial expressions, clothing adjustments – all testified to the feelings of guilt she was experiencing at being disloyal to Henry. She gulped. 'He wanted me to keep him informally . . . up to date with progress . . . to get a true picture.'

Henry's head snapped back against the door with a bang. 'So you are spying for him?'

Speechless, Jane held out one hand, then the other, as if trying to balance something.

'I'm the SIO. I'm the one who updates him.'

'I know, I know,' she said desperately. She covered her face with her hands and drew them down, dragging her features.

'Basically you've been giving me bullshit.' He sounded wounded.

'I was caught in the middle.'

'A rock and a hard place?'

'He's a chief super. What choice did I have? No, sod off, I'm not telling you anything? I don't think so.'

'You could have told him the correct route to get info about a case, to go to the SIO, in other words.'

'Not an option.'

'Or you could have told me what you were doing?'

She shrugged.

'Career plans?' he said, watching her face fall and knowing he'd hit the right button. He nodded understandingly, a sardonic look on his face.

'I wanted us to be all right, y'know, you and me, honest,' she pleaded.

'But at the same time you decided to snitch on me?'

'He has every right to know what's going on during a murder enquiry.'

'Yeah, he does, he's the boss, but it's my job to tell him, not for him to have moles operating like bloody informants. It's me who tells him, isn't it?'

'Yes.' Meek.

'But that's not the point, is it?' Henry moved away from

the door, sat behind his desk, swivelling his chair so he could see the shark on the wall. 'OK, you snitched. I can live with that. I can live with you not liking me, or wanting to rub my nose in it, and maybe I deserve it.' He could not remove the sneer from his face. 'I should've guessed it was him. He basically set up a two-bit journo to make me look a dick in public – and that really hurts.'

'You don't know he did.'

'Jane.' His look was withering. 'Don't be silly. The question about me being a stress-head? Where else could that have come from? Eddie Skirvin was prompted and that press conference was hijacked to take away all my cred. I'm waiting for my slot on TV's most embarrassing blunders now. Fuck!' He rubbed his eyes with the balls of his hands. He was exhausted. 'Dave Anger talked to the press and set me up . . . bastard.'

'It wasn't that bad.'

'Jane, fuck off,' he said, but not nastily, because his rage had dissipated away into despair. 'When I've bottomed this job – and I will – I'm off this bloody team. He can shove FMIT right up his rear end. Some comfy office in the back corridor of headquarters'll do me fine for the next three years. It's just . . . what have I done to him that's so bad?'

'You mean you don't know?'

'No,' he said.

'He says you shagged his wife.'

'Why can't even this be simple?' Henry thought as he faced Debbie Black in his office.

'Are you ordering me to go back to Harrogate again? Already?' she said indignantly.

'I don't think I've ever ordered anyone to do anything,' he said mildly. 'I want you to go back across there because you've established a good relationship with the Greaves family. And I want you to show Grandmother Greaves some mugshots, including George Uren, as per the Police and Criminal Evidence Act, to see if she can ID him as one of the guys who burgled her.'

'Why?' It was a very defiant word, because she did not want to go. 'You're just getting me out of the way, aren't you?'

'No, I'm not, but if it'll make you feel better, I'll order you to go,' he said finally, holding up his hands. 'I'm trying –

we're trying – to solve a particularly nasty murder of a young kid. You told me that Granny had been the victim of a bogus official job a few days before Jodie was snatched.'

'And?' Her face was set hard.

'It's something I want to follow up. I have a feeling that Uren could have been committing this sort of crime to fund his lifestyle. It's a hunch, just one of those old-fashioned cop things. Please,' he finished.

'Right, OK, I'll do it,' she relented. 'But on one condition.'

'What would that be?'

'A drink . . . and I promise not to get arseholed this time.'

'You're on.'

The next hour was spent trying to arrange an urgent meeting with SIOs from surrounding forces so they could discuss the possibility of a joint investigation and work out protocols and procedures. Times like this, Henry wished he had a lackey to run around for him, or was the correct term a 'PA'?

In the end he left messages with all the relevant detectives, none of whom he managed to contact personally, leaving him no further forward in the respect of setting up a cross-border enquiry. Such a meeting, though, was beyond urgent.

He sat back and the photograph he'd looked at in Dave Anger's office flashed into his mind. The wedding photo, bride and groom, both happy and blushing. He tried to recall the detail of the woman, the one he was supposed to have slept with, but it was only really a blur. He had not studied it carefully. So Dave Anger thought Henry had 'shagged' his wife. Why the hell did he think that? It was preposterous. Surely it would be something he would have remembered? Wouldn't it?

Henry had little time to ponder for the remainder of that day. In fact he had hardly time to take a breath and scratch his backside. There were so many facets to deal with, most of which revolved around dealing with a complex investigation which needed managing and leading.

He lorded it over the MIR all that afternoon, deciding to take a hands-on approach for a change. Much work was done with the family of Kerry Figgis, although the elusive real father remained that – elusive. House-to-house enquiries were expanded on Shoreside and Preston Road for other witnesses.

Nothing much seemed to be coming, though, and Henry was more concerned than ever about Kerry.

More was done with Jodie Greaves in terms of enquiries about the Vauxhall Astra that Uren had been driving, in an effort to find out who he had bought it from.

Everyone was kept busy, doing the routine stuff associated with such investigations, and Henry controlled it all, sitting there like Captain Kirk on the bridge of the starship MIR.

His next disagreement came with the appearance of DC Sheena Waters, something he had expected earlier, was prepared for, but not looking forward to. She marched into the MIR, all revved up and steaming to go.

'Why the hell did you bail Troy Costain?' she demanded. 'After all the kerfuffle about you being so upset because he'd stolen from your mum, and you go and let the little shit go! Now what's all that about, Henry?'

'Calm down, calm down,' he said, using the palms down gesture, 'he's only a crim.'

'He robs and terrifies old people,' she protested.

'Look.' Henry stood up. He had been sitting at the Allocator's Desk, sifting through actions. 'Try not to get upset . . . let's go to me office and have a chat.'

'No,' she said, clearly upset. 'He has a string of allegations to answer and I've spent all day gathering evidence to put to him, only to discover you let him go last night. And I was wondering why the custody officer hasn't been chasing my tail all bloody day. It's because there's no prisoner . . . so here, in public,' – she looked round the MIR and at everyone in the room – 'give me your reasons for letting him go.'

Henry tightened up, wishing he'd dealt with this earlier. 'When I said my office, it wasn't an option, Sheena,' words which, again, did not sit comfortably with him. Ordering someone to his office again. Not good.

'OK,' she relented, 'but it better be good, otherwise this is going further.' She marched out, Henry behind her, wondering whether he should leave his face set in a thunderous expression because it seemed to be its default position these days.

Sheena left his office not remotely satisfied. Henry's cooing, 'You'll just have to trust me on this one,' was not going down well at all. He realized that by letting Costain go, it would be impossible for Sheena to gather important evidence, because Troy would simply destroy it. What she did not know and what Henry did not tell her was, of course, that Troy was an informant and the reason why he had let him go. 'You'll have to trust me on this one,' did not do the trick. She was rightly miffed, because Costain was a good prisoner and there was the possibility of clearing up some serious crime on her patch.

As she left the office, Henry knew he had not heard the last of this. 'Oh to be a DC on NCIS,' he thought. 'Life would be so much simpler.'

A knock on the door made him jerk up his head. It was the one-man intelligence cell, DC Jerry Tope, who had so nearly invoked Henry's misplaced wrath earlier. He bore his usual sheaf of papers.

'Sorry to interrupt.' He was clearly afraid of Henry

'Come in, Jerry, it's OK. Sorry about earlier – wrong end of the stick.'

'No probs, boss.' He waved his papers triumphantly. 'Bingo.'

'Thrill me.'

'Your . . . er . . . hypothesis about burglaries?'

'Yep – shot to shit, I take it?'

'No – spot on, actually. I've looked at each of the disappearances in the other forces, and in each case there were several bogus official-type burglaries in the weeks prior to their abductions. I've hacked into the crime recording systems of each force, GMP, West Yorkshire, Cheshire – don't ask, but it's easy – and there's about forty burglaries in total, all very similar, all directed at old women.'

'Carried out by one man?'

'Two men. White males, thirty to forty years. All descriptions tie up. One could easily be George Uren. A ponytail is mentioned in some descriptions.'

'Any arrests?'

'Not a one. All undetected.'

'How much have they made?'

'Close to a hundred grand, mainly cash.'

Henry whistled. 'You've hacked into police systems that are not our own?'

'Basically, yes. Saves time, bureaucracy.'

'Brilliant. Illegal?'

Tope nodded. 'Extremely.'

'Can you be traced?'

'No,' he said confidently.

'Now we need those forces to do that trawl themselves and get each scene revisited for a full forensic hit, wouldn't you say?'

'Yep.'

'That'll be something for the big SIO meeting to action,' Henry said. 'If I ever get them off their lardy arses. OK, well done. I think we're on to something here.'

The debrief was at nine p.m. A round-up of the day's events and progress, or otherwise. Kerry Figgis was still outstanding and concern continued to grow; they were still no closer to catching the mystery man. He thanked everyone for their efforts and asked them to be back by eight next morning. They were all whacked after a lengthy day of graft, and they left a little subdued and dispirited by the lack of progress. Henry sensed a growing despair, one he was beginning to feel himself.

He spent the next hour with the policy book, going over everything that had been done, satisfying himself he'd covered all bases. He closed the book, knowing there were no obvious gaps in the investigation, but realizing there was every possibility this was going to be a long haul.

Closing his eyes, he pinched the bridge of his nose, a headache coming on. A combination of a day of bad food, too little sleep, not enough water, and stress. Henry was always close to the edge and had, through the years, been over it. He was determined that it was a place he would never visit again. It wasn't the stress of the investigation that was worrying him this time, though. It was the other things. If he could get rid of all that peripheral shite and be left with a complex murder investigation, he'd be tickety-boo.

He rolled his head, neck creaking. Why did everything creak now? Neck, knees, back. He was beginning to feel like a car that had reached that time in its life when things started to go wrong, when it became more expensive to maintain and run that it was actually worth. When a trip to the showroom was called for to trade it in for a new model.

Four years short of fifty.

The prospect of the half-century struck him like a rampaging elephant.

'Oooh, no, no, no,' he admonished himself, placing his hands on the desk to assist him stand up. 'No navel gazing for me,' he announced to his empty office. 'I'm going right now to increase my water intake for the day – disguised as a pint of Stella – then I'm going home, have a JD nightcap, leap into bed with my ex-wife and make hot lurv. She'll think all her birthdays and Christmases have come all at once, when in fact it'll be me.' He giggled, a noise which stopped abruptly as a large figure appeared at the office door, making him jump.

'First sign o' madness,' the man said with an American accent. 'Talkin' to yourself.'

Karl Donaldson stood there, his wide frame completely blocking the door. 'Mind if I come along for the drink, but I'll pass on the lovemakin', if you don't mind?'

Fifteen

'Sounds like you're havin' a great time.' Karl Donaldson took a sip of his mineral water and regarded Henry with a smirk of amused contempt.

Henry had just regaled his friend with the story of the last week, bringing him bang up to date, keeping everything in for Donaldson's delectation and delight.

'I wouldn't mind,' Henry pleaded, 'but I've obviously missed out on something. Having been accused of sleeping with a woman, I would at least have liked the pleasure.'

Donaldson chuckled. 'Your cock gets you into some scrapes.'

'Not this time,' Henry said fervently. 'He's barking up the wrong tree.' He took a deep, slow swig of his Stella, wiped his mouth with the back of his hand.

'You could take control of the situation, be proactive,' Donaldson suggested.

'What, sidle up to Anger and say, "I believe you think I screwed your wife?" I don't think so. Anyway, what drags you up to these parts, Yank? IEDs you say.'

They were sitting in the lounge bar of the Tram and Tower, Henry's local pub. They'd dropped Donaldson's Jeep off at Henry's house after Henry insisted the American should bed down at his house for the night, then adjourned to the pub for a couple of drinks. Henry noticed Donaldson wasn't drinking alcohol, remembering that last time they were in here, Donaldson had imbibed far too much. He was a big guy, but couldn't hold his liquor.

He looked at the American. Henry had good reason to suspect that this affable man was much more than he purported to be. Although Henry could never prove it, nor want to, he believed that Donaldson was involved in the sudden and violent departure from this life of some top-level international criminals, something that Henry had only recently started to realize; that he could actually be an assassin for the American authorities was never far away from Henry's thoughts. He certainly had the ability to kill, as Henry had experienced years before, when Donaldson had saved Henry's life by shooting a mafia hitman who was about to kill Henry.

One thing Henry did know for sure, though, was that Donaldson was a handsome swine. Women went gooey-eyed in his presence, and the fact he hardly seemed to notice women swooning all around grated Henry. Even now, in the Tram and Tower, every woman in the place was giving him sidelongs, making Henry green with envy.

'Yep – incendiary devices,' Donaldson confirmed. Since he had expressed an interest in them, Henry had sent him further details of them, as described in depth by an explosives expert from the forensic science lab.

'Why are they of interest to you?'

'Might have a link for you from across the pond,' Donaldson said, referring to the Atlantic Ocean and that big chunk of land three thousand miles away. Henry waited, raising his eyebrows over the rim of his pint glass which was against his lips. 'I spend my time looking at crime reports from around the globe,' he explained, 'but one in particular has been with me up here,' – he tapped his temple – 'for a while now; the murder of a Miami PD detective called Mark Tapperman.'

Henry took his drink away from his mouth. 'Tapperman? That name rings a bell.' His mind began the Rolodex shuffle.

'Let me save you time: Danny Furness.'

Immediately Henry remembered and as he did so, his mind recalled Danny Furness ... Danielle Louise Furness ... someone Henry hadn't consciously thought about for a long time now, but who he would never forget.

Danny Furness had been a wonderful cop and Henry had been happy to have her on his team when, several years earlier he had been involved in the hunt for a man called Louis Vernon Trent. Trent had escaped from prison in a most murderous and terrifying way and had returned to his old roost of Blackpool, determined to wreak revenge on all the people responsible for getting him sent to jail in the first place. Danny was the officer who had originally arrested Trent for a series of serious and escalating assaults on young children and got him sent down.

Trent's skewed mind had determined that one of the people who would suffer for his incarceration was Danny.

Danny had been part of Henry's team which eventually tracked down and rearrested Trent, but not before he had murdered several people, including a uniformed cop who'd had him cornered. Trent had subsequently escaped from police custody and had never been heard of since.

During the investigation to arrest Trent following his initial escape from prison, Danny had visited Florida on a related matter concerning a missing girl. There she had encountered Mark Tapperman.

Subsequent to all of this, Henry and Danny had embarked on a serious affair, which had ended when Danny had tragically died on Spanish soil.

'You OK, pal?' Donaldson waved at Henry, who had slipped into a trance of reminiscence.

'Yep,' he said, snapping out of his reverie. 'Just thinking about Danny.' He sipped his beer.

Donaldson eyed his friend sympathetically. 'Don't go there,' he warned.

'I won't,' he promised. 'But I do remember Danny talking about Mark Tapperman. He helped her out over there. Big guy, I believe. Built like a shithouse wall. I never met him.' Henry's eyes narrowed. 'You say he was murdered?'

'A few years ago . . . the day before the Twin Towers came down.'

'The tenth of September, then?'

'Yeah. He was investigating a homicide and, uh, he was murdered.'

'As a consequence of the murder investigation?'

Donaldson shrugged, frowned. 'Who can say? But there are some similarities between Mark's murder and your guy, Uren?'

'How similar?'

'Until we do a full scientific comparison, I'm only going off what I've read. Mark's body was found in a trailer park, a real trash trailer park, near Fort Lauderdale.'

'Uren's body was found in a bedsit.'

'Mark had been stabbed repeatedly and his throat had been cut open, his head almost severed.' Henry saw that the words were difficult for Donaldson to say, that he seemed to be choking on them. The American saw Henry's curious look. 'Mark was a good friend,' he explained. Henry nodded, understanding. Donaldson went on: 'So, stabbed, throat cut – and set on fire.' He paused for effect then added, 'Yeah?' to Henry's unasked question. 'Incendiary devices.'

'Bugger,' was all Henry could think of to say.

'From what I've seen, the devices look similar to the ones you found here in Blackpool.' Donaldson sat up, making Henry draw back instinctively. 'In fact, they look so similar I got Miami PD to send me one from the scene of Mark's death via the diplomatic pouch. It's in the back of the Jeep. Maybe tomorrow we could get a comparison?'

'Consider it done,' Henry said excitedly.

Donaldson relaxed. 'Last time I was in here with you, I got – as you so quaintly put it – bladdered.' Donaldson was collecting and using what he called 'quaint English terms', because he found them highly amusing.

'Pissed as a fart, I'd say.' So bad that he and Kate had had to put Donaldson to bed. 'And?'

'It won't happen again tonight, but I've had my fill of mineral water and as I'm not driving, I'll have a pint of Stella and a JD chaser. Your round, I reckon.'

'Big jump.'

'Big revelation coming . . . when you get back from the bar, I'll intrigue you further.'

Henry bought himself a pint, no chaser, two being his absolute maximum when driving, even though he realized that, as a cop, that figure should be nil. He carried the drinks back to their table where Henry saw that Donaldson was engaged in conversation with a woman, one of Henry's neighbours, who 'happened' to be passing the table on her way to the ladies, which were actually on the other side of the bar. She smiled at Henry, gave Donaldson a lascivious leer, then bounced off.

'She fancies you,' Donaldson said.

'As if.' He pushed the drinks across. 'You know, you could have any woman you wanted, couldn't you?'

'Guess so.' It wasn't an egotistical answer. 'Problem bein' I got a wife who'd kill me, and a wife who I also love.'

'Romantic fool.' Henry's face crunched up disgustedly. 'What's the revelation?'

Donaldson drank the beer deeply, said, 'Ahh,' then took a

sip of the JD. 'The murder Mark was investigatin' . . . was the murder of a nine-year-old girl, found stabbed to death in the back of a car and the car had been found burned out after . . . guess what?' He was clearly revelling in the old saying that knowledge is power.

'What?' Henry said eagerly.

'Before being found abandoned, the car in question had been pulled over by a highway patrol who had been mown down by the driver. Does that scenario ring any bells?'

'Jesus,' Henry said, remembering playing tig with the Astra in Fleetwood. 'How's the officer?'

'Died after being in a coma for six months.'

'I might just have that JD chaser . . . be rude not to, wouldn't it? We can always catch a cab home.'

'The murder investigation got nowhere?'

'Nah . . . it stalled with Mark's death. Some thought it could've been connected with the murder of a guy who owned a sex club, but only because Mark had been sniffin' round seedy clubs in Lauderdale after the girl's body had been found . . . prob'ly not connected.' Donaldson was starting to truncate and slur his words now, a sure sign that his second lager and accompanying chaser were having an adverse effect on his brain. The landlord had called time, and most of the clientele had drifted out.

The landlord called time again.

'We could have a lock-in,' Henry said. Somehow his weariness had evaporated under the influence of alcohol. He felt quite sprightly. 'The guy who owns the place knows me.'

'I could test another JD,' Donaldson said.

'Consider it done.' Henry, slightly ahead of his friend in the drinks stakes, wobbled towards the bar and returned bearing glasses.

Donaldson leaned forwards. 'Re our earlier chat, it's just come to me, the name of the person Mark Tapperman might have visited before his untimely death was John Stoke. We don't know anything more than that, never traced anyone of that name. Miami PD got that from Mark's wife. He'd been talking to her about it, but hadn't passed it on to his colleagues. He was a bit of a loner, Mark.'

'Oh, right,' Henry said, not really taking the information in;

a distraction had arrived in the form of a text message on his mobile.

'What is it?' Donaldson noted the expression on Henry's face. Henry handed the phone across. It read, u n me again, H. ull nvr ctch me.

'Time to go,' Henry declared, feeling uneasy. The number from which the text had come was not the same as the one from which the earlier texts had been sent. 'C'mon Karl, let's be having you.' He turned to the bar. 'Ken, can you bell a taxi for us?'

As ever after Donaldson had been drinking, it took a lot of manoeuvring to get him out of the pub. Rain lashed down outside, but as Henry stepped into the porch at the front of the pub ahead of Donaldson, he hardly had time to take in the weather.

Two hooded men came at him, wielding the think ends of sawn-off pool cues.

He didn't even see them properly. They were just a blur in the rain. He felt the first blow across his right shoulder and immediately sagged down to his knees. He covered his head with his hands, instinctively expecting a flurry of blows.

But something miraculous happened.

Karl Donaldson seemed to sober up in an instant. Maybe it was the conditioning his training had drummed into him, maybe it was the instinct of defending a friend, but unlike Henry, he instantaneously computed what was happening and with a roar Samson Agonistes would have been proud of, went into action.

Like an American football player (Donaldson did not understand the 'rugby' nonsense) – he powered into the attacker who had smacked Henry down. He drove his shoulder into the guy's guts and lifted him off his feet, depositing him on his back six feet away from where he was originally standing. With that player out of the game, Donaldson twisted and, like a Trans-Am express train, charged the other attacker, who was about to drive a cue down across the back of Henry's head. Donaldson roared as he ran, closing the distance in a split second and repeating his first move. This time the man was slightly quicker than his mate and managed to whack Donaldson across the back, a blow which had no discernible effect on the American, other than to get his 'mad up'.

Donaldson's shoulder went in low, driving a groan of pain and expelled air out of the man as Donaldson lifted and deposited him across the bonnet of a parked car, smashing the back of the man's head against the windscreen.

With the second man dumped, Donaldson turned to the slowly arising Henry.

The attackers did not need a second hint. The first one picked himself up off the ground, the second rolled off the car, and both fled into the night.

'Henry, pal.' Donaldson swayed slightly as the alcohol came back into play. 'You OK, buddy?'

Henry rose creakily, grateful to his friend who had saved him from another battering. He tested his body and found he'd been particularly lucky: nothing was injured.

'I'm not so bad,' he grunted, even though he was doubled over, hands on knees, snot dripping out of his nose, looking up at his concerned American cousin, who staggered slightly.

'Amateurs,' Donaldson said dismissively. Then he staggered backwards, lost his balance, caught his leg on the low wall of the porch and tipped over spectacularly into the small, neatly-tended garden, landing on his backside in a bed of flowers. He stared up, unable to keep his head steady, a ridiculous grin on his face.

In the shadows by bushes at the far end of the car park, a man hidden in blackness snorted and breathed in frustration, then melted away into the night.

FRIDAY

Sixteen

Both men had banging headaches the following morning, but there was no time to brood over hangovers. They were up at six thirty a.m., staggering around like zombies, until they emerged from Henry's house like Butch Cassidy and the Sundance Kid to face the onslaught of the day.

Deciding to collect Henry's car from the Tram and Tower after the morning briefing, they jumped into Donaldson's Jeep. The American drove them to the police station accompanied by the heart-tugging refrain of country music, making Henry feel inclined to suicide. He was relieved to arrive at the nick without a rope around his neck.

He briefed the team at eight a.m., and by eight thirty everyone was on the road, the whole investigation having gone up a notch. Once the MIR had quietened down, Henry and Donaldson scuttled to the canteen for black coffee and bacon sandwiches, that well-known cure for crapulence.

'Almost alive,' Henry said.

Donaldson's eyes were drooping, but he nodded. 'You're a bad influence.'

Henry shrugged. It was still nice to be considered such at his age. 'I try,' he said modestly. He folded the last of his toasted sandwich into his mouth and washed it down. 'Need to collect my car, then we need to get looking at a link between Uren's murder and Mark Tapperman's. Ironic, innit?' Henry snuffled a laugh. 'I can get a joint investigation up and running with the FBI, yet I can't get SIO's from surrounding forces to ring back with the possibility of putting a cross-border job together? It's obviously not what you know . . .'

The two men regarded each other.

'I drank far too much last night,' Donaldson admitted.

'Hm hum. Let's go and get the incendiary from the car and

207

hand it to Scientific Support.' He drank the last of his coffee. 'Any leads on it?'

'Could be linked to a white supremacy group in the southern states,' Donaldson began. 'They've been active over ten years, here and there.'

Henry's mobile squawked and a text landed. He read it with trepidation. Ull nvr ctch me. She ded. It had come from the same number as last night's taunting text.

He showed it to Donaldson, then decided to reply to it.

Who are you? he asked simply and sent it.

old frend, came the response, which he again showed to Donaldson.

'Crank?' he suggested.

'Or kidnapper?' Henry took a deep breath, wondering what he should be doing about the texts. If they were from a pay-as-you-go number, there would be little hope of tracing them. SIM cards were easy to register in false names. If they were from contract phones, which he doubted, there was a good chance of locating the source. 'I'll see what I can do about tracing these now,' he said. 'It's getting beyond a joke. But first let's get my car from the pub, then get your device checked out, then I'm going to see the Figgis family.'

'Holy shit!'

'Must've happened after we'd left.'

'You really have upset someone, Henry.'

They were standing on the Tram and Tower car park inspecting Henry's Ford Mondeo. The pub landlord, Ken Clayson, was with them.

'You not see anything?' Henry asked Clayson.

The bearded landlord shook his head. 'Not a sausage.'

The Mondeo, once a lovely shiny blue colour, had been the first brand-new car Henry had ever owned. He'd got a good deal on it and, though dubbed 'Mondeo Man' by his colleagues, had been pleased with it and looked after it well. Now, with a metal pole smashed through the windscreen, four tyres slashed, deep gouges scarred along each side and the headlights shattered, he did not really like it very much. He rubbed his tired face and groaned. He walked round the car and saw that the pole through the windscreen was actually a metal bar, possibly a piece of railing, with a spike on the end now embedded in the driver's seat. A warning? Threat? You next?

'It's got to be someone from GMP,' Henry said, shaking his head. Donaldson knew what he was talking about because he had been involved with that too. 'Or maybe an irate husband,' he muttered under his breath. 'Or maybe even my boss.'

'What you gonna do?' Donaldson asked.

'Report it as a crime, get CSI out, then get it towed to a garage and get it repaired. Claim on the insurance,' he finished. 'Going to have to get a runabout from work, I suppose. Bugger,' he blasted. 'Just what I need.'

Donaldson patted him on the shoulder. 'Cheer up, old chap.'

'Cheer up? Fuck off, Karl,' he said. 'And you can fuck off as well, Clayson,' he said to the landlord. 'If it wasn't for you, I'd only feel horrendously bad; as it is, your trade, the way you insidiously force drink down unwary men who should know better, is making me feel like my head's stuck down a bog.'

Clayson took it all in good part and invited the pair of them in for a coffee, gratefully accepted.

A cleaner, accompanied by an extremely loud Dyson vacuum, was working her way round the empty pub, ensuring that Henry, Donaldson and the landlord had to shout to make themselves heard. They had a general conversation about how crime had got out of hand and considered options for a new car for Henry; Henry also asked Clayson questions about the possible identities of his assailants last night, but he did not have any ideas. When his mobile rang, he excused himself and went to stand outside the pub in the spot where he'd been attacked.

'Hello . . . sorry . . . Henry Christie.' It was not a good line, lots of echo and fading signal.

'Mr Christie, this is Jackie Harcourt from the bail hostel in Accrington.'

'Oh, hello Jackie, sorry, Ms Harcourt.' Henry remembered her well. He had never heard her voice over the phone, but there was something strangely familiar about it.

'Remember me?'

'Yes, of course.' Bit of a chilly woman, he recalled. It was only a few days earlier he'd met her, but it seemed an eon ago. She had not been too impressed by Henry, and Rik Dean in particular.

'I'd like to see you,' she said quickly, as if, if she hadn't been quick, the words would not have come out.

'OK, when and why? I'm pretty busy at the moment.'

'Look . . . look . . .' Suddenly she sounded fraught. 'It has to be today, this morning, it has to be, otherwise forget it.'

'Are you OK? You sound upset.'

'I need to see you today. I need to see you about George Uren. Please. If not today, forget it.'

'All right,' he said, mystified. This did not sound like the in-control, businesslike woman who had expelled him and Rik from the hostel for stepping out of line.

'It's important,' she stressed, gasping back a sob.

'Where and when?' Henry said. Something told him it was more than important. 'Bearing in mind I'm in Blackpool. I can set off in a few minutes, though.'

'Right . . . er . . . not at the hostel . . . er.' It was obvious she couldn't think of anywhere.

'Do you know the Dunkenhalgh?' Henry cut in, realizing her thought process was addled for some reason. The Dunkenhalgh was the name of an hotel just off the M65 motorway on the outskirts of Accrington.

'Yes, I do.' She sounded relieved.

'I'll be there in an hour, traffic permitting. We can have a coffee there.'

'Yes, thanks, that'd be good.' She hung up. Henry checked and saw the number she had dialled from was withheld.

'Thank you too,' he said to thin air. Before going back inside the pub, he made a call to John Walker, the detective from technical support, had a quick conversation, then headed indoors.

'Yeah, yeah, I've seen someone fried,' Donaldson was telling Ken Clayson, the landlord. Their discussion had moved on to the death penalty. 'Jump about like catfish on a pole – zzzz!' Donaldson demonstrated, twitching in his chair.

Clayson winced uncomfortably. 'Ugh!'

'Sorry to interrupt such an intellectual discussion,' Henry said. 'Work to be done.'

'You really seen someone burn?' Henry's curiosity had got the better of him. They were on the M55, heading east into Lancashire, away from the flat coast towards hill country. Henry had commandeered Donaldson and his Jeep to drive him across to the industrial hinterland and Donaldson had agreed without a murmur of dissent. Now the big vehicle was ploughing its heavy way through a torrential downpour with the assuredness of a tank.

'Nah. Seen videos. Never been up close and personal, though.'

'Thought as much, you bullshitter.'

They lapsed into silence as they came to the end of the M55 and joined the M6 south, a stretch of motorway spanning the River Ribble, which held some shaky memories for Henry. Since those days the motorway had been widened and looked nothing like the carriageway on which he'd seen a bomb explode with devastating consequences.

'What does this broad want?'

'Hard to say. She sounded upset by something. I do think she knows more than she let on originally, though, but something held her back from blabbing. I could tell.'

Donaldson powered on to the M61. The rain continued to drive hard, the road surface running like a river, the day black. His headlights cut through the wall of water thrown up by other vehicles. He took a quick glance at Henry. 'Someone means business with you, Henry,' he said, changing the subject.

'I know.' He was glum, worried.

'Who is it?'

Henry made a raspberry sound. 'I've already speculated with you.'

'You think the guys who went for you last night are the ones who did your car?'

'Stands to reason, I suppose.'

'Or could it be someone else?'

'Fuck knows – but I'll find out.'

'How?'

'I'll find out – trust me.'

Silence descended again. He could have told Donaldson he had something up his sleeve to identify the car wrecker(s), but it was something he wanted to keep to himself for the time being.

Donaldson joined the M65, heading in the direction of Blackburn and Accrington.

'It's over three years since I spoke to Mark Tapperman's wife,' Donaldson said thoughtfully.

'You never told me he'd been murdered.'

'No real need. I knew you didn't know him, so he would've meant nothing to you. I don't tell you everything I know, pal.'

'And I thank God for that ... but there was the Danny Furness connection.'

Donaldson shrugged. 'He helped her out, is all.'

'Whatever.'

'He was a good cop, Tapperman. It must've taken someone very evil to get the better of him.'

'It's always the routine jobs that catch you out,' Henry said. 'Next junction.'

The Dunkenhalgh was a nice hotel, set in lovely wooded grounds close to the motorway. It had even been the location of several of Henry's drunken excesses during the earlier years of his service. He'd been to quite a few police functions there. He'd even had to work there on police business occasionally. Once, during the mid-eighties when he was on Support Unit, he'd spent a night there policing the local annual hunt ball at a time when anti-hunt protesters were causing a lot of problems. In the end, nothing happened that night, except that Henry and a couple of his wilder colleagues got drunk on duty and, to his everlasting kudos, Henry actually ended up getting a blow job from one of the lady hunt members on a four-poster bed in her room. It had been an exciting indiscretion, made all the more hazardous because her husband was on the dance floor and Henry's sergeant, a vindictive little man who despised Henry, was trying to find him.

Heady days, very special times, he thought as Donaldson drove up the long driveway to the hotel. How the hell he got away with some of the things he did he would never know. It was a classic notch on his headboard, one he occasionally relived with much pleasure and, sometimes, a cold sweat.

In those days of pre-marriage, he had often been wild and reckless. *So what's changed?* he asked himself, then realized at that exact moment, on a complete tangent, why Jackie Harcourt's voice was so familiar over the phone: she had been the crying woman.

Ms Jackie Harcourt was waiting in the conservatory, a mineral water in front of her. She looked perplexed when she saw

Henry had brought a colleague with him, and Henry saw her face drop. He introduced Donaldson and explained he was simply the taxi service, and that seemed to appease her. Donaldson took the hint.

'I'll get me a coffee,' he said, backing away.

'Do you want one?' Ms Harcourt asked Henry. He nodded. A waiter came over and took his order as he sat down on the opposite end of the comfortable sofa on which she was seated.

Her eyes did not meet Henry's, but she asked, 'Can we wait for the coffee to come before we start?'

'Sure,' said Henry, wishing he'd asked for a water now. He'd had so much coffee that morning, he was starting to shake.

He looked at her, reaffirming that she was a lovely-looking lady, even if her lines were slightly angular. She was wearing a black trouser suit with a buttoned-up peach blouse, no visible jewellery. 'Nice spot here,' Henry said.

'Mm. I use the fitness club . . .' she said quietly, looked down at the carpet. 'Or did . . . kinda let myself go to seed a bit recently.'

Henry would have disagreed.

The coffee came. Rich, dark, Brazilian, probably containing a double shot of caffeine. He sipped it and it hit the spot with a frisson. 'Now then, you have something for me?' he ventured. She nodded, still avoiding his eyes. Henry waited a couple of beats. 'And?'

Ms Harcourt sat up, fidgeting, pulling at her earlobes, her head bobbing as though an internal wrestling match was taking place. Finally she sighed whilst smoothing down her trousers.

'Remember you told Walter Pollack you'd come back to haunt him?'

'Yes – not my exact words, though the sentiment is about right.'

'I said it was a frightening thing to say.'

'So I recall.'

She paused. Her lips went tight, thin, bitter-looking. Her nostrils flared and she took an unsteady breath. She pinched the bridge of her nose.

'What is it, Jackie?' Henry said quietly.

Now she did turn and look at him. 'I'm glad he's dead,' she said passionately. 'So, so glad.'

'I take it you're referring to George Uren?' Henry said.

She nodded. 'But even so, the nightmare's not over.' Her voice was barely audible now against the background. She inspected her fingernails. 'Not for me, anyway.'

'Something happened between you and him,' Henry guessed.

'It did.'

Another pause ensued in what had become a very stilted conversation, but Henry knew not to push anything in case it all fell apart. It was an understatement to say his inquisitiveness was burning him up, but something was telling him he had to play this very cagily.

She continued. 'Whilst he was at the hostel I could sense he had a "thing" about me.' She tweaked her fingers on the word 'thing'. 'And it wasn't an ego thing on my part, God forbid,' she said defensively. 'I wouldn't want anyone in that place to have a "thing" about me, particularly him. Fact is, most offenders who come to the hostel don't even give me a second glance. They're all usually pathetic cowards, anyway. I'm just another authority figure and most of them despise me. But Uren . . .' She closed her eyes. Her body shuddered. 'The looks he gave me, the one-off comments, the sneer in his expression . . . he made me feel very uncomfortable and vulnerable.'

'Did he ever do anything?'

'Not while he was at the hostel.' She shot Henry a look of warning not to interrupt. 'Let me finish.' He nodded. She sipped her drink, hands quivering. 'When he did a runner, I was glad. He really, really made me scared, not like the rest of them. I was happy he'd gone.' She did more fiddling about, hesitating unsurely. 'He had a visitor once, a creepy guy who gave some details – all visitors have to sign in, but I didn't tell you that the other day because I was annoyed with you. I'm pretty sure the details are false, though. I've got the book with me, if it's of any use.'

'Why would it be?'

'Because George Uren came back to the hostel. He came back with the guy who'd visited him that time.'

Henry now knew what the punchline was going to be.

'They came back together, one night. I was on sleepover week with another staff member . . . there's always two of us. We have lockable en-suite rooms at the back of the hostel. The

214

other member of staff was asleep in his room . . . it was about two in the morning, something like that, my door opened, even though I knew I'd locked it, and Uren and his friend came in. They were on me before I'd even woken up properly.'

She sniffed. A tear appeared in the corner of her eye, balanced there for a moment, then rolled down her cheek. 'They put parcel tape over my mouth, tied my hands to the bed with it, and took it in turns to rape me,' she said simply. 'I've never told anyone.' Then she burst into a torrent of tears, a loud wail starting to build up inside her. 'I feel so dirty,' she sobbed. 'Unclean, ugly . . .'

Henry's face had set hard as her words were spoken. His mouth was dry and his heart was pounding with anger. This moment was always the most difficult to judge. Does the victim need the reassurance of the human touch, or does she want to be left alone, untouched? He slid along the sofa and went for option one.

The right one.

The rain had stopped and the grounds of the hotel glistened with droplets of water as the sun poked through and the clouds dispersed. Henry and Jackie Harcourt were walking on damp footpaths under the trees and she had, amazingly Henry thought, linked her arm through his. Her initial bout of upset had lasted a good ten minutes, but then she had got a grip on her emotions and said she needed air.

'I once went to a police-run awareness class about rape,' she told him. 'One of those "safe-women" things . . . don't seem to hear much about them, these days. One of the questions asked was, would you rather be slashed on your face with a knife and scarred forever, or raped? At the time I thought I would rather have been raped; now I know that a knife scar is only skin deep. Being raped wounds you deep down for life. I'd rather be dead, actually. I just can't get my life going again.'

She stopped and looked at Henry, as if daring him to challenge her.

All this, he thought, coming from a woman who was successful in her career, was good-looking, confident, seemed to have everything going for her. But Henry empathized with her. He, too, knew rape.

'I know what you mean.'

'Do you?' Her bright eyes played over him.

'Trust me,' he said. 'I do.'

She held his gaze and maybe saw some pain in him, too. She nodded, they walked on.

'They were silent and efficient, like they did it all the time. They didn't disturb the other member of staff next door, just held me down, raped me, took the tape off my mouth and forced themselves into my mouth, made me kneel down . . . they must have had keys – to get into the hostel and then into my room. Uren must've had them cut before he absconded, knowing he'd come back.'

The M65 was less than a hundred metres away, but the drone of the traffic seemed a million miles away from the world Henry and Jackie Harcourt were now inhabiting.

'After they'd finished, they gagged me again and tied me back to the bed, then they made themselves a cup of tea each, sat there drinking it, talking quietly to me, and then they left . . . but not before Uren's mate said that unless I stayed quiet, didn't tell anyone, they would come back and murder me. He even described how he would do it.'

'Who was his friend?'

'I don't know. A thin, weasel-faced man.' She stopped, closed her eyes and thought hard. 'Uren called him Lou, I think.'

'Lou? For definite?'

'When he came to visit Uren, and signed in, what name did he use?'

'It's here.'

She unfastened her shoulder bag and took out a hardback A4 size book. There was a marker tab in one of the pages. She opened it to that page and showed Henry, who read the name and tried not to blink: John Stoke. It was the second time in a matter of hours Henry had come across that name.

'I did something else,' she said. 'They left me tied up and I had to wriggle out of the parcel tape myself after they'd gone. I kept the tape.'

'Why?'

'I thought that if I ever built up the courage to do what I'm doing now, telling the police, it might have their fingerprints on it. They didn't wear gloves, you see.'

'Good thinking.'

216

'I did something else too.'

'Shock me.'

'I didn't wash the cups they used when they were drinking tea. I kept them in a cupboard, still with the dregs of tea in them.'

'Why?'

'DNA? And fingerprints on the cups . . . dunno. Did I do right?'

Henry regarded her with awe. 'You had the foresight to do that? That is brilliant, so fantastic, Jackie.'

'They're in the back of my car for you to take away.'

'That is remarkable,' he said.

'Bet you thought I was a bitch, didn't you?'

'I thought there was something lurking under the veneer, actually, but could never have guessed this was it.' They stopped and looked at each other. 'Why have you done this?' Henry asked. 'Why now?'

'Because it was killing me. It was ruining my life, socially and professionally, even though I did my best to cover it up. I'm as close as can be to a breakdown, I think, and I had to act to save myself.'

Henry stood over the CSI in the her office in the Pavilion Building at headquarters as she carefully examined the cups and the twisted parcel tape Jackie Harcourt had given him. She dusted them and lifted prints and also swabbed the cups for DNA, though she warned Henry a hit wasn't guaranteed. The fingerprints from the cups were good quality, though. The CSI transferred the lifted prints on their transparent tape on to the relevant form, which she handed to Henry after booking them into her record system.

He almost ran down the corridor to the fingerprint department where a senior fingerprint officer was waiting for him. Donaldson loped behind him, just as excited.

The SFO took the form and booked it into his system. 'Give me fifteen minutes.'

'Fifteen bloody minutes!'

The SFO eyed him.

'OK, fifteen minutes, but not one second longer.'

'Get a brew or something.'

'I'm all coffee'd out. C'mon,' he beckoned Donaldson. 'Let's have a stroll.'

Henry led the American out, emerging on to the edge of the sports field which lay between the MCU building and headquarters. The day was improving all the time.

'I don't want to put all my eggs in one basket, but, bloody hell, aren't fingerprints fantastic? You think crims would have learned, but prints come up trumps time after time. Amazing. One of those fantastic things in life – like a banana.'

'Eh?'

'Well, a banana's fantastic, too, isn't it? I mean, why a banana? It just doesn't make sense, but it's brilliant.'

'You're over the edge, buddy.'

Henry's mobile rang. It was the garage telling him how much the cost of repair to his car would be and that they wouldn't be able to start work until Wednesday next week. His enthusiasm waned slightly. 'Looks like I'll be in a pool vehicle for a week.'

He and Donaldson strolled around the perimeter of the sports pitch. His phone rang again and he took a message from the John Walker, the technical support officer, and made an arrangement to see him later. The pair walked on until Henry said, 'I wonder if Dave Anger's in?' They had reached the avenue which led from headquarters to the Training Centre, the residential student blocks nestling in the grounds underneath the trees. The FMIT block was one of these. 'Let's have a look.'

A couple of minutes later they were walking along the middle floor corridor towards Anger's office. The whole floor seemed deserted. Henry knew a murder had come in from the south of the county, so it was possible everyone was down there.

Certainly Dave Anger was not in residence. His office was empty. It was much as Henry had last seen it – tidy, with photos and certificates adorning the walls and his desk. Henry picked up the wedding day snap, which was actually laid face down on the desk. He showed it to Donaldson.

'I'm supposed to have slept with this woman,' he said.

'She looks nice. Good on you, as they say. Look at his sideburns, though.'

They were indeed comical viewed from the present day.

'And those lapels,' Henry smirked. 'And the kipper tie,' he added, and was going to say something about the brown suit and bell-bottomed trousers, when his eyes truly focused on Dave Anger's bride. He brought the photo up close.

'What is it?' Donaldson asked.

Henry continued to look at the young woman, then slowly placed the wedding photo down, took a step sideways and bent to inspect the photograph of Dave Anger's passing-out parade at Bruche, 1978. He peered closely at each female face.

'Henry?' Donaldson asked.

The hairs on the back of Henry's neck crept up as though Dave Anger had just urinated on his grave.

'Shit,' Henry whispered, realization dawning. He turned slowly to Donaldson, was on the point of speaking when his mobile blared out 'Jumpin' Jack Flash' again.

He answered it curtly, his eyes still on the photo.

It was Debbie Black speaking from Harrogate.

'Henry, can you talk?'

'Yep, go on,' he said absently, the photograph still in his hand.

'I did what you asked, showed Grandmother Greaves those mugshots.'

Henry had to think for a moment. 'Oh yeah, any luck?'

'She's a pretty good witness, actually – for her age.'

'Cut to the quick, Debs.'

Sounding slightly offended, she said huffily, 'She picked out Uren as one of the guys responsible for stealing from her.'

'Oh, brilliant,' Henry said, changing his tone. 'Starts to confirm our thoughts about how he had been making a living.'

'There's something else, though.'

'Hit me with it.'

'I showed her a range of faces, obviously, as you have to . . . and she picked out another one, the guy she says was with Uren when he committed the burglary. She said he looked younger on the photo and he'd changed a bit, but she was adamant it was him.'

'Who?'

'You're not gonna like this,' she said and gave him a name which sent a shockwave down his spine. Henry went cold. 'Right,' he said, 'make sure the ID is properly recorded, then get yourself back across here asap.' He checked his watch. 'I'll be briefing at five,' he decided on the hoof and finished the call. To Donaldson he said, 'Let's go and see if the finger-print meister has struck gold.'

He had.

'There are prints on the cups that belong to Jackie Harcourt,' he said. Henry had had the foresight to take a set of elimination prints from her at Accrington police station. 'There are other prints on one of the cups that belong to the deceased, George Uren.'

'Anything on the other?'

'Yeah – there are prints on the other cup belonging to this man.' He uncovered a descriptives form. 'I checked them on the automatic system, then did a proper job with my own eyes, just to confirm what the computer told me.'

Henry stared at the forms, which also contained a mugshot of the man. He picked them up, his hands shaking visibly. To Donaldson, he said, 'If I remember right, last night you told me Mark Tapperman had been investigating a guy called John Stoke. This morning, Jackie Harcourt showed me the entry in a visitors book to the probation hostel she manages. Someone using the name John Stoke.'

'Hell!' Donaldson uttered.

'John Stoke,' Henry explained, his voice on edge, 'is one of the aliases used by this man.' Henry indicated the forms in his hands. 'And it also explains why George Uren tried to run me down. This guy was the passenger – and he knows me.'

He handed the forms to Donaldson, whose eyes grew wide. He looked quickly at Henry. 'Him!'

'Yeah – things start to slot into place.' Henry's voice was desolate. 'Louis Vernon Trent . . . the devil's back in town.'

Seventeen

The cops knew something had happened, something significant, otherwise they would not have been brought back into the briefing room, summoned in from their tasks out on the streets without explanation. They waited expectantly, with subdued, little conversation, maybe a muted chuckle here and there, a silent, deadly fart let off by one who would not admit it, but not much else.

Five o'clock came and went.

At five fifteen, Jane Roscoe came in, wafted away the disgusting smell now hanging in the air, and muttered a half-baked apology for the delay. She set up a laptop computer and data projector, then beat a hasty retreat after telling the assembled detectives to be patient.

Henry Christie entered the briefing room at five twenty-six p.m., a folder under his arm, and strode to the front. Jane, Debbie and Karl Donaldson (who was attracting much attention from Debbie) came in behind and stayed at the back of the room, leaning against the wall.

Henry placed his folder on the table, picked up the remote mouse for the laptop, then raised his eyes to the audience. He noticed Dave Anger sidle into the room and take up a position next to Jane, arms folded, talking to her out of the side of his mouth. Henry put the man out of his mind. He had far more important things to do now than worry about a guy who obviously had massive self-esteem problems. He took a breath.

'Thanks for coming back in so quickly . . . I think everyone's here who needs to be,' he said, his voice steady. This was something he loved doing. 'But I thought it only fair to bring everyone up to speed with the latest development in this investigation, a development which I believe links the death of Jodie Greaves, George Uren and the disappearance of Kerry Figgis.' He pointed the mouse at the computer and right-clicked. The screen on the wall behind him came to life with the rich blue background of the constabulary, the force crest in the top right-hand corner. The corporate approach. 'We've put this PowerPoint together quickly, so apologies for any errors, but I'm sure you'll all get the gist of this.' He paused. 'As you know, our enquiries have been directed to try and find the man seen in the company of George Uren last Friday evening. The man we believe is jointly responsible for the kidnap and murder of Jodie Greaves from Harrogate, then the subsequent murder of George Uren and now the abduction – and possible murder – of Kerry.'

All eyes were fixed on him. The detectives were completely silent.

'From enquiries today, certain information has been uncovered which leads us to believe this is the man we are after.' This was the point at which technology usually cocked up. Henry gave a little prayer as he clicked the mouse. It worked. A name flew on to the screen: 'Louis Vernon Trent'.

He spoke the name out loud and heard one or who 'shits' and a 'Jeez' from the detectives. Most of the people in the room would either know, or know of, Trent. The man was notorious, to say the least.

Clicking the mouse again brought the most recent photograph of Trent on to the screen underneath the name. It was the mugshot taken when Trent was last in custody at Blackpool before he escaped and never been seen since, despite a massive manhunt.

'Trent,' Henry said without exaggeration, 'is one of the most dangerous men in the country.' He caught Karl Donaldson's eye across the heads of the seated detectives. 'Nay,' he corrected himself. 'The world. He escaped from custody here having been charged with a series of murders, including that of a police officer, as you'll all recall, and a catalogue of other violent crimes. Predominantly, though, Trent is a serial sex attacker who likes inflicting pain and suffering on his victims. He thinks nothing of murdering them, or murdering anyone who stands in his way. He's obsessed with children and is dangerous and violent to the core.' He raised his eyebrows. 'Because of that, I order every one of you to wear your stab vests from now on, and ensure you are in possession of your ASPs, cuffs and CS until he is caught. There is no room for heroes in this room, no room for false machismo, and because any one of us could now stumble across him, we must ensure we are protected. I speak from experience. Trent once tried to stab me, and if I hadn't been wearing a vest, I'd be dead now. Anyone found refusing this order will be off the investigation, OK?'

No one challenged him, even though detectives were notoriously lax when it came to self-protection because it didn't fit in with their Jack-the-lad personas.

'OK,' he said. 'Health and Safety briefing over ... down to business.' He clicked the mouse again and commenced a full chronological briefing on Trent, scaring everybody shitless as he trailed through the man's antecedents. It took twenty minutes to reach the suspected murder of a homicide detective in Miami three years earlier and the rape of a woman in Accrington eighteen months ago. 'We believe he probably came back to England after the murder of the American detective and could, quite easily, have been living among us ever since. He is a home bird and seems to feel comfortable in this area, which is where he was born. We are looking into links with abductions of young girls from surrounding forces and the possibility that Trent and Uren have been making their living by way of bogus official-type burglaries. Trent also preys on the elderly, by the way. He has no favourites,' Henry finished to a hushed silence. 'Any questions? I know I've rambled on a bit, but I think it was necessary.'

He right-clicked the mouse again and the presentation changed to a full screen photograph of Trent. Henry looked at it, then back at the squad.

'We now need to find him – and fast. After this briefing I'll be doing a press briefing – can't wait,' he said glumly. 'This will go out locally and nationally, I hope. We need to get the media and the public in on this, particularly if there is to be any hope of finding Kerry Figgis alive. We have to pull out all the stops. I believe Trent is still in the area. There are people out there who know where he is and there are people out there who you know can help us find him. I don't have to spell it out. It's time to call in all outstanding favours from the streets. Extra officers are being drafted in tonight, people being brought in on rest days ... I intend to flood the town with nosy cops who won't take "I don't know" for an answer.' He looked over to Jane, still next to Anger. 'DI Roscoe has all the new task allocations, so form an orderly queue at her desk.' People began rising before Henry had finished talking. 'Hold on, hold on,' he said, raising his voice, hands flattening everyone back down. 'The body armour instruction is non-negotiable, so Jane will check you're wearing before she gives you tasks.'

After the media had been wheeled in and out and the hunt for Trent revealed – a conference Henry was glad to get out of the way unscathed, after his previous mauling – he went back to his office, where he needed some peace and quiet to write up the policy book.

Peace and quiet were two things that did not exist in the world of Henry Christie.

He closed the office door, flicked the switch on his little kettle and, brew made, seated himself with an 'Ahh', sipping the tea whilst thinking about the events of the day and how he was going to translate them into police terms for the book. From the hungover trip to the Dunkenhalgh to see Jackie Harcourt with Karl, to the fingerprint idents and the discovery he was chasing Trent.

Trent would be forever linked with his memories of Danny Furness, and he cursed him for bringing those memories alive again. Henry had done some foolish things in the past where women were concerned, and while it could be argued that his relationship with Danny had been as ill-judged as any, he had deep feelings for her, and she was one of the women he believed he could have had a future with had her life not been so cruelly and tragically snuffed out.

He thought he had mentally buried her, but Trent had exhumed her, and Henry was having problems getting her off his mind.

'Come on, get a grip,' he told himself, opening the policy book with a sigh. 'Eeh, um.'

He picked up his pen and read through the log, and was just about to start writing when the door opened, his mobile phone rang and a text message landed. Immediate multi-tasking required.

Dave Anger walked in.

Henry answered the phone. It was John Walker, the technical support detective.

'Henry? You said you'd come and see me,' he said reproachfully.

'Oh, sugar,' Henry said, eyeing Dave Anger, who stood over him, arms folded. 'I forgot. Something came up, you might say. Sorry, pal.'

'That's OK, I know what's happening. I take it you're in Blackpool?'

'Yep.' He continued to look at Anger and mouthed, 'One sec,' to him.

'I'll come and see you.'

'No need for that.'

'No, I need to see you. I only live in Kirkham, so it's not too far out of the way. Be about forty minutes.'

The call ended. Henry said, 'Hello, boss.'

'I know you're busy right now,' Anger said coldly. 'Tomorrow, ten a.m., I want to see you in my office at Hutton, come hell or high water. There are things to discuss,' he concluded ominously.

'Such as?'

Anger considered the question with his bottom lip up over his upper one. 'Wait and see. Be there.'

He spun on his heels and left.

Henry middle-fingered the door space, shaking his head angrily. He thought he'd got his mind set to scribe up the PB, but Anger had thrown him off kilter, and for what? Screwing his wife? *Big effin' deal*, Henry thought. *Some people just take everything too seriously.* He shook his head and returned to the policy book, then remembered the phone text, which he thumbed to on his mobile phone with a slightly dithery thumb. Again the number of the person sending it was there, a number he did not know. The message read, no chnce ctchng me tosser.

He placed the phone down. Could this be Trent? He screwed up his face and thought about that one. Question was, how could Trent have got his mobile number? Not impossible to obtain, as he often handed it out, but somehow the scenario did not sit right.

He tabbed to the phone's menu and got into the messages folder, looking at his inbox. He had kept all the messages he'd received over the last few days. He read them one at a time.

Eight in total.

He'd received the first three whilst in Harrogate with the drunken Debbie: Gess who?, UR DEAD and have u chkd ur brakes? He'd got a further one, Watch ur bak, just before he'd been assaulted on the mezzanine by the guy in the balaclava. All had come from the same number.

Then he'd received three which read: u n me again, H. ull nvr ctch me, Ull nvr ctch me. She ded and, finally in response to his own text, one that read, old frend. Lastly he'd received one just before Dave Anger appeared in his office. These came from a different mobile number than the first four texts.

Eight texts, two different numbers.

Some threatening, some taunting. With the exception of the last one, they had all been received before Trent had been identified to the world, so it seemed unlikely that Trent would have sent the ones which said, u n me again, H. ull never ctch me, and Ull nvr ctch me. She ded., which struck Henry as odd.

The context of the first four messages were different than the last four, as they seemed to be aimed at Henry as an individual, whilst the latter ones were having a go at him as a detective.

That made him think they had come from different people, but where did that get him?

He called one of the numbers, then the other, but both phones were switched off and the nice lady at Orange invited him to leave a message. He declined.

Henry almost believed that Dave Anger could be the one who'd sent the threatening texts, but he dismissed that. Doing something like that would seriously jeopardize his job. He wasn't that stupid. Anger was more likely to screw Henry through the system.

That left Jane Roscoe's embittered husband, but more likely some dreg from GMP.

And the man in black who'd attacked him on the mezzanine – who was he? And the guys who'd laid into him outside the Tram and Tower but hadn't expected the American Express to smash them down, who the hell were they?

What a tangled fucking web I weave, he thought.

'Right, policy book,' he said resolutely, picking up his pen again to do what he had come into his office to do.

This time he managed to get a paragraph done. Not a quality piece of prose, admittedly, but one that hit the mark. He sipped his tea and looked up as another interruption came through the door in the form of Debbie Black. She plonked herself down on the chair opposite Henry. He placed his pen down and forced a smile.

'Hi.'

Debbie crossed her legs, making Henry wonder if he was about to be treated to a 'Sharon Stone', à la *Basic Instinct*. Trouble was Debbie's skirt was a bit too mid-length for such a display.

She leaned back, steepled her fingers under her chin and regarded him, a naughty smile playing on her highly kissable mouth.

'Drink later?' she ventured. 'You owe me, dumping me in Harrogate like that.' She pouted sexily.

'See how it pans out, eh?'

'No.' Her voice was firm. 'Later for definite.'

'Look.' He held out his hands, palms up. 'I can't really . . . I just can't.'

She squinted angrily at him. A shimmer of panic ran down his spine.

'Why not?' she demanded.

Instead of telling her the painful truth, telling her he was not interested, that he valued his home life too much, that he actually loved Kate, he said the first thing that came into his head because it was more likely to pacify her.

'It's Rik Dean,' he blurted. He saw her shoulders stiffen.

'What about him?'

'Well, he's a mate.'

She shook her head, not comprehending.

'He confided in me,' he went on, 'about you and him. You had a bit of a thing going, didn't you?'

With a folding of her arms, she uttered a snort.

'Basically, he hasn't got over you,' Henry said, 'and there was no way I could, y'know?' He shrugged. 'I couldn't get involved. He's a good friend and it would have gutted him.'

Debbie tilted her head, still squinting, but a different sort of squint now. 'He dumped me.'

'And he regrets it,' Henry said, shovelling like mad, the hole getting deeper by the second.

'He still hasn't got over me?' she asked in disbelief.

'No.'

227

'But he dumped me,' she insisted.

'Doesn't mean to say he did the right thing,' Henry said. It suddenly dawned on him that he was in extremely dangerous territory now and that a line needed to be drawn under it. Quickly. 'Yeah, look, so that's the reason, OK,' he said, attempting to draw that line, although it looked pretty vague and dotted to him at that moment. Inwardly he was cringing.

Fortunately, Debbie stood up, looking thoughtful. She wandered dreamily out of the office as though on a pink, fluffy cloud.

'Dangerous beauty,' Henry whispered to himself before banging his forehead on the desk and asking himself with each bang, 'Why' – bang – 'am' – bang – 'I' – bang – 'so' – bang – 'crap' – bang – 'at' – bang, bang, 'relationships?' He rubbed his reddening brow. He would rather be having a life-and-death struggle with a deranged serial killer than grappling with the emotions and complexities of the female of the species. 'Plasma screen TV, plasma screen TV,' he chanted in a sort of religious mantra.

The PB lay open in front of him, one paragraph completed, not a very good one at that. He picked up his pen and attacked the book with determination, finishing with a flourish of satisfaction about half an hour later, a mug of cold tea by his elbow.

Another intrusion.

It was John Walker, the detective from technical support.

Henry waved him in, told him to close the door, sat him down. 'You got something?'

'You need to see these.' He handed Henry a big envelope. Henry looked closely at what had been presented to him, feeling his heart skip a beat or two.

'Shit,' he said at length, looking at the detective.

'Yeah, shit,' he agreed.

'Anyone else know about this?'

'Nope?'

'Wife, girlfriend, boyfriend?'

'Not even him.'

'What are your plans for the morning?' Henry asked.

The DC shrugged. 'Day off, breakfast, newspaper, shopping, DIY, that sort of stuff.'

'Cancel all those plans.'

'OK,' he said without a moment of question. 'Why?'

'I need to tell you a story, then I need to phone the chief constable.'

'Whatever.'

Forty minutes later, the tech support DC emerged from Henry's office, somewhat shell-shocked by what he'd heard, but at the same time thrilled by what he'd been tasked to do.

Henry, equally shocked and a bit dithery, came out of the office a few moments earlier and made his way to the MIR, which was abuzz with activity following the earlier briefing. He found Karl Donaldson with Jane Roscoe at the office manager's desk. They had known each other a few years, having met through Henry. Donaldson was very much aware of Henry's affair with Jane.

He sauntered over to the pair and got a progress update. Little had moved on, but a lot of people were beavering away on their allotted tasks on the streets. Blackpool was pretty much locked down as cops went out banging on doors, calling in favours and doing a lot of shaking down in an effort to trace Trent, whose face was now plastered over the MIR walls.

The activity was satisfying. Henry was sure that if Trent was in town, he'd be flushed out or cornered soon. He had to believe that.

His mobile roared like a jet as an incoming text landed. He looked at it: ctch me if u can.

Donaldson and Jane watched Henry's expression alter.

'Problem?' the American asked.

'No,' Henry said, stern-faced. He walked out of the room.

Could it be that Trent was taunting him? He could not be sure, but from what he knew of the child molester, this was not something that fitted his behaviour pattern. Trent liked to assault and kill. That was his bag. It wasn't a game for him. He didn't like to leave clues, to play cat and mouse with cops. Cats usually caught mice, and he would not wish to jeopardize his freedom by playing silly buggers with mobile phones that could possibly be traced. He had been out and at liberty for a long time. Why would he want to lose that just for the sake of one-upmanship? He would not, Henry convinced himself. Trent wanted to stay free, not get caught. The more Henry thought about it, the less he believed Trent was the texter. But maybe the next twenty-four hours would reveal the culprit. Maybe.

In the corridor outside his office, he bumped into a constable coming out of the office. Henry did not know the officer's name, but recognized him as a member of the Support Unit, the bish-bash-bosh squad, as they were known, because of their somewhat hard-edged approach to policing. He was clutching a photograph in his hand.

'Help you?' Henry said.

'Yeah, boss . . . you got a mo?'

'Come in.' Henry led him into the salubrious interior of his office and plonked down at his desk, waiting for the officer to sit down opposite. 'Sorry, I don't know your name.'

'PC Fawcett . . . John Fawcett,' he said.

'What can I do for you, John?'

'I was at the briefing earlier,' he began hesitantly. He showed Henry the photo he was holding – one of the many Henry had hurriedly produced of Trent. Fawcett did not go on immediately. Henry waited for him to fill the gap. 'I've been looking long and hard at this photograph.' He waved Trent's face at Henry. 'And, well, I don't want to appear stupid or anything and I'm not a hundred per cent, but, do you remember when you busted into Uren's flat?'

'How could I forget?'

'I was one of the Support Unit officers covering the stairs.' Henry nodded, recalling him now. 'Just as you went into Uren's flat, a guy came down the stairs from the floor above.' The officer shrugged helplessly. 'I mean, it obviously wasn't Uren, so when he asked if it was all right to go past, I just said no probs. Took his name, let him go.'

Henry saw Fawcett's Adam's apple rise and fall.

'I think it was this guy.' He held up Trent's photograph.

It was a statement greeted by stony silence. For a moment, tumbleweed could have blown through the office on a whistling wind.

'You think?'

'A bit different-looking . . . but the eyes . . . yeah. I mean, we weren't actually given instructions about what we should do, so I let him pass, boss.'

On such simple things are suspects allowed to go free, and investigations are completely fucked up.

'How certain are you?'

Fawcett ummed and ahhed, then said, 'As I said, not a hundred per cent, but as certain as I can be in the short time I saw him in the crap lighting in the building. And,' he went on, dropping the bombshell, 'he told me his name was John Stoke, the name you said Trent uses as an alias.'

There was an extra long moment of dreadful silence as Henry digested this, then said, 'He came from the upper floor, you say?' trying to keep hysteria out of his voice.

Fawcett nodded.

'He could've been in one of the flats above?'

'Could have.'

Henry held back from standing up, towering over the PC and shouting him into a quivering mess because ultimately, it was he, Henry, who was to blame. Going gung-ho into the block of flats, not properly resourced, with only an 'on-the-hoof' plan put together, had meant he'd missed a simple thing: don't let anyone out until I'm happy as to who they are. It was one of those things the public would never believe the police would make a mistake on, but they did, often. The easy bits were the bits the cops got wrong, made themselves look stupid over. The building should have been tighter than a duck's buttocks and anyone should have been stopped, checked and verified. All the outer-perimeter people were looking for was someone doing a runner, not someone strolling out, having walked through police lines, passing the time of day along the way.

Sitting back in his creaky chair, Henry glanced out through the narrow window at the shark. Dave Anger would love to get hold of this one. Henry Christie, the incompetent bastard, had allowed one of the country's most wanted men to slip through his fingers. Literally. He could see the look of triumph on Anger's 'fizzog', as his dear mum would say, corrupting the French word 'visage' into a Lancashire speciality. Most definitely, Dave Anger had a 'fizzog'. Bile rose in his throat. Jane Roscoe's words, which summed Henry up, came to haunt him. 'Henry "Wing" Christie'. He looked at Fawcett, said, 'Shit.'

'Yeah, I know.'

'Sure it's him?'

'More or less.'

'OK – no problems, only solutions. Have you got anything on now?' Fawcett shook his head. 'Got a car?' He nodded. 'Let's go the MIR first and see what we've got on the other residents in the block of flats.' Henry rolled out of his chair. 'Onwards and upwards,' he said, none too energetically.

Henry checked the records detailing what had been done at the block of flats in which Uren's body had been discovered. The occupants of all but one flat had been accounted for and spoken to. A flat on the top floor was found to be apparently unoccupied, although it was rented out.

'What enquiries have been made with the landlord?' Henry asked Jane, whose job it was to keep up to date with everything that was going on.

She looked over his shoulder. 'Why?'

'Not sure yet.'

'The landlord has been spoken to,' she told him, 'but mainly about Uren's occupancy, nothing else. Uren rented the flat and lived there alone, by all accounts.'

'There's an unoccupied flat on the top floor – have we done anything about that? Found who was in it most recently? Have we asked the landlord who was in it?'

'I don't think so,' she said cautiously.

'OK,' said Henry, tight-lipped. 'Who's the landlord?'

Jane flicked through some sheets of paper on her desk and handed one to Henry. 'That's him.'

'Ugh,' Henry said, reading the name, and wishing someone had told him who it was. 'Why was I not told this?' he demanded of Jane. She half-shrugged. 'Right.' He turned to Fawcett, who was standing behind him. 'Got those car keys?' Fawcett nodded.

'What's going on?' Jane asked.

Henry tapped his nose and pointed a finger at her. He did not want her to know he had probably made one of the biggest policing cock-ups in history. Nor did he trust her not to run to Anger and tell tales. He turned to Karl Donaldson, who was sitting at Jane's desk. 'Fancy a jaunt out to see some of Blackpool's scum?'

'Sure,' he said, rising. 'What is it?'

'That kinda scummy stuff you find floating in stagnant water,' Henry said as a joke, which no one got. Donaldson just looked perplexed. 'Come on,' Henry said.

In the lift going down, Henry said, 'We missed Trent,' to his good-looking friend, using the royal 'we'. Not that he was ducking blame, but it was always good practice to spread it about where possible. He had always been contemptuous of bosses who were known to have Teflon-coated shoulders – meaning that no shit ever stuck. Now he wished he was one of them. He had clicked on to self-survival mode, and unless he could somehow pull this one back, questions would be asked in the corridors of power at HQ and he would be found wanting. He explained the situation to Donaldson.

'Shit happens,' the American said understandingly. 'Admittedly more often to you than anyone else, but it does. The secret is to hide it without causing a bad smell.'

The lift jarred as it reached ground level, the doors opening. Fawcett led them into the garage and to his car, an unmarked Vectra, which was still quite blatantly a police car. The missing hubcap was always a bit of a give-away. Fawcett jumped in behind the wheel, Henry next to him, Donaldson in the back.

'This is Karl Donaldson, by the way' he said to Fawcett. 'He's an FBI agent.'

'Ho hum,' the laconic cop said, unimpressed.

Eighteen

Blackpool had its full share of sleazeball landlords, and Larry Cork was no exception. Unkempt, unshaven, unwashed and whiffy, he was the stereotypical snivelling landlord, money-grabbing, back-stabbing, penny-pinching and priceless. Henry knew Cork of old. In his younger days the man had been a pretender to the crime throne of Blackpool, but hadn't really had the physical toughness to make good his threats. He had gradually disappeared from the mainstream crime scene, emerging as a landlord and buying up property left, right and centre around the resort. He and his sons – amazingly called Barry and Harry, who muscled for him – had made a killing in the 1980s on the back of DSS lodgers. That bubble burst, but Cork had made his dough. Now he ticked over nicely, owning a string of ramshackle flats, including the block containing Uren's, plus houses and a two amusement arcades in South Shore.

Henry had once locked him up for gross indecency in some public toilets on the prom, which added to Cork's sleaze. He enjoyed the company of other men and the excitement of meeting in public toilets. Henry held Cork in very low regard.

Detectives had interviewed Cork quite thoroughly about Uren, but he had not offered the police anything more than they asked. He told them that he did not know Uren well, that he was a good paying tenant, and he wasn't interested in his comings and goings. The perfect landlord. He wasn't asked any questions about the unoccupied, but rented, room on the top floor of the block of flats. Time to change that, Henry thought as he waited for Cork to answer the door of his flat on the ground floor of another block in North Shore.

Barry, Cork's eldest son, came to the door. He was a wide, strapping guy in his early thirties. He was as hard as nails, and as gay as his dad.

'Hello, Barry,' Henry said, holding out his warrant card.

Fawcett and Donaldson were at his shoulder. 'Need to see Larry, please. Name's DCI Christie, but you know that already, don't you?'

Barry opened the door fully, revealing himself to be dressed in a tight-fitting vest and leather jeans, body hair sprouting from all round the vest. Henry tried not to show his disgust. 'Dad's not in and anyway, he's already talked to the filth.'

'Need to talk more. Where is he, then?'

On the last word, Henry heard a toilet being flushed, a door opening and a growl of, 'Fuckin' piles playing me up again,' coming from the brown-toothed mouth of Barry Cork.

Henry gave Barry a blank stare.

Barry shrugged, eyed Henry's two companions – his gaze fluttering over Donaldson – and conceded defeat. 'OK, he's in.' He turned. 'Dad! Cops!'

Larry Cork came into view, zipping up and tucking his shirt into his loose pants. A cigarette dangled from his lips as though it had been stapled there.

'Can I help you guys?' he smiled. Then the smile fell and he scowled at Henry. 'You, you bastard!'

'Yep – how's it hangin' Larry?'

There was fire and caution in Cork's bloodshot eyes. His treatment at Henry's hands all those years ago had stayed with him. 'What do you want?'

'Just a chat about your tenants.'

'Don't like you, never have.'

'Feeling's mutual, Larry, but maybe it's time to move on. Let's not let the past colour the future, eh? There's been a murder on premises owned by you and by virtue of that you can't expect us not to be round to see you regularly, can you?'

'What do you want? I've already given a statement.'

'More depth . . . can we come in?'

Ten minutes later Larry Cork drove round with them to the block of flats where Uren's dead body had been found. Cork had identified Trent as one of his tenants, but said he didn't know of any connection between Trent and Uren. They had come as separate tenants, and Trent didn't use the name Trent anyway. He used the surname Stoke. He said he saw very little of him, and had certainly not seen him since Uren's body had been found.

Cork led them up from the front door, pausing at the floor on which Uren's flat was situated. The flat was still sealed as a crime scene.

'When the hell's that comin' off?' Cork asked, pointing at the tape stretched across the door. 'Money going to waste there.'

'Until our scientific people are happy there's nothing else we need,' Henry told him.

'Not good,' Cork said.

He took them up the next flight.

'How does Mr Stoke pay his rent?'

'Cash. Leaves an envelope for me in the lockable post box at the bottom of the steps.'

There were only two doors on the landing on the top floor. 'It's that one,' he said, 'and this is the spare key.' He handed it to Henry, who walked to the door and knocked on it. No reply. Last time he caught Trent, Trent was in a guesthouse in Blackpool. That was when Trent had tried to stab Henry, but instead the tables were turned when Danny Furness clobbered him with her baton and laid him out.

'Police – open up,' Henry called. Again, no reply. He put the key in the lock and opened the door to reveal a poorly-lit, dingy room which made the word 'basic' sound luxurious. A camp bed, a couple of old armchairs, rickety coffee table and nothing else, other than a kitchen sink.

'Nice,' Henry said, stepping over the threshold. The flat was empty, devoid of anything, including signs of recent habitation.

Donaldson was behind him. 'Could just be a bolthole,' he said.

'Did he ever have anything more here?' Henry asked Cork.

The landlord shrugged. 'How would I know?'

'Because you sneak around when your tenants are out . . . look, don't mess us about, Larry. We're chasing a murderer.'

Cork held up his hands in defeat. 'Fine, OK, it was always this empty. Never saw clothing, or food, or anything. I don't think he spent hardly any time here. Just paid his rent, which is all that bothers me. I wish all my tenants were like him.'

Henry, Donaldson and Fawcett exchanged a three-way glance. Henry sighed, dispirited. 'Let's get CSI up here to give it a once-over,' he said to Fawcett. To Cork he said, 'Thanks for your cooperation, Larry, but I have to say your choice of tenants is pretty fuckin' lousy.'

'I resent that,' he said haughtily, his cigarette bobbing on his lip. 'I check 'em all personally, references and everything. I run a tight ship here, despite what you might think, you homophobic bastard.'

'I'm not homophobic, Larry, but no one, and I stress, no one tries to put their cock into my hand. A mistake you made, if you recall? Little wonder you got bounced from here to kingdom come.' Henry's voice was rising at the memory of the little thing that had triggered his treatment of Cork when he'd arrested him.

'Boss?' Fawcett said.

'What?' Henry snapped.

'What references did Trent provide? Or Stoke, as he called himself?'

The three waited for Cork to respond. He scratched his dandruffed head, skin flaking on to his shoulder like a snow shower.

'Did he actually have any references, or did he just cross your palm with silver?' Henry asked him.

'I can't recall. Need to look at my files.'

'Larry, does it even bother you that a man's been murdered in one of your flats?'

'Not specially. Obviously I won't be getting any more rent off him, and I could do with the flat back to re-let it, and the fire damage has to be paid for, but no.'

After locking the empty flat, Henry pocketing the key, they all traipsed back to the Cork flat where his two sons were slumped on the settee watching TV, which was flicked off as the visitors returned. Both sons were smoking, had beers in their hands and neither moved. They were the antithesis of the stereotypical gay man, nothing remotely effeminate about them at all. The aroma of body odour hung unpleasantly in the air. Cork senior crossed to a desk on which was an expanding file jammed full of papers. He rifled through it, his grubby fingers emerging with a tatty sheet of paper.

'He filled this one out.'

Henry crossed the room and looked at it, some generic tenancy pro forma agreement, probably bought from W. H. Smith.

'Did Uren do one?' Henry asked.

'Yeah, it's in here, I think.'

237

Henry read the document carefully, touching only its edges, but it seemed to hold nothing further for him in the hunt for a killer and saving the life of a young girl which might already be lost. He passed the agreement over to Fawcett for his perusal.

'What you lot after?' The voice came from one of the couch potatoes, the most junior member of the family, Harry Cork. He was slumped like a piece of blubber across an armchair, beer resting on his gut and as much body hair showing as his elder brother.

'That fucker Stoke,' his dad replied. 'Him in the top flat.'

'Oh aye,' Harry said, losing interest. He broke wind, making Henry wonder how he, or any of the other two, managed to cop off with anyone else. They were gross and unpleasant and why anyone would chose to have dealings with them was beyond his ken.

Cork looked at Henry, shrugged.

'What's he done?' said Harry, surfacing again, a bit like a whale coming up for air.

'He did that murder,' Dad Cork informed him.

'Oh, right.' Disinterest returned. He slurped his beer.

'Well, if anything comes to mind, let us know, will you?' Henry said to Larry and handed him a business card. 'Call me, OK?'

'Whatever.'

'He's into kiddiewinks, isn't he?' Harry piped up again. All eyes turned to him and he looked round astounded by the attention. 'What?' he said.

'How do you know that?' Henry demanded.

'Oh no, nothing, nothing,' Harry blabbered, suddenly realizing he'd said too much.

Cork senior was glaring at Harry in disbelief. 'You pillock,' he uttered.

'Right,' said Henry, 'let's be knowing.'

'There's nothing to know,' Harry said.

'I beg to differ and I think an overnight visit to the cop shop's in order here, don't you? I think you're withholding information.' He turned to Fawcett. 'Call the van – three prisoners.' Henry had picked up on the fact that Harry had obviously spoken out of turn, revealed something he shouldn't have done. Being in such a desperate position himself – trying to save a career already going down the pan – Henry was ready to clutch at straws again. These guys knew something about Trent and if they didn't blab here and now, they would be dragged off to the nick, power of arrest or not. Henry was long enough in the tooth to cross that hurdle when he came to it.

'What for? We haven't done a fuckin' thing,' Larry protested. The older brother, Barry, rose to his feet. He was a big man, much lard on him.

'We're going nowhere,' he declared.

Henry stared at him. 'Sit down Barry, and listen.'

'Up yours, shitface,' he snarled. 'I'm going nowhere—' But suddenly he found himself back down from where he'd risen, with the help of Karl Donaldson's hand in his chest. He struggled a little, but Donaldson pushed harder.

Henry moved to stand at the door.

Harry Cork was on his feet now, not knowing what to do, but knowing he'd let something vital slip off his tongue.

Larry said, 'You had to open your silly gob, didn't you?' He hit Harry hard, ramming his fist into his nose. Harry stumbled back, caught the back of his knees on the coffee table and sat on it. The feeble piece of self-assembled furniture crumbled into matchstick fragments, but Harry was evidently more concerned about his nose, which had burst into Technicolor red.

Henry grabbed Larry's shirt at the chest and flung him back against the wall. His face was only inches away from Larry's, and his eyes were wild and desperate now. 'A man has been murdered and a girl has been kidnapped. She may still be alive,' he panted. 'If you have any information about Trent, Stoke or whatever his name is, fucking tell me now, Larry.'

'By bloody dose!' Harry screamed, trying to stem the flow down his face, neck and chest.

'How long for the van?' Henry said to PC Fawcett, who hadn't had time to shout for it yet.

Fawcett called in. 'Four minutes,' he shouted.

'Then let's chat for four minutes,' Henry said into old man Cork's fizzog.

Henry held on to father Larry; Donaldson stood menacingly over son number one, Barry; the youngest member of the family continued to blubber about his broken nose. He tried to stand, pick himself up from the pieces of the coffee table, and in doing so, inadvertently put his hand on the TV remote control, which clicked the TV on to the channel they'd been watching when Henry and Co returned.

'Aw, Jesus,' Larry moaned, sinking to his knees, covering his face as Henry released his grip.

Barry looked like a wild animal caught in a trap. He attempted to rise again, but Donaldson punched him in the chest and he went back down.

All eyes turned to the TV.

Harry tried to grab the remote control, but Fawcett kicked his hands from under him and he went down across the broken table again.

And there was nothing else to do but watch the horrific scene on the screen in front of them as a naked young girl, manacled to a wall, was savagely whipped until she could no longer scream, no longer even form a word. And then it got worse. And there was no doubt about it – what they were watching was for real.

Henry bent down in front of Larry. He could not begin to describe the repulsion he was feeling. He was short of breath and his heart was pounding in a way it never had before. He felt clammy, cold and very empty, yet at the same time filled with a simmering rage.

He spoke slowly.

'Does this have anything to do with Trent?' He lifted Larry's face up with the tip of a finger. 'Does it?'

'Yeah,' he whispered.

'Tell me.'

'All I know is, he makes films, sells 'em on. I mean, I don't know if they're real or not.'

'Liar,' Henry said.

'Yeah OK, they are real. I just watch 'em, that's all.'

'Tell me where he is,' Henry said softly. He could feel a desire to explode. He still had a fingertip under Larry's unshaven chin, which was coarse and sweaty. 'Tell me,' Henry insisted.

'He's a fuckin' madman.'

'I don't care. At this moment in time, I'm madder. Tell me where he lives.'

'I don't know, honest.'

'I do.' Harry, broken-nosed Harry, piped up. 'I followed him once,' he said through a mouthful of blood. 'I was curious.'

240

Nineteen

Conflicting emotions jostled for position inside Henry Christie. Part of him was deeply annoyed that he hadn't done the job properly when he'd gone to arrest George Uren. He hadn't thought it through, and if he had, Louis Vernon Trent could easily be in custody now. Or at the very least, that lowlife landlord could have been sweated earlier. Another part of him was truly excited. If it all came together, the cops were patient, and Trent hadn't already done a runner, one of the most wanted men in the country would soon be in his clutches. That prospect outweighed the negative side, but he knew he was fortunate to be in this position and was determined not to let the opportunity pass. And, all being well, he'd be able to stick two fingers up at Dave Anger, too.

It was ten p.m. Things had moved fast over the last few hours.

The trio of Corks were all in custody for various offences relating to child pornography and complicity in murder and kidnapping (though Henry knew the latter two allegations probably would not go far), and they were going nowhere for at least twenty-four hours.

A team from the surveillance unit had been brought in and were watching the address Harry Cork had given them. He had in fact pointed out the house in a quick, surreptitious drive past in a plain car with smoked-glass windows. Harry was now desperate to help the cops and Henry believed what he told them: they had only bought the videos from Uren, but Harry knew that the man called Stoke was supplying them. He had seen Stoke dropping off a package at Uren's flat one day. He hadn't even known that Stoke and Uren were buddies – 'honest to God' – but he did know that Stoke spent little time in the flat on the top floor. He had subsequently followed Stoke/Trent to a terraced house on Hornby Road, Blackpool, close to the town centre. That was the one he pointed out to the police.

Henry had asked Jerry Tope, the Intel DC, to do some quick utility checks on the address. The billing for gas, electric and council tax came back with the name reference Stoke. He had taken the place over two years before, a fact which sickened Henry. It meant that Trent had been living back in his home town, under an assumed name, right under the noses of the police, within a quarter of a mile of the station, making a living by stealing from old people and abducting children from surrounding forces.

But had he now gone? Had the police presence at Uren's flat spooked him? And was Henry too late to save the life of Kerry Figgis?

Karl Donaldson was along for the ride. Henry and he were sitting in an unmarked police car two streets away from the target address, speculating, hoping to accumulate. Not far away an armed team were also parked up, as well as other specialists, detectives and uniformed officers. Even a joiner was on standby to repair any damage that might be caused from the house entry. They were all waiting for the final decision to be made.

So far, the surveillance guys reported no sign of any movement from the address. No lights, no activity.

'It's chicken and egg,' Donaldson said. He shifted uncomfortably, having been hurriedly issued with a borrowed stab vest that was too tight for him. 'And what's the most important?'

Henry's jaw rotated. He knew exactly what Donaldson was obliquely referring to: obviously the most important thing was to save Kerry's life. That should override everything, even if it meant that Trent did not get caught . . . so should they wait? See if he entered or left the house? Or should they burst in, hoping Kerry might be in there alive? Not that there was anything to suggest she was in there. So many questions. Henry realized there was a good chance she was dead anyway, stats showed that . . . but, but . . . even if there was the faintest glimmer of her breathing, there was only one course of action to take. Even if she wasn't in the house, there could be clues to lead the police to her.

Henry nodded, agreeing with his inner gut feeling: better to lose Trent than a life.

'We go in.'

*   *   *

242

It was left to the specialists to get into the house. Once the exterior had been sealed, a team of Support Unit officers, armed with a door-opener, raced up to the front door. When they found it locked, they did the business. Within seconds the door was off its hinges. Immediately the firearms team burst through the gap into the house in a well-drilled manoeuvre, weapons drawn, full body armour protection, ballistic shields, torches and screams. They moved quickly but carefully through the ground floor, searching and securing the rooms one by one until they were satisfied it was all clear; the team at the foot of the stairs then got the instruction to move up, leading the assault on the first floor, which was also secured quickly with no trace of any occupants.

Henry and Karl Donaldson stood inside the vestibule, waiting for the rooms to be declared clear before stepping into the hallway, beckoned in by the sergeant in charge of the firearms team.

'No one ground or first floor, sir,' he reported. 'But there's a basement and an attic.'

'OK,' said Henry. 'Trent's a clever sod, so keep a presence upstairs and on this level. Don't stand anyone down yet. Let's have a look at the basement first, then the attic.'

'Roger,' the sergeant said sharply. He turned to direct his squad. The door to the basement ran off the hallway, under the stairs. Moments later the lead two firearms officers were ready to enter the basement. 'Go,' came the succinct order. The officer nodded and with Glock handguns drawn, ballistic shields in front of them, they tried the basement door – unlocked – reached through, simply switched on the light and charged down the concrete steps into the basement, followed by their back-up team.

It all fell spookily silent. Henry and Donaldson exchanged worried glances, then looked at the team leader who was at the top of the steps.

'Situation report?' the officer said into his radio.

'All clear . . . hell,' came the reply.

'Is there a problem?'

'You need to get down here . . . the DCI needs to get down here.'

Henry, his PR tuned to the firearms frequency, heard the exchange through his earpiece, as did Donaldson who had been loaned a PR.

The sergeant turned to Henry, who nodded and eased past him, followed by Donaldson. They went down the steep, narrow steps to the basement, hitting the stench as they descended. The four shocked-faced firearms officers who had made the entry, stood aside for them, allowing a view of the well-lit basement.

Trent's studio. His lair.

Sophisticated-looking video and DVD recording equipment. Two expensive cameras on tripods. Hundreds of DVDs and videos stacked up by a wall. A mixing desk. Spotlights. And the small stage in the corner of the room which Henry recognized because he had seen it on Cork's TV set, the one with the girl manacled to a metal ring in the wall.

She was still there, kneeling up to the wall, hanging by her wrists, which were chained to the ring that looked like a towel rail.

She was dead. Her head lolled through her arms, her lower legs starting to show signs of decomposition. She almost looked like she was praying. Her little naked body was stripped of flesh where she had been whipped and tortured.

'Boss.' Someone tapped Henry's arm. He tore his eyes away from the girl. One of the firearms team pointed across to another corner of the basement, the only poorly-lit area. Henry walked across and found a blanket draped over something. He lifted it carefully, then reeled back instinctively before regaining his composure and looking again at the two small bodies on top of each other, decomposing. One was nearly a skeleton; another still had quite a lot of flesh and skin on the bones.

He dropped the blanket, horrified.

'You guys – well done, but out, now, please,' he said to the firearms team. 'The attic needs sorting, please.' They did not need telling twice, withdrawing silently.

Henry and Donaldson looked at each other.

'Three dead girls,' Henry said, unnecessarily.

Donaldson's jaw jutted.

'And he's not here – unless he's in the attic.'

'No,' said Donaldson.

Henry turned to the body of the girls chained to the wall. 'I don't think that's Kerry Figgis. That's the girl on the Cork's video . . . could be the one from Manchester, maybe.'

'Which means Kerry could still be alive. Maybe she's with Trent now.'

'A plus point . . . and another plus point,' Henry said, stunned by his thoughts. 'I know that Jodie Greaves died in the back of that Astra, and she went through hell, but at least she didn't have to suffer this. Not that it's any consolation . . . fuck, just look at these poor kids. Shit.' Henry was close to tears. 'He cannot be allowed to escape.'

'Maybe we're not too late,' Donaldson said.

'How do you mean?'

'Because there might still be a chance of him returning here. I know it's a long shot, buddy, but just suppose he hasn't seen us here,' Donaldson said urgently, making chopping gestures with his hand to emphasize what he was saying. 'These unfortunate kids aren't going anywhere, so is there anything lost in shutting up the house, getting the door repaired – there's a joiner with us, isn't there? – and maybe waiting a few more hours. Whaddya think? Kerry isn't here, so it's not as though we've totally lost her yet; you did the right thing coming in, now let's continue playing out our luck. You never know. He might just come back, whistling a happy tune.'

SATURDAY

Twenty

A lone in the darkness, he was aware of the sound of his breathing, the beat of his heart, even the noise of his eyelids coming together as he blinked. All magnified, all giving away his position, or so it seemed.

He looked around the living room, his eyes now well adjusted to the dark, the heavy curtains cutting out most of the illumination from the street outside. It was a normal room. Three-piece suite, TV, DVD, pictures on the walls. A normal room in a normal house in a normal street in Blackpool – a far from normal town. But hadn't 25 Cromwell Street been a normal address? Yet what had Fred West's home revealed? A trail of multiple murder stretching back over many years.

At least this house had only had its current owner in for two years. There would not be a legacy of lifetime killing here, just that of forty-eight months. What Trent could have achieved in that length of time was pretty terrifying, though. Three corpses in the basement for starters. Would more be found?

Sitting there, one floor above, Henry was certain that more bodies would be discovered.

A scraping noise made him stop breathing, listen intently.

Nothing. It was nothing.

As much as he could, he relaxed in that normal room.

His thoughts stayed with those bodies, the remnants of three young girls, murdered by the hands of Louis Vernon Trent and probably George Uren. Their terrible fate made Henry surge with anger. Kidnapped, abused, probably filmed, kept alive for how long? Months, possibly. Then murdered. His eyes moistened as his imagination ran riot. They had been given no chance and no hope. Plucked from the streets, from surroundings they knew well, felt safe and comfortable in. But in an area in which two ruthless predators swooped to survive; firstly by targeting old people, stealing from them, terrifying them

249

and destroying their lives in the process; then pouncing on the young and ending theirs just to feed their perversion.

Henry knew he was the last hope for all those victims. If he missed Trent this time, he would never see him again, of that he was certain. He had disappeared for several years once already, but then come home to build a lair in which he lived with impunity. If he could do it on his home soil, he could do it anywhere. He would learn by his mistakes and would never be found again, and he would still go on living at the expense of the defenceless.

A car drove by. Its headlights sent brief rods of light through the chinks in the curtain.

Henry stayed still, checked his watch. It was a few minutes after midnight, into a new day, and although he had been there for less than an hour, he felt that the chances of Trent returning were ebbing away. Part of him believed Trent would not show, because he was a feral animal with highly developed senses that kept him one step ahead of the game. If he hadn't already gone, Henry was sure he would intuitively know that his lair had been invaded and would not come back.

Henry had bustled everyone off the property, got the joiner in to do a quick repair to the front door, and the house was back to square one, on the face of it – with the exception that Henry was sitting in the living room, and everyone else, including a bleating Karl Donaldson, had been withdrawn. Henry had been insistent with Donaldson, who said it was foolish just to have only one person in the house. He and Henry had almost had a stand-up row about it, before Henry agreed to a suggestion made by the American which was a bit of a compromise. The nearest plain police car was at least a quarter of a mile away. Others were even further away. Their personal radios were all on a single talk group and ordered not to transmit anything unless urgent.

Another hastily-devised plan, Henry thought, leaving him exposed and a little nervous. He was prepared to give it until daylight. If Trent had not returned by then, it would be all hands to a manhunt.

To Henry, the return seemed unlikely, but it was worth a try.

The time passed on. Henry settled in for the wait, yawned. His earpiece fell out. He replaced it, screwing it in. Sometimes he thought his ears were not the right shape for anything other than good quality headphones.

'DCI Christie – contact call,' Henry whispered over his PR.

'Received,' comms answered.

He settled back. His stab vest was not the best thing for comfort, especially with the covert cuff/baton/CS harness hanging under his left armpit.

Twenty minutes later he found himself nodding off, the toil of the long hours beginning to play on him. He struggled to keep his eyes open.

'Shit.' He took some deep breaths. 'Not good.' He sat up and urged himself to keep going. He went ten more minutes before his head fell forwards, the earpiece came out, and he jerked his head upright, rubbed his eyes hard.

Then he sensed something dreadful, but before he could react, his head was yanked backwards and a knife placed across his throat.

'Long time, no see,' Louis Vernon Trent whispered into Henry's ear. 'If you move, I'll slit your throat.'

He could feel the narrow, fiercely sharp blade digging into his skin, not quite cutting the surface. Trent was standing behind him, leaning forward so that his head rested on Henry's right shoulder. Trent's breath was warm on his ear, the man's left hand on Henry's forehead, holding his head back.

'This is a good trap,' Trent said.

'Yeah, I scream, they all come running.'

'They being?'

'Lots of cops.'

Trent thought about this and pressed the knife harder into Henry's skin. 'Do you know how long it takes to slit a throat? Before they come, that's how long it takes . . . and actually, it's not that good a trap.' His voice was quiet, no more than a whisper. He seemed calm and relaxed. In control.

'Good enough for you.'

'What, you alone in this house? I don't think so.'

'How do you know I'm alone?'

'Watched you all coming and going. I have a friend next door, nice old lady, until she saw you lot and asked me why all you nasty policemen were raiding my house. Now she's a dead old friend.'

'Why come back?' Henry asked. 'If you knew we were here?'

'Need to get my money before leaving. And I knew *you* were here. Couldn't resist one last chance to kill you, could I, Henry?

I always wanted it to be Danny, but she came to another sticky end, so that's all right. Just had to have the last word with you.'

'Ego,' Henry said.

Trent adjusted his stance slightly, getting a better hold on Henry's head, the knife digging deeper. It felt sharp and deadly. Henry's nostrils flared. Just one cut – zip – and he was dead, or at least bleeding to death. 'Ego?' he laughed. 'You're the one with the ego problem, if you think you can catch me all by yourself, with the nearest help, what, three minutes away. You'll be dead, I'll be gone by the time they land, when they realize you haven't made that last contact call.'

Trent's face was right next to Henry's. He could feel the skin of the man's face next to his. He could smell him.

Henry moved his right hand a fraction.

'So where've you been?' Henry needed to keep him talking.

'Around . . . left a trail behind me . . . such memories.'

'Including a cop in Florida?'

'He was getting too close.'

'That why you came home?'

'Where the heart is . . . now I have to uproot again, and it was going so well.' Trent stiffened, the knife at Henry's throat cutting in now. Henry gasped as a trickle of blood dribbled down his neck. Trent relaxed, and the knife came off. 'Time for me to go, Henry. Don't want to look a gift horse in the mouth.'

'So you kill me, set me on fire, is that it?'

'Could be.'

'Where'd the incendiaries come from?'

'America – small-time white supremacists. Idiots, but their hearts are in the right places, I guess.' He twisted the knife and scraped it across Henry's skin. 'I'll make sure you die quickly, Henry . . . sort of.' He stuck the point of the blade into the soft fleshy part underneath Henry's chin. 'It'll go behind the Adam's apple, right through, and I'll dig around, and blood'll fly everywhere.'

'Thanks for that – just like George, eh? Why kill your buddy?' Henry's right hand moved an inch more as he slid it across his stomach towards his left arm.

'He panicked. It was obvious you wanted him and I knew he'd crack if caught. A weak man. I had to shout at him to run you down, and then he didn't do it well . . . he would have crumbled, and that would have been the end of my quiet life, occa-

252

sionally fulfilling my desires and making recordings for posterity.'
He was speaking in a cold, matter-of-fact way about filming his killings. The voice of a psychopath, a man whose beat was Psycho Alley, who could see nothing wrong in the way he lived.

'How many desires did you fulfil?'

'Since coming home? Maybe ten, twelve. Lost count. Don't keep a tally. Most of them are downstairs in the walls.'

'And Kerry Figgis, where is she?'

'How should I know?' He pulled Henry's head further back, stretching and exposing his neck further. 'As soon as I saw you in Fleetwood, I knew you'd come to me sooner rather than later. You're the only one capable, I think. All the rest are idiots. So you have to die, Henry, then I truly believe the police will never, ever catch me again.'

'Why the texts, though?' Henry gasped.

'What texts?

Henry's right hand edged under his jacket.

The point of the knife pressed into his neck.

'I like this part,' Trent said.

'You're fuckin' bonkers.' Henry's fingers had got as far as touching the base of the CS canister held in the covert harness.

Trent's face was side by side with his, cheek to cheek. He pushed the knife in a little further, pricking the skin. Henry jerked. Trent chuckled. 'That was nothing. Just imagine the knife plunging into your neck.'

He raised his head away from Henry, obvious that he was steadying himself for that thrust into Henry's neck, to end his life once and for all.

'One more thing,' Henry said urgently, his voice desperate. 'Just one thing.' His hand was now wrapped around the CS canister.

'What?'

'What did you do with Jodie Greaves between kidnapping her and me stumbling on you?'

'Henry,' he said patronizingly, 'you truly do not want to know, other than that she was lovely. She would have been a star.'

'Bastard,' Henry said.

On that word, the light came on in the room as Karl Donaldson stepped through the door. Trent looked up and saw what looked like a space-age ray gun in Donaldson's right hand. At the same moment, Henry snatched the CS canister out of the harness, twisted away from the knife as far as he could and, trying not to spray himself, aimed where he thought Trent's face might be and pressed the spray button. Donaldson aimed the weapon at Trent and pulled the trigger. But it was no gun: it was a taser. Two hooks shot across the room, attached to minutely thin wires, and snagged into to Trent's clothing. Fifty thousand volts of electricity arced across his body at the same time as the spray from Henry's CS hit him full in the face.

The joint effect was stunning.

The charge sent Trent writhing across the room with an unworldly shriek and floored him like he'd been hit by a demolition ball, the knife flying out of his hand. The CS took immediate effect, eating like acid into his eyes and nose, making him scream and claw at his face.

Henry leapt to his feet, and staggered across to the fireplace which he used to hold himself up.

'I love it when a plan comes together,' Donaldson beamed.

'Fuck me, Karl,' Henry said, 'he nearly slit my throat. Fuckin' Yanks, always leavin' it to the last minute.'

'Pal,' Donaldson said soothingly, 'a miss is as good as a mile.'

One of the cruel hands of fate Henry believed he had been dealt in life was that he was useless at golf. No matter how he tried – and he had tried – throughout his life, he had failed humiliatingly. He thought he had a good, easy swing, but the problem was when that little white, bastard of a ball was placed in front of him, it all went, as his colleagues say, 'shit-shaped'. His attempts at the game were so disastrous that in order to compute his score, he always used the following equation: think of a par, double it and add two and, without fail, Henry's score could be fairly accurately estimated.

It was this equation that he applied to, yet amended, in relation to Louis Vernon Trent, for the benefit of the custody officer. 'Think Hannibal Lecter times two, add a dash of Ian Brady, then a smidgen of Jeffrey Dahmer and you'll be somewhere in the region of how Trent operates.' Henry dabbed a piece of tissue on the nick Trent had cut into his throat; he could still feel the line of the blade where Trent had held the knife across his windpipe. In his imagination, he felt it tearing his throat out. 'He'll kill you, or rip off your face, at the drop of a hat, so never deal with him unaccompanied.'

The burly sergeant seemed contemptuously unimpressed.

'I mean it,' Henry said mildly.

'OK, boss.'

Right now, Trent was in a cell. The door to it was wedged open and two strapping PCs sat outside in the corridor next to each other on chairs positioned directly opposite the door. They kept a constant vigil on him – suicide watch – as per force instructions regarding murder suspects. Trent had been stripped and every orifice had been searched. The police were as sure as they could be that he had nothing secreted in his mouth, nose, ears or arsehole that he could use to harm either himself or anyone else. He had been given a paper suit and slippers before being marched down to trap one, the nearest cell to the custody office door. He had acquiesced to everything in a muted, but resentful way, which made Henry worry slightly.

Henry had questioned him – off the record and highly illegally – during his recovery from the horrible effects of CS, firing him questions about the whereabouts of Kerry Figgis, but Trent refused to talk and Henry wanted to spray him again, but realized that torture would get him nowhere. The only thing Trent said was that he wanted a solicitor and a doctor. It annoyed Henry that both requests were being complied with. The doctor would be half an hour, the solicitor one hour.

In the meantime, Henry debated whether or not to get a superintendent's authorization under PACE to conduct an urgent interview. This could take place without a solicitor for the purpose of saving life.

Would it achieve anything, he was wondering. He looked thoughtfully at Donaldson, who had taken a back seat as Trent was processed through the custody system.

The American sidled up to Henry. 'How are we going to explain me and the taser, H?'

Henry shrugged. That would be a bureaucratic nightmare of bullshit at the very least, and he didn't want to think about it just now. 'Minor matter,' he said, brushing the issue aside for the moment. 'We'll think of something.'

'Still, can't argue it was a good idea me sneaking back into the house to hide in the kitchen. You'd be dead otherwise.'

'Yeah, I'm glad I thought of it,' he said tiredly, remembering Donaldson's insistence. 'As brave as I am, I didn't really want to be all alone in the house with those bodies in the basement and the possibility of him showing up – even if you obviously fell asleep under the kitchen table,' Henry admonished.

Donaldson sniffed resentfully. 'He was a sneaky son of a bitch himself. It's no wonder the firearms guys missed the hole in the wall.'

On a further, more detailed search of the house following Trent's arrest, officers had discovered that a hole had been made in the brickwork in the attic wall which divided Trent's house from next door, a hole just wide enough to allow a grown man to clamber through easily enough. A stack of cardboard boxes had hidden the hole from cursory inspection. As the firearms team had initially been searching for a man, they had missed the hole during their brief attic search. They had also found a bundle of Bank of England notes totalling thirty-five thousand pounds, proceeds of Trent's crime spree against old people, and four passports in different names. Unfortunately, they had also found the old lady dead next door, stabbed innumerable times.

'He must have been watching our every move from next door,' Henry said. 'Saw us come and go and set up our little sting. If he hadn't been so greedy, he could've walked.' Donaldson nodded. 'But he needed the dosh to set up somewhere else . . . and he couldn't resist getting one over on me, one of the few people who've stood in his way and lived, I guess. This one's for Danny Furness.' Henry sighed, reflecting a second.

'It's a pity he saw fit to kill the old lady next door,' Donaldson said. 'You know – I think I'll apply for an extradition order for this guy back to the States to stand trial for Mark Tapperman's murder when you've finished with him. Florida is a pleasant little state which still fries its killers. Now there's one execution I would go and see.'

Henry regarded Donaldson pensively. 'You're a bit of an enigma, aren't you Karl?'

'Hell, why?'

'Well, big old friendly Karl, yet you sneak about like a ninja.' Henry's eyes narrowed. 'More to you than meets they eye, isn't there?'

'Don't push it, Henry.' Donaldson said uncomfortably.

The English detective gave a short titter. 'I won't. I probably don't want to know . . .' His mobile phone rang, breaking the slight tension between the two. Henry answered it and within moments his face had darkened, all thoughts about the clandestine activities of his pal gone from his mind. 'OK, OK . . . stay there . . . I'll be with you in five.' He finished the call.

'Problem?'

'Need a motor.' Henry looked round and saw PC Fawcett strolling unsuspectingly into the custody office. 'You still got a plain car?' Henry pounced.

'Uh, yeah.'

'Come on – I need you.' To Donaldson he said, 'You too, job on.'

'Look, I don't know, I don't know – it could be summat, it could be nowt. It's just weird, that's all.' The words were spoken by a harassed Troy Costain. 'You asked me to check out Callum Rourke and that's what I've done, and I've ended up followin' him here, doin' your dirty work.'

'OK, well done. Now tell me what happened.'

They were on Shoreside, having met up with Costain following the hurried phone call he'd made a few minutes earlier. They were outside the grounds of the primary school on the perimeter of the estate, a complex of low-rise buildings surrounded by high, anti-vandal painted walls and railings. Henry was talking to Costain in a huddle, the other two, Donaldson and Fawcett, still in the unmarked police car.

'Uh, well, I don't know the twat that well, other than the bit o' smack I've dealt him, so I asked about, unobtrusively, like, but no one else seemed to know much about him either.'

'Just hit the nail on the head, Troy. It's freezing out here.'

'Yeah, well, I went and sat outside his house, well down the road a bit, wonderin' how t'get something on him, y'know – just to please you, because I'd robbed your mum. Then, I dunno, about half an hour ago, there's no lights on in the house and the front door opens and he sneaks out and starts walking. I think, odd, so I follow him, y'know, in and out of the bushes and all that crap. Dead jumpy he was, always looking back. Could tell he was upta no good . . . but I like an enigma, and I stick with him and follow him here.'

'Where is here?' Henry looked round.

'Just on the other side o' the school's like a little cul-de-sac of lock-up garages. Half of 'em are derelict, but some still have doors on and are used. He went to one which was padlocked, unlocks it, goes in, pulls the door down behind him.'

'What's he doing?'

'No bleedin' idea, but I think it's sus. This time o' night? This is a pretty dodgy estate, this.'

'Tell me about it. Have you had a listen?'

'Didn't want to get spotted, so I called you, like you said – any time.'

'Show me.' Henry jerked his head at his companions for them to get out of the car and tag along. Costain led the way around the perimeter of the school, up a back alley, then down a narrow ginnel which led out on to a colony of garages. In the past, they had been allocated to houses in adjacent streets, but over time they had become neglected. Now, though still owned by the council, they were only used by anyone who could be bothered sticking a lock on them. Henry had been here before. He had once found a stolen Land Rover in one; another time he'd discovered four pedigree poodles which had been stolen from a woman in Cheshire.

'It's that one,' Costain pointed. 'Third along.'

Henry glanced at Donaldson and Fawcett, did a quick explanation, which drew a wide-eyed response from Fawcett, who looked first at Costain and then in awe at Henry, putting two and two together. Henry clocked Fawcett's response and whispered a warning in his ear. 'You say fuck all – understand?' To have Costain revealed as a source would be damaging to both Henry and Troy if the wrong people found out. Henry because he would end up being chewed up and spat out for committing a major disciplinary offence, and Costain because he might end up dead for being a grass.

He told Costain to stay put, then indicated for the other two to follow him towards the identified garage. As with all the others, it was single, just about wide enough and long enough to accommodate a medium-sized saloon and little else. There was a light showing under the door and Henry could hear an engine running and thought he could also make out the sound of muffled music. He waved for Troy to join them. 'What's at the back of the garage?' he whispered. 'Is there any way out?'

'Just a brick wall, as far as I know.'

Henry assessed the garage door. A common-or-garden metal up-and-over door, nothing special. It had a handle in its centre about two-thirds of the way up, and extra security was provided by a padlock on one edge of the door, which had obviously been removed to allow Callum to get in. He was contemplating how difficult it would be to rip the thing open if it was locked from the inside. With four pairs of strong hands, he sussed it would be pretty easy. Even if it was locked, they would be able to twist and wrench it open, he was sure. He guessed that, at best, it was secured with only a flimsy latch.

He turned the handle slowly and pushed the door, found it to be unlocked. It moved easily and with one more heave, he opened it.

There was a car inside with its engine on – a silver-grey Toyota – parked nose in. Two people were inside on the front seats. Immediately Henry noticed the hose coming out of the exhaust pipe, fed into the interior of the car through the rear side window. The inside of the car was clogged with dense exhaust fumes and there was music playing, that old funeral favourite, 'Angels' by Robbie Williams.

'Driver's side!' Henry yelled at Fawcett, whilst he himself dashed to the front passenger door and yanked it open, hoping he wasn't too late. He had dealt with this type of suicide before and it always surprised him just how quickly the fumes killed.

'Shit,' he cursed. He wafted away the pungent smoke and plunged his head and shoulders into the car, grabbing the seemingly lifeless, naked, and trussed-up body of Kerry Figgis. Her wrists and ankles were bound by parcel tape.

At the same time, from the opposite side, PC Fawcett had opened the driver's door and was trying to manhandle Callum Rourke, the boyfriend of Kerry's mum, Tina, out of the car. He had been affected by the fumes, but put up a fight and tried to punch Fawcett. Donaldson came in behind the young cop and helped subdue the man.

Meanwhile, Henry eased his arms under and round Kerry's naked body, her head flopping worryingly against her chest and his shoulder. He manoeuvred her carefully out of the car and down the side of the garage into the fresh air, where she started to cough horribly across his clothes, but he did not care, because the only thing that mattered to him at that moment in time was that Kerry was alive.

'It's OK, it's OK,' he said gently to her, then caught Troy Costain's eye. They regarded each other with expressions on their faces that defied words.

'Nice one,' Henry said to him.

Twenty-One

It was nine fifty-five a.m. Henry Christie stood at the entrance to the FMIT block at police headquarters at Hutton, a large reinforced envelope in his hand. The campus was quiet, being Saturday morning, and no one else was to be seen or heard. He had not yet had any sleep since he'd nodded off and then been so rudely awoken in Louis Vernon Trent's living room, but his mind was active, as the night since had been so frantic and stressful. Now he was all set to meet Dave Anger, as instructed.

He was nervous but, at the same time, certain.

Using his swipe card, he stepped into the building and trotted up the stairs to the first floor, walking along the narrow corridor until he reached Anger's office. The door was open and the superintendent was at his desk. Anger did not look, even though he must have at least sensed Henry was there.

Henry did not move, did not knock or cough, just waited.

Finally Anger raised his head. His piercing, angry black eyes turned to Henry.

'Come in. Sit,' he said tersely. Henry did as ordered, sitting down primly on the low, pink-cushioned chair that was a feature of the whole complex. Someone must have bought a job lot of them years before, and they were ubiquitous. He placed the envelope on his lap.

Anger made a weary, psychological one-upmanship show of finishing some report or other just to show Henry where his place was, closed the folder, tidied the desk, then rose and closed the door softly, before returning to his chair.

Henry blinked dumbly.

'Well, you've gone and done it, haven't you?' Anger said, 'And I couldn't be happier.'

'If you mean I've caught Louis Trent and arrested someone else for the crimes I was originally investigating for you, and saved a young girl from certain death, then yes,' Henry nodded enthusiastically, 'I've done it. Good result, I'd say, despite the odds.' Henry looked meaningfully at Anger, who sighed.

'Not even that lot can save your sorry arse, Henry.'

'And why's that?'

'I'm afraid you're going to be transferred off FMIT. You'll be starting work on some pen-pushing, half-baked project in Corporate Development starting Monday. Where you can't do any harm.'

'And why's that?' he said again.

'Because officers who assault prisoners the way you do are not fit and proper to be on FMIT, nor or they fit to be police officers full stop. You assaulted a prisoner, namely Troy Costain, in front of a witness, then compounded this by allowing him to be released on bail. I suspect this was because you did a deal with him so he wouldn't complain about you. Am I right?'

'No comment,' Henry said, realizing who had grassed on him. Sheena Waters, the woman DC so aggrieved that Henry had released Costain, had gone straight to the big cheese. Henry didn't bear her a grudge, though.

'And there's more . . . it just gets better and better. Allowing a member of the public, ie your friend Karl Donaldson, to be an unauthorized part of a police operation and – and! – to allow him to use a taser. Fuck me, Henry. Hanging offence. You are well and truly stuffed. Try and wriggle out of that one. Any comment now?'

'Nope.'

'However, you're not suspended, but you'll be working in the Best Value department of Corporate Development, just for the time being.' Anger smiled nastily. 'I knew that if you had enough rope, you'd eventually throttle yourself and give me a legitimate reason to bin you.'

'It's a pleasure.'

'Jane Roscoe'll be taking over your investigation. She'll be given temporary DCI and you'll be returned to your actual rank of inspector.'

'What a surprise.'

'Professional Standards will be getting my report first thing Monday morning.' He tapped the file he had been working on. 'Expect an early visit from them.'

'I'll look forward to it.'

'You can't believe what this means to me, Henry,' he gloated.

'Huh, don't bank on it.' Henry inspected his nails, raised his head and looked levelly at Anger. 'When are you going to tell me what this is all about? I think I've a right to know, because it's not really about my lack of professionalism, is it?' His eyes roved the desk and he clocked that the Anger wedding photograph was no longer there. The Bruche passing-out parade was still on the shelf behind him.

'Believe what you want. I think you are a crap detective, not fit to be on FMIT; you're a loose canon, and certainly not chief inspector material, and as long as I've got a hole where the sun don't shine, you'll never achieve that rank if I have anything to do with it. Then again, there's every chance you won't be a cop any longer when PSD have finished with you, so that won't be an issue anyway. And I don't like you, you're right – but my report will be purely objective, based on fact.'

'That's nice to know.' He paused, took a breath. 'Any chance of you reconsidering?'

Anger almost bayed with laughter. 'When the devil's home freezes.'

'Is there anything I could do to make you change your mind?'

'Don't be pathetic,' Anger spat derisively. 'Now get the hell out of here, take the weekend off – enjoy it – and come back into the big house on Monday morning and tootle up to Corporate Development.'

Henry made to stand up, then sat back. 'There are a couple of things, actually. I won't beat about the bush.' He had practised this in his mind a few times, but he knew this was one of those occasions when he'd just have to wing it. 'I've been receiving text messages over the last week, threatening and taunting ones, from two different numbers. I don't suppose you have any ideas about them, do you?'

'Why the hell would I?'

'I've tried to ring the numbers back, but haven't got any replies. I've sent texts to each one, too.'

Anger shrugged.

'I tried this morning, too – but still got no reply, though the phones did ring out.'

'What are you getting at, Henry?'

'Thing is, sir, as you know, it's possible to get cell-siting approved to trace the location of mobile phones, which is accu-

262

rate to a matter of metres. And, so long as the phone is switched on, it doesn't matter whether the phone is being used or not; the phone companies have the technology to pinpoint them from the pulses they emit. Amazing stuff. But you know all that.'

Anger remained motionless, his facial expression revealing zero.

'The chief has authorized us to get Orange to do a cell-siting for the two numbers this morning. They're both pay-as-you-go numbers, you see, so there's no contract address or anything for either of them.' Henry forced a smile and took a breath. 'I phoned both numbers this morning from a withheld number and hung up when they went to ansaphone,' he said. 'Other thing is, my car got damaged a few times over the last week, which was a real pain, so I did something about that, too. Called in a favour from a guy in tech support. Like I said, technology is amazing, innit? I got him to fix up a couple of them mini cameras inside my motor, so that if anyone damaged it, they'd get filmed. And then, would you believe it?'

'Believe what?' Anger's face had gone slightly green.

'My car gets smashed up in a pub car park and we get some fantastic pics of the offender in full flight.' Henry took the envelope and pushed it across Anger's desk. 'Want to look? They're very clear.'

'I don't think so.' His mouth had turned down at the corners. He looked as though he was going to puke.

'The cell-siting pinpointed the offending mobile phones to this building. I know it's expensive and only usually used for life and death situations, but the chief made an exception in this case. He believed it money well spent to catch a high-ranking officer harassing and threatening lower-ranking officers. That and the damage thing.'

He and Anger stared at each other across the expanse of the desk. Henry's face remained impassive, even when he said, 'Touché.' Anger's face tensed continually at the jaw line, but something in his eyes said, 'Beaten.'

'I'm having marital problems,' Anger said simply. 'After over twenty-five years of marriage, she's left me ... it all started going horribly wrong just about the time I transferred here from Merseyside.' He wiped his face with his hand. 'Then when she found out you were on my staff, she started taunting me about . . . about, well, you can guess.'

'We had a one-night fling at Bruche,' Henry said. 'I've never seen hide nor hair of her since. I didn't even know you then.' He didn't mention he'd been into Anger's office on two occasions recently inspecting his treasured photos. Nor did he mention that she was a one-night fling that had ended up with him on top of her on the bonnet of the Commandant's car.

'You'd think you two were still at it, the way she talks,' Anger said sullenly. 'I hate you, Henry. It feels like you're responsible for my marriage collapsing.'

Henry did not go into counselling mode. He simply said, 'Are the phones in your desk?'

Anger opened the top drawer and took out two mobile phones, which he dropped on to the desk with a clatter. They were old handsets, bulky, but still serviceable. He pushed them away from him.

'Did you organize my beatings, too?'

He sneered. 'Henry, if anyone's going to have the pleasure of kicking the shit out of you, it's me. I wouldn't sub-contract that to anyone.'

'Fair do's.'

'Can we do a deal?'

It was Henry's turn to stifle a laugh. 'I'll take my chances in Corporate Development and with PSD. And anyway, it's not up to me.' He stood up and opened the office door to reveal Chief Constable Fanshaw-Bayley standing in the corridor. Behind him was John Walker, the tech support detective. 'Did you get all that?' Henry asked.

Walker said, 'Yep – it's all on tape.'

Henry opened his jacket and slowly removed the wire he had been wearing, which he bundled up and gave to Walker. 'Thanks for your time,' he said. Then to FB, he said, 'I'll leave it with you, boss.'

He walked out without looking back at Dave Anger. FB stepped into the office and closed the door softly.

At Blackpool Vic, Rik Dean was awaiting one last visit from the consultant. He was expecting to be discharged later that afternoon. Henry had been with him about half an hour, bringing him up to speed with the investigation he had missed out on.

'. . . Looks like Callum Rourke has been abusing little Kerry right under Tina's nose, or maybe she knew, I don't know. Something we'll have to delve into. Seems Kerry wanted it to stop, Callum continued the abuse, so she threatened to tell the police, which panicked him, which is why he flipped, abducted her and then tried to kill himself and her. He spun us a pack of lies on the night she disappeared, but I got lucky,' Henry admitted, not mentioning Troy Costain. 'I mean, I'd definitely got tunnel vision, and though I hadn't really liked young Callum, I was convinced Trent had snatched her, even though it didn't totally fit the pattern. But he doesn't abduct all the girls in the world, does he?'

'Just a coincidence, huh?' Rik was sat upright on his bed, fully clothed, waiting for the almighty consultant. Bandages showed around his neck and shoulders, and his arm was in a sling to ease the pressure on his neck. He still looked pitifully weak, however. 'You did a good job, H,' Rik said.

'Almost got you killed along the line, though.'

'The routine ones are always the ones that bite your arse. Don't blame yourself. One o' those things. At least I live to fight and love another day.' He paused. 'You still don't know who's out to beat you to a pulp, though, do you?'

'Nah,' Henry answered absently. 'Gotta be someone from Manchester, I reckon. I'm pretty much running out of suspects – though there is one irate husband still on the prowl.'

'How do you feel about it?'

'Threatened,' he shrugged. 'I'll just have to take more care, be ready.'

Henry excused himself after a few minutes, stating he had a lot of work to do, which was true. He wandered slowly through the hospital, feeling pretty happy with things until he reached the main entrance foyer at the front of the hospital. There, eyes raised up to the information and direction boards, stood a spectacular-looking Debbie Black, dressed to maim, if not kill. Before she spotted him, Henry dived into the newsagents and grabbed a magazine from the shelves. He hid behind it as he saw Debbie find what she was looking for on the boards, adjust her clothing with an all-over quiver of her body, and set off down the corridor. It was clear to Henry where she was headed – to Rik Dean's ward. There was no other reason for her to be here.

Henry replaced the magazine on the shelf and scuttled quickly out of the hospital, hoping that Rik Dean would not hate him too much.

As he drove away, the figure who had been watching Henry, also got into a car and began to follow, slotting in two cars behind. The person's breathing, as ever, when Henry Christie was in view, was shallow and juddery. One day, that person thought, Henry Christie would get more than just deserts for all the suffering he had caused. He would get dead.